What readers say abou

Absolutely brilliant! —Bri(

a thoroughly engrossing time trave... as it started. —Nan Hawthorne, *An Involuntary King*

a delightfully intricate tale of time travel, life lessons, challenges of faith, and redemption...moving, witty, and captivating...a page-turner...I highly recommend this novel. —Jennifer, Rundpinne.com

Vosika spins a captivating tale.... The pacing flows from a measured cadence...and builds to a climatic crescendo reminiscent of Ravel's Bolero. I become invested in the characters. Both Shawn and Niall are fully fleshed and I could imagine having a conversation with each. Write faster, Laura. I want to read more. —Joan Szechtman, *This Time*

fast-paced, well-written, witty...Captivating! —Stephanie Derhak, *White Pines*

Ms. Vosika wove these aspects...together in a very masterful way that...kept me spellbound. I could hardly put it down. —Thea Nillson, *A Shunned Man*

Original & intelligently written. I couldn't turn the pages fast enough. —Dorsi Miller, reader

Ms. Vosika spins the web so well you are a part of all the action. If you love history, romance, music and the believable unbelievable...this book is for you. I couldn't put it down until I closed the cover on an ending I never expected. —Kat Yares, *Journeys Into the Velvet Darkness*

...best time travel book I have ever read. Fantastic descriptive detail and a sweet love story are combined beautifully. —Amazon reviewer

some of the best writing it has been my pleasure to read.... —JR Jackson, *Reilley's Sting, Reilley's War,* and *The Ancient Mariner Tells All.*

a very exciting tale.... —Ross Tarry, *Eye of the Serpent,* and other mysteries

Vosika is a master at creating engaging characters...a riveting plot, well-drawn cast, and the beautiful imagery of Scotland. —Genny Zak Kieley, *Hot Pants and Green Stamps*

I love books on time travel, but this is so much more. The characters come to life in your heart and mind. —Jeryl Struble, singer/songwriter, *Journey to Joy*

One of the most intriguing stories of Scottish history I have ever read...riveting. —Pam Borum, Minneapolis, MN

I found myself still thinking about the characters after finishing the book. —Goodreads reviewer

To My Children

The joys of my life

The
Minstrel Boy

Blue Bells Chronicles Book Two

by

Laura Vosika

Gabriel's Horn Publishing
in association with
Night Writer Books
www.gabrielshornpress.com
www.nightwritersbooks.com
www.bluebellstrilogy.com

Acknowledgments

Writing a book, despite the name on the cover, involves many people. My thanks and love to my children: Karl, Caoimhe, Kian, Cara, Michael, Matthew, Connor, Liam, and John Paul.

My thanks and appreciation to the Night Writers of Maple Grove for their invaluable advice: Ross, Judy, Genny, Judd, Jack, Janet, Lyn, Sue, and Stephanie. You are all a great blessing in my life.

Thank you to Cindy, Pam, and Courtney, for their encouragement and support. Thank you to the many, including readers too numerous to mention, who have encouraged me every step of the way, and the many kind words.

Thank you to Deb, my editor, who has put so much work into this book with me, and to Stephanie, for her extra work and help on it.

The Minstrel Boy

The Minstrel Boy to the war is gone

In the ranks of death you will find him;

His father's sword he hath girded on,

And his wild harp slung behind him

~Thomas Moore (1779-1852)

Prelude

Inverness, Scotland, Present

I sit in shock for three days after Shawn's disappearance. At least, they say I'm in shock. Maybe I am. Everything swirls, silent, unsettled, like being underwater. My motions are slow. I see him throw the ring, turn back for the child; I see the horse, the sword flashing down.

The police put out alerts. His picture is everywhere. But they've called off the search. They're coming to the castle again today. I've hardly slept. I shower, I struggle to braid long, tangled hair. My head spins in exhaustion, despite coffee from Shawn's black mug with the gold trombone.

Celine's voice filters through. "Hide Bruce's ring." I stare blankly as she tugs it off my finger. She tucks Niall's crucifix inside my black sweater. "Don't let the police see them, Amy."

Conrad, Dan, and the police burst into Shawn's suite. Celine sits beside me in the window seat, a comforting angel, her long blonde hair falling like a shield between me and them. Conrad storms and rages. It's his way. Dan shouts angry, hateful things about Shawn, and it's awful because they're all true. But still. A man I loved—whatever that says about me—just died. Dan doesn't know he's dead. Dan thinks it's a normal disappearance. As if any disappearance is normal. Their voices batter me, a dull roar like surf pounding the shore.

"He comes back from the castle confused?" the older cop at the table asks. "Miss Nelson? Miss Nelson, are you listening?"

I nod, trying to keep stories straight. Niall came back from the castle. But they think it was Shawn. Shawn kept so many lies spinning in the air. I can hardly keep this one story straight; the truth and what they think and what I have to pretend to believe.

"And he passes off counterfeits to yer man, Jimmy?"

"I don't know," I say. "He told you he got them from the pawn shop." 'He' is a safe word. Shawn gave Jimmy counterfeits. Niall told them Shawn got counterfeits from the pawn shop. They think it was Shawn telling them. A headache digs a sharp nail in my right temple.

"Jimmy turns up behind Eden Court, and Shawn pulls a knife?"

"No." Niall pulled the knife. But they think it was Shawn. I nod.

"Well now, is it yes or is it no?" the cop demands.

"Yes." I draw a shuddering breath. "It was self defense. There were two of them, attacking him."

"He told you to buy train tickets to Stirling. Why did you do such a thing for a man who was clearly confused?"

Conrad stops pacing long enough to say, "He was obsessed with Bannockburn." He paces again. His hands flutter like angry crows.

"So Mr. Kleiner comes back from the castle obsessed. He'd hit his head, had what appeared to be an arrow wound."

"No...." I shake my head. Niall had the arrow wound.

Celine squeezes my hand, warning me.

"The doctor stitched it up. If it wasn't an arrow wound, what was it?"

"*I don't know.*" I sigh. *The doctor's a smart man, recognizing an arrow wound in the twenty-first century. MacDougall shot Niall during a cattle raid in 1314. I drift away inside, seeing Niall last week outside the pawn shop, running his hand down my hair to my waist, talking about French shampoo. I still don't know what he meant. I smile, remembering.*

"*'Tis naught to laugh about!*" *The older cop explodes from his seat, slamming his palm on the table.*

I jump.

"*Why would you leave a clearly disoriented man in the wilderness?*" *the cop demands.*

Even shy Celine looks up in shock. "Leave her alone!"

"*I don't know,*" I say. *My lip trembles. "He didn't seem disoriented. It was so important to him." Then the tears come, flooding down my cheeks. I'm exhausted from days of questioning, scared of making a mistake or mixing up stories. I'm alone and pregnant, missing Niall, grieving Shawn; my body shakes, convulsing with noisy sobs, as Dan and Conrad and these cops all witness the most humiliating moment of my life.*

"*You've got to stop crying now, Miss,*" *the older cop shouts. "Just answer the questions!*"

I don't know if he's angry, or flustered by a hysterical woman, or both. I cry harder, wiping at my running nose, burying my face in my hands.

Aaron bursts through the door, looks from the mess that is me to the cop, and yells, "Enough! Leave her alone!"

Dan lights into Aaron. "We need to know what happened to Shawn! Get Celine out of here and let them do their job!"

"*Can we all just settle down!*" *the cop yells.*

Celine pulls me close, pressing my head against her shoulder.

Conrad stops pacing. "Knock it off, Dan." His white eyebrows bristle.

"*If she could just answer the questions!*" *shouts the cop.*

"*I've told you everything I know!*" I burst from the window seat. *Humiliation flares into anger. "Have I done anything illegal?"*

The older cop slaps his notepad on the table and pushes his hand through his thin, brown hair, glowering.

"*He was told not to leave town,*" *Dan snaps.*

"*I didn't know that!*" I shout.

Conrad glares at the cops. "It was Shawn who caused trouble, not Amy. You're asking the same questions over and over. It's getting us nowhere. You need to go."

Everyone freezes. Conrad has no authority to kick them out.

"*Clive.*" *The younger cop glances at me. His dark eyes pierce mine, startling me. Something trembles inside me. He breaks the look, turning to the older cop. "She can tell us no more. We've done enough." They look like reprimanded school children, the older, paunchy one, and the tall, broad one. Gripping their notebooks and caps, they leave.*

They think I'm crazy. But they're gone.

I go down for lunch. The orchestra descends on me. I retreat to the safety of Shawn's suite. They want answers, and I'm not good, like Shawn, at thinking up lies. I can't tell them they'll never find him. Because Shawn Kleiner, the notorious twenty-first century musical phenomenon is dead.

And has been for 700 years.

Stirling Castle, Scotland, 1314

On a stool before the great head table, surrounded by long trestle tables teeming with hundreds of knights who had fought at Bannockburn, Niall plucked his harp, harmonizing as he sang the Falkirk Lament *in tribute to those who had fallen in battle, who were not here to share the feast.*

With his eyes closed, Niall saw not the great hall of the medieval castle, not the platters of roast and venison and serving boys rushing with food, but the great concert hall half a country and seven centuries away, where he'd last played the Lament, *not the tapestries on the castle walls, but the curtains soaring to a ceiling high above; not the fires blazing in the hearths, but blinding electric spotlights. He heard not the shouts and laughter of victorious knights, but the swell of a hundred musicians, trumpets and flutes and nasally oboes all backing the plaintive lament, Amy's violin singing sweetly behind him, and the thundering applause of a crowd as big as Bruce's entire army. Shawn played on the edges of his mind. They had thought it was Shawn they applauded. His fingers drifted up the last arpeggio, and became still, letting the notes shimmer in the air, missing that concert stage seven centuries away.*

He opened his eyes, disoriented at seeing the great hall around him, the sconces and surcoats and wolfhounds and weapons. The sweet scent of rushes mingled with the tantalizing odors of meats, vegetables, breads, and ales. Men jostled at the tables, eating, drinking, and roaring with laughter and talk.

At the head table, piled high with roasted boar and glazed fowl, sat Robert the Bruce, King of Scots, surrounded by his brother and his earls. A thin crown of gold circled his graying auburn hair. Sunlight, strong even late in the evening, shone through the windows of the hall and glinted off the rearing lion, picked out in thread of gold, on his tabard. He leaned back, looking pleased.

Several seats down from him, beside her father, Allene beamed with pride. Niall smiled at her.

Bruce rose from his seat. A hush came over the great crowd.

Tearing his eyes from Allene, Niall scrambled to his feet, surprised.

Like a master musician, Bruce let the silence hang, looking around the room, meeting half a dozen eyes, before lifting his chin. "Niall of Glenmirril, come forward."

Niall set his harp down by his stool, and crossed the small space to bow low before his king. "Your Grace." As he rose, a tall, elegant woman glided up behind Bruce's chair. She wore a fine russet surcoat. Neat, tawny hair showed under her snood, framing a patrician face. Her golden-brown eyes met Niall's.

A smile lit his face. "Mother!" He had left her weeks ago at Glenmirril.

She inclined her head gracefully. "Our King bid me come with all haste." She rounded the head table to stand before Niall. Bruce hefted a sword from beside his chair and handed it across the table, laying it across his mother's outstretched hands.

He recognized it immediately. "Father's sword," he whispered.

"Kneel," Bruce commanded.

Niall dropped to one knee, his head bent as the sword brought memories rushing over him: his father, tall and strong, with golden-chestnut hair like his and Shawn's, carrying him on his shoulders into Glenmirril's great hall; his father's laughter, becoming quieter over the years as his brothers died; his father in Glenmirril's courtyard, taking the crucifix from around his neck, and placing it over Niall's head, whispering, "Guard it, treasure it," before mounting his hobbin, and following the Laird, through the gatehouse, to fight at Falkirk.

It was the last time Niall had seen his father.

"Rise, Niall of Glenmirril," Bruce said, "an able bard, an able warrior, both of which have served my army well. Rise and take your father's sword. You have well earned the right to carry it into battle."

Niall rose, accepting the sword from his mother. "Your father would be proud," she whispered.

"You have shown honor and courage." Bruce said. "You brought men we sorely needed to Bannockburn. You inspired my troops with songs of victory on the eve of battle. You fought boldly and well. Your ruse of having townfolk storm out from Coxet Hill helped us win a great victory. You threw yourself before a charging knight to save a child."

Niall bowed his head, swallowing. Shawn had done all of that.

♫

Chapter One

"I can't stand the thought of leaving." Amy was aware she'd said it at least three times. She and Celine sat together under an oak, next to a tree stump overlooking the steep slope of the battlefield where Shawn had died. A small band of trees separated them from the parking lot of the white, stuccoed Heritage Centre. Just a week ago, when she and Conrad and the police had arrived for the re-enactment, the museum had been housed in a restored medieval fortress, dark and forbidding, built by Edward II after the battle.

Across the field, a statue of Robert the Bruce presided over the country he'd saved. Before the re-enactment, it had been Edward II, helmet in the crook of his elbow, glaring across the land he'd conquered. Amy tore her eyes from the statue, turning to Celine. "There are too many questions. I hoped coming back here one last time would settle them. But it hasn't."

Celine took her hand. "You needed a break from it all, regardless of what you find here." She met Amy's eyes. "You needed a break from his things, too."

Amy gave a sardonic laugh. "You don't know the half of it. I drink from his mug, I sleep with his robe. I don't even know right now if I loved him or hated him, but I can't stop opening his drawers and touching his clothes and taking out his trombone."

"You loved him for two years." Celine spoke as softly as the dappled sun shimmering on her blonde hair. "He's the father of your child. Still," she said, "you needed a breather. As to the questions, let's try again."

"We went over them a dozen times on the train and last night at the hotel." Amy sighed. "But fine, the ring. How did he get Bruce's ring?"

"A token," Celine suggested. "Didn't kings give tokens like that?"

"I guess. But for what? Not for bravery in battle. He died." The word choked out. Amy pressed a hand to her mouth. She blinked back tears, focusing on the sunny hill and field where Bruce's small army had defeated England's might, seven hundred years ago. It had been marshy, then. She'd watched men struggle in the sucking ground, and warhorses fight against it under hundreds of pounds of armor, knight and trappings. She'd seen Shawn fall in it, a sword slashing down over him.

"Something he did before the battle?" Celine suggested. "Bringing Hugh and his men?"

"That could be." Amy nodded, pushing back the emotion, trying to think rationally. "But what changed him enough to do a king *any* service worthy of a gold ring and to actually apologize to me?"

"Tell me the story again." Celine closed her eyes as if listening to a passage of music. "Start with when he wakes up in the tower."

"Well, he'd leave the tower, everyone would think he was Niall, and he'd get sent on Niall's trip. He'd have seemed a little strange, and they'd figure it was because Niall had a head injury and infection. The Laird would send

Allene with him. Nobody else knew the way. It was a three or four day walk through wilderness." Amy rose abruptly, pacing a small area before the tree stump in agitation. "But what *happened* in that time to change him so much?"

"A long trip through the forest," Celine mused.

"With a pretty girl," Amy scoffed, throwing herself down on the stump. "I can only imagine."

"Medieval times, though." Celine opened her eyes. "She'd have slapped him if he'd tried anything."

"Which might surprise Shawn, that someone wasn't impressed by his attention, but hardly change him enough to apologize." Amy tried to imagine a medieval wilderness. "There'd have been wild animals. And Niall said there was likely a traitor from the castle hunting him."

"Well," Celine said, "he was out of his element, everything out of his control for once. Maybe it shocked him into thinking about how he's lived."

"Maybe." Amy stared across grass bending in a soft breeze, and daisies white as snow, into the past. In the early days, when she still saw mostly his public persona, she'd gone to his house to work on arrangements. His suitcase had been flung open on the dining room table. The smell of roasting chicken had drifted in from the kitchen. He wore jeans and a t-shirt, his feet were bare, and his chestnut hair hung free to his shoulders. Music books were piled next to the suitcase. Clothes were strewn over the couch and table.

"Going somewhere?" she asked.

"California." He named a talk show. "What should I wear?"

"I don't know." Amy poked among the polos and dress shirts. "I never watch her. When did this happen?"

"Yesterday. She had a cancellation, and my publicist got me in."

"A trombone player with a publicist!" Amy shook her head.

Shawn grinned. "That's why I'm an original." He lifted a tuxedo shirt, frowned, and tossed it onto a pile Amy concluded was the no's. "Admit it, it's doing wonders for the orchestra. Did you see the sales on our CD?"

"The soundtrack?" Amy boosted herself onto the table, watching him pack. "That's because the movie is taking off."

He'd tossed a pair of slacks into the suitcase. "And because I'm plugging the orchestra on these shows. Because a bunch of teenage girls will buy anything they can get with my name and picture on it."

Amy had rolled her eyes. "Arrogant much?"

"So he reaches the camp." Celine's words cut through the memory, jolting Amy back to the field where Shawn had died. "And he carves this apology on a rock."

"What?" Amy blinked in the Scottish sun. Green summer leaves rustled overhead.

"You said Hugh built his camp around a gigantic white rock."

"Right." Amy nodded, pulling herself from the memory. "He liked to keep it shining white, clean, perfect. Niall said Hugh is—was—a giant of a man, and Shawn risked his anger to carve the apology on his rock."

"I don't know." Celine's eyebrows furrowed. "Maybe you'll have to be content that he *did* apologize. What other questions?"

"Iona J. I keep wondering if it has anything to do with the apology or them switching places to begin with."

Celine leaned back against the tree. "Iona J was part of the apology, right?"

Amy closed her eyes, reciting. "*Shawn K. Stirl C. 6.21.1314. A, so sorry.*" She opened her eyes, turning to Celine. "*So* was underlined three times. The last words were *Iona J.*"

"Aaron has run dozens of searches." Celine stared up into the leaves overhead. "On every combination of Bannockburn, Glenmirril, Iona, and Campbell. It could be the island. Or a girl named Iona. The J might be a last name. But he's finding nothing."

"Even if someone named Iona J knew something, Shawn couldn't have known that in 1314." Amy reached inside her dove-gray t-shirt for the crucifix Niall had left her. She studied the miniature carved Christ.

"Even if you could figure out what he meant," Celine asked, "would it do any good now?"

"I guess not." Amy bit her lip, her eyes locked on the crucifix. Niall had worn it always. He'd planned to give it to Allene, but had left it with her instead, telling her to sell it, if need be, to care for her child. It had been a long time since she'd felt so cared-for by Shawn. Her thoughts drifted back to that day at his house.

Shawn had laughed when she'd called him arrogant. "I told Conrad what I'd do for the orchestra if he hired me, and it's happening." He'd thrown a dark blue polo in the suitcase, and turned his back on the mess. "So. The arrangements. My next project is love songs."

Amy raised her eyebrows. "You're pulling my leg." She'd gone out with him him once, in thanks for a kindness, but resisted a second time.

"No. I'd be doing more with your leg than pulling it if I were half the player you think I am, but I do have a few sincere moments." He pushed the clothes off the table, onto a chair, and handed Amy a list of songs. He stuffed the last of his clothes in the suitcase, and jammed it shut.

"*Unchained Melody* and *Don't Forget Me When I'm Gone.*" She studied the titles. "You'd hardly put them in the same category, never mind on the same CD."

"That's just it!" Shawn joined her at the table. "Love isn't all mellow and romantic. Sometimes it's raw, hard, painful." He leaned close, contemplating the list. His chestnut hair fell forward. She could smell his shampoo and aftershave. "Maybe I should keep them all and plan a series." They threw ideas back and forth for awhile, before Shawn said, "Let's just pick one and start. *Don't Forget Me When I'm Gone.*"

She reached for a pad of staff paper. "Trumpets, trombones, horn?"

"I want a tuba," Shawn said. "I want that deep sound."

She glanced at him, waiting for the off-color joke. He shuffled through a pile of music, found a fake book, and opened it to the song. "Intro?" he asked. "Or jump right into the melody? Why are you staring at me like that?"

"Nothing." She didn't want to put the idea of off-color jokes in his head or make him think that's what she wanted. "Just so many ideas. But here's what I'd do." On a fresh piece of paper, she sketched a plan. "With the climax here." She wanted to bite back the word.

But he seemed engrossed in her ideas, and missed a second opportunity he would normally have taken. "Yeah! Yeah, that's good! How about this?" He jotted a few adjustments under her outline. "See how it grows from the melody in just one trumpet to thick block chords at the climax!" He laid the pencil down, meeting her eyes. "Shall we start?"

They did, and she'd disappeared into a Brigadoon mist of notes and melodies, Shawn walking in the magical world beside her, sincere, respectful, admiring—nothing like the man she'd refused to date, the man who wore selfishness like a badge of honor, who strutted around the orchestra hall like he owned it.

On the field of Bannockburn, she snapped her mind from the past, back to Celine, forcing herself to face reality. "He's dead. But it's eating me. If I could just stay a little longer, maybe I would find the answers." She tucked the crucifix back inside her shirt. Shawn would have stayed if he felt like it. Niall would have stayed if he thought it necessary.

Amy stared out over the daisy-sprinkled hill where they had fought, where Shawn had died, and two words drifted through her mind. *Why not?*

Stirling Castle, 1314

The pounding in Shawn's head ebbed away to a dull thud. Soft strains of harp music lilted somewhere far away.

Drunk again. *Why do I do it?*

But that didn't seem right. It wasn't alcohol—he didn't think. It had been weeks since he'd had a drink. Mead. Ale. He drifted through pleasant thoughts of bluebells, rolling hills, and mead in front of the fire. Gutting a deer. Playing harp. He shook his head, groaning at the renewed pounding. That wasn't right, either. He didn't play harp. He couldn't guess who was. He wasn't even sure it was real. Waiting for battle.

That was really not right! He tried to push himself up, but pain shot across his midsection. The harp music stopped abruptly on a seventh, begging for resolution. Shawn collapsed back into feather pillows; tried to rub his eyes, but his arm was heavy. He groaned, deep in his stomach, and dropped the arm.

A lilt of Gaelic brushed his ear. He rolled his head. *No, that form of the dative wasn't used till the 1700's.* That was his father talking. His father had been dead a long time. And the voice was a woman. *Will he stay awake this time?* He didn't know if the words were Gaelic or English. He only knew what they meant. He lifted his arm this time, despite the heaviness, and dropped it with a thud across his forehead.

"Aye, he's waking, sure," a man said.

Slowly, Shawn remembered the child, and Amy running for him; sure he could make it; throwing himself between the boy and horse, sunlight flashing off a long blade. He remembered Niall's face floating above him; a rough ride, jolting pain with every step. But now he lay in something soft.

"A hospital, right?" His voice cracked, like an old man's, from disuse. He pulled in a heavy breath, and lifted one eyelid, still shielded by his arm.

"What's he saying?" asked the woman. Allene.

"He thinks he's in an infirmary in his own time." That was Niall.

Shawn dragged his resisting arm off his eyes, and cracked them open, squinting. Light and dark floated before him.

"Shawn?"

"No," Shawn croaked, resisting the truth. "Like Oz, right?"

"What's he saying now?"

"I've no idea," Niall said.

"Just a dream." As light and dark coalesced into shapes, Shawn made out two faces, nothing more than blurs. But he knew who they were. He rolled his head, trying to escape the pain. "I'm not in Kansas."

"Oh, aye!" Niall's voice rose. The taller shape lightened and Shawn made out two dark spots—they must be eyes—in the pale blur. "That's something they say!"

"What does it mean?" Allene asked.

Shawn turned his head, gasping as a shock of pain ripped through him. She was there, a pale oval face surrounded by a red halo.

"I don't know," Niall answered. "But they said it often."

"I'm not sure I believe your story."

"There he is."

She sniffed. "It doesn't mean he came from another time. Do you take me for a fool?"

Shawn drew in a ragged breath. He pushed himself up, sending another searing pain across his stomach. The fuzzy shapes that were Niall and Allene edged forward and shifted into focus. Her eyes became pools of blue, her lips a red rosebud. The auburn halo shimmered into a cloud of hair. She and Niall edged arms under him, despite his protests, and helped him sit up. He shouted in pain.

"Gently, Niall," Allene chided. Something cool and damp brushed his forehead. Shawn closed his eyes, breathing deeply in relief.

"We thought many a time we'd lost you." Niall pulled back.

Shawn studied him. His features became clearer. They'd met only briefly, in the midst of battle. But Shawn knew him. He'd lived his life, traveled with his betrothed, trained and fought with his kin. And Shawn knew the face well. It was his own.

Inverness, Present

"You can't throw away your job and stay alone in a foreign country!" Conrad stomped the length of Shawn's blue-toned suite, his white hair bristling, his arms flailing. "How will you support yourself?"

Amy perched on the periwinkle cushion in the window seat, unbothered by Conrad's tirade. While he paced and muttered, she studied Shawn's suite, the best the castle-turned-hotel had. It had been the chambers of a lord. Its heavy mahogany furniture, and silks, paintings, and wallpaper in shades of blue, stood at odds with the sleek black computer and printer on the round table in the middle of the room. Frescoes adorned the ceiling. Gargoyles grinned down from the corners. A calm had come over her an hour ago, as she'd packed Shawn's things, as she'd lifted Niall's crucifix—the one he'd bought at the pawn shop—off the wall. Maybe she was still in shock.

"What do you hope to accomplish?" Conrad demanded.

Amy shrugged. "I don't know. I just need to stay."

"But you're having a *baby!*" He launched back into his pacing.

"Not for seven months." Maybe she shouldn't have told him that detail. He was right. She should be home to have a baby. Dana, her best friend, had reminded her several times that she didn't know any doctors here and had no way to get to the hospital when the time came. Her left hand touched the garnet ring on her right, tracing the sharp cut of the stone. She lifted her head and spoke, trying to sound strong. "I've looked into renting a house. Niall gave me money." She didn't worry about it being Shawn's money. After all, it was Shawn's baby. And Shawn had no more use for it.

Conrad stopped. His arms gave an especially energetic burst, one hand landing on his head as if trying to pull it off. "*Shawn* gave you money. There was no Niall." His snowy white mustache trembled. "You're overstressed."

Amy said nothing. Early evening light skimmed through leaded glass panes and skipped off the stone on her finger. Niall's crucifix hung safe under her black t-shirt. They told her the truth.

Conrad spun to her. "What will you do when it runs out?"

Amy's long black hair grazed across her back as she turned to look out the window. "I'll have students by then." Her stomach trembled. She wasn't sure if it was morning sickness or fear. Bannockburn wasn't so large. Maybe there wouldn't be any students.

"Have you talked to your parents?"

"No."

"Why not, Amy? You're so young to be here all alone."

She used Shawn's tactic of evading. "I'm almost twenty-five."

"They must be worried sick."

Her stomach twisted into another knot. She lifted her eyes to him. "Why? What did the news say in the States?"

"That he disappeared."

She bit her lip. "Did they say I left him in the tower?"

"What's that got to do with it? He disappeared at the re-enactment."

Panic lodged in her throat. "Have they mentioned my name?"

"No." Conrad fell back to pacing, muttering, and staccato outbursts.

She tried to relax against the blue cushions, watching the sun, bright as midday, pick out a palette of colors in the walled garden below. Niall had made a plan, and it seemed to have worked. Shawn's plans had always worked out, too. The problem was, she didn't really have one, herself. And this time, things had spun out of even Shawn's control.

So what she hoped to gain by staying, when the orchestra flew home tomorrow, she couldn't say. She just knew that not even deadly medieval destriers could tear her from the place she'd last seen Shawn and Niall. She needed to know something, anything, about what had happened. She needed to be near them both.

Conrad's tirade burned itself out with a last burst of, "This is *crazy!*" He sagged into Niall's office chair. Amy's heart sank. Despite his white hair and lined face, he had never looked old. Until this moment.

And she had brought it on.

No, she corrected herself angrily, she had not. Conrad's shoulders sagged. Events beyond her control, beyond even Shawn's control for once, had brought it on. She left the window seat and crossed the room. "Conrad." She rested her hands on his shoulders. "I'll be fine." She knew she was trying to convince herself as much as him.

He turned to her. The bags that had not been under his eyes three days ago, unnerved her. She clutched his hand, lifted to his shoulder. "Conrad, you and this orchestra are the world to me, but I have to be here."

"I know." He squeezed her hand with bony fingers. "He drives me mad, gives me more headaches than anyone, always up to something, but he reminds me of myself when I was young."

Amy smiled. "And he would have been just like you someday, full of energy and life, and still in control of everything."

"You're speaking as if he's dead, Amy. He's just missing."

But she'd seen him fall under the hooves of a horse.

Conrad squeezed her hand. "Where did he *go?*" he asked.

"I don't know," Amy lied. She'd seen the sword slash down.

"I love Shawn," Conrad sighed. "Like a son. Despite everything."

"You couldn't help but like him," Amy agreed.

"He was always happy. Always cracking a joke. Didn't take life, or himself too seriously. He was reliable. Well, in professional matters. When he said he'd do something, he did, and he did it well." Conrad rose, and walked the length of the room, his head bowed. "He got the best out of people." He stopped at the window, staring out over the broad green lawn. "He gave us confidence. We were just a little Midwestern orchestra, struggling to keep an audience. But Shawn came. He believed in us, and we changed."

"Yes." Amy nodded. "He made everybody feel like they mattered."

Conrad turned from the window. "I remember the day he auditioned. I had just passed you in the hall, and heard all the garbled, mixed-up noise of two dozen trombones doing scales and lip slurs. It was beautiful."

Amy smiled. Only a musician, she thought, would find the sound of two dozen trombonists warming up beautiful. She did, herself.

"This cocky young fellow walks in," Conrad said, "his hair too long, looking so confident I almost thought he was going in there to audition them himself, except he was swinging a trombone case. I got the check-in list from Lindsay, and came back, and it had gotten quiet in that room. I couldn't figure out why. Then I heard this tone! Like the heavens had opened and Gabriel had come down with his horn. Incredible! If you could mix gold and honey together and turn it into a sound, that's what it was! He played *Blue Bells.* I heard humor in it. He played *Czardas,* and I could almost feel the gypsies around me, see their skirts swinging, feel the heat of the fire and hear it crackling, he brought it so to life. He played *Body and Soul,* and I knew I'd do anything to hear that sound every day, and I grabbed the contract off Lindsay's desk. I already had plans." His eyes shone. "I knew we could feature a sound like that."

"We could and we did," Amy said, "and it changed everything." Her own life, most of all, she thought, her hand coming to rest on her stomach.

"Yes. And the funny thing is, I knew before I opened the door who was playing. He has such a gift, Amy, in his music, in the way he connects with people. I knew from what I'd seen in the hall we'd have a strong personality on our hands, and I was already thinking of you. I had this gut feeling you were just what he needed. You're two of a kind in so many ways, genuinely likeable, such gifted musicians. When you started arranging together, it was all I knew it could be, more than either of you could be alone. I was so sure there'd be a day he'd settle down and stop this nonsense."

"Conrad, I wish you'd been right."

Conrad sighed. "He was more than I bargained for. I really believed you'd pull him together."

Amy stared at the floor. Her long hair fell heavily, shielding her face. "Not even close."

Conrad closed the short space between them, and gripped her shoulders. "He didn't *want* to be pulled together. He just wanted to keep swimming farther out, where no one could reach him. That wasn't your fault."

Amy twisted the ring on her finger, unable to meet his eyes. "I left him in the tower. That *was* my fault."

"I'm sure he gave you good reason." Conrad's hands fell from her shoulders. "Probably pushed you too far just like he'd pushed half the orchestra too far. He was on the brink of getting fired." The conductor paced the room once and sank back into the chair. "Now he's gone without a trace and one of my best players is leaving. I'm worried about you, Amy." He lifted watery blue eyes, begging her to come home. "You need to be with your friends and family."

Amy rested her hand on his shoulder. "I'll be fine, Conrad." She hoped it was true.

Conrad squeezed her hand. "Is there anything I can do for you, Amy?"

"Funny thing is," Amy said, "all I can think of right now is Miss Rose."

Stirling Castle, 1314

"Welcome back to life," Niall said.

"Some welcome," Shawn muttered in Gaelic. He peered around the dim room, a small stone chamber barely big enough for the tester bed and wardrobe. They'd propped him against pillows, with a linen sheet and fur over his legs. He fingered the long white nightshirt he wore.

Niall and Allene still had blurred edges, Allene in a long cotehardie of sapphire over a pale blue underdress, and her hair bound back in a long auburn braid. Niall wore a rough brown vest over a full-sleeved white shirt, brown hose, and leather boots. Shawn studied him, curious about the man whose life he'd been living, the man about whom he'd made so many judgments. Light shimmered at the edges of a tapestry, suggesting a window behind it. The whole thing had the close, heavy air of a sick room. He prodded his side tenderly. "What happened?"

"Big horse, big knight, big sword," Niall said. "You got in the way."

"There was a boy."

"I got him. He's safe. Would you'd been as nimble of foot as I."

"Niall!" Allene gasped. "'Twas a brave thing to do!"

The corner of Niall's mouth quirked up. He met Shawn's eyes; they recognized one another's humor.

"Had I been as slow as you, the child would be dead," Shawn retorted.

"Had I been...."

"Stop it!" Allene snapped. "He is ill. Find a servant to bring broth."

"And leave you alone with him? 'Twould be improper with any man. Especially him."

"I've my knife," Allene replied.

Shawn groaned. The incident by the stream was best left unmentioned till he was well enough to defend himself. "I'll get broth myself. Where is it?" He pushed himself clumsily off the pillows, gritting his teeth as pain seared his midsection, and pulled weakly at the furs.

Allene fussed over him, shoving his legs right back into the middle of the bed and yanking the furs over him. "You'll go nowhere."

"I have to get up," Shawn protested.

"Why?" Niall asked. "You've nowhere to go."

"Prevent blood clots."

Niall and Allene looked at each other, uncomprehending, and Niall turned back to Shawn. "You can't go anywhere."

"Why not? Where are we?"

"Stirling Castle," Niall said.

"Stirling. We won?" Shawn straightened, brought up short by the shot of pain through his side. "History said we lost!" He turned to Allene. "I remember! You got them to storm out from Coxet Hill!"

Allene smiled. Her forgiveness of his past misdeeds swept over him. "Aye." Her eyes softened. "It made the difference."

Niall stepped forward, breaking their eye contact. "The English thought 'twas another army. Edward fled and left his troops in disarray."

"Stirling is ours, then," Shawn said. "So why can't I leave? Walking around is the best thing."

Niall and Allene looked uncomfortably at one another. "You must tell him, Niall," Allene prodded.

"What?" Shawn demanded. "Am I scheduled to be hung and drawn for...."

Allene's eyebrows drew down. She shook her head sharply.

"You don't exist," Niall said.

Shawn shoved the furs off and swung his legs, bare under the nightshirt, over the edge of the bed. He grunted in pain, but didn't let it stop him. "Can't we say I'm your cousin from Edinburgh? Does Edinburgh exist yet?"

Niall sighed, and looked at Allene. "He's much to learn." To Shawn he said, "Hugh had ever a mind for a good jest. He saw possibilities in us looking alike and hid me. There are now those who saw me felled from a near-mortal wound, and up again the next day as if naught had happened."

"Good joke." Shawn pushed himself to his feet. Pain pierced his side.

Allene hovered, fretting. "You dasn't get up! You're ill!"

"Leave him be," Niall said.

Shawn gripped his injury, half-doubled over. "I need to get back to that tower."

Again, Niall and Allene glanced at each other. Niall cleared his throat. "We do not yet have a treaty with the English. We're still at war."

"But we won," Shawn protested. "You said Edward ran off the field screaming like a little girl. No offense or anything, Allene."

"We are at war until we have a treaty." Niall spoke firmly. "At present, a score of Englishmen will run from two Scots. It didn't hurt for the English prisoners to believe a Scot can recover in a day from an injury such as some saw you—me—sustain on the field."

"Yeah, okay, so they saw that. Now I need to go to Glenmirril."

"You cannot just walk across the country by yourself." Allene shook her head at his failure to grasp the obvious. "We'll not be going back till after the festivities."

"And when is that?"

"A week."

"A week!" The injury drew Shawn up short. He pressed his hand to his abdomen, squeezing his eyes tight.

"You're not fit to travel, regardless," Allene pointed out.

"I have to get to that tower." Shawn opened his eyes. "The orchestra is leaving...." He stopped. "How long have I been here?"

"You've been in and out of fever for weeks," Niall said.

"They're gone." Shawn drew in a deep breath, easing his hand from his side. He'd get to the tower, go to sleep, and wake up with everything right again. He'd missed his chance on the battlefield. But if it had happened twice, it could happen three times. "It doesn't matter," he muttered. "I'm rich. I can get on a plane and fly back."

Allene leaned close to Niall, her red curls brushing his cheek and her eyes on Shawn. "He's of a mind he can fly now?"

"You can't leave this room," Niall said. "The Laird has decided there could be uses for having two of us, unbeknownst to others. Besides, we can't let the prisoners know the truth now. They are scared of us, and we'd fain keep it so."

"Uses?" Shawn sank back on the bed, his hands planted on the edge for support. Standing up for two minutes was enough exertion for one day. "*Uses?* We saved the battle, we changed history. Isn't that enough?"

Niall didn't answer. Allene looked carefully away.

A wave of dizziness swept over Shawn. He tried to swing his legs into the bed, and failed. Allene swept back into her element, fussing, lifting his legs into the big feather mattress, spreading furs over him, plumping pillows. "There now, back to sleep," she said. "We'll talk on the morrow."

"I'm going to Glenmirril *on the morrow*." Shawn glared.

Inverness, Present

"Why *are* you staying?" Celine stood with Amy under the high walls of Inverness Castle, shining red in its spotlights. Below, the River Ness floated in moonlight. "Conrad's worried. He thinks you're in shock."

Amy wrapped her arms around herself. "I'm *sure* I'm in shock. I've spent days crying, trying not to be hysterical, touching all his things, being interrogated by Dan, Conrad, the police, even Caroline." Amy studied Celine. Streetlights turned her hair to a silver waterfall down her back, almost to her knees. The niggling suspicions of recent months came back. Amy frowned, and spoke quickly, brushing it aside. "King David had a castle here. Niall told me on the train how he watched Bruce's men destroy it."

Uncertainty flickered across Celine's china blue eyes and fragile features, and she, too, spoke quickly. "Let's go."

They headed down the hill. The Bluebell Inn, where Shawn had thrown his party, stood at the bottom. Amy's footsteps slowed. Celine tugged her arm once, then stopped. Amy watched the patrons inside the lit pub. "I know his parties so well," she said softly. And abruptly, more loudly, "Let's go in."

"Why?" Celine asked. "It can only hurt."

In the light pouring from the noisy pub, Amy studied Celine's pale skin and china blue eyes. She wondered if they were both thinking of Caroline. "Like pulling a splinter," she said. "Yeah, it's going to hurt, but you just have to." She climbed three wide, wooden stairs, and crossed a porch into a world of mahoganies and rich greens, lively with song, laughter, revelry. It must have been the same that night. She'd heard how he'd played with the band, played a raunchy striptease on his trombone, making eyes at Caroline.

While a few patrons idly studied her, Amy peered into the back recess of the pub. The poker game, where he'd gambled away his trombone, would have been there, at the large wooden table. People would have held their breath, waiting to see what would happen when Jimmy claimed Shawn's trombone.

"Can I help ya, love?" A woman leaned over the bar, giving a pleasant smile. Her white peasant blouse stretched tight and low. Just Shawn's type.

"A bottle of wine." Amy spoke impulsively. The orchestra was leaving. It was her last night with a friend, before she was alone. "To go."

The woman raised her eyebrows. "We dinna usually...."

A barman pushed through double doors from the kitchen, wiping his hands on a towel. His eyes fell on Amy, roamed her face, her hair. He touched the woman's arm, not taking his gaze off Amy. "It's yer man's girlfriend. Give 'er a bottle of wine. 'Tis the least we can do."

The woman's smile faded. She stared at Amy as if at a curiosity, and nodded. She disappeared into the back, and returned with a bottle of Merlot. The word hit Amy like a cold wave from the loch. Shawn had brought Merlot, her favorite wine, to their last picnic in the tower.

It felt like his fingers reaching from the grave.

She took it in a trembling hand, and hurried from the pub.

♫

Back in Shawn's suite, Amy pushed a corkscrew into the bottle while Celine searched Shawn's room, turning up a single wineglass. "You never said why you're staying."

"I don't know." Amy poured Merlot into Shawn's black mug with the gold trombone. "It occurred to me when we were at the field. And back at the hotel, Conrad was ranting and raving, you know how he does. I was staring at Niall's crucifix, and this peace surrounded me. The words came out like someone else was saying them, and I knew it's what I have to do."

"Aren't you scared?" Celine held out her wine glass. Amy tipped the bottle. Blood-red wine flowed smoothly over its lip.

"To death." Setting the bottle down, Amy clicked her mug to Celine's glass, and they drank, reminiscing about the orchestra, concerts, Niall and Shawn. "Everything I felt for Niall," Amy said, "is so mixed up with thinking he was Shawn. I don't even know if it's him or Shawn I really miss."

"Niall was kind." Celine's voice held a note of wistfulness. "He's what Shawn convinced people he was." She sipped her wine. "Your new place is arranged?"

Amy nodded. "The hotel manager has a friend going on sabbatical who needs someone to stay in his house." They fell quiet, sitting on the bed. One question burned on Amy's mind, buzzing alongside just enough wine to broach the awful question. She took a hasty sip of the Merlot and lowered the mug to her lap. "Please, tell me the truth. I got this feeling, a couple months ago—Shawn and you...."

Celine hung her head. Her face turned red. Tears slid down her face, but no sound came out.

Amy felt a fist sink in her gut, the wind knocked out of her.

Celine looked up. Wrinkles creased her forehead. "He told me you broke up. He told me over and over, till I believed him. Amy, I...." She dropped her face into her hand. The Merlot trembled in her glass. "I'm so ashamed. I shouldn't have been so stupid, but I *wanted* to believe him."

"I know how convincing he was." Amy's hand slid into hers, more angry with Shawn than Celine. "What about the rumors?"

Celine wiped at her nose, avoiding Amy's eyes. She whispered, "He told me they were nothing. He promised me it was all an act that got publicity and sold CDs. He swore he'd never cheated on you. Ever."

Stirling Castle, 1314

It was a week before the Laird, accompanied by Hugh, appeared in Shawn's room. They wore tunics and trews. A heavy tartan covered Hugh's shoulder. The Laird, though dwarfed by his brother, was as big and gruff as always, red and silver hair springing up like a mane. The scar running down his left cheek gave him a fierce look. He limped, thanks to an English knight swiping at his leg during the battle.

He dropped into a large chair. Hugh stood by the door, arms folded across his massive chest, his head cocked to one side. Shawn, ever a good judge of mood, felt relief in his presence, despite his size and pose. He'd lived with Hugh in the woods. He'd proven himself.

He hoped.

With the tapestry removed, strong light and fresh air poured into the room. MacDonald, his eyebrows hovering like angry hawks over piercing blue eyes, studied Shawn, from his linen shirt to his leather boots. Shawn twisted uncomfortably on his hard chair. Tell the truth, Niall had advised. Looking from Hugh to the dirk tucked in the Laird's boot, he hoped Niall knew what he was doing.

MacDonald spoke. "The likeness is uncanny. Though I should have known Niall would never cross the loch."

"Why wouldn't...?"

The Laird gave Shawn a stare hard enough to freeze the words in the air, and turned to Hugh, his voice slow and heavy. "You'd no idea?"

"Allene said he'd been seeing double and acting strangely since the head wound. You spent time with him yourself and thought 'twas Niall."

"Aye." The Laird frowned at Shawn. After another moment, he said, "The twenty-first century. Niall has ever loved a jest."

"'Twould be unlike him to make quite such a wild claim," said Hugh. "And at this of all times."

MacDonald nodded and turned back to Shawn. "Explain yourself."

"How?" Shawn spread his hands. "We went to the castle, I fell asleep in the tower and woke up with Allene throwing cold water on me."

Hugh coughed into his hand. A corner of the Laird's mouth quirked up. "Aye, Allene might do such a thing." He studied Shawn for several more minutes. Icy sweat prickled Shawn's forehead. His usual iron nerves didn't stand up so well to cold steel in the room. "Tell me about it." MacDonald's eyes were hard.

Shawn knew it was a test. Niall had not left Allene alone with him; neither had Allene left Niall alone with him. Shawn understood. They'd been given no chance to create a story together, though Niall hardly seemed the sort to pull such a trick on his chief. Still, there was a reason this man remained the chief. Shawn cleared his throat. "What do you want to hear? History?" He had no Gaelic word for technology or science. "Art?"

"Tell me about your life." The Laird and Hugh listened, arms folded across beefy chests, with a question here and there, sharp eyes rarely blinking. Shawn suspected every word was imprinted on their minds—high school, America, cars, trains, planes, orchestras, radios, plumbing, electricity, internet, television, the modern Edinburgh and Stirling. Allene brought food while he answered their questions. MacDonald gulped his mead and set the mug down with a thump. By the door, Hugh clamped his arms more tightly over the tartan crossing his chest.

Shawn dared a word of his own. "You're going to compare this to what Niall says." He looked to Hugh. "You understand he spent less than two weeks there and won't know all this. He might not have seen planes. He wouldn't know about men on the moon."

The Laird frowned. "Your history said we all died at Bannockburn?"

"That's what I remember," Shawn said. "Would I be stupid enough to tell you that when it obviously didn't happen? I think Niall and I changed history."

The Laird fixed Shawn with an unnerving stare. "Yet with all these wonders, your people know nothing of moving through time? You'd no control over this?"

Shawn lifted his hands in resignation. "Look, ask Niall about me. I was rich and famous and powerful in my time. I lived in a place a lot nicer than this." He gestured around the room. "I mean, don't get me wrong, castles are cool, but I am *not* looking forward to using that toilet when it gets cold! People don't get hacked to death in my time. Or slapped around and thrown in cellars to sit in their own filth. I never went hungry in my life until I came here. Why would I stay if I knew how to get away?" On a roll, he indicated his injury. "In my time, I'd've had medical care and *antibiotics* to kill the fever a lot quicker. I'd have a *physical therapist*—and she'd probably be really cute. I'd be outside instead of locked up!"

"Enough." MacDonald's one word carried more weight than Conrad's ranting and pacing and flailing. Shawn stopped.

The Laird lifted himself from the chair and limped toward the door.

"Hey, you can't kill me." Shawn rose, gripping the aching wound. "This was not my fault! I had no control over this!"

The Laird pierced him with a glare. He dropped quickly into his chair, but he persisted. "Didn't I get your daughter safely to Hugh? Didn't I prove myself at Bannockburn?"

Hugh opened the heavy wooden door. He and the Laird slipped out. A key clicked in the lock behind him.

Shawn dropped into his chair. "Oh, damn!"

Chapter Two

At the airport, musicians gripped Amy's hand, where she stood at the end of the long line winding slowly toward security.

"Take care of yourself," Aaron said. "You sure about this?"

"I'm sure." Amy turned to Dana, her best friend, not sure at all. "You're not going to cry, are you?"

Dana sniffed and brushed her eye. Her cinnamon puff of hair hung limp, a striking contrast to its usual moussed spikes. "I can't believe you're not coming home. How are you going to take care of yourself?"

"I'll be fine." Amy heard her own voice come out too loud, trying to convince herself. Even now, her stomach was doing back flips, and she wanted to get the fastest cab back to the hotel, grab her suitcase, and race back to safety, her job, her second family, her cozy apartment with its lace and warm colors and purring cats greeting her each evening.

"You don't have a job," Dana objected. "You don't have a doctor. You've never even *seen* this house. A year, Amy! You leased it for a year without even looking at it."

Amy's heart pounded faster. "Yeah, I know I should have looked first. But it's a long train ride. It'll be fine." She hoped it would be. Dana was right. It had been foolish to accept a place sight unseen. Her parents would be quick to say so. "I'll find a doctor."

"But you're all alone. What will you do?"

"Practice, paint, write music, visit castles." Words rolled off her tongue, anything to stop Dana. She was close enough to tears and turning back without the reminders of how rash she'd been. "Really, Dana, I'll be fine."

"But what about me? Who will I go to movies with?"

"You'll never lack for company. I'll be back in a year." They hugged one another tightly, and Amy turned to Celine.

"I'm so sorry," Celine whispered.

Amy's smile slipped. "I understand."

"How can you?" Celine asked. "I was so stupid."

"He lied to you, too." She squeezed Celine's hands. Her stomach clenched in anger, but it was at Shawn.

Celine gave a last watery-eyed glance as Aaron reached for her hand, and led her to the x-ray machine. She hopped on one foot, struggling with her boots, looking back. Amy waved.

"Good luck, Amy!" Jim, the portly trombonist, engulfed her in a warm hug. "You were right about Shawn, you know."

Amy pulled back, thinking of the rumors. "Right about what?" she asked warily.

"You always said there was someone different in there." Jim's normally jovial eyes became serious. "After the concert in Edinburgh, I bumped into his bag backstage, spilled everything. I was picking it up, when this card fell out, thanking him for playing flute for kids at a hospital."

Amy's shoulders relaxed. She smiled. "Yes. I've caught him doing a few good deeds in secret."

"Did he get mad?" Jim asked with a chuckle.

"Yeah. You, too?"

Jim nodded. "Yep, he blew. Grabbed it out of my hand, shoved it back in the bag like I'd caught him with drugs. Then he made a joke, laughed."

"That's how he was." Heat prickled her eyes. He'd had an infectious smile, the kind that made everyone around him smile, too. "The storm clouds always passed like a breeze in August."

"I finally understood," Jim said, "why you thought there was more to him. You were right."

Amy brushed at wet eyes. "Thank you," she whispered.

"If anyone could have saved him from himself, Amy, it was you." He patted her shoulder. "But he made his own choices."

Amy stared at the floor, biting her lip to stop the trembling. She'd also made hers, and he'd ended up dead.

"They'll find him." Jim hugged her again.

Rob laid his hand on her arm as Jim moved on.

"Rob." Amy sighed. "They're waiting for you."

"Come home with me." He squeezed her arm. "I'll take care of you."

"You've offered three times," Amy said. "I'll be fine."

His face turned red, a striking contrast to his blond hair. He trailed to the end of the line of musicians removing their shoes and sending their baggage through security. "You can't do this, Amy!" he insisted.

She bristled, not wanting to hear her own doubts spoken aloud. "Before Shawn, I believed I could do anything. I can do this."

"I didn't mean that," he protested. "I just meant, you shouldn't be alone. You're overstressed. How will you support yourself?" They were all the things Conrad had said, but Rob said them with a possessive hand on her arm, his head bowed close, his lips near her ear. "You have...."

A garbled voice, heavy with a Scottish accent, erupted over the loud speaker, swallowing his words.

"You can't stay," he said, when it stopped.

"I can't leave." She edged away from him.

"Where are you going to live? You can't have a baby here."

"Rob!" She backed up another step, trying, and failing to evade his reaching hand. "I've arranged a house. They have hospitals and doctors!" But panic climbed up her throat. She hadn't looked into insurance. She should beg Conrad for her job back, get her things from the hotel and book the next flight home.

As the line moved, pulling him closer to the x-ray machine that would tear him from her, he became more insistent in his whispered attempt at privacy in the crowded airport. "Why are you doing this? Come home with me and give me a chance."

"Rob." Her heart shifted from *allegro* to *vivace*. She pried his fingers off her arm. "You and I never had anything. A talk behind the castle. A hug in the tower when I was scared."

"We held hands," he reminded her.

"You can't just claim me like this!"

"I'm not *claiming* you. I *care* about you."

"Sir, your shoes."

Rob twisted his head from security to Amy and back to security.

"I'm sorry, Rob," Amy said, and meant it. "Call me, but don't push for something we never had."

He fixed her with a meaningful gaze. "When you get back...."

"Sir." The man at the x-ray machine spoke more firmly.

Rob removed his shoes, stumbling on one foot, and tossed his carry-on into the x-rays bins, craning his neck to look back at her. She waved to the other orchestra members, filing away on the other side of the divide. Her heart bolted from *vivace* to *molto presto*. Her pulse pounded. She wanted to chase after them, forget her suitcase, forget this insane idea, and just go home. Yes, Shawn would have followed whatever whim struck him.

But look where he'd ended up.

Stirling Castle, 1314

Shawn paced the room restlessly, despite the pain cutting across his stomach. Panic swelled his throat. He snapped his fingers over and over. "Think, think, think. I'm going to die. They're going to hang me!" The only thought that came to mind was leaving Amy a message. He looked around the chamber. His eyes fell on the wardrobe. A knife sat on one shelf. He frowned. Just walking was a challenge. He could hardly take on the guard outside. They must have realized that.

He picked it up, ran his finger along the blade. It was sharp and strong. He'd left her a message once. He searched the room, his hand clamped to the aching wound, and chose his spot, behind the bed, near the floor, where the Laird would never see it. He glanced up, checking for security cameras, before remembering where he was, and started carving his mark, the mark he'd always used to sign his letters to Amy.

Bannockburn, Present

Amy stood in the doorway of her new home, framed by a cheerful blue door, wondering what in the world she had done. Shawn's trombone dangled from one hand, and her violin from the other.

"Where would you like these, Miss?"

She turned to the taxi driver, waiting with the suitcases. Shawn's mother, Carol, had told Conrad she could take Shawn's things. She was glad to have the trombone. It had been a third person in their relationship, always there, dictating so much of their lives. It also stood as a stark reminder she had not yet spoken with Carol. The weight of that call hung over her. Carol's faith defined her. She'd be disappointed to learn Amy was pregnant.

But the call had to be made. Amy glanced at her watch, and added six hours. It would be evening there. She'd just start some tea and then do it.

"Miss?"

"Oh, sorry. Just inside. Thanks." She carried the trombone in herself, as if it held Shawn's spirit. The driver dropped the suitcases in the small foyer with a pair of soft thumps, touched his cap, and bade her farewell.

She closed the bright blue door, and leaned against it, sighing. It felt good to be alone. Dana was right, she chided herself. Not the smartest move, accepting a place sight unseen. But as she looked around, she thought her trust had been well-placed this time. A living room with a fireplace opened up on her right. The hall ran down to a kitchen.

Leaving the suitcases, she went to look. It had an old, but clean, stove with a white kettle on the burner, small table with two chairs, and a compact washer tucked under the counter. She edged aside lace curtains at the back window, revealing a small patch of garden, closed in by six foot brick walls.

After filling the kettle and lighting the stove, she turned back for the suitcases, bumping them up the stairs behind her. A glance around showed a bathroom and three bedrooms, one with a rolltop desk and tables. She chose the larger bedroom, and soon had the bed made with a new set of linens.

She stood back, studying her peach and lace bedspread. She wished, yet again, that she'd gone home with the orchestra, to her own apartment. She shook her head—it was too late—and hung her black concert blouses in the closet and put her few clothes into the dresser. A folded sheet of paper fell from her suitcase. She glanced at it—Niall's history of the crucifix—and put it in a drawer with the garnet necklace he'd given her. He'd gone back to Allene. She felt wrong wearing it.

She set a small framed picture of herself and Shawn, taken just months ago at Castle Tioram, on the dresser. She touched his face through the glass, remembering the night in the ruins. He'd been loving, kind, and funny, and she'd believed they'd finally turned a corner, and all would be well again as it had been in their first eighteen months, when they'd written music side by side and gone to movies and carnivals and danced to slow strains of music, wrapped in one another's arms in his living room with only the firelight from the hearth. Her hand settled on her flat stomach. She *had* to call Carol. She twisted her thumb under her palm, feeling the ring. It had been less than a week since he'd thrown it. It felt like a lifetime.

Downstairs, the kettle whistled a high C. As soon as she settled her nerves with some tea, she'd call. Taking Shawn's black mug, she hurried to stop the shrieking kettle. As she poured the steaming water, her phone trilled.

Names jumped through her head. Was it Conrad calling to encourage her to come home? She might give in. The police with more questions? She couldn't keep any more stories straight. Her parents? She couldn't tell them what she'd done. A glance at the caller ID brought a warm gush of relief. She lifted the phone and hit *talk*. "Miss Rose!" The name filled her with the same magic, warmth and images of summer gardens it had since she was three.

"Amy!" Her old teacher's voice was as rich and melodic as the low register of her violin. "I've just talked to Conrad. Why in the world didn't you call me immediately?"

Tears stung Amy's eyes. It had been a year since she'd spoken with Miss Rose, more than twenty since she'd first walked into her apartment, but she could almost smell the cinnamon and gingerbread. The last weeks and months with Shawn rushed up on her. "I couldn't tell you," she confessed. Rose was a romantic. They'd dreamed big, she and Rose, over gingerbread and tea after Amy's lessons, or riding the subway to auditions, about the great future awaiting Amy. "I messed up." She took her tea to the front room.

"Messed up?" Miss Rose spoke incredulously. "He disappeared, Amy. How's that your fault?"

Amy bowed her head, in the quiet of her new living room. The familiar pain stabbed her heart. "Not that. Not just that." She brushed a hand under her nose, fighting the urge to sniff. "I'm pregnant."

"Pregnant?" There was only the briefest pause before Rose said, "We'll get through anything together, right? How are you feeling?"

"Fine," Amy said, and immediately laughed, scorning her own answer. "I mean, no morning sickness. I don't feel so great about *being* pregnant. I'm a mess about Shawn."

"Well, of course! I can't imagine."

"It's not everything it looks like, though," Amy said. "I broke up with him. He's not coming back." Her voice caught; she brushed at her eyes.

"Hm. What do you mean, not coming back?"

"I don't know." She stumbled on her words. "Rose, I saw things at that re-enactment. I can't explain. I just know he's not."

"What do the police say?" Rose spoke brusquely.

"They say there's nothing more they can do." Taking strength from Rose's calm, Amy's eyes traveled over her new brick fireplace, and the painting of a castle over the mantel.

"Have you called your parents?"

"No."

A small silence, quick as an eighth rest, fluttered between them, before Rose asked, "Why not?"

Amy cleared her throat. "You know my parents."

"Yes," Rose said, like the sigh of a bow on the softest *pianissimo*. "But I've never been sure you do."

Amy paced the small living room. "I'm coming to know them better, the more I avoid that call." She touched the dark-hued mantel. "My mother is going to be upset about how this makes her look." She ran a finger over the smooth stone statue of Bruce on the mantel, a reproduction of the one at the field. "Has—um—what's been said on the news there?"

"It's been a bit of an uproar." Rose spoke mildly. "Shots of the re-enactment. Crying fans. Interviews with the police chief."

"Nothing about...." Amy hesitated. She gave herself a mental kick. She could trust Rose. "Nothing about me leaving him in the tower?"

"Mm." Rose made the sound she once had when listening to Amy play exercises. "It's been mentioned."

Amy groaned. "My parents are going to have a fit."

"They haven't mentioned you by name," Rose assured her.

"It doesn't matter. My parents' friends know who 'the girlfriend' is. My mother's going to say I shouldn't have done it."

A soothing noise came over the line, whisking Amy back to the china teapot with red roses sitting on a lace doily in Rose's Greenwich Village apartment. "If you left him, Amy, he gave you good reason. Last we talked, he was whisking you off to Hawaii and you were writing music together. You two made that orchestra something special."

Amy ran her hand across the soft leather couch standing against the inside wall. "Everyone thinks it was all Shawn."

"Oh, he was instrumental. So to speak." Rose chuckled at her pun. "But it was the music. If he thought it was all him, he deserved a night in a cold tower."

"It wasn't that." Amy moved on to the lace curtains at the front window, and touched the suede wing chair. "He was drinking more and more, gambling. Cheating. I think."

"Oh, honey." The word came like a bow pulling a silken thread of sound from a string, surprising Amy. She realized she'd expected her mother's response. *You must be wrong.* Or, *What did you do to make him cheat?* "No wonder you left him," Rose said. "You deserve better."

"But I'm not sure." Amy emphasized the last word. "So many things seemed off for so long, but I only know for sure about...."

"Where there's smoke, there's fire." Rose brooked no argument. "Trust yourself, Amy. If he was doing everything on the up and up, you never would have thought he was up to that. Now, my time's running out. So I need to tell you quick. Conrad said you want me to come over."

"No." Amy shook her head, though she wanted it more desperately than she'd wanted the scholarship to Juilliard, more fiercely than she'd wanted the job with the orchestra, and almost as deeply as she'd wanted to believe Shawn was, at his core, who he showed her in private. "No, he shouldn't have told you that. It's expensive."

"Well, the thing is," said Rose, "you have wonderful friends in that orchestra, and it seems they bought me a ticket. But I can tell them...."

Amy gasped. "They bought you a ticket?"

"They didn't want you to be alone."

"They really did that for me?" Amy blinked back tears of emotion.

"It seems they did. Shall I see if the airline will give them a refund?"

"Of course not." Amy laughed. "But—you have rehearsals and jobs."

"I've worked hard for thirty years. I can afford time off. I'll be there the day after tomorrow."

"I've put everyone to so much trouble." The familiar guilt rose in Amy. "I should just pack up and come home."

"I think not. Your heart is telling you what you need. Now about your parents. Call them, Amy. Only the most selfish person would worry about their friends right now instead of their daughter. So just do the right thing and don't worry what they say. Shall I bring some gingerbread?"

"Yes." Amy smiled, the worry dissipating. "Please. I'll meet you at the airport, and I'll have tea waiting at home." With plans settled, Amy ended the call. She felt better. Maybe she could even call Carol. As soon as she finished her tea, she told herself, she would.

With her mug in hand, she wandered to the oak bookshelves stretching on tiptoe all the way to the ceiling, crowded with books of every size and color. She ran a finger along leather and cloth bindings, head tilted, to read titles. *An Antidote to the English: The Auld Alliance 1295-1560. Scotland: An Autobiography.* The second shelf held books on medieval Scotland, and the third, a dozen volumes on cairns, standing stones, and ghosts. She pulled out one after another, skimming the contents for Glenmirril or Iona. She found a reference in *Mysterious Scotland,* a heavy tome whose leather binding smelled of age, and curled her legs up into the chair, chiding herself she should call Carol.

A page or two, she promised herself. With a sip of the tea, she stared at the word *Glenmirril.* She'd left Shawn there barely three weeks ago. She closed her eyes, swallowing over a knot in her throat. Not only was she pregnant, she was responsible for Carol losing her only son. Carol would never want to see her again. And they'd been close.

She opened her eyes, not wanting to read about the castle after all, and flipped through the pages, scanning ghostly lore, then abruptly slammed the book shut. She *had* to call Carol. *As soon as I finish the tea,* she told herself. And she was being ridiculous about the book. She opened it again, paging through to the chapter on Niall's home.

Glenmirril is riddled with interesting stories. Its very name dates to a strange event in 1296. She touched the words. Niall would have been six. He would have been there. *When Edward I stormed up Loch Ness, the people of Glenmirril prayed for, and, they say, received, a miracle. A mist rose so thick and so high that it shielded the castle from Longshanks.* Wondering if Niall remembered the event, she turned the page, but the book skipped onto other tales.

Among Glenmirril's colorful stories is Murtagh MacDonald, killed at Culloden, who returns each April 16 to play his pipes until midnight. In the fourteenth century, a mysterious Brother Andrew disappeared from the north tower the night of June 8th never to be seen again, and a woman who drowned in the sixteenth century still calls for help on misty nights.

With Glenmirril's ghostly cast roaming her mind, Amy closed the book, and pushed it back on the shelf. In the last days of June, sunlight blazed through the lace curtains at the window. But a rumble in her stomach, and faint nausea, told her it was past dinner. As soon as she got dinner going, she told herself, she'd call Carol.

Stirling Castle, 1314

"*Planes?*" The word felt curious on Niall's tongue.

"*Planes, airplanes!*" MacDonald barked.

"Did you see any such thing?" Hugh's arms clapped like steel across his chest. A stormy countenance replaced his usual humor.

"No." Niall shifted uncomfortably on his chair. He'd spent the time they'd been in Shawn's room praying he'd made the right choice in telling the truth. "But I was there only briefly. They spoke of flying home once. I thought they spoke as we do, as in fly from this place, leave."

Allene turned from the window where she gazed out over the hills and fields stretching toward the site of their recent victory. "He spoke of flying home in his room. D' you remember, Niall?"

"Aye." Niall nodded. He, too, had been little more than a prisoner, guarded at all times, until the Laird could speak to him. Allene stayed always by his side, hearing every word he spoke to another. He found no fault with MacDonald for taking precautions. He'd thought of finding a more believable story, but could think of none. The clans all knew one another. They knew their own genealogies. Gossip traveled just as fast without the internet of Shawn's time. It would be difficult to create a background for Shawn, and being any sort of English in this time and place was a likely way to die.

Besides, he didn't like to lie. A jest perhaps. Out and out lies, never. "What did he say, Allene? We were both so surprised that he seemed to think he could fly."

Allene's eyes grew bright. "*Get on a plane and fly home!* Those were his words."

Niall straightened in his chair. "I did see something! 'Twas in the hills, large and silver, roaring overhead. I was more of a mind to find Hugh at the time, and it was so far away, I didn't think much on it. Could that be what he means? Ask him what color it is, and what sound it makes! A roar, like a dragon, and smoke streaming from its tail."

"From its tail?" Allene looked doubtful. "'Tis unlikely."

A servant arrived with food, and over the meal, Niall continued telling the Laird and Hugh all he remembered. "Did he mention *photographs*? They're miniatures, but perfect, and no paint. A lass held up a silver box." He demonstrated with his hands. "It flashed, and they said she was taking a picture. I saw many pictures, of Shawn especially."

"Eclectic city?" The Laird's attempt at the word came out slowly.

"Electricity," Niall corrected. "Torches burn without flames. Boxes make music without minstrels."

"Impossible," muttered Hugh.

"Those are *radios*," Niall continued, oblivious of the interruption. "Others have moving pictures. It all works with electricity. They need a rope attaching them to the wall."

Allene fingered the corded belt around her waist, and touched it to the rough stone wall several times. Niall smiled. She blushed and turned her back quickly, staring once more through the arched window at the open fields. "'Twas no such rope, Allene," he said. "These ropes had bits of metal at the end that went directly into the wall."

"So the walls are the real wonders," said the Laird. He rose and limped to the wall, running his hand up and down the stones.

"What are they made of, to cause such things?" asked Hugh.

Niall sighed. "I was there so briefly, I can't possibly understand. Ask Shawn. But they were smooth, not stone."

"No weapons?" Hugh returned to his main interest.

"No. The men carry naught. They've no guards at their doors."

"*Cars*," said the Laird. "Tell me about them again."

Niall told him again about the enclosed metal wagons hurtling down the road with no horse. "They are controlled with a wheel inside. Some had two benches, but there are *buses*, too, which hold a hundred men. They have roofs and doors and are two stories tall."

"Houses on wheels?" Allene's eyebrows rose high.

Niall took a sheet of parchment, dipped a quill in ink, and sketched several cars, inside and out. Allene came from the window, the Laird hobbled over from his inspection of the wall, and Hugh left his post by the door. They leaned over his shoulder, examining the drawings. "Ask him to draw some. I suspect he'll have difficulty with a quill, as his people do not have them."

"No quills," Allene breathed. "How do they write?"

"Small sticks called *pens*." Niall held up his hands, showing the size. "Ink flows, in many colors, and never blots. Ask him to draw the clothes Amy wore." He sketched again.

Allene gasped. "She went about in her knickers! How can this be true? How can any of it be true?"

"How can I make it up?" Niall jabbed the quill into its holder. "I may jest, but have I ever tried such an elaborate jest? And 'twould be poor form in the midst of our troubles."

"Aye," agreed Hugh. "'Twould not be in character."

"Still," insisted the Laird, "with all this knowledge, he says they've no control over moving through time, so how did it happen?"

"For all their knowledge," said Niall, "they haven't wisdom, necessarily. Do we not have stories of men disappearing into underground caverns and coming out years later? Seven years, or two hundred?"

The Laird chuckled. "Niall, you've ever scoffed at fairy folk."

"And I do still. Yet there *are* stories of such things. Shawn's people believe only what they can see and create. They've little faith in things they can't see or take apart or understand with their own senses. They scoff even more than I at fairy folk and moving through time. I found only one man who thought with any seriousness on it, and even he was doubtful."

"And Amy?" Allene's voice became low and less than friendly, and Niall suddenly wished she were not hovering so near his shoulder. "She thought you were Shawn, did she not? Did you tell her the truth?" He searched for words, and when his search took too long, he found his ear pinched and yanked upward between her fingers. "What did you tell her?"

"Allene, leave the poor man be!" her father snapped. "Give him a chance to speak!" But he, too, waited in significant silence while Niall tried to phrase his answer. Hugh's face became grim.

"I asked what their people believed about changing times," he said, "and she became so upset, I stopped asking. She said they would lock me up if I said I'd done that. So I didn't say it. I felt I'd little choice but to be Shawn."

Allene's fingers tightened on his ear. "Did being Shawn include kissing her?"

Niall cringed, wishing Allene wouldn't cut so directly to the heart of things. He wished the Laird and Hugh would grant him two minutes' privacy with Allene to explain. But the Laird stared stonily, and Niall looked back and forth between them, caught. He tugged, trying unsuccessfully to free himself from her grip. "They were betrothed." It wasn't quite true, but he was tired of shocking them with things of Shawn's world. Then again, he didn't like lying. "Well, not exactly, but they behaved as if they were."

"Meaning she kissed you." Her voice gave no quarter.

"Well, aye," Niall mumbled. "But she was mad at Shawn, so not for several days."

"Did you kiss her back?" Her voice grew sharper. Her fingers pinched his ear harder.

"Now, Allene," said Hugh, "I've heard someone was kissing Niall—that would be Shawn—on Coxet Hill the night before the battle."

Niall slapped his hand on the table and bolted upright out of his chair, knocking it backwards, and breaking free of her grip. He rounded on Allene. "You kissed that chanty wrassler!"

She backed up a step. "I thought 'twas you!"

"And she thought 'twas Shawn!"

"But you knew you weren't Shawn." She raised her chin defiantly.

"And he knew he wasn't me!"

"Aye!" She jabbed him in the chest with a triumphant finger. "And he stopped me! Did you stop her?"

"Aye, I stopped her."

But his pause, brief as it was, was long enough to cause Allene's eyes to darken. "How *quickly* did you stop her?"

He cleared his throat. "*Very* quickly."

"Five seconds?"

"Aye," he agreed, hoping to end the conversation.

She punched him hard in the chest. "Five seconds! You let her kiss you for five seconds!"

"Maybe only two!"

She punched him in the chest again, knocking him a step backward. He caught himself on the fallen chair and regained his balance. He looked helplessly to the Laird who only tried not to smile. "D' you know how long five seconds is when kissing!" Allene demanded. "'Tis hardly a peck on the cheek!"

"Maybe only one! D' you think I was counting?" He backed around the table, around the Laird, and Hugh.

Allene marched after him. "And what were you doing while she was kissing you? Kissing her back?"

"How long did it take Shawn to stop you!"

"Three seconds!"

"You were counting?"

"Stop, both of you!" MacDonald's face glowed red. "'Tis no matter. She didn't know, Allene, as you didn't yourself."

"What was I to do?" Niall demanded, safe on the other side of the Laird. "'Twas after the concert, everyone was excited, I wasn't thinking clearly, and how was I to explain stopping? Tell her who I was and be locked up? Had I done so, I'd still be there, and you'd all be dead at Bannockburn!"

"Och, I'm to believe you kissed another lass to save all Scotland!"

"'Tis true!" Niall glared at her and seated himself again at the table. "And what purpose did your kissing serve?"

She harrumphed, glaring back at him. "I've not kissed him since."

"And I've not kissed her."

Allene picked up the fallen chair and set it with a thump back at the table. "How could you? She's not here!"

"Stop!" the Laird roared. "Niall, tell me about these concerts."

"Is she pretty?" Allene pouted.

"Beautiful," snapped Niall. "And kind. Not once did she punch me." He rubbed his chest irritably.

By the door, Hugh gave a sound like a snort, that Niall suspected was an attempt not to laugh. He threw Hugh a dirty look, too.

Allene sniffed, and turned her nose up, pretending not to listen while Niall described the theater. "Instruments of brass and wood, a dozen drums, lights shining in our faces, and a crowd the size of Bruce's army watching, clapping for everything."

"And this trollop sat right behind you the whole time?" Allene snapped.

Niall ignored her. "They've large sackbuts and trumpets that can play any note at all. A hundred of them play together at once. The harp was almost as tall as I. Ask him about Celine, the lass who played the harp."

"Was she beautiful, too?" Allene demanded.

"Very! Hair to her knees like an angel, and her harp inlaid with gold."

Allene fell silent while he told them more, and finally, the Laird said,

"Enough. We must decide what to do. His presence has already convinced the English we're a strong and hardy race to be feared." He chuckled. "Imagine thinking a man cut nearly in half could be up and walking the next day. 'Tis to our advantage they continue to think so. We've no way of getting him back, and we'll not look a gift horse in the mouth, aye? We can make use of this." He pushed himself up from the table, and headed for the door.

Niall rose. "But will he agree to whatever you've a mind to do?"

Hugh's eyes widened in surprise.

MacDonald turned back, stunned. "Do you forget I am the Laird, Niall?" His eyebrows hovered low over piercing eyes. The scar running from temple to jaw turned whiter. "Here, he'll do as he's told, regardless of how things are done in his time." He reached for the door handle. "I'll ask him those things. Will I send a guard to protect you, Niall?" He chuckled at Niall's glower, and slipped out the door with Hugh, leaving Niall to face Allene.

Inverness, Present

With vegetables and beef sizzling on the stove, with nothing left to put it off, with shaking hands, Amy called Carol. The phone rang. She hoped Carol wouldn't answer. But it clicked, setting her nerves jangling. She gripped the phone in one hand, and Niall's crucifix in the other.

"Amy." Carol's voice sounded ragged and thin. But warm.

"Carol. Hi." Amy drew in a breath. The crucifix bit into her palm. "I'm sorry I didn't call sooner."

"Oh, Amy, don't apologize," Carol said. "I can't imagine what you're going through, yourself. How are you holding up?"

Typical of Carol, Amy thought, thinking of someone else even in her own distress. Her hand relaxed on the crucifix. There was no need to admit she'd broken up with Shawn. She almost confessed, *I left him there.* But the world thought he'd disappeared later, at the re-enactment. "I'm...okay," she said.

"Are they still looking for him?" Hope fluttered in Carol's voice. "Is that why you stayed?"

"Uh, yes." Amy sprinkled seasonings on the stir fry. She couldn't tell Carol her son was dead, could only leave her hanging in limbo, praying and waiting for news Amy alone knew would never come. She set the spice bottle down hard, asking herself again what she expected from her rash decision to stay. But she felt at peace being near Shawn and Niall—even if they were both dead.

They talked briefly about the investigation, till Amy could put it off no longer. "Carol, there's more. It's going to disappoint you," she said. "I wasn't living a way you approve of." She hesitated. "I mean, with Shawn."

Silence hovered, before Carol said, "You drank, too? Or...you don't mean *drugs*? He didn't do *that,* did he?"

A flush warmed Amy's face. She gave the stir fry a quick swish with a spatula. "No!" Before she could lose her nerve, she said, "I'm pregnant."

"Oh." Carol fell quiet, then suddenly laughed. "Oh, thank goodness! I mean, of course I didn't approve of—all he did. But—I'm going to be a grandmother?" Her voice shimmered with hope.

Amy let out her breath. "You're not upset? This isn't...." She stopped herself saying, *This isn't how I planned to live my life.* It would sound like she was blaming Shawn, which wasn't fair, and the last thing a grieving mother needed to hear. And even as she half-blamed him, she also wished she'd accepted his invitation to his room, in the castle hotel. She wanted that last memory.

"Upset?" Carol sounded perplexed. "Well, of course I wish he'd lived differently, but—were you afraid to call because of this?"

"You're so religious," Amy said weakly. She edged the vegetables up the side of the pan, letting the meat cook longer. "I thought...."

"It's not like I don't know what the world is today," Carol said. "And my faith tells me not to cast stones." She paused, and added, "I mean, I would have *liked* the normal order, but...well, maybe it's wrong, but I actually feel like you've just handed me a gift, in the face of him disappearing." Her voice caught. "For all his faults, Shawn loved life. He'd never willingly disappear, and I've spent every day since Conrad called afraid I'll die alone, no husband, no son, no grandchildren. I didn't know if you'd want to keep in touch." Her voice caught. "If he never comes back."

"Of course I do," Amy said in a rush. "Carol, you're closer to me than my own mother." Tears stung her eyes. "I was afraid I'd lose you, too, when I told you."

"No, never," Carol said. "But...if they don't find him...you'll meet someone new someday. Can I still see my grandchild?"

"Someone new?" Amy pushed the spatula through the chunks of beef. The oil crackled and spit. "I'm barely thinking two minutes ahead, never mind to someone new."

"But there will be someday," Carol persisted. "And when there is...?"

"Yes, I want you in this baby's life." Amy hesitated, then rushed into the question. She had to ask. "I know it's strange, but did Shawn ever mention Iona to you? Or someone named Iona?"

Silence hummed on the line a full ten seconds, before Carol asked, "Where the Scottish kings are buried? No. Why?"

Hating the evasion, Amy said, "Nothing. Just something he said—before he left. Nothing important."

They talked briefly before saying good-bye. Amy slid the phone closed, tapping it against her mouth. Even now, she was equally glad she hadn't gone to Shawn's room. She missed him, loved him, and hated him all at once, her gut still screaming that Caroline had been with him, while her mind yelled just as loudly, *You're paranoid and crazy. Caroline, Shawn and Rob* all *told you she was with Rob!*

She must be wrong, she thought. It was hard to understand, when she felt so normal, why she kept jumping to wrong conclusions. Maybe Shawn had told Celine the truth that he'd never cheated before. Things had gotten bad after the abortion a year ago. She slammed the phone down on the counter and snapped the burner off. "Listen to me make his excuses," she muttered.

As she searched the cupboard for a plate, her mind turned to all Niall had told her about the trip Shawn would have made through the mountains with Allene, still trying to guess what had brought on the apology. She tried to picture the Shawn she had known, alone with an attractive young girl, reaching Hugh's camp some days later, changed enough to risk carving an apology on Hugh's precious stone. It made no sense.

She found a plate and served up her dinner. There had been so much good with him—notes under the door, secret trips out of town, working together. And so much bad—the twisting in the gut trying to believe crazy stories, yet finding it impossible to doubt the hurt and innocent look on his face. Life hadn't been normal since she'd let herself get sucked into his world. But it hurt just as much when he suddenly disappeared.

She wanted to yell. She still had things to say. She wanted to hear the words *I'm sorry*, and the truth—one she could believe. She'd never hear those things now. So what had been the point of staying?

She sank into one of the rickety chairs at the kitchen table, staring blankly at food that no longer looked appetizing. Rose would be here soon, she consoled herself, and it would be okay. It always was, with Rose.

Stirling Castle, 1314

Niall and Allene stared at one another after the door shut.

"I thought 'twas you." Allene turned to the window, her arms wrapped around herself. "You knew 'twas not me."

"I'm sorry." Niall rested his hands on her shoulders.

She shrugged them off. "Did you fancy her?"

"She was fair, she was kind," he said. "And she did no wrong. She was upset she'd kissed me when she learned I was betrothed." He hesitated, but he'd always been honest with her. "They thought I was Shawn and that it was my bairn. I didn't know if I could get back or if Shawn would return to make her get rid of this child, too. I did what I could to provide for her."

He edged his shirt apart at the neck. She stared over her shoulder, and touched the base of his throat. "Your crucifix."

"'Tis worth a great deal then. We are to give all we have. We are to care for the widows and orphans, and in the world she lives in, that is what she and her child are, now that Shawn didn't get back." He hesitated, before telling her the rest, softly, hoping she wouldn't hear. "I asked for her hand, if I couldn't get back."

She turned to him, her eyes sad. His hands fell to hers.

"You are long gone in her time," he said. "But d' you see, I did all I could to come back to you."

She lifted her hands to his shoulders, and he kissed her, his hands in her hair, for much longer than five seconds.

Chapter Three

Edinburgh, Present

So slender she might fade into the very air, Miss Rose nonetheless filled the airport with her presence. Her smile, her laugh, her dress of layers of sheer, floating cream, and her cherry-red hat with a wide brim turned heads. She walked arm in arm with a teenager in fatigues, laughing together as if they were old friends. As travelers dispersed, a little girl broke free from her mother, and ran to Rose, throwing her arms around her waist. Amy's violin teacher waved farewell to the girl in camouflage and leaned down to return the child's hug. Then she lifted her head and saw Amy.

Her face lit with even more than its usual animation. "Amy!" She spoke to the girl. "This is my friend I told you about. She plays the violin like an angel! I've known her since she was younger than you!"

She waved good-bye to the child and spun Amy into her arms, planting a kiss on each cheek that knocked her red hat to the floor, releasing her hair into a dandelion puff too dark to be called strawberry blonde, and too light to be called auburn. "I've missed you so much! How *are* you?"

"Fine! Wonderful now that you're here!" Amy brightened, swept into Rose's energy.

"Have a good visit, Rose!" a middle-aged man called.

Rose turned to him. "You, too! Come and meet Amy! Isn't she pretty with her beautiful long hair? And so talented, too."

Amy blushed.

The man shook her hand. "A pleasure to meet you! Rose couldn't stop raving about you." A woman who might be the man's daughter bounced up and down, calling to get his attention, and he bid them farewell.

Rose scooped her hat up off the floor, linked her arm in Amy's, and steered her through the crowded airport, greeting half a dozen brand new friends as they weaved their way through the crowd to the baggage carousel. There, Rose heaved a floral suitcase off the belt, and, taking Amy's hand, charged through the airport, while Amy nearly ran to keep up. "I have orders from Conrad to treat you like royalty." She threw open the glass doors, bursting into the early July day. She lifted her face to a blazing blue sky. "Heaven! You've landed in heaven, Amy. I can't wait to see your house. Shopping or lunch?"

"Lunch." With anyone else, Amy might have prevaricated. Rose demanded and got answers. "There's a good pub near Edinburgh castle."

"And then we shop." Rose leaned half-way into the street, straining on tip-toes, and with sheer force of personality, brought a taxi screeching to a halt. She tossed her bag in the back seat, and soon had herself and Amy settled and the driver heading into Edinburgh. "Have you painted lately?"

"I haven't had time."

"Hm." Miss Rose made the sound that told Amy she knew there was more to the story. "You have time now. You were very good. We'll be getting you some supplies. Where's the nearest music store?"

Amy settled back against the taxi seat, relaxing in Rose's presence. "Rose, are you even like this at funerals?"

"I guess I must be," her teacher replied. "Because if he's not coming back, we rather are in the middle of a funeral."

"Do I have your permission to grieve?" Amy regarded her wryly.

"Oh, certainly!" Rose waved her hat, fanning herself. "In fact, you're under strict orders to grieve. But I've known you since you were three, Amy. You need your painting and music. Are you still writing?"

Amy shook her head. "We hadn't started the new CD." She turned quickly to stare out the window, hiding the tears she blinked back. "It was going to be Broadway hits." She'd been looking forward to it. Outside, fields flashed by. "I haven't composed without Shawn since—well, since college, before I even met him."

"You're not letting that talent go to waste," Rose informed her. "I expect a song before I go. And a painting. Horses? You're particularly good at those. What else would you like to see and do?"

When the taxi had dropped them at the pub, Rose pulled dozens of brochures from her straw purse and spread them over the table, taking Amy on a dizzying potential itinerary that left her almost as exhausted as if they'd actually visited each of the places. Amy was grateful when the waitress appeared with fish pie, coffee, and a glass of wine for Rose. Gathering the brochures, Rose flashed a smile. "Thank you, dear! It looks delicious! What's the best place in Scotland? What should I absolutely not miss?"

"Inverness," the waitress said promptly. "Shopping, theater, hiking, boating, anything you want."

"Inverness it is," Rose announced. "Thank you!" She turned to Amy as the waitress left. "Shall we take a bus or train?"

Amy picked up her fork. "You never run out of energy, do you?"

"Nope, and I don't intend to." Rose sipped her wine. "Glenmirril's in Inverness, isn't it?"

"You want to see Glenmirril?" Amy lowered her fork.

Miss Rose set her wine down. "That traumatic? What happened there, Amy?"

Amy stared at her fish pie. "I left him."

"You justifiably walked away. He's a grown man. Why didn't he follow you out of that tower?"

"He wanted to finish his picnic."

"His choice. He could have called a cab."

"His jacket was in the car," Amy said, "with his cell phone and money."

Rose sniffed. "He could have walked home. But what I want to know, Amy, is, *what happened* in that tower that upsets you so much?"

Amy pushed at the fish with her fork. "What did the news say?"

"That he was injured, had a fever and behaved strangely afterward, and then disappeared."

"That's about right."

"Amy, why won't you look at me? How was he injured?"

"An arrow," she mumbled.

"Like a bow and arrow?" Rose asked incredulously.

Amy lifted her eyes. "Rose, the news didn't say everything, because they don't know everything. It wasn't Shawn who left the tower with an arrow wound and a fever."

"What?" Rose leaned forward. "Metaphorically speaking? They kept saying he came back a different man."

"No." Amy shook her head. "It really wasn't him. It was a man named Niall. Did you watch the last concert?"

"*I am Niall Campbell, born in 1290, heir to Glenmirril.*" Rose leaned back in the booth. She closed her eyes, as she always had when Amy played a passage, and she was searching her fluid, colorful mind for ways to transform it from good to great. "*This is who I am.*" She opened her eyes, flashes of bright blue. "Yes, I watched it. In fact, the whole world has watched it about four million times, now, on YouTube. Two dozen of those were me, wondering what on earth he was doing."

"He was telling the truth," Amy said.

"So who *is* Niall Campbell? Don't the police know it wasn't Shawn?"

Amy shrugged. "I told them what he said. They don't believe it."

"You told them he said...?" Rose waited for her to fill in the blank.

"I told them he said he's Niall Campbell born in 1290, and wanted to get back to save the Scots at Bannockburn."

"Hm." Miss Rose swirled her wine. "No wonder they don't believe it. But *you* believe he wasn't Shawn. Why?"

"He had scars on his back. He didn't behave like Shawn. He was obsessed with Bannockburn."

"So he wasn't Shawn. And the police didn't run a search on this Niall because they believe it *was* Shawn."

Amy nodded.

"Did *you* Google him? Niall, I mean?"

"No." Amy took a bite of her fish. "He told me who he was."

"And you believed him?"

Amy set the fork down, leaning across the table. "I wish you could have met him, Rose."

"You believe him?" her teacher asked again.

Amy felt light inside, remembering Niall's smile, his hand on her hair. "I believe he was sincere. He was kind."

"Hm." Rose tasted her fish, eyebrows drawn. "So Shawn disappeared from *the tower*, and this Niall got shot with an arrow, had an infection and disappeared from the re-enactment?"

Amy stirred milk and sugar into her coffee. "Do you think I'm crazy?"

Rose frowned. "I've known you too long to think that. But it's a strange story at best. And if it's true, what *did* happen to Shawn? Where he is?"

Amy sipped her coffee. "He's gone." Tears stung her eyes. She set the coffee cup down with a clatter, and pressed a hand over her face. "And this child is going to grow up with no father."

Rose rounded the table abruptly, sliding onto the bench beside Amy, and put an arm around her. "I know it's not what you wanted, but thousands of children grow up without fathers, and it's not perfect, but they're okay."

"Remember my friend Colin, years ago?" Amy sniffed. "He hated not having a father." She bit her lip, trying not to sniffle. "I swore I would never do that to a child, and it's exactly what I've done."

"But *you* didn't do it," Rose insisted. "I won't even pretend to guess what happened, but he was gambling, drinking, cheating. You know what I think you need?"

"A therapist." Amy pressed a hand to her mouth. "Mental help."

Rose sniffed. "No, you don't need a therapist. You need to figure out why you accept so much blame. Then quit doing it. You need to go back to that tower."

Amy shook her head. "No."

"Because you can't face the place he disappeared or because you can't face your guilt? Unjustified guilt, I might add."

"I'm just not going back." Amy tried another bite of her fish pie, but her appetite was gone.

"Pick somewhere else, then. Because we won't be sitting home. After lunch, we hit the thrift stores and find you something fun to wear. No black, no sweatshirts."

Amy swallowed a smile. Only Rose could say such things without raising ire. As she had through fifteen years of lessons, she said, "Yes, Miss Rose."

"You're not waffling out of this," Rose warned. "Pick a place."

Stirling Castle, 1314

With Niall's drawings in one hand, the Laird glowered at Shawn's sketches of buses and twenty-first century clothing. Hugh, Niall, and Allene clustered around, studying his attempts to depict modern life.

"Okay, so I'm not an artist," Shawn said irritably.

MacDonald's eyebrows snapped down into a deep V over his nose. The scar running from temple to lip turned white, silencing Shawn.

Shawn came as close as he ever had to flushing, as he scrutinized his artistic efforts. Amy had a stroke of genius when it came to capturing images on paper. Ink splotches covered his work which, even with a ballpoint pen, would have been little better than stick figures and boxes with circles. Lines meandered between thick and thin, the quill and ink uncontrollable in his unpracticed hand. He ventured again. "You don't, uh, hang people for being unartistic, do you?"

MacDonald scowled at him. "For you, we'll consider it."

"Father!" Allene reprimanded. "You can see 'tis as Niall drew."

"I see you were right in saying he's no idea how to use a quill." He turned to Shawn. "Are you literate?"

Shawn's eyes widened in offense. "Are you...." He searched for a Gaelic word for *kidding*. "Are you jesting?"

MacDonald's eyebrows dipped lower still. The scar turned whiter. "We *do* hang men for disrespect."

"Sorry," Shawn muttered. "Everyone's literate in my time."

MacDonald stabbed a finger at his art. "You can't even use a quill!"

Shawn spread his hands. "We don't *have* quills."

"I told you they didn't," said Niall.

The Laird frowned. Shawn watched warily as he clasped his hands behind his back and strode to the window. Sweat prickled his back under his heavy linen shirt. He exchanged glances with Niall and Allene. Their faces gave him no clue.

"Can you speak Latin?" MacDonald turned back.

Why the hell would anyone want to speak Latin, sprang to Shawn's tongue. A shadow flickered across Niall's face. Shawn re-phrased his initial thought. "No."

"No, My Lord," Niall corrected.

When Shawn didn't respond, Allene raised slender eyebrows. "You'd best adapt to our ways while you're here."

Shawn's eyes flashed across the knives in Niall's and MacDonald's boots and at MacDonald's belt. "Yes, My Lord." Humility galled him.

"French?"

"A little." Enough to charm women, Shawn thought. Certainly there was no other use for the language.

"I believe the word you're looking for is *chan eil*. No." Hugh grinned in response to Shawn's glare.

"Can you fight with a sword?" MacDonald asked.

"No." Shawn's irritation mounted. Most people had been impressed at all the things he *could* do.

"Do you know where the Lammermuirs are? The River Esk? Do you know of James Douglas?" The Laird fired one question after another at him. "Can you ride? Can you hunt?"

Shawn shook his head at each, feeling steadily more like a recalcitrant schoolboy, rather than the accomplished phenomenon he'd been—would be—in a mere seven centuries. His anger deepened with his feeling of ineptitude.

MacDonald threw up his hands. "What *can* you do?" He turned in annoyance, to stare once more out the window to the blue sky beyond.

Shawn looked to Niall, searching for a clue. Niall looked away. Shawn turned to Allene. She smiled reassuringly.

Minutes ticked by, while Shawn's hands grew clammy and his insides curled in tight knots. Finally, MacDonald turned from the window. "Allene, you'll tutor him in penmanship and languages each morning and evening. Especially the bollox he's making of our native tongue."

"I grew up speaking Gaelic!" Shawn objected, his nervousness forgotten in his anger. "My Gaelic is flawless!"

"Flawless twenty-first century Gaelic, perhaps," Niall reminded him. "But very peculiar to fourteenth century ears."

"Hugh," the Laird said, "you'll school him on geography and clans."

Shawn half-rose from his chair. "Why? I'm going home."

Hugh gave a sharp shake of his head, warning him. He sat back down.

"Niall, you'll teach him to fight and ride."

"Ride!" Shawn shot to his feet. His chair scraped backward, tottered, and regained its balance. "Not on a horse! I don't do horses!"

"You'll do as I say." MacDonald's hand fell on the hilt of his knife.

Shawn's anger overrode the threat. He planted his hands on the table. "Why? Why do you want me learning all this? I'm going home!"

"Sit down," Hugh rumbled. His hand on Shawn's shoulder added weight to his suggestion.

Shawn sank into the chair, glaring at MacDonald.

Storm clouds rolled across the Laird's face. "We've no way of *getting* you home. You'll live as Niall. You must know all he knows."

"I don't *want* to live as Niall," Shawn informed him, his eyes burning.

"As you wish." MacDonald spoke mildly.

Shawn leaned back smugly in his chair. Niall and Allene glanced at one another.

"Hugh," MacDonald said, "put a hood over his face and take him to the dungeons. We've no explanation for his presence. We'll have to hang him."

Shawn felt the blood drain out of his face.

"Yes, My Lord." Hugh laid a hand on his arm. "Come along, Shawn. Hanging's not so bad. 'Tis the drawing and quartering you mightn't care for."

"I'll live as Niall," Shawn said hastily. "I love quills! I love Latin!"

Inverness, Present

In the small, crowded office they shared at precinct headquarters, Sergeant Chisolm slapped a manila folder on his partner's desk.

Inspector MacLean looked up, scowling. "I'm working." He pushed the folder off his report. "What is this?"

"Shawn Kleiner." Chisolm dropped into the wheeled office chair at his own desk, twelve inches from MacLean's.

"Him." Irritation flashed across MacLean's face. "Case closed, is it not?"

"It is. The orchestra's gone home." Chisolm leaned forward, piercing MacLean with a meaningful gaze. "Ninety-eight of them."

"Counting tickets is not my business." MacLean jotted on his report.

"There are a hundred in a symphony orchestra," Chisolm pressed.

"Kleiner didn't go home." MacLean looked up. "Who else?"

"The girlfriend stayed." Chisolm looked smug.

"Did she now?" The irritation smoothed off MacLean's face. He set his pen down. "Did she take time off?"

"Resigned her post entirely."

"She didn't," MacLean breathed. "Why?"

"Thought you'd be interested." Chisolm tapped the file smugly. "She's let a house in Bannockburn. As to why, I couldn't say."

MacLean frowned at the papers cluttering his desk. "You've thought all along she knows something she isn't telling."

"She was too nervous," Chisolm said.

"She'd had quite a few shocks." MacLean rubbed his chin.

"Too careful choosing her words. 'Tis odd, quitting your job and staying behind."

MacLean tapped his pen on his desk. "When your boyfriend has just disappeared under such circumstances? Maybe she wants to be nearby." He took his cell phone from his pocket, clicked a few buttons, and stared at the screen, frowning. He stowed it back in his pocket and asked brusquely, "Do we call her in for more questioning?"

"The case is closed, Angus. She's done nothing illegal. And she's out of our jurisdiction now, is she not?"

MacLean frowned, leaning back in his chair. "She is. Keep me updated all the same, will you?"

Stirling Castle, 1314

MacDonald set Shawn straight to work. Niall led him, still moving gingerly with his injury, around the castle compound in the mist before dawn, learning every building. He attended Mass as the sun rose. Through the morning, Allene supervised his attempts with a quill, making him copy French verbs and Latin prayers, even as he repeated them aloud, perfecting his speech, straining his ear to capture every idiom and nuance.

He spent afternoons in his room, learning hand to hand combat with MacDonald, Hugh, or Niall. His back ached from falling on the stone floor as they came at him time and again, the Laird always with a new surprise, Hugh with brute force, and Niall with lightning strikes.

And while they grasped his wrist to yank him off the floor, they battered him with questions. *Which way are the Cheviots? Name Bruce's sisters. Where has Elizabeth been held these many years? Do you even remember who Elizabeth is?* And their wooden practice swords flashed again, striking, and the cry of, "You're dead! Watch, man, *watch!*" rang in his ears.

Before dinner, he practiced pieces Niall played on harp. He retaliated by taunting Niall with a recorder they found. "*You* learn something. Keep your fingers in place. The melody goes up by a third there, can't you hear that? Wrong fingering." The Laird grumbled about the time. But Niall took Shawn's part. "You never know what will be of use."

With his face hidden by a hooded robe, Shawn watched from the corner of the courtyard one day, learning faces and names, as Niall's mother, with her entourage, departed to visit kin on her way back to Glenmirril. She hugged Niall warmly, and mounted her horse, and with several dozen men, rode out through the gates of Stirling. In the shadows, Shawn thought of his own mother. He wondered if Amy would stay in touch with her, be there for her, now that she was all alone.

Most nights, he ate in his room, while MacDonald quizzed him on politics and battles, but he spent two evenings in the great hall in Niall's place, enjoying his time with Allene and the men from Hugh's camp, and swilling his ale deeply. The men called for the song he'd played the night before battle, and he consented, taking Niall's harp and singing. The whole hall joined, Bruce and his brother Edward standing and lifting stone goblets high, bellowing the refrain. *And stood against the English might, and sent them fleeing home!* Shawn met Allene's eye. They both turned away uncomfortably.

Amy was ever on his mind.

So was his loneliness.

"Don't dare make me look bad by eyeing the lasses," Niall had warned before Shawn had gone down to dinner. His hand had rested on the hilt of his knife, and his usual humor had been absent. "Anything you do will be attributed to me." All the same, Shawn didn't think Niall would appreciate him smiling at Allene.

Niall stood atop the ramparts with him each evening, naming hills and rivers, making him repeat it back until his head spun with names, directions and landmarks, and his dreams were filled with Galloway Hills, lineages, rivers, King Alexander, John Balliol, and all that Niall knew.

The Laird watched, assessing every moment and, Shawn was sure, hearing every word. His neck itched, feeling a phantom rope, wondering what the Laird was deciding behind those fierce, lowered eyebrows.

Falkirk, Scotland, Present

What am I doing? What am I doing? What am I doing! The words pounded through Amy's brain, beating down as hard as the glaring sun, as she crossed the broad lawn sweeping before the Callendar Park mansion with its broad wings and fairy tale turrets. An art bag, loaded with new supplies, hung on her shoulder. Heat prickled her neck.

"I'm so glad you picked a place." Rose clutched her broad-brimmed hat to her head. A breeze swirled her skirt around white Victorian boots. "I was beginning to think I'd never get an answer out of you."

Amy lifted her sunglasses to peer at Rose with a mischievous smile. "Self preservation! I can't afford any more of your shopping trips!" She settled the glasses back on her nose. The truth was, as she'd lain in bed, holding the crucifix Niall had left, staring at the leafy silhouette of the tree outside her window, her mind had drifted, like a twig on a river, between the two banks of Shawn and Niall, and an urge had grown in her to see the place Niall's father had died. Yesterday's research had led her to Callendar Park, a likely site for the battle of Falkirk that had claimed James Campbell's life.

Pausing before the mansion, Rose studied Amy's denim capris and royal blue sleeveless top that stood out like a sapphire against her long black braid. Self conscious under the appraisal, Amy pushed a long tendril of hair, curling with perspiration in the warm day, behind her ear.

"You're beautiful," Rose announced. "Black and gray are elegant, of course. Very much what your mother might wear. But don't you feel better in these bright colors than you did sitting in church in black?"

"In my defense," Amy protested, "I came on an orchestra tour. That means lots of concert black."

"And now you feel beautiful in bright colors!" Rose didn't ask.

The sun blazed in the blue summer sky. Amy laughed. "Yes, Miss Rose."

"Oh, stop that!" Rose laughed, too, and linked her arm in Amy's, steering her past the mansion, toward the loch. "What sparked your interest in Falkirk?"

"Well, there's lots to draw." Amy couldn't resist teasing Rose. "You did tell me I would be drawing while you're here."

"I also told you to call your parents," Rose reminded her, "and you haven't. It's taken some doing on my part, these last few conversations with your mother, to convince her to give you time. Since when have you wanted to draw a ditch?"

"It's not a ditch," Amy objected. "It's Antonine's Wall."

"It *was* Antonine's Wall," Rose sniffed. "It *is* a ditch. Historical value aside, you wouldn't choose to draw a ditch. So why Falkirk?"

Yes, why? Amy asked herself. There was nothing to be learned here. It didn't even directly relate to Niall or Shawn. "The mansion, gardens, swan boats," she said. "They're all perfect for drawing." As they approached the pond, she added, "It'll make a beautiful water color, don't you think?"

"Hm." Rose shaded her eyes to scan people paddling swan boats on the smooth, blue surface, past the small island in the middle. "You made the mistake of leaving me a whole day to read."

Amy narrowed her eyes at Rose. There was no way she could guess.

"It didn't go over my head that one James Campbell of Glenmirril died here in 1298." Rose pulled a brochure from her straw purse to fan herself. "Was he Niall's father or brother?"

"Father." Amy clamped her mouth tight, but the word had slipped out. She cursed her tendency toward full candor. Maybe she ought to have moved half an inch in Shawn's direction on the honesty spectrum. "I mean," she hedged, "I mean—Rose, why are you hounding me?"

"A man who looks like Shawn claims to be Niall Campbell of Glenmirril, who would have been eight when James Campbell of Glenmirril died at Falkirk, and here we are," Rose replied. "A convoluted path, but I hardly think coincidental. And you were quick to say James was his father."

On the loch, a couple on a swan boat laughed. Amy spun and marched for the woods. Rose hastened after, reaching for her arm. "You're right," she said. "Listen to me, going on at you. I'm sorry. I know things were rocky with Shawn, but it's still a loss. And traumatic, the way it happened. But something isn't sitting right, and you won't say what. I guess I'm just trying to get you to talk to me, like you used to."

Muggy July air filled Amy's lungs. She hurried toward the shady woods. "Talk about what?" she asked. "He's done some horrible things this past year, and my gut says there's more. My head tells me I'm a fool to still feel anything for him, but I do. What must people think of me?"

The shade of the grove welcomed them. The glare of the sun settled into a leafy green filter of pale light on the dim path, but the air still clung, damp and heavy. Amy flapped the neck of her shirt, trying to cool herself.

"Don't worry about anyone else," Rose said. "They don't understand if they haven't been there. But you're hardly the only one to love longer than you should have."

"Have you?" Amy demanded. "Do you have any idea what it's like?"

"You know I was married?" Rose queried in return.

"You mentioned it years ago." Sweat trickled down Amy's back.

"For five years." In the dim copse, Rose removed her hat, fanning herself. Her reddish hair gave a puff with each flap of the hat. "The night I met you was the worst night of my life."

"That's hard to believe." Amy stopped on the shady path, studying her friend. "I remember it like it was yesterday. You were playing by the Christmas tree, in white lace while all my mother's friends wore black and bottle green velvet. And you kept looking up at me and smiling."

"Yes, I did." Rose laughed, a cheery sound on the quiet trail. She linked her arm in Amy's and began walking again. "I felt better when you smiled back. You looked so lonely sitting up there."

"What happened that night?" Amy asked.

Rose sighed, staring up into the leafy canopy as they walked. "He was like a prince in a Disney cartoon. Tall, good-looking, talented, cheerful. Everyone loved him. He could romance like he had a team of Hollywood scriptwriters behind him. He made me feel like a princess."

As if on cue, a bird warbled high in the trees. "My friends started saying they'd seen him with other women," Rose said. "I didn't believe it because I'd known someone good and kind for eight years."

"What finally convinced you?" Amy's feet scuffed on the soft forest path.

"I found a note. One he couldn't explain away." Rose smiled. "In retrospect, I should have enjoyed the show, watching him squirm and try to come up with a story. It was really quite funny." The smile drifted away on the sound of a sigh. "To someone who wasn't in the middle of heartbreak."

"Yeah." Amy's heart squeezed as if she were still hearing Shawn's lies, torn, wanting him to be the man who had brought so much joy into her life. A rabbit darted from the foliage. "With voicemail and travel and time differences, an agent *might* call at two in the morning."

Rose laughed. "These men are masters of stories that *might* be true. And we *want* to believe them. Life with him was so good, I wanted it to last forever."

Amy nodded. "That's how it was with Shawn, the first year and a half."

"But I knew that night at your parents' party that it was over, and it felt like having my heart ripped out and put through a meat grinder. Nothing ever hurt so much in my life. It's so hard to reconcile the person you thought you knew with the monster staring you in the face. Makes you a little crazy."

"A lot crazy," Amy said softly. "My head tells me I shouldn't waste tears over him when he made me feel that way."

"The head and the heart play at two different tempos." Rose stopped, peering through foliage and pine trees. "Is this the mausoleum the brochure mentioned?" She veered onto a side path, charging uphill.

Amy followed, pushing at ferns that hung over onto the narrow path, to a massive round edifice like a Greek temple. Its gray stone base, covered in graffiti, rose above her head. Columns stretched higher yet, supporting a flat roof. Rose marched up to it, touching it and studying its surface, before turning back to Amy. "The head reaches the *fine* first. It takes time for the heart to get there. It's often many pages behind."

"Doesn't make for very harmonious music," said Amy.

"Every great piece has some dissonance. Goodness, it's hot!" Rose disappeared abruptly around the tomb.

Amy glanced up at the dappled green filtering down through the trees. A shaft of light skimmed down one side of the mausoleum, turning it silver, highlighting the ugly scrawls that defaced its timeless beauty. She seated herself under a tree, and pulled her sketch pad and pencils from her art bag.

The air grew warmer. Midges swarmed around her face. She waved them away, disrupting their dance and thinking of those long-ago Scots, waiting in formation with their pikes. James Campbell, maybe in chain mail and leather boots, stood among them. Did he swipe at midges, too? Did he think of his sons, executed by the same English waiting across the field to kill him in his turn? Did he think of Niall and Finola, his children back at Glenmirril praying for his return?

Humidity filled Amy's lungs. She breathed deeply, pulling in sticky air. The image was disturbingly vivid. Here where James had died, she could almost see him watching her—an older, grayer version of Shawn and Niall, with weathered skin and laugh lines crinkling into sorrow around his eyes. Trying to shake the feeling, she set her charcoal pencil to the paper, sketching the crypt with firm strokes.

Rose returned from her inspection of the monolithic tomb, settling herself beside Amy. Her white skirt pooled around her. "It's like people," she said.

Amy's pencil paused. She looked up into Rose's eyes, blue as the hot July sky above. "What's like people?"

"The battle of Falkirk." Rose dug in her purse. Brochures in vivid reds, blues, and greens spilled like jewels over her white skirt. She snatched one up, waving it triumphantly.

Amy laughed. "Rose, only you would come up with such a comparison. How is the battle of Falkirk like people?"

"You seem to think you need to sum Shawn up and place him in a single column, good or bad. Like accounting. One final answer."

"Well, it would be easier." Amy sketched in the foliage hanging over the mausoleum. "Then maybe my heart would hurry and reach the *coda* and I'd feel sane and happy like I used to."

"But life isn't so simple." Rose fanned herself vigorously. "It's more like music. Majors, minors, tri-tones. They all work together."

"And what does this have to do with a medieval battle?" Amy paused in her drawing to wipe a bead of sweat slipping down her temple. "Besides, I'm not really seeing any good in this one, in particular."

"What do you know about it?" Rose asked.

Amy laid the pencil down. "Their own lords deserted them!" Her voice shot out a third above normal, as if it touched her personally. But it did. She had known, almost loved, Niall, even promised to consider marrying him. And his father had died here, maybe lay here still, bones beneath the earth. It *did* touch her personally.

Rose frowned.

Amy cleared her throat. She tried to speak as if it were inconsequential —just meaningless words in a history book, not someone's life, not a boy of eight left fatherless. "It was a horrible defeat. There's nothing good in that."

Rose tapped the brochure. "But defeat here was only one movement! It wasn't the *fine*."

"It was for...." Amy's jaw tightened. She looked down to her sketch pad, taking an intense interest in shading the columns.

"For Niall's father?" Rose arched one eyebrow. "You speak as if you knew him."

"Don't be ridiculous." Amy's pencil came down hard, making one column too dark. She scrubbed at it with an eraser, only smearing it more. "What good do *you* see here?"

Rose leaned forward, the brochure crumpling in her grip. Her eyes shone. "William Wallace kept fighting. Almost single-handedly. How did his example change everyone around him? How did it shame and inspire those run-away lords? He made them believe they *could* win against the most powerful nation in the world! How did that change history?"

The eraser in Amy's hand sagged to the drawing pad. Niall had changed history. But maybe Wallace's persistence against impossible odds had inspired him to push forward, even in the face of waking up in the wrong century. He could have given up. He could have settled into Shawn's life of ease and plenty. Amy wiped her hand across her perspiring forehead.

Rose lifted the brochure. "Edward II had a hollow victory here. His men were hungry, deserting. He left and didn't come back for three years, which gave the Scots time to regroup."

Amy nodded. "Okay. But Shawn...."

"There was good in him, too, Amy." Rose gripped her arm. "Don't hate yourself for mourning him is what I'm trying to say. He made people happy."

"In more ways than one." A diminished note of bitterness colored Amy's words.

Rose snorted. "I'm sure. Did you think he'd change for you? His type rarely does, and it's not because you weren't good enough. He had a reputation, which I'd hoped he'd put in the past. That aside, the last time he played at Lincoln Center, he held his taxi for my friend, went out with his umbrella to meet her, and had the taxi take her home first. He paid the bill."

"He had plenty of money." Amy dismissed his good deed. "You know, I'm not sure you're helping. It would be easier for me to just hate him."

"But you don't," Rose pointed out. "And you hate yourself for *not* hating him. And you shouldn't." She lowered the brochure. "Kindness always matters. My friend is arthritic. What he did meant a great deal to her. That's part of who he was, Amy. It's okay to grieve that."

Amy stared at the half-drawn picture on her lap. Tears pooled in her eyes. "He was tormented," she said. "His father's murder really messed him up. I think I saw the person he would have been, even tried to be." She closed the drawing pad. "But Niall's father died, too. And...." She stopped, breathing heavily in the heat. She couldn't tell Rose Niall had been kind and good; she couldn't say she'd known him personally.

She lifted her eyes to Rose. A man bolted from behind a tree, charging with a pike, mouth drawn in fury. Amy scrambled to her feet, the sketch pad and pencil falling to the dirt path.

"Amy!" Rose leapt to her feet. "Are you okay?"

The man disappeared, leaving only herself and Rose by the decaying tomb, amid the leafy trees and birdsong.

"I'm fine!" Amy grabbed for the sketch pad, the pencil, the art bag, shoving them at one another. "Sorry. It must be the heat." Or an overactive imagination. Shawn had always said she imagined things. "We better head back, maybe get something to drink." Struggling to breathe in the damp air, Amy plowed down the forest path, fleeing the ghosts of Falkirk.

Stirling Castle, 1314

With a glance at Shawn, Niall hefted a wooden sword from the pile Hugh had left in the dewy grass at the edge of the field. "Ready?" Across the field, other men practiced, their swords crashing against one another.

"Breeze." Shawn smirked. "Hell, this isn't even real." Being outdoors lifted his spirits, even if the Laird had insisted he wear a heavy steel helmet that covered most of his face, and made it impossible to flirt with the women in their flowing skirts and sleeves nearly sweeping the floor. But the early morning breeze and grass under his feet still beat another day quoting Latin prayers, surrounded by the same four stone walls.

Niall smiled and tossed the sword. It jolted into Shawn's hand, jarring his arm and wrenching his shoulder as it slammed into the dirt, dragging him off balance. Pain shot across his abdomen. He righted himself and shot Niall a dirty look. "This weighs three times what the real ones do!"

"Only twice as much," Niall corrected.

"How am I supposed to fight with this?" Shawn gestured angrily at it.

"Picking it up would be a good start." Niall reached for a second weapon. He swung it in a lazy arc.

"No." Shawn clamped his hands on his hips, glaring through the helmet's slits. "This is ridiculous. Get me something that weighs what the real ones do."

"Have it your way." Niall's wooden sword flashed high in the air.

"Hey, hey, *hey!*" Shawn threw his hands up over his head. "Where's the chivalry! You attack an unarmed man?"

"You're unarmed because you'll not pick up your weapon!" Niall lowered his sword, but pushed his face in Shawn's. "Is that going to work in battle?"

"What if they gave a war, and nobody came?" Shawn countered. With his leather-booted toe, he kicked at the offensive object. "Ride the peace train. You people are behind the times. Downright medieval."

"So you've said. Pick up your sword."

Grunting and clutching the wound that still gave him sharp twinges with exertion, Shawn heaved the thing from the dirt with both hands.

"Maybe you should try swinging it first," Niall suggested.

"Yeah, you think?" Shawn slashed it through the air a few times, its weight like lead in his arms. "Why do they make them so heavy?"

"Build up strength. If you can fight with this, you stand a better chance of survival with enemies coming at you. Now, see the pell?"

"The stick guy over there?" Shawn nodded at the six foot post with a shield stuck to its front. A large blackbird sat atop its helmet.

"If that's what you call it. Hit it. Three points for head, shoulders, or abdomen."

"Let's start on my level," Shawn suggested. "How about three points if I manage not to let him hit me first?" In the distance, men shouted and called as they drilled.

Niall quirked a smile, though he fought it back. "How about a point if *I* don't hit you first? You're the most ill-mannered student I've ever been unfortunate enough to be saddled with."

"And you're the most humorless sword instructor *I've* ever been saddled with."

"You've had many?" Niall raised one eyebrow.

"None, thank God."

"It shows."

"Mr. Motivation, aren't you?" Shawn scratched at his back, where sweat prickled under the thick gambeson. "I'm not seeing you as a successful leader in the business world."

"I'm in the business of staying alive, and I find the prospect of dying in battle to be powerful motivation. You ought to, as well." Niall swung his sword at his side. "Hit the pell."

With a grumble, Shawn hefted his sword to his waist and managed to fling its tip at the post. It struck what would have been a man's knees before sagging to the ground. The bird atop the pole flapped its wings, scolding, but didn't budge.

"Hm." Niall frowned. "Worse than I expected."

"You don't read parenting books do you?" Shawn hadn't felt inept in years. Heat flushed his face under the metal helmet. His embarrassment came out as anger. "Here's where you say rah, rah, good effort!"

"'Twas a poor effort if any at all." Niall selected another weapon from the pile and tossed it at him. "This one's a little lighter."

They worked while the sun climbed high in the sky, till Shawn's muscles screamed in pain, till sweat ran down his back under the padded gambeson, till his mouth was dry as sandpaper, and a headache throbbed in his temples, till he vowed he'd take the wooden sword to Niall as soon as he had the strength to swing it. They worked to the sound of men and horses racing at quintains across the field. Finally, with the sun blazing directly overhead, Hugh approached, swinging a leather bag.

"Dinner." Niall grinned, lowering his sword. "And I daresay some ale."

"I daresay it's high time." Shawn tugged his helmet off. Light and air and a full range of vision had never felt so good. "You people have a startling lack of awareness of the dangers of *dehydration*." He used English where there was no Gaelic.

"What's that?" Niall asked.

"Lack of water."

"Aye, well, we're not given water breaks in battle, are we?" Niall hailed Hugh. The giant of a man tossed the sack the last couple of feet, and Niall caught it easily.

"Progress?" Hugh asked.

"Barely."

"I object!" Shawn flung down his sword. "I scared off that crow!"

"No, it was flying home to get its friends to come and laugh at you, too." Niall chuckled, pulled out a bundle of bannocks wrapped in a kerchief, and tossed a couple to Shawn. He wolfed them down. Hugh took a long draft of ale from the skin he carried, before passing it on.

Shawn hesitated only a moment before deciding he'd risk germs over dehydration. The ale slid down his throat cold and wet and more glorious than anything he'd ever drunk. His irritation with Niall slid away as quickly. A broad grin covered his face. "Whew, that's good!" he shouted. "What do you guys put in this stuff?"

"Hard physical labor," Niall said dryly.

"It makes everything taste better," Hugh added. "After you eat, Allene's ready to work with him on his script and Latin."

"*Veni, vidi, vici,*" Shawn muttered. "*Carpe diem.* Fish today."

Hugh shook his head and walked away. Niall slung the pack of food on his back, and they walked together to a tree on the edge of the field. Shawn sank in exhaustion to the ground, leaning against the broad trunk. He closed his eyes, feeling the hot noon sun shine bright against his lids, while sword-fighting instructions and Latin and clans marched through his weary mind. Bruce, Turnberry Castle, Elizabeth, Marjory, Douglas, Conrad at the castle hotel, Dan, his own small mansion on its spread of trees and fields, parties, the orchestra and Rob and Dana laughing, drinking freely of champagne.

"Why did you treat Amy so poorly?"

"Huh?" Shawn jolted, surprised at his feet jarring against soft earth, and the tree rough against his back, trying to remember where he was.

"She was—is—kind. She deserved better."

Shawn said nothing. His aching body and exhausted mind hovered between the medieval field, gambeson, helmet, and wooden sword, and his twenty-first century home with its modern appliances and his first party there, just before Christmas, where he'd so recently been in his sleep.

"'Tis none of my affair," Niall apologized.

"No, 'tis not," Shawn mimicked. His irritation from the morning returned. He dropped his head back against the tree, staring up into the foliage overhead. A bird sang, and far away, a sheep bleated.

"Still," Niall said, "it seems we'll be spending a great deal of time together. She wasn't your sort. Did you love her at all?"

"That's right, this is the age of chivalry and romance, isn't it?" Shawn spoke with derision. "You'd care about a thing like that."

"Is there a time when one wouldn't?" Niall asked. "Do men not care about love in your time?"

Shawn shrugged. "Yeah, I guess." The bird sang, a trilling pitch as beautiful as the clink of champagne glasses, as light as the laughter at the Christmas party. Shawn drifted back into the night. It had been the first big party in his new home, after a big write-up in a national paper, when his first CD and his recording with Mannheim Steamroller had taken off and he'd made himself the 22-year-old owner of a small mansion on twenty acres.

He'd invited the whole orchestra. Amy had gone ice skating with him just a week before. He was sure she'd come. He found reasons to be near the door, hoping, waiting. It was easy at first, with people arriving, needing to be let in. As the party reached full swing, and his guests demanded his attention, it became harder.

His eyes wandered past whomever he chatted with, searching the growing crowd of musicians, neighbors, and children. He drank more and grew more lively as the night wore on. When groups began to leave, he knew she wasn't coming. Dana sidled up to him, touching his arm. "Hey." She lifted a martini glass. "Where's the Christmas spirit? Why are you looking so down at your own party?"

"Only thinking you're leaving soon." He put a smile on his face. Nobody ever found him down. "That would bring anyone down. You know you have beautiful eyes?"

She rolled those eyes. "As does every woman, according to you."

He grinned. "Just because I notice doesn't mean it isn't true."

"Want some help cleaning?" Not waiting for an answer, she circled the great room, gathering dishes, and carried them to the spacious kitchen. He followed with a few wine glasses. "Are you disappointed Amy didn't come?" she asked over her shoulder.

"Amy who?"

She laughed. "You think you're fooling anyone? Get those plates from the table." He obeyed, amused at her taking charge. She plunged her arms deep into the sink full of suds. "It's your house. Grab a towel and start drying. You think I don't see how you look over my shoulder at her all the time? And how you try to wheedle information from me about her? I don't blame you. She's sweet."

He set wine glasses on the expanse of granite counter, and threw a handful of streamers in the garbage. "Do I look like I do sweet?"

She had looked up from the dishes. For once, she didn't smile. "Maybe something in you knows that's exactly what you need."

"Did you love her?" Niall's voice yanked him back to the medieval field.

"Yeah, I did." Shawn leaned against the tree, staring up into fluffy clouds. He'd felt like a better man with her, like maybe he could be all the good she saw in him. "She was exactly what I needed."

Chapter Four

The nightmare jarred Amy awake, as it had each night—the child crying, horse rearing, sword slashing; the dead kings of Iona surrounding Shawn in mouldering shrouds. She jolted upright in bed, breathing hard, icy sweat beading her forehead. She smelled blood. She heard the screams of men and horses. And saw Shawn, stumbling. Falling to one knee.

She felt in the dark for the lamp. Light flooded the room. She startled at the flash of white tangled in the peach and lace bedspread, still seeing the clinging grave clothes of long-dead kings.

It was only Shawn's robe.

She touched it. It was soft, warm, and whole, and smelled faintly of his aftershave. She looked around, at white walls, worn blue carpet, the framed photo of herself and Shawn on the dresser, trying to pull herself from the nightmare. Lace curtains fluttered at the window. The moon glowed silver outside, tangled in leafy tree branches. She laid her hand on her flat stomach. Her child would never know its father. *There'll be other people to love you,* she promised silently. Still—fathers mattered.

She swung her feet to the floor. His trombone case stood in the corner. She hefted it onto the bed, and took his trombone out, smiling as she thought of the day she'd handed it to Niall. The shock on his face had been priceless, especially knowing now that he'd thought he'd be locked up or shot if he couldn't play a concert. She worked the slide. It was sticky. Shawn would hate that. She blew in the mouthpiece, producing a rough foghorn of sound. Not wanting to disturb Rose, she lowered it to her lap, seeing Shawn at the jazz club, and prancing across the stages of concert halls. He had been born for this. It was part of him.

Her mind wandered to the women storming the stage, the way he'd kissed them. It hadn't bothered her at first. She'd accepted his explanation. *It's an act, that's all. We're selling tickets like hotcakes!* It was after finding the woman's name on his phone, and the story sounding off, that his act had started bothering her, regardless of how many tickets it sold.

Irritated at the memories, she stowed the trombone back in its case, and went instead to pick up the photograph off the dresser. Tioram's stone walls rose behind her and Shawn. Its green slope raced down to the camera's lens. April's stiff breezes had blown Shawn's golden chestnut hair, and she had huddled into his arm. His smile had looked more genuine, more relaxed, than usual. It had been a good week, just the two of them, no unexplained absences on Shawn's part. He'd told stories of fishing trips with his father in northern Minnesota. He'd found a way into Tioram, despite its barred entrance, and they'd spent the night.

She turned her right hand, looking at the Bruce's ring, which Shawn had thrown to her. "Why couldn't you have been like that all the time?" she asked his image, and set it back down.

Stirling Castle, 1314

"It's a bloody prison!" Shawn slapped down the quill, and rose, almost throwing himself into his favorite seat on the window sill. He glared at Niall, polishing the great sword on his lap to a high sheen. "And who studies Latin at this time of day!"

"'Tis no prison!" Allene scoffed as she jabbed his quill back in its holder. Rosy sunlight streamed in the window at an hour much earlier than Shawn would have willingly witnessed. "You're well fed and let out often. Have you no dungeons where you come from?"

"*When* I come from, Allene," he corrected. Sitting on the sill, watching dozens of workmen scurry through the early morning mist below, he looked to Niall for support. Niall raised his eyebrows, and grinned, rubbing a cloth over the blade, but offered no help.

"You'd best be careful saying such things," Allene retorted.

"Yeah, okay, I won't say it outside this room." He swung his feet to the floor, biting off each of the next words. "But I barely leave. And even when I do, every minute of my time is under someone else's control. Every minute," he emphasized. "That makes it a prison."

Allene tossed her head. Niall rose, placing his father's great sword in a chest. "Well, I've good news. Have you noticed the activity outside?"

"Yeah, it's hard to miss, when I'm locked up here like Rapunzel. What's up with that?" He hoped it wasn't a hanging. Especially his.

"Festivities to celebrate our victory," Allene said.

A weight lifted off his shoulder. He'd live a few more days.

"Bruce has asked me to play harp." Niall smirked as he closed the lid on the chest. "He thinks I play well and foresee the future."

"If only he knew." From the window, Shawn rolled his eyes at his mirror image. "The original words were a lament about the slaughter of the Scots. *I* changed that. *I* gave them hope and inspired them."

"I thank you for the boost to my reputation." Niall bit back a laugh.

"You ought to learn the piece I played in case he wants to hear it again," Shawn said.

"I've stumbled through it a few times already, but perhaps you can teach it to me as you played it. I've time tonight."

"I'll check my blackberry," Shawn muttered, staring out once more to the castle grounds and the hills beyond.

Niall and Allene exchanged glances. "Berries?" Allene whispered.

Niall shrugged and added, "I'm also to take part in the tourney."

"The tourney? What, that jousting stuff? You do that?" Shawn turned from the window. His eyes fell on Niall's bare forearms, knotted with muscle he'd never noticed before. What was it he'd originally thought of Niall? A namby-pamby? Because he hadn't gotten to first base with Allene? He realized with a start that this man was strong, and skilled, and he was just as glad to be on his good side, never mind where he'd gotten with Allene.

"All men of rank do." Niall crossed the room to a closet of dark wood. "The Laird says you're to wait in my tent and can take a turn going around the grounds while I stay out of sight."

"He ought to let me do it more. Lot of good I'll do anyone when I can barely find my way around the castle."

Allene rose from the table, joining Niall at the wardrobe.

"D' you not yet understand that our lives hang in the balance?" Niall looked back over his shoulder. "The Laird needs to know he can trust you. Why d' you think he's here every night talking with you?"

"My charming personality?"

Allene coughed delicately into her hand before reaching into the wardrobe. Niall arched one doubtful eyebrow, as he, too, pulled out clothing. Allene carried a bundle to the bed, laying out a gray robe, and two surcoats in royal blue and white.

Shawn touched one gingerly. "My dad would have killed to see this," he whispered. Awareness grew in him, and he looked from one to the other. "You better not be expecting *me* to joust. I don't even know which end of a horse to get on." He thought painfully of Amy. She had loved horses.

Allene ducked her head, hiding a smile.

"I'd not sully my name by having you fight in my stead." Niall laid two hauberks on the bed with a heavy chinking and clattering of chain links.

Shawn snorted. "So far everything I've done has made you look better. Miracle recovery, my hairy...." He looked from Niall's suddenly stern face to Allene's hastily lowered eyes. "...knuckles."

"There's much to be done before the tournament and feasting. Allene, leave us while Shawn changes."

Allene crossed the room.

"Is the Laird done having her make sure we don't compare notes?"

At the door, Allene gave him a tight frown.

"Can you blame him?" Niall asked. "'Tis a wild tale from a stranger, and we've cause to be wary these days."

Shawn grunted his concession. Satisfied, Allene left the room, while Niall named the various articles of clothing for Shawn. "You'll wear a cloak and hood over them while I show you the grounds. Learn every face. Listen carefully."

"I don't get it." Shawn shrugged out of his vest. "War's over, we won." He tossed aside his much-worn linen shirt.

"We are at war till we have a treaty." Niall removed his own vest. "Edward refuses to recognize us as our own country, he names us rebels, and would hang any one of us for treason." Niall spat out the last word.

"But what exactly does the Laird want with me?" Shawn examined the scar the sword had etched across his abdomen. It ran, red and puckered, around the left side of his waist and across his stomach. "How am I going to explain this when I get back?" he asked in irritation.

"*If* you get back," Niall said. "'Tis a fine battle scar. Ladies love them."

"I thought you were far too pure to think about what ladies love."

Niall grinned. "I'm only trying to be helpful to those among us who think of naught else." He tugged his shirt off over his head, and donned a fresh tunic.

Shawn rolled his eyes. "Well, thanks for thinking of me, but *I've* never had to rely on battle scars to attract women." He yanked a linen tunic over his head and tugged it into place.

"But then, your usual barbaric tactics don't work so well here." Niall handed him a padded gambeson.

Shawn wiggled into it. "My tactics are not...."

With a pointed glance at the long scar on Shawn's palm, Niall dropped the hauberk over Shawn's head with a heavy chinking and enough force to buckle Shawn's knee. He staggered under the weight and caught himself. He struggled to get his arms through the long chain link sleeves, feeling for a moment suffocated in the dark weight of the thing, before one arm, then another, found a sleeve and worked through, and he came up for air, shaking like a dog emerging from water. "Allene told you about that?" Shawn took an inadvertent step backward.

"'Twas your good fortune you'd just saved Scotland and were in no condition to fight or I may have killed you." Niall spoke with a pleasant smile that left Shawn little doubt he meant every word. Niall slipped his arms into the sleeves of his own gambeson.

"Yeah, well. Thanks, I guess." It was a subject best avoided. "How do you move in this stuff, let alone fight?"

"Years of training." Niall donned his chain mail and surcoat.

"Yeah. Well. I can't do anything for you people. I can barely move. I don't know what the Laird is thinking."

"He does not yet know how our likeness may serve, but feels it too good a chance to pass, and best to be ready. We've no way to send you back, and no way to explain your presence." Niall tweaked Shawn's mail shirt, settling it into place, and reached for the blue and white surcoat.

Shawn squirmed in head first, while Niall sighed at his ineptitude. "If I can figure out the internet, you can certainly put on a surcoat with more grace than that."

Shawn's head emerged from the long garment, and his arms popped out. "I did pay some attention to my history. They never put these things on by themselves."

"I just did." Niall tossed the robe at him, off to one side. Shawn lunged with a clink of mail, caught it, and pulled it on, while Niall issued instructions —who they would meet, how to recognize people, the lay of the buildings, the day's events. "Memorize everything. Keep your face covered. Your dirk."

Shawn tied his boots. "It's a festival. Why do I need weapons?"

Niall took two from the wardrobe, flipping them one after the other, at Shawn. He jumped aside, letting them land on the bed. "Safety first," he snapped. "Don't you people know anything? Someone will get hurt."

"One in each boot."

Grumbling, Shawn lifted the robe and shoved them in, swearing when he poked himself.

Niall laughed. "Now draw!" He ducked suddenly.

"Huh?"

Niall was behind Shawn, knife to throat. "You'd be dead had it been real."

Shawn shrugged him off in annoyance.

"D' you not wish to stay alive till we can get you back!" Niall demanded. He stepped back and said, "This time, draw!"

Shawn stooped and pulled a knife from his boot.

Niall whipped him around, knife to throat again. "No!" he barked, backing up. "Fast! Can you not understand? People here will kill you!"

"It's a bloody *festival!* Why would anyone want to kill me!" Shawn stabbed his knife back in the boot.

"'Tis 1314. We're at war. Now draw!" Niall lunged.

Shawn spun to the side, whipping the knife from his boot, and Niall danced backwards, grinning. "Better. But you're fortunate 'twas me your friends met in the alley after the last concert, not you."

"What friends?" Shawn kept the knife up, wary.

"Put up your hood." Niall tucked his knife in his boot, and took his father's sword from the chest. "Let's go." He told the story, as they circled down the tower stairs, out into the courtyard, and among the buildings, jostled by crowds of workmen and knights, of Jimmy and his friend behind the theater.

Shawn fell silent beneath his gray hood.

"Did you know you were giving them counterfeits?" Niall asked. "Mind now, the armory's here. King Robert resides there."

"Are you my judge and jury?" Shawn's voice came out muffled from under the hood. "Someone gave them to me. I didn't have anything to replace them with, and the guy was going to beat me to a pulp."

"Aye, me too." Niall paused before adding softly, "I wonder, had he enough chivalry to leave Amy be when he was through with me?"

The possibility bit into Shawn's neck like cold fingers.

"The dovecot and gardens that way," Niall said. "You're watching?"

Shawn only vaguely processed the words *dovecot* and *gardens,* his mind locked on Jimmy. It had been barely two months since he'd played poker with the man at the Bluebell Inn. Even surrounded by his friends, even with his own six feet and strong build, the big Scot had made him nervous. Something in his sullen eyes and tense manner suggested the slightest provocation would spring him over the edge from man to unbridled beast.

A horse trotted up, chestnut fetlocks clopping into Shawn's limited view along with a man's foot in a stirrup and the green hem of a surcoat. The horse's hooves sent sharp reports off the cobblestones, and echoed off the nearby buildings. Its sweat filled Shawn's nose. "Niall Campbell! Well met! Who is your friend in the robe?"

Shawn lowered his head, keeping his tell-tale face out of sight. In the dark of his hood, he thought of Amy, shorter, slighter, and pregnant, facing Jimmy alone in the empty lot behind the theater.

"A monk of Monadhliath," Niall said. "He's taken a vow of silence."

"Good brother," the man said. "The monks of Monadhliath are renowned for their prayers. Perhaps we've you to thank for our victory." Leaning down from his horse, the man clapped Shawn on the back with an affectionate force that, added to the weight of his chain mail, nearly sent him flying, and knocked his thoughts back to the present. Make that the past, he thought wryly.

"He may not speak for a year," Niall reminded him. "You're in the lists, Roger?" Shawn resisted the urge to throw back his cowl and see if it was Roger from Hugh's camp, and greet the man he now considered a friend. The voice sounded similar. At the same time, a pain stabbed his heart, thinking of Adam around the campfire, Adam who had so often fallen asleep on duty and been set to scrubbing Hugh's great rock, the Heart; Adam with seven daughters and a bairn on the way, one he would never see. His thoughts jolted back to Amy and his own child he might never see.

"Aye. We're each to joust against an English prisoner. Bruce wishes to keep us of a mind they are a strong nation, yet. You, Niall?"

"Aye. It's been some time since I jousted, but I've had a chance these past weeks to practice tilting."

A pair of workmen carrying rolls of brightly striped tenting silk edged past them in the narrow street. A fat chef hauling a gigantic basket full of rolls hastened after them, the smell of freshly cooked bread lingering on the air as he passed.

"Amazing, that!" Roger said. "Hugh says the sword went half through you. I saw it myself, from the schiltron, saw you run toward that horse and the sword come down. Yet here you are, riding and training the men and traveling to England with Lamberton weeks ago already."

"We Scots are hardy!" Niall replied. Shawn heard a smile in his voice. "The English must know it. For the sake of Scotland, tell the story to all."

"There are those as say 'tis not possible," Roger said.

"Oh, I've the scar to prove it," Niall assured him. "If any doubt, I'd be happy to show it to the lords and put rumors to rest."

Vow of silence, Shawn told himself. He didn't particularly look forward to anyone, lords or otherwise, prodding the vicious scar. Even as the ugly possibilities with Amy and Jimmy gripped him, he dearly wished to give Niall a solid kick under the table, figuratively speaking, for making promises for him. Roger trotted away, clopping on the cobblestones.

"I'm not taking my shirt off for a bunch of guys," Shawn hissed.

"The baker is there." Niall pointed, ignoring him. "The chapel is on the green."

"Okay, so don't answer, but I'm still not taking off my shirt to show off an ugly scar. What about Amy? They didn't hurt her?"

"Amy didn't care for me carrying my dirk," Niall answered. "'Twas my good fortune and hers I did. They didn't believe I wasn't you." Shawn heard dry humor in Niall's voice, though he saw little more than the cobblestones passing under his feet. "Amy was upset and winded from a long run to the train, but they did her no harm. Mind the building on the left. 'Tis where they card wool. The butcher is beyond it. 'Twas Roger of Ayr we met in the street. His father fought with William Wallace. His grandfather supported the Competitor, Bruce's grandfather."

"My head is still spinning with the last four nights of clan history," Shawn complained.

"You must know it." Niall's voice brooked no argument.

Shawn grumbled, silenced by a group of men in belted tunics and hose struggling by with boards and trestles. He and Niall followed them out the castle gates.

"They're setting up tables for feasting," Niall explained, and returned to his who's who, quizzing Shawn as they crossed a field still dewy in the early morning, to a contingent of Scots, with their horses tied up.

Shawn stopped with a clink of the mail under his robe. "You said...."

"Dry yer eyes." Niall patted a horse's nose. "You're not going to fight. But you must learn to ride, and we've a wee bit of time before the jousting. You'll have the whole afternoon free to walk around the fair." He spoke briefly with one of the men, before leading two horses to a distant stretch of meadow. He tossed a helmet up. "Take down the hood and put it on. It'll cover your face."

They spent the next two hours riding in circles around the meadow. Niall trotted along on a glossy chestnut stallion, quizzing him on the names of Highlanders and expressing amusement and irritation at Shawn's discomfort.

"I *was* just sliced nearly in half a few weeks ago," Shawn groused. "And somehow you're the hero and you've got a problem with me?" The smell of sweat—horse and man—filled the air. "I never cared for horses." It would have been a perfect day for Amy. His heart squeezed painfully, ashamed his actions had endangered her. He'd never meant to hurt her.

"Whisht." Niall chuckled, and clucked for the horse. It trotted to him, with Shawn clinging on awkwardly. "Reins, not the pommel. Back straight. You're not a sack of turnips. Name my brothers and sister."

"James, Adam...."

"James, Thomas."

Shawn tried again. "James, Thomas, Will...."

"James, Thomas, Finola," Niall corrected. "Let go of the pommel."

"James, Thomas, Finola, Will...."

"Think, think! You must know this! James, Thomas, Finola—that's Gil's mother—Adam, William, Robert, Alexander, me. Heels down. Name them again. And dismount properly this time instead of sliding off like a drunken Sassenach."

"What difference does it make as long as I end up on my feet?" Shawn threw a leg over the horse's rump and slid off the beast, hitting the ground with a bump, and catching himself against the horse. It snorted and snuffled at his face. He warded it off, grimacing.

"I'd be shamed to have anyone see me fall off a horse like that," Niall said. "You may have to be me at any point, do you not see?"

"Yeah, I see." Shawn patted the horse's nose cautiously. "It's been real, it's been fun," he told it. "You know the rest, right?" He turned to Niall. "I can't really see a time when I have to ride a horse or pretend to be you."

Bannockburn, Present

With chamomile tea steaming on the end table, and the last shadowy wisps of the nightmare warning her she wouldn't sleep yet, Amy threw kindling in the hearth and stirred it into a small, cheerful blaze. It would be mid-morning in the States—a perfect time to call her parents. She could tell Rose by breakfast that she'd done it.

Instead, she chose a book from the professor's shelf and settled into the arm chair. The wall lamp spilled warm light over *Tales of Bannockburn,* but her thoughts jumped from the pages before her to the photograph of Shawn upstairs, to Niall on the train, and back to the book. She made herself skim its pages. A parliament at Cambuskenneth. Raids on Northern England. The Declaration of Arbroath. She sighed, her mind straying back to the nightmare. She wished it would loosen its grip and let her sleep. But she knew the pattern. So, with eyes that refused to become drowsy, she read twenty pages on the days after battle, of Bruce's clemency toward Marmaduke, and his grief over the death of his cousin, the Earl of Gloucester, though the man had fought against him.

A tale is told, said chapter twenty, *of a joust after the battle. Bruce held a tournament, pitting his Scots against captured English knights. Despite a severe injury at the recent battle, one young noble took part. He was knocked from his horse and, failing to rise, was carried from the field into his tent. Almost immediately, he emerged, blowing kisses to the ladies.*

A smile tugged at the corner of Amy's mouth. It sounded like something Shawn would do. But he had died at Bannockburn. She pressed her hand to her mouth, remembering him in his better moments, wielding a giant spatula over a grill, promising the first and biggest burger to her young cousin.

The book made no mention of Niall or Glenmirril. It shouldn't surprise her, she thought, but it was still a disappointment. Sleep fluttered further from her keyed-up grasp. Niall had mentioned jousting with his foster family. She tried to picture the man she had known so briefly, who had played harp and touched her hair in the alley, mounted on a horse with a lance.

She gave her head a shake. He was gone, back with Allene. Shawn was dead. It did no good to sit and think about them. She had to do something else. Her phone lay on the coffee table. She picked it up, scrolling through her text messages. Celine had left a funny story about Conrad. Rob wanted to know if she'd considered coming home, yet. Dana asked if she'd found a doctor. She bit her lip, missing Dana, missing their movies, lunches, going to Shawn's jazz gigs and barbecues, rooming together on the orchestra's tours. She clicked through her contacts to Dana's name and hit *talk*.

Stirling Castle, 1314

Despite his complaints, despite a morning's enforced company with a horse, and the oppressive heat inside layers of jousting gear, mail, and a monk's robe, the fresh air lifted Shawn's mood.

A whole afternoon at a tournament and fair, without being quizzed, challenged, trained, questioned, warned, or flung to the floor by a wooden sword, was a treat, even if he must spend it hidden under a monk's hood. Rarely, in his previous life, had he so looked forward to something.

The sun blazed. Sweat streamed down inside his garb. But in the excitement of booths and steaming food and ladies in flowing sleeves and long skirts and knights in chinking, clinking mail, he forgot the discomfort. He trailed in Niall's wake, now and again introduced as the faceless, nameless monk of Monadhliath, under a vow of silence, through a throng on the broad lawn below the castle that increasingly included men dressed for jousting in hauberks and colors and coats of arms, with huge swords at their sides. Snatches of conversation drifted to him, comparing competition times, opponents, and weapons.

Niall led him into his tent, at one end of the jousting field. It felt like an oven, with its blue and white silken walls trapping the heat. "You'll have a good view," Niall said. "Watch through the flap and learn."

"It's been fun," Shawn said. "If a little different. *Bhris a' chas*, I guess."

"I'd hope not to break a leg." Niall frowned.

"Good luck," Shawn clarified with a grin. They shook hands, and Niall left. Shawn settled onto a stool, studying the dim interior of the tent. His father would have given anything for this chance. He himself wanted mostly to be back where he belonged, onstage, playing his trombone, begging Amy for a second chance. He leaned forward, squinting one-eyed through the narrow slit of the tent's flap into glaring sunshine. Niall had chosen his place early and well, on a slight rise which gave Shawn a clear view down the length of the jousting arena, to King Robert's dais at the far end. A colorful swirl of ladies swayed like flowers in a breeze on the king's platform, under his canopy. Shouts of men and the clink of tackle sounded through the silken walls.

Alone, Shawn dropped his chin onto his fists. Amy would be alone, too. Or would Rob have moved in? He'd long ago seen Rob's feelings. And Amy would be smart to accept. His mood sank like England's warhorses in the carse. Rob would love her and care for her as she deserved.

He pictured them sitting together on the plane, flying home. Rob would comfort her. If she even needed comfort. They'd be happy together with his child. *His.* It had begun to matter, fiercely, since Niall had confirmed for him that she was pregnant. They'd use the money Niall had given her. His child, his money. His jaw and eyes had narrowed when Niall told him. "You did *what?* You took *how* much? That was my *money!*"

"'Tis no use to you," Niall had pointed out with a shrug that enraged Shawn further.

"What if I *had* gotten back? I almost did!"

Allene's hand had dropped, soft as a ripple on a pond, to his sleeve. She'd ignored Niall's sudden tension. "You'd have let her fend for herself now?"

Shawn had sagged, closing his eyes on his stone prison and the wooden table. The man he had been, yes, that man might have. *Would* have. Behind his lids, he saw that man, not fun-loving and living life to the fullest and on his own terms, as he'd once seen himself, but small, mean, selfish.

Even cruel.

He'd opened his eyes. "No." He swallowed hard, stared a moment at the scarred table, before raising his eyes to Niall's. Humble words did not come boldly from his mouth. "Thank you...for taking care of her." He'd tried to justify his anger. "It's just, I'm not used to people helping themselves to my money." He'd shrugged, hoping the explanation satisfied.

A roar erupted outside, jolting him from his morose thoughts. He peered through the narrow slit in the flap. Thundering away from him, down the lists, was a black-armored knight astride a black horse, and charging toward his tent on the other side of the list, with equal intensity, a knight in a green tabard, leaning low over his lance, head down. They clashed a hundred yards from Shawn, and the man in green hurtled to the ground with a sickening crunch. Shawn turned his head, grimacing. This was their idea of fun? It made his drunken night with Caroline look downright sensible. As the crowd cheered, men raced to the fallen knight. With much effort on their part, he climbed to his feet and clanked off the field.

The black knight removed his helmet, revealing the haughty smirk of Edward Bruce. He cantered up the list and down again, waving and grinning. Shawn edged forward, twitching the flap wider. Edward, on his black charger, skidded to a stop before the king's stand, and dismounted with a flourish. His mail chinked as he climbed the stairs to the platform, where he claimed his prize, an all too friendly kiss from the queen of the tourney.

Shawn settled back into the dim tent and his thoughts. He wanted to get back to Glenmirril, but he had no sense they'd be returning soon. Short of making a run for it, pursued by men with weapons who knew how to fight, in a country he didn't know, he had no chance of countering MacDonald's wishes. And for what? A hope, nothing more. The time switch had also happened at Bannockburn, so Glenmirril wasn't the only way. Maybe he'd find himself back in his own time at any moment. He searched for some logic or pattern to the switches, but none appeared.

A roar went up. The announcer's voice, a rich bass, carried across the field. "My Lord Niall Campbell of Glenmirril against Sir Charles of York, prisoner."

Shawn put his eye back to the tent flap. Before him was the back of Sir Charles, arms encased in long mail, a red plumed helmet and red and white surcoat flowing on either side of his horse. The animal snorted, bucked its head, and skittered sideways. Puffs of dust billowed around each impatient hoof. Far down the list, in front of the king's stand, Niall waited, regal in blue and white. His hair fell to his shoulders. His horse stood like a statue. He bowed to Robert, bowed to the queen of the tourney, and raised a hand to the crowd. They cheered. Even from this distance, Shawn could see the grin on Niall's face. He enjoyed this! Niall lifted his helmet onto his head, settled it firmly, and reached down to the boy beside him for a lance. He gripped it under his arm, and gave a nod to the tourney master.

Nearby, the English prisoner hefted his own lance. A trumpet blared. Hairs prickled on Shawn's arms. Sweat prickled his back. His muscles tensed till they hurt. The English prisoner, astride his huge bay shouted, a muffled sound from inside his helmet. He kicked his mount viciously and shot away in a cloud of dust. Niall snapped into action, dropping low over his horse's neck. Hooves pounded. Dust swirled, and the two crashed like a Ford and Chevy, a crunch of metal, a shock of impact. The Englishman wavered in his saddle, and Niall thundered past, pulling off his helmet as he skidded to the near end. He shook his head, turned to his tent, and grinned. The horse snorted, as if in victory. Shawn swore it smiled, with large bared teeth. Wheeling the animal to face the king, Niall waited while the Englishman replaced his shattered lance. Niall's horse stood serenely, animal and master alike exuding confidence.

Niall pushed his helmet back on. His hair flowed from under it. The trumpet blasted. Niall shouted, leaned low, and charged. There was another crunching impact, and a woman screamed. The dust cleared to the sight of the red knight mounted and Niall on the ground, a puddle of blue and white. Shawn's heart jumped. He pressed close to the tent's opening. The medieval equivalent of medics swarmed the field. Niall's prone form was lost in their midst. Then they were bustling toward the tent, gingerly, striving for speed. Shawn barely yanked his cowl up before they pushed through the flap. They laid Niall on the cot. They fussed. They shouted orders. They felt bones. Niall lay gray against the pillow, his eyes closed. He didn't move.

Bannockburn, Present

"Amy? Amy!" Dana's squeal erupted on the line. "Travis is home on leave. We're at an art gallery opening." Amy heard voices in the background. It was easy to picture Dana, her short hair ruffled and moussed, her freckled face smiling, answering the phone in the middle of something fun and exciting, her arm looped through her boyfriend's. Dana rattled on about the show for a minute before asking, "How are you? Have you seen a doctor? I put a box of baby clothes in the mail for you. And the cutest crib set!"

"I feel great." Amy kept her voice down, not wanting to disturb Rose. "I found a doctor. How's everyone there. Celine, Aaron? Jim?"

Dana chatted at length about Jim's new grandson.

"Sue? Jason?"

"Sue's great. Who's Jason?"

"In the percussion. You don't...?" Amy stopped. He'd been at the table with Niall. He'd been excited about the re-enactment because his ancestors had fought at the battle. A wave of sickness washed over Amy, remembering. They'd fought for the English. But she had to be wrong. "Jason Bohun?" she tried. Her vision darkened around the edges.

"Never heard of him. Amy, you'd *love* this gallery. Remember when we went to that art museum?"

"Yeah, those two professors," Amy said faintly. Panic rose in her chest. Dana had no memory of Jason.

Dana laughed. "They were something! That was just before Shawn's first barbecue. Do you remember that obnoxious apron he wore? And he had like a thousand condiments."

"And that music he had playing." Amy's voice echoed in her own ears, her mind stuck on Jason. But Dana would think she was crazy.

"He couldn't believe no one wanted to hear a ukulele!" Dana jumped from one reminiscence of Shawn to another. His appearances on talk shows. "He was *so funny*. I could hardly breathe when he started cracking jokes." His CDs. "He knew how to pick pieces." His arrangements. "I can't believe how fast he could write."

"Yeah." Amy's voice got quiet.

"Have you heard anything?" Dana asked.

Amy bit her lip. She wanted to say, *He's dead. I'll never hear anything.* But they all thought he was only missing. She looked at the ring he'd thrown.

"Amy, are you there? What are the police doing?"

Amy crossed to the window. "There's nothing they *can* do, Dana."

"But there has to be! They can't just abandon him. You stayed to make sure they find him, right?"

"It's an open file." Amy inched aside the lace curtains. Charcoal gray etched the lowest edge of the eastern sky. "He's not their only case." Agitation churned her stomach. She couldn't tell Dana he was dead, couldn't tell anyone why she thought so, when there was no body. She'd end up accused of murder if she insisted he was dead. Enough people would figure he'd given her good reason. She'd as good as killed Jason, too, leaving Shawn in the tower. But he'd given her plenty of reasons to leave him.

"Amy?"

"I'm here." She dropped the lace curtain back into place. Thoughts of Shawn's strange stories filled her mind, the time he'd insisted two liquor stores didn't carry his brand of beer and the third had been inexplicably closed. Agitation swelled into anger. He'd been with Celine. The anger grew, turning to acid in her stomach as she stared out at the night's star-sprinkled black veil lifting to gray. "I have to go."

"You'll stay on them, won't you? Make sure they keep looking?"

"Yeah, Dana, they're doing what they can. I have to go, okay?" Ending the call, she stared silently out the window for several moments, before she removed the ring from her finger, turning it, studying it, and wondering, who had Shawn really been in the end? She wasn't even sure who he'd really been from the start.

Stirling Castle, 1314

The sweat increased on Shawn's back, in the dim, stifling heat of the silken tent as he pressed himself out of the way. He wished, suddenly, that he had the least bit of modern medical knowledge. But he could only wait, trying to go unnoticed, while they hovered. MacDonald barreled in among them, Hugh close on his heels. "Niall! Niall lad! Can you hear me!" And then, "Out!" The Laird barked the word. All action stopped.

"D' you not hear him!" Hugh spun on the men like a charging bear, and they scattered. Sunlight flashed through the tent's opening as they ran, and the flap fell to again, dropping darkness around them.

"Now!" The Laird rounded on Shawn. Shawn backed up a step. MacDonald dropped his voice. "Get that robe off and walk out there. *Now.*"

Shawn's heart pounded. Sweat slicked his hands. He tore at the robe, fumbling it over his head, even as Hugh's meaty hands grappled to help him. "You're not expecting me to joust, are you?" The robe fell to the floor, revealing Niall's blue and white tabard over Niall's hauberk.

"Go," MacDonald hissed.

Hugh pushed him to the tent's entrance, throwing aside the flap and holding Shawn's hand high. Shawn squinted into the glare of the afternoon sun. "Nothing can stop a Scot!" Hugh bellowed to the crowd. "See, he's well!"

Men roared and whistled, and women clapped. Children jumped up and down on the side of the lists, screaming, "Alba! Alba! Alba!" Hugh picked up Niall's helmet from the dust where it had rolled, and pushed it into Shawn's hands.

Shawn blinked in the bright sun. "You're not expecting me to joust, are you?" he hissed again, trying to smile and wave at the crowd through his panic.

"You'll be fine, Lad," Hugh muttered through his teeth, also waving and smiling, and he gave Shawn a shove on the back.

Shawn tucked the helmet under his arm, and took Niall's flowing hair, Niall's face—his own—out of the tent. The showman took over. He'd find an excuse not to get on a horse. With his heart racing, sweat itching under the heavy mail, and a huge, false smile on his face, he strode forward, his hand lifted high. He blew kisses to ladies, and strutted the length of the lists with hundreds, thousands, of people leaning over the ropes, cheering, screaming. *Niall! Niall Campbell! My Lord Niall!*

He shook hands with men and boys hanging over the ropes, stood on tiptoe and waved to people farther back, blew a kiss to a blushing girl. Then Allene was skipping down the stairs from Bruce's dais, flying across the field in her sapphire dress, the sleeves nearly sweeping the dusty ground, rising on tiptoe, meeting his lips in a swift, dry touch. She gripped his arm, a smile on her face, and hissed, as she pulled him along, "Don't overdo it, Shawn!

Enough with the ladies, aye!" She smiled brightly, leading him up the platform to King Robert.

From the list below, the red knight gaped. "You can't...you were...."

Robert stepped forward, his face awash in pleasure. "'Tis my Bard of Bannockburn! An able musician, an able fighter." He turned to the crowd, gave a half rest of silence, and then roared, "You can't keep a Scot down! Mark it, Englishmen!"

The previous enthusiasm paled in comparison to the new eruption of cheering. "Niall! Niall! Niall!"

Shawn forgot it was not him they cheered, buoyed by the roar of the crowd that was his own natural habitat. He waved again. Allene grabbed his hand before he could blow another kiss, and turned him to the king.

"You seem not to be the victor," Bruce said. "But such remarkable fortitude deserves its own reward. What will you have from the queen of the tourney? Another ring? A jewel? A horse?"

The queen, the girl, was beautiful, with blonde hair shimmering down her back. Allene cleared her throat.

"Uh, yes." Shawn wiped the infatuation off his face, but the girl smiled and blushed. He looked to Allene, unsure what to pick, forbidden Edward's choice of a kiss from a beautiful girl. Allene looked demurely at the floor. "A horse," he said, unsure why he'd pick such a thing.

"A horse it will be," the girl said. "Choose from those in the stable on the morrow." Her voice was light and sparkled with humor. She stepped forward, an angel with an ash blonde halo, and lifted her slender, drooping hand. He took it, and kissed the cool fingertips, before lifting his gaze to hers. She had beautiful eyes.

Bruce cleared his throat. "You'll play for the banquet tonight."

"Yes, Your Grace." Shawn bowed, buoyed by the cheers, honors bestowed by a king, and the prospect of another night feasting with beautiful women.

Bannockburn, Present

A second cup of chamomile tea, steaming in Shawn's black and gold mug, did nothing to settle Amy back to sleep. Rose wouldn't rise for another couple of hours. Amy forced herself through a chapter of a book on Iona, finding no clue to Shawn's message, before restlessness drove her back to the kitchen to refill the mug. His meaning hardly mattered now. Anger, love, and sorrow stirred inside her more strongly than the tea swirling in the wake of the spoon.

Finally, irritated with the walls of her own home, with early dawn turning the world outside dove-gray, she opened her closet. Her hand hovered over a soft gray top with a wide belt. But the brightly-colored clothing purchased on her shopping spree with Rose brought a smile to her face. Her hand slid back and forth over the hangers, before settling on a ruby red silk tunic with gold embroidery. It was more daring, more off the beaten track than she'd ever worn.

She liked it. She grabbed it quickly, before she could change her mind, donned a pair of leggings, and braided her hair into a thick rope down the length of her back. With her art bag slung over her shoulder, she threaded through Bannockburn's quiet streets, a morning choir of birds chirping as she passed on her way to the battle field.

In the dewy grass, looking across to the great statue of Robert the Bruce, she pulled out her pad and pencils, smiling at the memory of Rose charging into the art store, threatening to buy one of everything unless Amy told her exactly what she wanted. Within minutes, an outline of horse and rider filled the page.

She studied the sketch. The day of the re-enactment, the sun had blazed down on a statue of King Edward II of England, although nobody but her seemed to remember that. She had to be crazy, thinking history and a statue had changed before her eyes; thinking a member of her orchestra had disappeared. Shawn had often said she imagined things. Yet the image of the other statue was so clear.

She flipped to a fresh sheet, closed her eyes, and searched her memory. Edward's statue had been much like Bruce's. But the pedestal had been black, and square. She opened her eyes and sketched quickly, shading each stone with hatch marks. Edward sat astride his horse, heels down like Bruce. But he held his helmet in his left arm. Soon, he filled the page, his hair frozen in the act of blowing in the breeze—like Shawn's. Her pencil paused. Edward's eyes, so vivid in her memory, looked cruel. Maybe it was the weak jaw or the sardonic twist of his mouth. She studied the picture. Maybe it was only that she remembered the story: the statue was built on the spot where Edward had killed the last Scot.

She set the pencil down. It couldn't be possible to remember the statue and story in such detail, or to be buffeted by such strong emotions, thinking of Niall being that last Scot under Edward's sword, if none of it had happened. She touched the crucifix under the red silk tunic. She'd assumed, with the change in history, that he'd survived. But she didn't know.

Her hand fell from the crucifix. Irritation, both at herself and Shawn, shot through her. Of course it was real. Of course she could trust her own senses. And if she could trust her senses on such a crazy story, she could certainly trust them about Shawn. But except for Celine, there was no proof. Only a twist in the gut. She could touch the crucifix and ring, proof of Niall's existence, but Shawn, Rob and Caroline all said she was wrong about her suspicions.

Her mind traveled farther back. "He must be having an affair," she'd joked to Dana after a movie one night. "I can't believe how long it takes him to run to the store for beer."

Dana had laughed. "He's gone what, less than an hour?"

"The store's just down the street," Amy argued. "And there are always strange things happening. Police cordoning off the parking lot. Power outages when he goes to pay."

Dana laughed. "You really think he could get to the store *and* meet someone in such a short time?"

She shrugged. "I guess not. But I've never had the power go out at a store. It's happened to him twice."

But Dana was right. It would be impossible to buy beer and meet someone in such a brief time. So why did her gut still churn at the thought of those night runs for beer?

She looked back at her sketch pad. Shawn hadn't thought much of her drawing. She thought it was quite good. She'd captured the cruelty in Edward's eye, the twist of his mouth, the arrogant set of his shoulder and lift of his chin. She smiled. For the first time since the re-enactment, she wanted to do more of something. She wanted to stop grieving, at least a little.

Stirling Castle, 1314

"Impressed with yourself, are you?" Allene's voice slapped Shawn as he entered his room, flush with ample ale and the victory of playing for a king, being feted by knights and earls for his hardiness, and blushed over by women.

His eyes adjusted to the dim light, the room shaded once more by a thick tapestry over the window. Niall lay in the bed, eyes closed, his breathing shallow, his face gray. Hugh and Allene sat on either side of him. Even in the weak light, he could see red rimming Allene's eyes. "I hope you minded Niall's words not to sully his name."

The glory of Shawn's night tarnished.

"Only barely." MacDonald pushed through the door behind Shawn, sparing him a scathing glower. "Had I not been there, mayhap 'twould be a less satisfactory answer. Is he no better, lass?" He eased the door shut.

Allene glared at Shawn. "He's not come around."

Hugh reached across the bed to touch Allene's hand. "You cannot blame the lad, Allene."

The Laird's hand fell on Shawn's shoulder. "Aye, 'tis not his doing." His hand slid away, and he joined Allene and Hugh at the bedside.

Shawn dropped into a chair against the wall, deflated. He watched the three of them, hovering over the still shape, and wondered what his future here held, without Niall. He didn't think Hugh, MacDonald, or Allene felt quite the concern for him that Niall might. Niall was his only connection to his real life. He couldn't do the things this world expected of Niall. He hunched over, hands clenched together between his knees, watching. Allene brushed a cool cloth over Niall's forehead, crooning. MacDonald took his still hand, whispering, "Come on, Laddie. We need you, Niall."

Shawn searched his mind for any medical knowledge he might have gleaned. He must have picked up *something* useful, in twenty-four years in the future. Concussion, contusion, skull fracture? He wasn't sure what a contusion was, and he could do nothing about a skull fracture. Internal bleeding? Broken rib? A punctured lung?

"Hygiene!" He sat up straight. "Did you clean him well? Make sure the water is boiled."

MacDonald and Hugh turned to him. Allene continued to stroke Niall's forehead. Shawn leaned forward, speaking quickly, not sure boiled water and washed hands would help a skull fracture or internal injuries. "And don't let them bleed him. Do you still bleed people?"

"Aye." The Laird turned to Hugh. Allene looked up. The three spoke silently to one another with their eyes, and MacDonald turned back to Shawn. "I've sent for the physician. Tell me why I shouldn't."

"It'll kill him." Shawn spoke without thinking, even as he realized it might not kill him. "At least, it won't help," he added lamely.

"Why should I trust you?" The Laird's red and silver beard bristled.

"Niall told me what kind of man you are."

"Was." Shawn stared at the floor. "I got Allene to Hugh."

"Aye, he did," Hugh vouched. "He fought off a wolf."

"I hunted with them and learned to fight," Shawn added.

"I saw a man of honor and valor in my camp," Hugh said, "whatever Niall says he was in his own world."

Shawn looked to the Laird, desperate to be believed. "Don't you understand there's nothing like this in my world? Do you understand what it is to be thrown from the safety of my time into something as brutal as a medieval battle and step forward and do it anyway?" When the Laird said nothing, Shawn tried again. "Are you afraid I don't have Niall's best interest at heart? Do you think I'd hurt him?"

Again, MacDonald, Hugh, and Allene exchanged glances.

Sweat gathered under Shawn's arms.

Finally, Hugh spoke, his voice low and gravelly. "I trust him."

Slowly, Allene nodded. "I've spent weeks with him, Father. I trust him, too."

MacDonald hung in a chasm between his doubts and their trust.

"I've done everything you've asked," Shawn persisted.

"You'd no choice," MacDonald said. "I am the law for my clan."

Shawn lowered his eyes, resisting the urge to say, *And I was the law in mine.* Instead, he said, "You have to trust me." He heard the pleading in his voice. He'd never pleaded in his life. He'd ordered. He'd commanded. He'd bullied. He looked at Niall, still and gray in his blue and white surcoat, and was happy to plead. "I don't know much about medicine, but I know bleeding is bad."

A knock fell on the door.

"'Tis the physician." Allene and her father stared at each other.

"He may just have a concussion," Shawn said. "Try to wake him up."

"Malcolm." Hugh laid a hand on MacDonald's arm. "You must decide."

The knock sounded again.

The Laird stared at Shawn. His face seemed to age in that moment. His cheeks sagged, and his eyebrows fell. "You're certain?"

Shawn nodded.

The knock sounded, louder.

"Go," whispered MacDonald. His hand tightened on Niall's arm.

"Me?" asked Shawn.

The Laird nodded. "Go to the door. Show him your face." He stared at the floor. "Tell him his services are not needed."

Shawn stood. The trembling of relief and fear started on his insides, and spread to his legs. What if he was wrong and Niall died anyway? He opened the door to a robed physician with pointed, gray beard and piercing eyes.

"I'm fine," he said, and in the face of the man's confusion, eased the door closed. He returned to Niall's bed, and felt his pulse. Why he hadn't thought to do it first, he didn't know. And immediately on that thought, came the answer—he didn't have a clue what to do with the information, anyway. But Niall's heartbeat pulsed steadily in his wrist. "It's strong," he told Allene and MacDonald. At their blank looks, he said, "That's good. His heart is strong." He sank into a chair, unsure what to do next.

MacDonald rose from his seat by Niall, and settled a hand on Shawn's shoulder.

"I'm sorry," Shawn said. "I wasn't a doctor. I don't know these things. I just know bleeding is bad." He looked to the dim light showing around the tapestry at the window. "That thing. Can we take it down? Give him some air?"

Again, the other three hesitated.

"Please?" Shawn said. "We're very healthy in my time, and we're big on fresh air. Can we at least try?"

The Laird nodded. Hugh rose, stretching on his toes, and pulled the tapestry down. Warm evening air streamed in on a sunbeam.

Allene lifted Niall's hand, pressing it to her cheek. The four of them sat, not speaking, while the light waned in the arched window, and the hills outside glowed first with evening light, then turned purple, and finally, black, and disappeared altogether.

Bannockburn, Present

Far away, a portly woman in a t-shirt and broomstick skirt, a kerchief on her head, followed leisurely after a bounding golden retriever. Longing for her cats filled Amy. The dog loped up, sniffing at her ruby red tunic. Shawn had talked once about getting a dog. But he traveled too much. She smiled, remembering a day at the pound. It had been a good day—one of many good days. If only he could have stopped his lying. If only he could have listened, just once, up in the tower. The dog licked her, its big tongue leaving a wet trail on her cheek. She pulled back, laughing.

The woman bustled up, apologizing, calling, "Cullen, get off her."

"It's okay." Amy scratched the dog's ears. "He gave me a laugh."

"You're the American." The woman grabbed the dog's collar. "You moved in up the way."

Amy nodded, thinking she shouldn't be surprised how word got around. She held out her hand. "Amy Nelson."

The woman shook her hand. "Ina MacGregor." She sat down in the grass next to Amy. "If you're herself, you'll surely be needing a laugh."

Amy bit her lip. Her thumb strayed under her palm, feeling Bruce's ring.

"Och, I've overstepped my bounds, now, I have." Ina pushed a gray curl back under her kerchief. The dog gave a short, deep woof and nudged Amy's knee. "He's wanting you to throw him a stick." Ina picked one up, handing it to Amy.

Amy threw it. It arced, black against the morning sun, across the field where men had died. Cullen bolted after it. "It's okay," she said to Ina. "I was more surprised that, well, apparently you know exactly who I am."

"Och!" The woman shook her head. "'Tis not even a month, a big name like him disappearing. There was talk when you moved in. 'Tis the way it is here. No harm meant, ye ken." She patted Amy's hand.

"No harm taken." Cullen bounded back across the grass, grinning and drooling around the stick. Amy threw it again. "I've found people here very kind."

"'Tis a great loss," the woman said. "My husband died last year. 'Tis not quite the same, mind you. But bit by bit, the shock wears off, and ye'll feel ready to step back into life. Take yer time. There's a lovely church down the street where I found a great deal of peace, if you'd like me to take you there."

"I *would* like that." Amy found herself surprised at her own reaction to Ina's offer. She hadn't been to a church since meeting Shawn. Cullen returned with his stick, dropping it, wet and slimy, in her lap, and licking her face enthusiastically. She threw her hands up, laughing, and gave him a hug.

Stirling Castle, 1314

"Niall is needed at Council." The Laird's hand fell on Shawn's shoulder.

Niall had lifted heavy lids in the night, while MacDonald and Allene slept. "Welcome back," Shawn had said. "You impressed the whole crowd by walking right back out of your tent after that fall. You had a great time playing harp at dinner. They think you're *Superman.*"

"Superman?" Niall squinted in the dark and took a heavy breath. Shawn wondered if he understood anything or had lost his memory. Then Niall smiled and reached out a hand. He and Shawn gripped one other's wrists. "Thank you," Niall whispered.

"You feeling better?"

Niall nodded. He opened his mouth to speak, but nothing came out. Shawn hurried to scoop water from a bucket in the corner. Lifting Niall under the shoulders, he eased the dipper to his mouth. Niall whispered another thanks, and laid back, breathing heavily. Soon, he'd drifted back to sleep. It was enough. With relief, Shawn had known he would be okay.

Now, Niall opened his eyes at the Laird's words. The older man's face lit up, but he spoke quietly, wary of being overheard. "Niall, laddie!" He looked to Shawn, amazement in his eyes. "He'll be aw' right!"

A twinge of guilt touched Shawn. He hadn't done much, and didn't know if his actions had made any difference, anyway. But maybe they had. And it was to his benefit that MacDonald recognize his loyalty.

Niall twisted in the bed, trying to rise. Hugh clambered from where he'd dozed in a chair by a chess table. "You're awake, Niall!" Allene woke, where she slept in a chair, and with a yelp of joy, kissed him multiple times, while he tried to fend her off.

"Allene, now," her father said. "The man has much to do." With Hugh, he lifted Niall to a sitting position. Niall's face lost what little color it had had, and he suddenly vomited, once, twice, three times, retching more deeply and doubling over farther each time. Allene fussed and flurried to the bucket in the corner, grabbing rags and cleaning him up with a stream of meaningless, comforting chatter.

He tried in vain to brush her off, embarrassed eyes meeting Shawn's. Shawn grinned. Niall, the great Niall Campbell, was embarrassed. "Do you want a nice cup of warm tea and a cookie?" Shawn asked.

Niall managed a scowl before retching again, while Allene carried on, wiping him up.

"You must get up, Laddie," MacDonald insisted.

"Father, he's ill!" Allene argued. She dipped her cloth in the bucket. Shawn turned away, reminding himself to make sure the water was replaced before drinking from the pail again. She wrung the cloth over the chamber pot, and dabbed at the stains running down Niall's nightshirt. "How is he to go to a council? He's not fit to be out of bed."

"Stop fussing, Allene," Niall said. "I'm fine. Bring my clothes." He braced himself on her arm, pulling himself to his feet. His knees promptly buckled, and only Shawn's quick movement saved him from collapsing and taking Allene down with him. Shawn eased him back onto the bed. "Give me a moment," Niall said.

The Laird looked from Shawn to Niall. "Can he?" he asked Shawn.

Shawn bit back the impulse to say, *Why are you asking me? I don't know anything.* But he'd apparently been right about bleeding and fresh air. Vomiting likely meant concussion. And Niall was obviously weak. "He needs rest," he decided.

"I'm fine!" Niall snapped. But his head hung. He gripped the sides of the bed with stiff arms, trembling at the exertion.

"Uh-uh, back in bed." Shawn couldn't resist a smirk. "Allene, are there clean nightshirts? Give it a few days, Niall. What do you have to do at the Council?"

Niall submitted, with a glower, to Allene tugging his nightshirt off and replacing it, and having his legs pushed unceremoniously back under the covers. "Be there. Advise if asked. Though how you're to do that, I don't know."

"I'll be there, Laddie," the Laird said. "Else we must tell them you're ill and explain how it happened you were fine last night."

Niall relaxed his head on the pillow, too spent to argue. He gave a last weak attempt at a glare, and closed his eyes.

"Quick, Lad," the Laird said to Shawn. "D' you understand all that's at stake?" He pulled up a chair and pushed Shawn into it, drawing himself up knee to knee in another one.

"I think so. We won, but we're still at war, thanks to Edward refusing to admit he lost."

"Given a chance," Hugh rumbled, "he'll yet hang our king as a traitor."

"And all of us," Niall said weakly from the bed.

"'Tis the first council of a united Scotland, including those Scots who fought against the Bruce," MacDonald explained.

"*What?*" Shawn demanded. "We're having a council with *traitors*?"

"Sh," said the Laird. "D' you not see? Scotland has been divided long enough against itself. King Robert believes mercy and forgiveness will unite us and make us strong. You must know who you're talking to, Lad, as Niall would."

So began another long lecture, punctuated with Niall's comments, and sometimes with his deep breathing as he slipped back into sleep. Sir John Stewart of Menteith, Alexander MacDougall—"Thieving MacDougalls!" Niall muttered—the Earl of Ross, had all fought against Bruce. The Laird quizzed Shawn till he could repeat their descriptions and backgrounds.

"The MacDougalls?" MacDonald prodded.

"Alexander MacDougall," Shawn chanted. "Son of Ruadhri, son of...."

"Son of Raghnall," Niall corrected.

"Ronald was the son of Summerfield."

"Raghnall, not Ronald." Hugh shook his leonine mane.

"Somerled, Lad, Somer*led*," MacDonald bellowed. "You can't be making such mistakes! Niall knows this!"

"Somerled," Shawn said. "Somerled. Was he a king or something?"

Hugh heaved a sigh. "King of the Hebrides in the 1100's."

"Got it," Shawn said. "And MacDougall accepted Bruce's offer of peace."

There were those who had been loyal all along: Edward Bruce, head-strong and outspoken; James Douglas, a military genius, large and powerful, recognizable by his black hair; the Earl of Lennox; Angus Og, Lord of the Isles, whose stature belied his fierce fighting ability; William Lamberton, the bishop who had traveled to London after the battle; the other Neil Campbell, Bruce's most loyal supporter since the days of Brander Pass and hiding in caves.

"He's lived hard," the Laird said. "He'll look older than his years."

Shawn saw no diplomacy in saying that, to him, everyone here lived hard and looked older than their years.

When Shawn had stumbled through enough correct answers, Allene handed him one of the ever-present dirks. "You must keep one about you at all times," she admonished. "'Tis not wise to go about unprotected."

"You don't yet understand," Niall said weakly. "This is not your world."

Shawn pushed the dirk into the top of his boot, with the Laird still questioning him on politics, and names.

"Enough, My Lord," Niall croaked from the bed. "Trust him. Say as little as possible, Shawn. Listen well, especially to those who were enemies."

Bannockburn, Present

As they walked the mile to the church, with Cullen tugging at his leash and sniffing each green-leafed tree, Amy wondered what she'd been thinking. She hadn't been to church in years. She didn't belong there.

Ina chatted about the battle of Bannockburn, unconcerned with Amy's silence. "Many fascinating stories associated with it," she said. "St. Fillan, now. The Bruce was a devout man, they say. He asked for the Mayne to be brought to the battle."

"The main what?" Amy asked.

Ina laughed, a comfortable, motherly sound. "Mayne." She spelled it. "His arm bone."

The dog stopped to sniff a bush. Amy stared at the woman. "Bruce wanted a *human bone* at the battle?"

Ina smiled. "Fillan's left arm, during his life, glowed with a holy light so he could study into the night. It was a treasured relic, said to grant miracles." She yanked at Cullen's leash. "Come on, you. Enough of that."

They walked on, the dog's attention easily diverted to new trees, as Ina continued. "Well, the abbot, ye ken, dinna want to risk the English capturing the Mayne. So he brought only the case in which it was kept. But the night before battle, while Bruce prayed in his tent, there was a great crack and flash of light from the case, and when Bruce opened it, there was the Mayne, back where it belonged."

"So he saw the victory as a miracle?" Amy asked.

"Oh, aye, 'twas a miracle, indeed," Ina said. "St. Columba's relics were at the battle, as well. Abbot Bernard used them to bless the troops. So really, now, though Bruce was a military genius, I personally believe he also deserves credit for being wise enough to ask a little help from above." She gave a significant glance upward, nodding sagely. "Can ye ever imagine, pitching five thousand men against twenty thousand?"

Amy didn't have to imagine. She'd seen it.

Stirling Castle, 1314

"They refuse a treaty?" Edward Bruce bolted straight up from his place at the long expanse of table.

Shawn closed his eyes, swallowing, and opened them again to stare at a man who should be long dead.

A shorter man rose also, drawing all eyes to him. "We defeat him soundly and yet he refuses us?" Fire burned in his eyes and crackled in his voice. "Does he refuse our terms or any terms?"

The Laird leaned close to Shawn. "Watch everyone. Watch their faces. Watch their eyes." Obediently, though he had no idea what he was looking for, Shawn scanned faces. MacDonald had verified several identities for him. Some were easy to pick out from the descriptions given, and others' names had been used already. Sir John of Menteith's eyes sidled side to side. He leaned to the Earl of Ross, whispering. MacDougall must be the man with the dark hair springing back from his forehead, and yellow teeth, on Shawn's right. Douglas leaned forward, listening intently, his black hair falling to his shoulders, and his beard thick for a man only on the edge of thirty. A battle scar ran down another man's face, and his eyes failed to look the same way. Regardless, he was not a man with whom Shawn would tangle. He continued scanning faces, all the while listening to the Bishop's report.

"All terms, My Lord," replied Bishop Lamberton. "They regard us as rebels, and your Grace an imposter." He nodded at Niall. "My Lord Niall traveled with me and was my ears at Edward's court."

"Ah, my bard who inspired my men to victory." Bruce leaned forward, peering at Shawn. "My Lord Bishop says you excel at gathering information."

Shawn rose, bowing to the King. He wondered how Amy had reacted to Bruce's ring. The last thing he remembered was seeing her hands close around it, before the heaving, black chest of the warhorse had filled his vision, colorful trappings whirling like a tornado around him, and the flash of the silver blade.

MacDonald nudged him.

"My Lord Niall," Robert pressed. "What did you learn?"

Shawn blinked and cleared his throat. "My Lord...King." His voice came out less than his usual bass. This man speaking to him had been born over seven hundred years ago, the stuff of history books. Yet he stood before him in the flesh.

Fear gripped him. Niall had briefed him. He'd spent several nights at dinner with these men. But speaking before them all, giving information he really knew very little about, information that might determine their course of action, was a test like no other. Still, years on stage before thousands must count for something. He took a breath and spoke with confidence he didn't feel. "I found the ladies enthralled with a Highlander at Edward's court."

Several men smiled. Edward Bruce and Angus Og leaned forward. MacDougall scowled. Shawn noted them all, adding, "And lasses the world over do like to talk."

More men smiled. "Allene will understand, no?" said the Earl of Ross. The Laird cast a ferocious eye on him.

"The feeling is strong in England," Shawn reported, ignoring Ross. Niall had heard it from several amorous women. "Edward's men encourage him to refuse us. They don't care—uh, they care not—because they are far south and nothing, uh, *naught* we do affects them in London." His heart pounded, hoping it was enough, but Bruce waited. He continued. "The ladies view the conflict here as a thrilling story, no more. They attend court and eat well and follow their entertainments. They've no incentive to push Edward to treat with us. It simply does not affect them, whereas knowing their king gave in to those they name rebels will be felt a national shame."

The men rumbled.

"Even so!" boomed Edward Bruce. "Did I not say 'twould be so?"

Shawn sank into his seat, grateful to be out of the spotlight.

"We should have invaded immediately," spoke the other Neil Campbell. Beside him, Edward Bruce nodded vigorously, glaring at those who had prevented his eager hand from pursuing the English after Bannockburn.

"They may want peace," said Lennox, "but we need it more than they. We've not their numbers. How are we to invade London?"

"Give me men!" Edward Bruce bellowed. "I'll march on London!"

"My galleys will harry their coast," shouted Angus Og.

"We can not afford more war!" Lennox raised his voice to be heard.

"We cannot afford *not* to make war," argued Bruce's friend, Neil. "'Tis the only language they speak."

The Bruce leaned back, an elbow on his chair, a hand on his chin, regarding each silently. Light poured through the tall, narrow windows and winked off his crown. Shawn watched, noting who took which side, who spoke with whom, the undercurrents running between each. It was a skill he'd perfected, in ruling the orchestra. He would not be Niall's equal in combat, at least not soon. But he might be of use all the same, he realized.

MacDougall turned from the ongoing debate. "How's your arse, Niall?" An evil gleam, that might have been humor in another man, lit his eye.

Shawn regarded him thoughtfully. MacDougall had shot Niall while Niall retrieved MacDonald's cattle from the MacDougalls. Shawn took an instant dislike to the man. "A strong diet of Highland beef cures all ills," he replied. "And we do seem to have a goodly amount of it at Glenmirril." He smiled, taking care not to let it touch his eyes, and turned away.

"Last words?" Robert asked, and all argument stopped.

"War," stated Edward Bruce. Neil Campbell and Angus Og nodded.

"Peace," said Lennox.

Robert's eyes fell on Shawn. "You've not spoken, Niall. What say you?"

"I say...." Shawn paused. This world, he realized, wasn't so different from his own. There were wars aplenty there—then. And he'd never given a thought to a single one. "I say the ladies of Edward's court speak true. They'll not care until it touches them."

Nods went around the table. But all voices stilled and all eyes turned to the King.

Bruce spoke. "We cannot reach London. But we can make them fear war, can we not?"

"What have you in mind?" asked Angus Og.

Shawn listened, watching the men around him, while Bruce outlined a plan. Angus Og and the Earl of Ross would harry England's coasts, while Edward Bruce, the Earl of Moray, and James Douglas raided the north of England.

Lennox still objected. "Will it not merely provoke retaliation, your Grace? We need peace."

"It is for peace we do it, Lennox." Bruce's eyes blazed. "I wish more than a pause in the fighting. We must force a treaty from them so we can have *permanent* peace!"

Shawn scanned faces one last time. All but Lennox were now in agreement, and he wondered what he'd just brought on himself. He didn't expect he'd be so lucky as to survive more medieval battles. And there seemed no intention of going back to Glenmirril.

Shawn realized with a start that Bruce was staring at him. The king turned his gaze to the Laird. "My Lord of Glenmirril," he said.

MacDonald rose, bowing. "Your Grace?"

"A word with you after the council." Bruce's eyes flickered back to Shawn, his brows knit, before signaling the Chancellor to close the meeting.

"What have I done?" Shawn hissed at MacDonald. His heart pounded. "Is he going to hang me?"

Bannockburn, Present

"He was quite the character now, was he not," Ina said.

A wave of anger flashed over Amy; anger for all the awful things Shawn had done and been that had led to that moment in the tower; for bullying her into the abortion; for refusing to listen; even anger for being giving and kind so many other times that she loved him despite it all. Images of him and Celine wavered before her. For a brief second, she wished she'd been the one on the charger, swinging the sword herself.

But she nodded politely. "He was one of a kind." Maybe it was her own fault. Dana never would have put up with his lies and stories. But it had been Dana who kept saying, "Shawn loves you. He would never hurt you."

"I have his *Greatest Hits of the 40's.* My husband loved the big bands. It gives me so much happiness, hearing it."

The anger subsided a little. Amy remembered every minute at his side, arranging those pieces. "Shawn had a way of making people happy," she agreed. She wished that was the whole story, instead of only the good half.

"Here it is now." Ina stopped in front of a steepled brick church, with a statue of Mary high up in an arch on the front wall. "Did you stay in case they find him?"

"I don't know." The breeze pulled a long strand of hair from her braid. Amy pushed it behind her ear. She and Ina stared at the church, in awkward silence. She didn't belong here, Amy thought. She'd messed up in so many ways, God couldn't possibly want her there. Maybe Ina would leave, and she could slip away without going in.

Stirling Castle, 1314

"Wait here, Lad," MacDonald murmured in Shawn's ear, and left him to make war talk with men whose names he barely remembered.

"How many d' you think Douglas will take on the raids?" asked Ross.

"A dozen like Niall would do it," spoke up Lennox. "Imagine being cut in half and up and walking the next day!"

"Incredible!" Lachlan, a fresh-faced youth from Glenmirril, joined the men in the hall.

"We Scots are hardy!" Shawn spoke with gusto, but his eyes darted to the door through which MacDonald and Bruce had disappeared. He couldn't possibly have done anything to deserve hanging. Unless Bruce knew he wasn't Niall. Nerves quivered in his arms.

MacDougall turned from a nearby group. His black eyes glittered. "'Tis not possible. Surely the injury is not what you claim."

"I saw it myself," piped Lachlan. "'Tis all they say and more. His insides were spilling out."

"They were?" Shawn turned to the young man in astonishment. He remembered nothing beyond the sword slashing down.

MacDougall dismissed Lachlan without a glance. "Show me," he ordered Shawn.

"Here, My Lord?" Shawn put on his most surprised expression, hoping to dissuade the man.

MacDougall's heavy brows lowered over darkening eyes. "I say you're lying. I'll not believe it till I see it."

"Prove him wrong," said Lachlan.

MacDougall smirked, waiting.

Shawn bristled. "I'm not in the habit of proving myself to petty cattle thieves." He cocked one eyebrow.

All heads turned. MacDougall's smirk slid into something sinister and deadly. He touched the hilt of his dagger. "You'll prove yourself one way or another."

"That determined to see me take it all off?"

MacDougall pulled the knife. A circle formed around them, strong, bearded men shoulder to shoulder, cutting off his escape, watching with interest, whispering to one another.

Shawn eyed the dirk. He really should learn to keep his mouth shut, he thought. He couldn't fight the man. He laughed suddenly, derisively. Thank goodness Niall had been inconvenienced. "Have it your way." He lifted his shirt and turned, playing to the crowd, showing the thick red scar running across his torso, and halfway around his side.

"Satisfied?" His eyes spit contempt at MacDougall. "Don't ask again. People might talk." He dropped the shirt and turned on his heel, shoving through a gap in the crowd, hoping the kid, Lachlan, had his back.

Bannockburn, Present

Ina waits all too patiently, while my nerves stretch taut. I smile, unable to go in, unwilling to embarrass myself by walking away after I said I wanted to come.

Just as an awkward moment is about to get even worse, she grabs my hand. "I shouldna be botherin' you with personal questions. It's just— you're so alone." Her heart is in her eyes. "If you want to talk, I'm here."

My irritation melts like mist on a hot morning, touched at her caring. I squeeze her hand. "Thank you."

She gives me a quick hug and hurries away, Cullen tugging at the leash to reach some exciting new smell. I turn, facing those huge front doors, suddenly grateful to her for staying, for forcing me to go in. Maybe it's okay...somehow...even though I've ignored God for so long.

I enter cautiously. I sit in the back pew, as far from the crucifix as possible, staring down the long rank of pews marching to the altar. Shafts of sunlight drop through stained glass windows, picking out the gold threads in my red silk tunic. Silence hangs around me, peaceful as a summer dawn.

Why did I stay? Stupidity? A ridiculous whim I'll regret? My mind jumps like a cricket to Caroline, Shawn, Celine. Rob said Caroline was with him that night, so why am I angry at her? But it seems strange she'd go with Rob. He's not her type. And it's not his style. But Rob wouldn't lie to me. Confusion pounds at my head as I try to find the truth in this dark maze.

And Celine—she should have known Shawn was lying. It should have been obvious we hadn't broken up.

Anger swells, knotting in my stomach. I squeeze my eyes, seeing red behind my lids. I want to burn the clothes he left behind, especially the shirt he wore to the Blue Bell with Caroline; burn it, send her the ashes, hope she chokes to death on them.

Guilt chases right after the anger, guilt for sitting in church full of hate and anger. How's that for a fine way to spend time with God? Some days, I'm mad at Him, too. I wonder if this is His punishment for all I've done, for going against my beliefs, having an abortion. I'm mad at Him for letting Shawn into my life, for not knocking some sense into me sooner, for letting me let myself get drawn in and stupidly believing that other face he showed me. I'm mad at Him for all of that even as I blame myself for every stupid step along the path that brought me here.

I pull my drawing pad from my art bag. Keeping my hands busy keeps the worst of the agitation at bay. I sketch a quick outline of the altar. I stare at it, at Christ on the crucifix, sad eyes gazing down, but my mind is on Shawn. He created such a wonderful world for the two of us. I wish it had been real. I wish he could have been all he pretended to be, all I fell in love with. Or at least, that he could have been honest from the start about who he really was.

I press a hand suddenly to my temple, where a headache throbs. Listen to me! This is why I can't be mad at Celine. I saw who he was from the start and still, I believed every lie. He was so convincing, eyes wide, so surprised and hurt I could doubt him.

I wanted to believe as badly as Celine did.

I try to force my thoughts away from it. I outline the figure on the cross before lifting my eyes to the spacious ceiling rising loftily above my head. But the thoughts won't let me rest. I'm alone, pregnant, with a child who will never know its father. I did that to my child by leaving Shawn in the tower. Rose is right—I deserve better. Still, I'm angry at myself for leaving him. I didn't have to storm out. If I hadn't, he'd be here, alive. I think about my child, our child, and how I'm going to explain some day why *his father isn't here.*

After another minute of watching dust motes, I lift Niall's crucifix. What would Niall do? He'd forgive. The answer is easy. But does forgiving stop the pain and anger that torment me day and night like wild beasts? I sleep with his robe, I drink from his mug. I have nightmares of him being buried, surrounded by dead bodies, women, but he's too full of life and keeps trying to get out. I can see I'm dreaming an allegory. His own behavior killed him. Yet I still blame myself. I still can't believe someone as full of life as Shawn could die, that this crazy thing could happen.

I study the crucifix. The detail of Christ, in such a small carving, is amazing, the thorns of the crown, the folds of the loincloth. I turn it over. A thin piece of inlaid white wood runs down the back, held in by thin metal bands, top and bottom. Apart from the heavy ring on my finger, and the garnet necklace Niall gave me, it's my link to sanity, physical proof I'm not crazy.

I run my finger down the white shard in the back of the cross. An idea drops into my head. My eyebrows draw together. I wonder if I can find more proof. Shawn died in 1314. So he must have been buried. Maybe I can find his grave. There are archives and records. I can go to Iona. Maybe he was buried there?

No. I press my fingers against my forehead. He carved the word before he died, so it's not about where he's buried. The puzzle makes my head hurt. I try to put the pieces together, but nothing fits. I slap the sketch book closed in frustration.

Rose will be awake by now, wondering where I am. I tuck the crucifix inside my red silk collar and lift my eyes to the altar. I wonder if God was any more vocal in answering Niall's questions. Because with me, He's silent. Maybe I should forget it, admit there's nothing to be done here. I should pack up, go home, apologize for making such a fuss, and accept this horrible new nightmare-reality.

But I can't. Not yet. I'll maybe, at least, just see if I can find out where Shawn was buried. Rose will be pleased if I suggest another trip. The dead would have been taken to Stirling Castle. I'll at least try.

And here, in this place, I'm at peace with that.

Stirling Castle, 1314

"What did Bruce want?" Shawn demanded. Hours later, after a feast of many courses, jugglers, and playing harp, they hurried back through stone halls, past tapestries and arched windows, to Niall's room. "Is he going to hang me?"

"Keep your voice down," MacDonald snapped. "I said we'll discuss it with Niall. Are you always so impertinent?"

"As often as possible." Shawn glared back. "Especially when it concerns my neck."

"I'll hang you myself," MacDonald muttered. "Now, did you notice who was missing?"

"How could I possibly notice who *wasn't* there?" Shawn thought his powers of observation had been quite acute, given the circumstances.

But MacDonald was not so easily impressed. "Did you not *listen* when I told you the clan histories! Think back! Young MacDougall was not there. Why is he not swearing fealty? I don't trust the man."

"You wouldn't trust the pope himself if he was a MacDougall."

"Och, now, don't be irreverent. A MacDougall could never be so holy as to be a priest, let alone the Holy Father." He snorted in amusement. "Good could as soon come from a MacDougall as a man could fly."

"I did tell you we fly across oceans in three hours."

The Laird snorted again. Shawn assumed it was for lack of a better answer. But MacDonald added, "Don't be saying such things aloud. Walls have ears." At Niall's chambers, he opened the heavy wooden door.

Shawn's spirit revolted at entering the room again. He'd spent too much time there. But he had no choice. He followed MacDonald in, biting back his complaints. Allene sat by the window, poking a needle in and out of white cloth. Hugh looked up from pieces laid out on the chess board. Niall sat, his legs dangling over the edge of the tester bed, its rich blue hangings pulled back to let in air. He appeared in better health. An empty bowl sat on the stand by the bed. But his face was still pale, and his arms trembled. "How was it?" he asked. "What's next?"

"Raids on England," replied the Laird.

Allene sighed.

"I expected naught else." Hugh pushed a queen across a diagonal.

"Bruce wants something with you, Niall," Shawn put in.

Niall leaned forward. "What does...?"

"Edward will not recognize us." MacDonald raised his voice. "Your information on the English court had its effect."

Niall glanced curiously at Shawn, but addressed MacDonald. "I'm sorry the information was not of a different ilk. Would that the people were pushing Edward to accept our terms. But they are self-centered fools living idle lives with no concern for aught but their own pleasure."

Shawn believed Niall would have spit, had he been outdoors.

"I'm sorry the information was gotten with any hint of untoward behavior with women." MacDonald's eyebrows bristled.

Allene lowered her mending, frowning at Niall.

Niall grinned at her and turned back to MacDonald. "I've spent years in your care, My Lord. I value your daughter and my betrothal to her. You can be sure 'twas no more than winks and pretty words."

"They can go a long way," Shawn said.

The Laird harrumphed.

"Sorry for trying to help," Shawn muttered.

"I can assure you, My Lord," Niall added, "Allene has no cause to fear my fancy turning toward such lasses."

"We've other matters." The Laird wandered to the window, looking out to sky and hills alive with vibrant hues in the late evening sun. "Duncan MacDougall is not here."

"Is he a fool?" Hugh asked.

"Have you spoken with King Robert?" asked Niall.

"Aye."

"And while he was," Shawn said, "MacDougall questioned you being cut nearly in half. He insisted on seeing the scar. So if anyone asks, remind them they've already seen it."

The Laird nodded approval. "Aye, 'twill work. As to MacDougall, the absence of his son does not go unnoticed. The Bruce has ordered you to Creagsmalan to see what is afoot."

"What's Creagsmalan?" Shawn asked.

Allene resumed her sewing. "Duncan MacDougall's castle."

MacDonald noted Niall's condition, and added, "I've asked him for a few days to make alternate plans to train the men. Shawn, you must take over Niall's duties so he can continue to rest."

Shawn groaned. "I've always found running from a fight a healthy habit. I don't suppose that's what you want me to teach them?"

Niall rolled his eyes, and spoke to the Laird. "Assign Roger to aid me. I mean him. Roger can work with the younger ones. Shawn, you deal with the older ones. Stay on their backs. Yell a lot. 'Work harder!' and 'Swing like you mean it! Do you want the English dogs to rape your mother!' 'Twill work for a wee bit."

"Watch that the formations are tight," Hugh added.

"My Lord," Niall addressed MacDonald. "There's time to work with him tonight before I'm—he's—due on the green on the morrow. Pull him aside now and again as if you are conferring about the men, and tell him anything else he should be doing." Niall's face paled. The trembling increased in his arms. "What did you call this?" he asked Shawn.

"Concussion." Shawn gave the English word and returned to Gaelic. "A blow to the head. The brain swells, and that's a problem considering your head was already plenty big."

Hugh guffawed, and pushed a pawn forward.

"Says 'Shawn Kleiner the best of Scotland' gamboling in the meadow with lasses falling out of their dresses all over him." Niall snorted.

"Lasses fall out of their dresses in your time?" Hugh looked up with interest.

"Hey, those were promo posters!" Shawn said. "People loved them!"

"People meaning you," said Niall.

"How long must he rest?" the Laird interrupted.

"Look, I'm no doctor. But you can see he still looks pretty bad. Even worse than normal. You don't want him re-injuring his head before it's healed, and he's off to do just the sort of things that might do that."

"How long?" As Niall's trembling grew, the Laird moved to the bed, and helped him back under the covers.

"I think they usually say a few days to a week," Shawn said.

Niall threw an arm over his eyes, and groaned. "How are we to hold the Bruce off for a week?"

"We don't have to," Shawn pointed out. "I stay in the room and you leave when you're ready. It's not like they've got GPS."

Allene's needle paused, a gleam of silver thread trailing from it. "What is...?"

A knock at the door interrupted her. All five exchanged glances.

Niall pulled the covers over himself, and the Laird twitched the bed hangings closed, covering both Niall and Allene, sitting on the other side of the bed, as Shawn crossed the room. He opened it to the one man he'd truly come to hate in this place: MacDougall.

Chapter Five

"Mary Queen of Scots was crowned here as an infant in 1543," the tour guide announced. With the rest of the group, Amy and Rose filed past him, into the chapel at Stirling Castle. Two little boys bounced in with their parents. One of them dashed to the front of the chapel, shouting, "Look at the ceiling, Mam, look!"

Hefting her backpack higher on her shoulder, Amy looked up to the polished wood overhead. Three tapestries caught her eye. While Rose, her floral skirt swirling around her ankles, followed the tour guide, Amy studied them, losing herself in the burst of colors of the flowers and the men's tunics and hose. They gathered around a unicorn, a shock of white amid the color, aiming spears, while dogs strained to reach the unfortunate animal.

"Lovely, aren't they?" She started at the tour guide's voice beside her. He was in his twenties, tall, thin, with a thick, long mop of curling black hair.

"The tapestries?" she said. "They're amazing!"

"And full of symbolism. The medieval mind thrived on symbolism."

Her head tilted, she studied the tapestries anew, wondering what Niall would see there that she didn't. He felt too real, warm, and alive to be labeled a medieval mind.

"You're American?" The guide leaned closer.

She nodded, offering her hand. "Amy."

His smile grew. He held onto her hand. "Colm. A pleasure."

"Thank you." Heat climbed up her cheeks. She wore a long, fitted top found on yet another shopping trip. "The pink is so striking with your hair," Rose had insisted, and Amy had been surprised at the attractive face looking back at her from the store's mirror. It had been a long time since Shawn had told her she was beautiful or complimented her eyes. The mirror told her they weren't bad. They were wide, dark blue, and edged with thick, dark lashes. And now, Colm stared deeply into them. She slid her hand from his, blushing.

"You've got a lot to carry," he said.

"Just some things I picked up while I was in town." Amy touched the strap of the backpack. She'd opened a bank account that morning, and, pleased to find royalties flowing in, both from CDs and the trading cards some entrepreneur had made of the orchestra's members, had bought score paper, a laptop, and acrylics. "I paint," she explained.

"People, landscapes?" His eyes brightened with interest.

"Nature, animals." Her shoulders relaxed. She realized she'd expected him to scoff—as Shawn had. Pleasure rushed through her at his acceptance. Emboldened, she nodded at the unicorn tapestries. "I'd love to paint these."

Colm's head bowed close. "When you do, I'd love to see them."

The two little boys bolted up to him. "Did anyone *die* here?" the older one demanded.

"Are there *ghosts*?" asked the younger.

Colm squatted down. "We've our share of ghosts—the Green Lady for one. And a soldier who comes out now and again from the stairs outside. We're going there now. I'll show you." He gave Amy a last smile and let the boys drag him to the door of the chapel.

"I think he likes you," Rose whispered, joining her.

Amy blushed. "He's just doing his job." They followed the group out into the courtyard.

"Hm." Rose glanced up at the sun, and put her straw hat back on her fluff of red hair. "Is that Shawn talking? I saw what happened."

"Rose, it's all too recent with Shawn. I'm not interested." Amy strained to hear Colm's stories, listening for any mention of Bannockburn.

It wasn't long before, walking backwards across the cobbled bailey, Colm said, "Bruce and his men stayed on a bit after the battle. If you look to the right...."

Amy lost his next words as Rose leaned close, whispering, "Which was in June. So your Niall might be here in his own July in 1314."

Amy glanced at her. "You said he obviously wasn't from 1314."

"And *you* said there *was* a historical Niall Campbell who fought at Bannockburn. He might be here with Bruce's army."

A shiver went up Amy's arms. She wondered if she walked in their ghostly footsteps even now, if they were all around her, divided only by time. She studied the buildings all around them—the great hall, the chapel, and the windows of the palace—as if she might see Niall looking down. "Do you think any trace of his time would have survived?" They followed the group into a cool, dim tunnel running under one of the castle buildings. Small chambers opened off the passageway.

"I think our guide would be happy to have coffee with you and tell you all about it." Rose winked.

Amy bit her lip, daring a glance at Colm. He stood at the door of a chamber, one of the boys hanging on his hand. He beamed at her. She gave a quick smile, and ducked into the nearest room, with displays on medieval music. She barely saw the placards on the walls. Her thoughts flew back to Niall. He had walked here!

"Go ask him." Rose followed her in.

"Later," Amy whispered back. She read the placards. They all focused on the courts of the many James's. Her hand drifted to her stomach. It had been Shawn's father's name, handed down generation after generation from his Scottish ancestors. She read the last placard. There was nothing about Bannockburn.

Disappointed, she followed the group back out into sunshine and gardens. Through the rest of the tour, Colm said no more about Bruce's time. Finally, he led them up to the windy courtyard overlooking the countryside. "Questions?" He looked around.

Hands waved. Rose wandered off again. Amy leaned on the stone wall, looking out. A graveyard wrapped around the ground directly below the castle. Beyond it spread the gray-roofed town, the River Forth snaking through the land like a giant anaconda, and further yet, the Wallace Monument rising on a hill. More hills climbed beyond that. With a touch of vertigo, she pulled back.

One of the boys jumped up and down, waving his arm. "Did James really keep lions in that courtyard?" he asked. "Did they *eat* anyone?"

His brother waved with equal vigor. "Did James really stab Douglas with a poleaxe and throw him out a window?" He leaned forward, eyes wide.

Colm nodded. "Yes, James II stabbed Douglas with a knife. His captain of the guard used the poleaxe, and he was thrown from the window into the Douglas Garden below."

The boys exclaimed in excitement, and Colm moved on to the next question. When the last of the tour group wandered off some time later, he joined Amy at the wall. "Any questions I can answer?"

She felt a little guilty accepting his attentions, but she'd come to find out what she could about Shawn. "What was here in 1314?" Bruce's ring weighed heavily on her finger.

"Wooden stockades, wooden buildings." Colm leaned on the stone wall, the breeze rippling his dark hair, and indicated the green below. "Armies would have camped down there, maybe trained or jousted."

Amy looked down, imagining knights and pikemen as she'd seen them the day of the re-enactment. Niall had said he trained men. She wondered if he'd spent time on that lawn. "What about the castle buildings? Which ones were here in 1314?"

"Nothing."

Amy's attention snapped back from the green below. "Nothing?" Her hopes sank. "How would you find out about the people who were here then? What happened to the men who died at Bannockburn?"

He pointed down into the countryside. "There was a place down there that became known as Polmaise—the Pool of the Rotting—because so many English knights were left unburied."

"But what about Scotland's dead?"

"Barbour only mentions William Vipoint and Walter Ross. I imagine they were taken home to their families."

"What about those who weren't knights?"

"A mass grave, I'd think."

"A mass grave?" The words came out faintly. "There'd be no remains left at all."

"No, I'd think not," Colm agreed, cheerfully.

The thought of Shawn dumped in a communal pit made her feel ill. "Do you know where that grave was?"

"No idea," Colm admitted. "I've never thought about it."

"How would I find the names of the men who were buried there?"

Colm thought a minute, before saying, "Archives, cemeteries, historical research, archaeological digs, maybe. But there'd be nothing left here."

Stirling Castle, 1314

MacDougall did not wait for an invitation, but pushed his way in, slamming the door behind him. Hugh looked up from his chess board. His eyes darted to the chest that held Niall's sword. The Laird turned briskly from the bed, as Shawn stepped between it and the intruder. His thoughts leapt to Niall's lessons on drawing a dirk. But MacDougall towered over him and outweighed him. His coarse black hair and yellow teeth, the rough material of his shirt and vest, everything about him, held a black aura of threat.

"Pleasant family reunion," MacDougall sneered. "When are the happy nuptials, My Lord?" He turned to Shawn. "Or are you finding his daughter unsatisfactory after London's women, Niall?"

Shawn bristled, but said nothing.

"My daughter and Niall will wed when we return home." The Laird ignored MacDougall's intended slight. "What is it you wish?"

MacDougall dropped into a chair without invitation, and kicked his heavy boots up on the table. He inserted a yellowed nail in his teeth, picking out his meal. "I hear Bruce has a mission for young Campbell."

Shawn and the Laird glanced at each other. Word traveled fast. "That would be summat to discuss with the Bruce," the Laird said.

MacDougall chuckled. "I think we know well this is not a decision in which the Bruce will include me, though it involves me and mine. It seems he thinks Niall knows his way around my son's land."

"The Bruce thinks a great many things," the Laird said. "Speak to him directly. Niall, show him the door."

Shawn took a step toward the door.

"I care not what the Bruce says." MacDougall dropped his big feet to the floor like a small earthquake. His finger fell from his mouth, and if the effect had been even vaguely amusing, it was gone. Even Jimmy would not like to meet this man in a bad mood. The same finger stabbed the air toward Shawn. "Messengers have already left for Creagsmalan. No sight of Niall Campbell will be tolerated anywhere on my lands."

MacDonald stared with a smooth countenance, giving nothing away.

"Shall I make myself more clear?" MacDougall glared. "I would fain see Niall carrying on at his normal duties each day and at dinner each night. 'Twould be a shame if anything were to happen to his lovely bride to be." He rose to his feet.

Hugh rose, too, sending the chess board flying with a clattering of stone pieces on stone floor.

MacDonald's face turned slowly red. The scar across his cheek turned white against the rising color. His hand fell on the hilt of his knife. "Don't be threatening my daughter, MacDougall. If aught should befall her, you'll find out why the loyal Scots won at Bannockburn."

MacDougall lifted a lip in a sneer. "And how would that help your daughter, even if I were afraid of you?" He stormed out the door, slamming it behind him.

Niall was immediately out of the bed, shoving at the entangling blue curtains, his head swinging toward the chest that held his sword.

"Niall!" Allene reached for him across the bed.

Shawn put a hand on Niall's arm. "You're not going to do anything to him in the shape you're in."

"And you'll do naught to him on your best day!" Niall snapped.

Shawn's eyes became hard.

"Niall!" barked the Laird. "You'll go back to bed. You—as far as anyone else knows—will be working with the men for several days still, and at dinner every night. She is in no danger."

"Take her back to Glenmirril immediately," Niall said. "Or send her with me. I'll deliver her safely home before I go to Creagsmalan."

"Is the answer not clear?" MacDonald asked. "Shawn will continue to work with the men after you leave. MacDougall will see you at dinner every night."

"And how are we to explain that to the Bruce?" demanded Niall.

"What a tangled web we weave," Shawn quoted, shaking his head.

"And do you want that pig to think he's cowed us!" Niall asked.

"Niall, 'tis but a setback. Are we no smarter than a man who didn't have the sense to side with Bruce to begin with? We'll think of summat." The laird looked to his daughter, on the other side of the bed, her face pale against her blazing hair. "Allene will be safe."

Bannockburn, Present

The sun rose early on the battlefield of Bannockburn, sending ethereal light through the mist hovering over the grass. Amy watched it swirl around her toes, bare in her sandals, contemplating her failure at Stirling. Rose walked beside her. Colorful flowers blossomed on the hem and bodice of her white sundress. "Did you find what you wanted at Stirling?" She clutched a white lace shrug around her shoulders.

Amy shivered, despite a long cardigan over her denim capris. "What makes you think I wanted to find anything?"

Rose gave a Mona Lisa smile. "Glenmirril, Bannockburn, Stirling, Falkirk, they're all connected. I heard you ask Colm what was left of that time. Not like I didn't see the connection the minute you suggested it. You were never one for out and out frivolity. Do you think our historic Niall Campbell died there?"

"I don't know." Amy's heart gave an extra, hard knock against her ribs. She hoped not.

"And no matter how much I twist it around in my mind," Rose added, "as irrational as it sounds, I think it ties in somehow with Shawn. It has to. So what were you hoping to find?"

Amy studied Rose. But her face, a pleasant mask in the cool, misty morning, gave nothing away. Amy picked her words carefully. "I want to know what happened after the battle."

"To the historic Niall Campbell?"

Amy nodded.

"Hm. Your boyfriend disappears and you're interested in the fate of a fourteenth century warrior."

Amy said nothing. They reached the statue of Robert the Bruce, its white stone pedestal floating above the gloam. "A great man." Rose tipped her straw hat back to look up at it. "An amazing victory." She circled the statue, and returned to Amy. "Let's say," she said, "just for argument's sake, that everything your Niall told you is true. We know he wasn't Shawn. That's a given. But let's say he really did go to sleep in 1314 in his own castle—the same place Shawn slept that night. If Niall woke up in Shawn's place, and Shawn disappeared, there's really only one logical conclusion."

Amy tightened her arms around herself. Somewhere far away in the pea soup, a sheep let out a stuttering mewl. Pink clouds streaked the horizon.

"So Shawn wakes up in Niall's time looking like Niall—who's scheduled to fight at Bannockburn." Rose ran a hand along the white pedestal, her back to Amy. "Which means Shawn gets sent there instead. Which would explain why you say he's not coming back."

Amy closed her eyes, seeing the sword slash down over Shawn. She pressed a hand to her stomach and another to her mouth.

"Even though, of course, none of this can be true." Rose turned from the stone and peered at her with concern. "It can't be true, right? Tell me this isn't true."

Amy swallowed. Her mouth moved, but nothing came out. She tried again, neither agreeing nor disagreeing. "Someone named Niall came back from Glenmirril with me. Shawn never turned up again. Niall disappeared at the re-enactment."

"Into thin air, according to reports." Rose's eyebrows puckered.

"The place was surrounded by police trying to get him." Amy stared into streaks of pink brightening to baby blue, avoiding Rose's eyes.

A trio of birds burst into song.

"Okay," Rose said slowly. "So let's say it's true for argument's sake. The dead would have been taken to Stirling."

Amy nodded, dropping her gaze to the thinning mist around her ankles.

"But," continued Rose, "there's nothing to be learned there about the men who died at Bannockburn, and definitely not about Shawn."

Amy lifted her eyes to the statue of Bruce, towering high above her, staring out sternly over his country. She stretched her hand high, touching cool white stones. "Imagine," she said, "if the English had won that day. This would be a statue of Edward II, on the spot where he killed the last Scot." The sick feeling flooded back, of looking at the man who had committed such a deed.

"Which would include Niall Campbell of Glenmirril," Rose said.

"But if history changed," Amy said, "then Niall's fate changed." She hoped it had. It was crushing, thinking they'd both died. Her mind flew to Allene, weaving an image of the two of them co-existing side by side in time, in grief. It felt for a moment as if they all surrounded her, Niall, Allene, and Shawn, only a sheer veil separating them, rather than seven hundred years. Her thoughts spun in circles. *We do exist side by side, but they're bones somewhere under my feet while I'm alive, alone.*

Her breathing constricted. A faint moan touched her ears, and ribbons of mist twisted themselves into a man on the ground, gripping his side, his face as pale as the mist. She yanked her hand off the stones, realizing she was breathing hard. She closed her eyes, willing her breath to slow. It was nothing but mist and the lowing of a cow, somewhere out in the countryside.

"Niall was important enough to be mentioned on the Glenmirril tour," Rose said. "Certainly we can find out what happened to him. Maybe it'll tell you what you really want to know."

Amy turned, her eyebrows drawn in thought. Across the field stood an entire museum devoted to the battle of Bannockburn. She wondered why she hadn't thought of it sooner.

Stirling Castle, 1314

Within a day, Niall was itching to get out of bed. Dressed alike, he and Shawn trained the men in shifts. After resting from his early morning work,

Niall came, in the gray guise of the silent Brother Andrew, as they now called their alter ego, down to the wide meadow stretching below the volcanic rock that lifted Stirling Castle high against white clouds and blue summer sky. Shawn followed him into the silken tent, and donned Brother Andrew's robe as Niall discarded it. Wearing a duplicate of Shawn's outfit, Niall left the tent, followed by the hooded monk.

Shawn had exhorted the men to greater strength and quicker moves, with no real idea what they should be doing. Niall moved among them, correcting stances, showing them how to put weight behind the thrust of a knife, adjusting the angle of a boy's pike, admonishing the men in schiltrons to pack themselves more tightly. Shawn followed, a silent monk absorbing every word, to the place where the jousting had taken place only days ago. Men thundered down the list, tilting at a ring, while Niall thundered equally at them to keep their heels and heads down. After an hour, Shawn whispered from under his hood, "You're getting pale."

Niall waved him off. "I've no need of a nursemaid. Your job is to learn."

"Your job is to recover. Time to switch."

Niall stabbed him with a vicious glare, but followed him back toward the tent, threading among throngs of men in schiltrons, on horseback, or fighting one another with wooden swords. "Lift your arm higher!" Niall stopped to bark at a gangly teen. "Use your height!" He pushed himself into the boy's face. "This English dog is going to rape your sisters if *you* don't stop him! You want that?"

"No, My Lord." The boy turned red. He wiped a belled linen sleeve across his forehead, and threw himself back into the fight, hacking and slashing. Niall became steadily more pale.

"Time to switch," Shawn hissed. "You're going to drop right here."

"Faster," Niall barked at the boy. He and Shawn pushed through a group of horsemen. "Get back to work," Niall yelled over his shoulder.

In the tent, Niall dropped to the cot, his breathing quick and shallow. Shawn pulled off the robe, and tossed it at him. "Put it on, Brother Andrew. Any last minute hints on teaching something I know nothing about?"

"Yell a lot," Niall mumbled. "*Sassenach, English dogs.*" He dragged himself up long enough to struggle into the robe, and dropped back on the cot with a heavy thud.

With Niall's face safely covered, Shawn stepped back into the warm July air, tied the flaps securely, and spent the next hours yelling, "This English dog is going to kill your mother!" Or daughter or sister. He watched the older men carefully, noting who consistently had the upper hand, studying every nuance. "Watch Carmag!" he yelled at a small thin man with a wisp of beard. "See how he swings?" And to another, "Do you see Roidh letting up on the attack? No! Follow through, man, follow through, keep on him!"

He slipped back to the tent, to find Niall snoring. He wanted to drop himself. Sweat covered his back, and his muscles cried for rest. He re-tied the flaps and went out for another two hours.

When Brother Andrew appeared at his side in late afternoon, he was more than ready to switch. Niall pulled off the robe as soon as they were safely enclosed in the dim tent. "Allene has left food." Strong color had returned to his face. He burst with energy.

"You're awfully eager to be out there," Shawn said.

"Of course I am," Niall answered. "They're my men. D' you think I don't feel Adam's loss and grieve for his widow and daughters and new bairn? The war is not over, and I want each of them here when it is. I know their fathers, mothers, wives, sisters, and children, d' you see?"

Shawn nodded, staring at the bread on the table. Weak light poured through the silk of the tent. He barely knew a thing about the men and women in the orchestra he'd considered his. He didn't even know if Rob had sisters. He remembered meeting a brother after a concert. Or maybe it had been a cousin. And Rob's father—had he sold instruments at a music store? Or been a school teacher? He couldn't remember. "Tell me about them," he said.

Niall sat down on the chair, and handed Shawn a trencher of meat and turnips. "Taran, he's the boy, the tall gangly one. His mother was a beauty in her day. She nearly died giving birth to him. I was but a boy at the time, but I remember her screams still. His father came back from Stirling Bridge with one eye, proud to have fought with William Wallace. He taught me to gut a fish, back before Taran was born, when he didn't have a son and I didn't have a father. Taran's sisters are younger, one shy and quiet, the other full of fire."

While Shawn wolfed his bread in the dim light filtering through the tent walls, and gulped cold ale, Niall told of Roddy who had won a cow on a dare, by swimming across the loch; Charlie, whose two high-spirited daughters had surprised everyone by going to the convent; Ronan, who had a knack for getting into fights, and yet managed to be a great favorite, still, with his quick wit and generosity.

"There was a bad year," Niall said, "some time back when I was off fostering. The harvest was poor, the MacDougalls had taken our cattle again. Ronan had a sheep, just one, and he took it to the widow Muirne and her six children. He pushed it in her back door and disappeared. He got very thin that winter, but the widow and her children ate well. D' you see him out there now, fighting, the tall thin man with the long, graying red beard? I'd lay down my life for him, knowing what he did for them."

Shawn set down the empty trencher. He didn't like the hard knot in his throat. He'd bought a plane ticket and slid it under Amy's door. He hadn't been entirely awful. But he wondered if he would have done it, had it meant not eating that week.

Probably not.

In the dim interior of the tent, he made an internal vow to be more like Ronan. If he ever got back to Amy, everything he had would be hers. He wondered what she was doing, alone and pregnant, how she'd used the money Niall had given her, or if she'd sold the crucifix or ring.

"Tell me more about yourself," Shawn said.

Niall waved off the request. "I'm expected back with the men."

"You're their future Laird. They'll wait. I'm supposed to be you. Tell me more. Favorite color. What do you do in your spare time? Where do you go on vacation?"

"Vacation?"

Shawn realized the modern Gaelic word he had just used would mean nothing to a medieval Scot. "Your annual two weeks paid time off." He slugged back a draft of ale, laughing at his own morbid humor. Obviously, nobody got two weeks off here, paid or otherwise. "It's when you get to lounge on a warm, sandy beach sipping a margarita and do nothing all day."

"A margarita? What's that? Doing naught for a whole day?" Niall shook his head. "You don't get bored?"

Shawn laughed. "I don't get bored doing naught," he mimicked. "It's called relaxation. Besides, you don't just sit and stare at the walls. You *do* things, just not work things. Movies or ice cream...."

"Ice cream?"

"Or swim." Shawn stopped. "Wait. What was Old MacDonald...."

"That's the Laird," Niall said sternly. "You'll not call him that."

"Yeah, what was he saying about you and water?"

Niall gulped the last of the ale. "Your turn to rest."

"You're not going to tell me? Then how am I supposed to be you?"

Swiping his sleeve across his mouth, Niall rose.

"Must be a phobia or something," Shawn said. "You embarrassed? Lots of people have phobias. No big deal. I'll help you. I'm a great swimmer. I was a fish in another life."

Niall pushed through the tent flap. It dropped back in place, leaving Shawn alone in the weak light. He sighed, pulled the hood over his face, and collapsed into well-earned rest.

Bannockburn, Scotland, Present

The Heritage Centre was quiet, early in the morning. Amy settled her stomach with a hazelnut mocha latte and jelly-slathered toast at the cafe, while Rose browsed the gift store. When she finished, they paid their fees and slipped under the great two-handed sword of a life-size William Wallace, into a world of medieval weaponry—maces, daggers, and claymores. Weapons gave way to a wax woman, frozen in the act of raising a crown high over the kneeling Bruce's head. Long golden hair flowed down the back of her royal blue cloak.

"Isabel MacDuff," Amy read.

Rose scanned the placard, paraphrasing. "...paid heavily for defying her husband...claimed the MacDuff family's hereditary right to crown the kings of Scotland. Edward II made her live in a cage on the walls of Berwick Castle." She made a sound of disgust. "Cruel!"

Amy studied the silent figures, trying to see, in the wax depiction, the world and people Niall knew. But their clothes and stances made them foreign to her twenty-first century mind; as foreign and strange as men swinging swords and wielding bloody daggers against one another. She tried to imagine Niall doing such things, the Niall who had played the harp and leaned over a candlelit table at the Two-Eyed Traitor. She couldn't.

They resumed their tour, following a set of blue and red placards showing the concurrent movements of Bruce and Edward II as they marched toward their great clash. She knew it from Niall's research, while he'd been with her. The events leading to the battle hadn't changed.

"It's early for tourists," a voice said behind them.

Amy spun to see a young man, just over the edge of heavy, with nondescript brown hair and a friendly, open demeanor that saved him from being plain. "Amy Nelson." She held out her hand. "I'm not officially a tourist anymore. I live down the road."

"The American who moved in." He shook her hand. "Mike."

"And this is my friend, Rose."

"Ah, yes, now we heard you had a visitor."

"It seems everybody knows everything here." Amy looked to Rose, her eyebrows arched in question.

"Well," Rose said, "when you go out to the battlefield and church every morning, I take walks and chat with the neighbors. You didn't think I sat home, did you?"

"I know you better than that. I'm only surprised they remember you," Amy teased.

"We do talk a bit." Mike grinned. "Do you have questions?"

"What—um—where were...?" Her heart kicked an extra two beats. There was no reason he should be suspicious of such a question, she told herself. "I heard Bannockburn's dead were buried in a mass grave. Where would that have been?"

Mike lifted his hands in resignation. "That's lost to history. Now there was a place called Polmaise...."

"The Pool of Rotting," Amy finished.

"You know about that?" His eyebrows shot up.

"The tour guide at Stirling mentioned it." The thought of Shawn in such a grave made Amy feel sick. "Who eventually dealt with that?"

"Bruce's army and the nearby townsfolk, I'd think."

Amy hated to think of Niall burying hundreds of rotting bodies. She hesitated, before asking her next question, but decided there could be no harm in it. "Does Iona have any connection to Bannockburn?"

"Iona?" His voice rose a perfect fifth at the end of the word.

"Iona?" Rose echoed.

"I've never been asked that," Mike said.

"Why Iona?" Rose demanded.

"Just curious," Amy said hastily. "Something someone said. It doesn't matter."

Rose narrowed her eyes, a promise of questions to come.

"Well, now," Mike interjected, before Amy could slide away from the topic, "Columba's relics were at Bannockburn. And Columba founded the monastery at Iona."

"Wasn't that hundreds of years before Bannockburn?" Amy asked.

"Oh, aye. Sixth century. But if it's a connection you're wanting, it's all I can think of." He smiled. "I'd be happy to show you around."

Despite his youth, Mike had a thorough knowledge of Bannockburn and the museum. While Rose asked a dozen questions, Amy's mind jumped between his tour and Iona, trying to follow Shawn's trail. He'd woken up in medieval Glenmirril, no doubt with a hangover, and sometime during his few days at the castle and in the wilderness, he'd discovered something about the island refuge of a sixth century monk important enough to try to tell her?

It made no sense.

Mike stopped before a floor to ceiling aerial map. "Something we're rather proud of." He beamed, pointing out the high school and housing developments—including her own—built over large portions of the battlefield.

"Isn't this your house?" Rose picked out Amy's street.

"I'm living on top of the actual battle?" Amy asked.

Mike nodded enthusiastically, but seeing the look on her face, added quickly, "We've no trouble with ghosts, now!"

"Oh, no," she said. "It's not that." In truth, a thrill trembled through her to find she was living on the site of the battle she'd watched, to feel it might appear before her again, to hope she might see them, Shawn and Niall, reach out to them again. "I just didn't realize." It was yet another thing she couldn't tell anyone.

"That's grand, then!" He led her to another wall. "It's something, now, isn't it!" His face glowed, as he showed off a ten foot wall mural depicting horses, schiltrons, footmen, archers and pikemen all tangled in a deadly game of Twister ranging over a great expanse of boggy carse. While Rose peppered him with questions, Amy studied the intricate scene, picking out faces among the warriors, searching for any who might look like Niall. Ridiculous, she told herself. The painter hadn't actually been there. Still, she searched.

"But how did Bruce beat an army three or four times the size of his own?" Rose asked.

"He chose his ground well." Mike pointed a stubby finger at the River Forth. "See how he forced Edward's army into this narrow bog where they couldn't fight well? And on the second day of battle, despite outnumbering the Scots several times over, Edward turned and ran. A strange thing to run from such a small army."

He couldn't know, Amy thought, that the medieval Edward had run from a small army magnified by twenty-first century gawkers and re-enactors. It must have seemed ten times its real size.

"We don't have many Americans so interested in this battle," Mike commented.

Rose flashed a bright smile. "She knew someone who was there."

"Rose!" Amy's head snapped up from her study of the mural. She turned to Mike, saying hastily, "She's joking."

"Well, yes, of course." He cocked his head, frowning at Amy. "I dinna for a moment take her seriously."

Amy swallowed. She gave a sharp twist to the ring on her finger. She should have laughed it off. "I'm doing research." The lie flowed smoothly, unexpectedly, disconcerting her. She'd never seen any part of Shawn in herself. In the case of lies, she didn't want to. But the truth would hardly do, through no fault of her own.

His smile returned. "On the battle?"

"On a man named Niall Campbell." She could hardly claim to be researching a medieval Scotsman named Shawn Kleiner.

"She wants to know what happened to him after the battle," Rose added.

Mike rubbed his chin, studying the mural as if it held the answer. "Do you mean Bruce's friend and brother-in-law?"

"I don't know," Amy admitted. "Was he?"

Rose leaned forward. "From Glenmirril."

"Up on Loch Ness?" Mike shook his head decisively. "No, the one I'm talking about was from Lochawe."

Amy took his meaning—wrong man—though she had no idea where Lochawe might be.

"I don't know any other Niall Campbell," he said. "Though I've a friend who knows Glenmirril well. I could ask him, if you like."

Amy nodded. "Yes! Thank you! I'm back often enough."

"Ask him about Iona, too," Rose said.

"I'll do that," he assured them. "Now if it's the aftermath of the battle you're wanting, come this way." He led them to another wax scene. "The Declaration of Arbroath, 1320."

"1320?" Amy's eyebrows puckered at the five men in mail and colorful surcoats. One gripped the hilt of a great sword, point on the floor. Another leaned over, setting his quill to the declaration. Amy turned to Mike, about to ask what had happened in the years in between.

He'd straightened his back and lifted his chin. "An open letter to the Pope." He gazed into a distant time. His chest swelled. His voice took on a powerful orator's tone that belied his vanilla pudding looks. *"The deeds of cruelty, massacre, violence, pillage, arson, imprisoning prelates, burning down monasteries, robbing and killing monks and nuns, and yet other outrages without number which he committed against our people, sparing neither age nor sex, religion nor rank, no one could describe nor fully imagine unless he had seen them with his own eyes."*

"Wonderful!" Rose clapped.

Mike's gaze returned to the present. A faint grin and blush spread across his face. "I know the whole thing, but most people willna stand still long enough to listen."

A smile broke across Amy's face. "That's a shame. You have a real gift!"

The blush deepened on his round cheeks.

"Those things happened?" she asked.

Mike nodded as vigorously as if he had seen them with his own eyes. "Hammer of the Scots was too kind a name for Edward Longshanks. And his son was no better, but that he was so inept we regained what Longshanks took. His men liked to nail our priests to the church door and burn it around them."

Amy felt sick, thinking of Niall in such a world. Even if he'd survived Bannockburn, his eventual fate might be crueler than death on a battlefield.

"How can men be so brutal?" Rose asked sadly.

"But from these countless evils we have been set free," Mike quoted. "And the most beautiful part, to my mind, if you promise not to run for another thirty seconds." He waited for their acquiescence, before adding, "And you must promise to hear trumpets and violins swelling in the background as I say it. For it deserves that."

Amy smiled over the ill feeling. "Everyone seems to know everything about me here, so you know I can imagine violins. Go ahead."

He squared his shoulders, looking again into a noble past. *"For as long as a hundred of us remain alive, never will we on any conditions be brought under English rule. It is in truth not for glory."* He paused. *"Nor riches."* Another pause. *"Nor honors that we are fighting."* He stopped, lifted his chin, and his next words rang out a third lower, with the power of an opera singer. *"But for freedom."* He looked her in the eye. *"For that alone, which no honest man gives up but with life itself."*

The words hung in the air, shimmering with a life of their own.

A broad smile crossed Amy's face. "Wonderful!"

"Well done!" Rose gushed.

He bowed, grinning from one to the other, and added with pride, "They say 'tis the basis of your own Declaration of Independence."

"I can see that." Amy studied the men leaning over the document. Maybe Niall had known some of the signers. She returned to her original concern. "But what happened between 1314 and 1320?"

Mike shrugged. "Raids, the Bruces led the Irish against England. You'd have to go to the library or online, maybe to castles or archives, to research that in detail. We don't cover that here."

Stirling Castle, 1314

"D' you never rest, man!" Ronan exploded that night in the great hall at Shawn's elbow. He swung to the Laird, his stringy red-gray beard brushing his chest. "Going non-stop since dawn, and look at him, fresh as a bluebell!"

The Laird smiled. He'd just roused Shawn from a nap in the tent, and sent Niall to his chambers for his own much-needed rest. After dinner, Shawn would don a helmet to cover his features and subject himself to more riding instruction at Hugh's hands. "That's our Niall," MacDonald said.

Ronan left, threading through the hall with loud exclamations of Niall's hardiness. "And just days after being knocked from a horse!"

People whispered, staring at Shawn. Beside him, Allene leaned toward her father. "Brother Andrew is aw' right?"

"Aye," the Laird said softly. "He's asleep in his chambers. His color is good. It seems our friend was right in saying he needed rest rather than bleeding."

Allene looked to Shawn with growing kindness in her eyes. "Thank you," she whispered. "I couldn't bear to lose him."

Me, neither, Shawn thought. Niall was his only thread to his own life, tenuous as that was. He hesitated only a second before asking, "What's with Niall and water?"

Her lips tightened. "He'll not go near it."

"Yeah. I kind of figured that much out for myself. I was born for water. Get him to let me help him."

"He won't." Allene ended the conversation with a turn of her head.

He pulled his eyes from her, and ate, picking hesitantly with his fingers. The Laird leaned close. "The Bruce wishes him to leave soon."

"He's still getting weak and shaky fast," Shawn objected. "He needs more rest."

"There's too much to be done," MacDonald retorted. "We haven't that luxury."

"He's in no shape to go yet." Shawn felt a prickle on his neck and looked up. Across the room, MacDougall's eyes fell on him. He met the black stare with a solid gaze of his own, until the man turned away. Shawn leaned back to MacDonald. "You have to hold Bruce off a couple of days at least."

Inverness, Present

"Inspector MacLean, phone!"

"Can it not wait?" The big officer rubbed his short black curls vigorously with a towel as he strode through the police station, calling answers back to other officers and a reporter who ran to keep up with him. "It's been a rather long day." He paused at the door to the office he shared with Clive, turning long enough to tell the reporter, "The rest of them can fill you in. I've work to do."

"No, it canna wait." Clive shut the door, closing them in. "Are the boys safe, Angus?"

"All three heading to hospital, but they'll be fine," MacLean said.

"You're quite the hero."

"I'm quite the swimmer and too bull-headed to quit, is all."

"So far it's stood you in good stead," Clive said. "Hopefully it continues to, as we'd not like to lose you."

Inspector MacLean grinned. "There are those as say I'm too stubborn to die. I think you're stuck with me awhile." He glanced around the sparsely furnished office and tossed the damp towel on top of a filing cabinet. It barely missed the wilted fern. "Who's on the phone that willna wait till I'm in a fresh uniform?"

"Oh, he'll wait. I'm thinking it's you who'd rather not."

"Is that so?" MacLean raised dark, questioning eyebrows as he picked up the phone. "Inspector MacLean. Can I help you?"

"It's Mike. Are you sitting down?"

MacLean dropped into his swivel chair, pushing through papers that had collected on his desk. "I'm sitting. Clive assures me this is big enough I'd rather hear it than rush home for a hot bath and whiskey." He grinned. Clive was already pouring a tumbler of smooth amber that would do well in lieu of the trip they'd wanted him to make to the hospital himself.

"Much rather. We've a new neighbor who sits at the battlefield every morning. I've just finished showing her around."

The smile fled Angus's face. "Did you now? Clive told me she stayed on. What else do you know?" He took a long drink of the whiskey.

"She's let a house nearby. She'll be staying for some time."

"Now why would she do such a thing?" He spoke more to himself than Mike.

Clive raised his eyebrows, as he refilled the inspector's glass. "Did I not say you'd want to hear this?"

"She often stops in the cafe and has a hazelnut mocha. She's very interested in the Battle," Mike said. "Not surprising, I guess, considering her boyfriend disappeared at the re-enactment."

"But what does she hope to gain?" MacLean tapped his fingers beside the newly-filled glass. "Does she think he'll come back to the field?"

"I'd not know, but she was quite disappointed we've nothing on the years between the battle and the Declaration of Arbroath. She wanted to know where the dead of Bannockburn were buried."

"Why on earth would that matter?" Angus asked. "I'd think she's bigger things by far on her mind."

"I've no idea," Mike said. "She also asked if there's any link between Iona and Bannockburn."

Angus scratched his head. "Iona?" He turned to Clive. "Can you look in the reports and see if there's anything about Iona?" He spoke into the phone again, while Clive tapped at his computer. "Did she say why?"

"No," Mike answered. "Certainly no harm done. Eccentric at worst. Her friend joked that she knew someone at Bannockburn—at the battle, you see—

and she seemed quite concerned that I understand it was only a joke."

"Odd." Angus took another swallow of whiskey.

"I'd a feeling certain of the Inverness police would be interested."

"Very. Unofficially, of course. Thanks, mate." Angus dropped the phone in its holder, and turned to Clive. "Anything?"

Clive shook his head. "I'd have remembered such a thing."

Angus drank another half glass, staring thoughtfully at the ceiling.

"Home now?" Clive asked.

"We've no more official business with her?" MacLean slid his desk drawer open and took out his cell phone. Clicking through to his albums, he stared at a picture: a drawing of a woman with long black hair.

"I'd be hard pressed to think of a reason to talk to her again." Clive leaned over to see the phone. "What have you there?"

Angus clicked a button. The picture disappeared. He laughed. "Another time. I've been told to take a day or two to recuperate from my swim. I believe I'll take my hols in Bannockburn."

Clive's easy friendliness disappeared in a wary dip of eyebrows. "Tread careful now, Angus. We've no business with her."

Angus gulped the last of his whiskey. "You promised me a ride home. I'm wanting that hot bath quite badly. I've an early start tomorrow."

Chapter Six

"It seems like the place to say good-bye." Rose sat on the tree stump under the small copse at the edge of the battlefield. "As much time as you spend here."

"Here and the church." Sitting under a tree overlooking the steep slope of Bannockburn field, Amy sipped her hazelnut mocha, then gave a laugh. "And thrift stores, since you came!"

Rose studied Amy's royal blue top. It's long sleeves extended past her wrists, and it emphasized her slender form. "You look beautiful. Those bright colors go so well with your hair."

A small blush of pleasure climbed Amy's cheeks. She turned away, looking into the morning mist that filled the lower half of the field, like a cauldron of boiling magic. "Rose, I'm so glad you came."

"Glad enough to finally tell me everything?" Rose asked.

Amy's hands tightened around her cup. "I told you everything."

"Except one thing. Do you *believe* Shawn disappeared into 1314?"

Amy fixed her eyes on the mist. "I never said he did. I told you the facts." A bird trilled in the tree above her.

"And that's what the facts imply."

"Several people have said I'm..." Amy cleared her throat. "Overstressed. Because I told them those facts. Because I said Niall gave me money."

"*I* haven't said you're overstressed," Rose pointed out. "You say it wasn't Shawn, you gave good reasons, and I believe you. You've always been clear-headed."

Amy turned, finally, to meet her teacher's eyes. "Time travel, though. Does a clear-headed person believe in time travel?"

"While you've been out on your morning walks," Rose said, "I've done a lot of reading. Is Einstein clear-headed enough for you?"

"He believed it as a theory," Amy countered. "What if someone told him it really happened to them? Would he still believe it?"

"He'd ask the right questions." Rose sipped her coffee. "He wouldn't blindly believe anything he was told. And you haven't, either."

Amy said nothing.

"Your behavior says you believe it, even if you won't say the words," Rose said. "You're searching for Shawn or Niall or both of them. We've been to the place Niall's father died, and the place the battle was fought over. You asked where Bannockburn's dead were buried. You said Shawn's not coming back."

Amy's lips tightened against the shot of pain through her heart.

Her teacher rose from the stump, and settled on the ground beside her, pulling her head down onto her shoulder. Hot tears slid down Amy's face. Her body trembled. The memory of his last moments was horrifyingly vivid. She wiped at her nose.

"You've always been cautious," Rose said. "You wouldn't believe it if it weren't true."

Amy heard the sound of hiccuping sobs, and realized, with shame, that it was her. "I'm sorry," she tried to say, but it came out on another sob.

"Don't be." Rose held her while she cried, stroking her hair. "You lost someone you loved for a long time, and you can't even tell anyone."

"No." Amy wiped at her nose again, tried and failed again to stifle the sobs, and sagged onto Rose's shoulder, letting them rack her body. The last time she'd cried in Rose's arms, she'd been twelve. Colin's horse had died. She and Rose had spent her lesson crying, talking, and eating gingerbread.

"I wish I had some hot tea," Rose murmured.

"You're thinking of that day," Amy managed to say with a small laugh.

"Of course I am." Rose smoothed Amy's hair. "Although Shawn, no matter what he was up to, is still a bigger loss than Colin's horse."

The last sob ended on a laugh. "He'd be so pleased to know that."

"Hm! He ought to be grateful he still outranks a horse. Cheating on you! I've guessed enough. Now, tell me everything straight up."

Amy drew in a deep breath. She wiped the back of her hand across her eyes, and told the whole story, including the apology carved on Hugh's rock, and the events at the re-enactment. She showed Rose the ring and, trying not to knock over her coffee, took the crucifix from her neck. She gave it to Rose. "It's Niall's. He left it with me to sell in case I need money to take care of the baby." She bit her lip, not wanting to cry again.

"What do you know about it?" Rose studied the crucifix.

"Not much," Amy admitted. "Some monks made it for his father. He left a sheet with it's history, and places I could sell it."

"Don't sell it." Rose returned the crucifix. "If he managed to cross back, why didn't Shawn?"

"Let no good deed go unpunished." Amy's voice caught again. "He threw himself between a knight and a child who wandered onto the field." She stopped, feeling the pain stabbing again, feeling the tears coming on.

"He was killed," Rose said softly.

"There's no way anyone could have survived it." Amy drew in a deep breath. The sun had climbed, the mist had cleared, and something had lightened inside her. "Do you know how good it feels to tell the truth? Only Celine and Aaron know. It was awful trying to keep stories straight for the police. And everyone keeps telling me he's only missing and may turn up anytime." She straightened, meeting Rose's eye. "If I tell anyone Shawn's dead, I can't explain why I think that."

"Yes," Rose agreed. "Be careful. Deep as my faith in you is, even I'd have had trouble believing it if it had been the first thing you'd said to me."

"Rose, what in the world do I *say* when people tell me he may turn up?" Amy gripped the mocha as if it were her last hold on reality.

"Say thank you and change the subject." Rose glanced at her watch. "These planes are under the impression they must keep schedules, and I'm afraid theirs is interfering with mine right now."

Amy laughed even as she brushed at the last of the tears. "Maybe you could call and let them know they'll have to hold the plane for you."

"I have half a mind to do just that. Come on, now, help me up. The taxi will be at your house in an hour."

Climbing to her feet, Amy helped Rose up. They crossed the parking lot, coffees in hand, past the white stuccoed museum, while Rose issued orders.

"I like the song you wrote. Now do another one. I want a painting from you as my Christmas gift. A bird would be nice, so get going on that." They crossed the main street and headed into Amy's neighborhood. "And your parents. Amy, you have *got* to call your parents. What must they think, the way I keep putting them off and telling them any day now?"

"What *will* they think?" Amy returned. "They'll have a fit."

"You can't run from these things," Rose reprimanded as they reached Amy's street of look-alike row houses. "You tell them, or I will."

"Oh, Rose, don't."

A black dog raced up alongside them, barking. Rose reached down to scratch its ears. "Hi, there, Max. It's nice to see you."

"You know him?" Amy asked.

"I see him every morning. Say hello. He'll be your friend for life. Now what are you so scared of?"

Amy scratched the dog's ears. "They'll disown me." Shawn had threatened her with that fear, the first time she'd been pregnant.

"Hm." Rose climbed the stairs to Amy's bright blue door. "And if they do?"

"Well, they're my *parents,* Rose!" Amy slipped the key in the door and let them in the front hall, dim after the morning sun. Sadness suddenly overwhelmed her. In just minutes, the taxi would take Rose away, and leave her alone. It wouldn't take long to throw her things together and go with her.

"Exactly." Rose strode to the kitchen, where she lit the burner and started the kettle. "If they're real parents, they're not going to disown you over being pregnant. Not in today's world, certainly. I can't help but notice, Amy, that it's not your mother you told Conrad you wanted. So what if they really disown you? You have a good job."

"I have no job at all," Amy pointed out. "I take it we're having tea before you leave."

"Yes. Because tea and gingerbread make everything better." She opened a cupboard and took down a plastic container of their favorite treat. "You have skills, a degree, royalties. You can get a job. If worse came to worst— which it won't, because you're resourceful and hard-working—I'd buy you a plane ticket to New York, and you'd stay with me until you win your next audition. Which you wouldn't have to do, because Conrad will take you back faster than a thirty-second note."

"You're right." Amy set out two plates, contemplating Rose's words.

"I usually am. Would you get the mugs, please?"

Amy opened the cupboard. She stared at the rose-covered china teacups sitting on the shelf, then laughed. "Rose, where in the world did you find them? They're just like the ones in your apartment!"

Rose beamed. "Gotta love those antique stores! I thought they'd make a nice going-away gift for you."

"I love them," Amy said. "They feel like home." She realized, at her words, the deep truth of Rose's statement. Rose was home, not her parents.

The kettle began a slow, steady hiss. Rose's hand hovered over the handle. "Remember how we used to wait until it sang?"

Amy smiled. She hadn't smiled as much in the past year as she had since Rose's arrival. "When I was six, you told me it was an opera singer turned into a kettle by an evil wizard with a magic flute."

"Hm, yes, well, I think that's true." The pitch of the kettle climbed steadily up a gliss, until it pierced their ears, and, laughing, Rose took it off the burner. The sound fizzled away in a sigh of relief. "I believe her name was Madam Orloff Kazarsky, and she got him mad by running off with his son."

"I remember sitting at the top of the castle in Central Park when you told me that story."

"Those were wonderful days." Rose smiled as she tipped the kettle over a china cup. Steaming water billowed over the teabag. "You've put up notices for students, and thanks to my well-endowed mouth, all of Bannockburn already knows you're the best violin teacher available for miles, anyway."

Amy bit back a smile. "Thank you, Miss Rose." She'd said it at the end of every lesson for fifteen years.

"Thank *you*," Rose returned. "As soon as my taxi leaves, you're going to take your painting supplies, get on a bus, and go find a bird to paint. And call your parents."

"Yes, Miss Rose." Amy smiled, stirring milk and sugar into her tea. "Now tell me, what are you doing when you get home?"

"A few weddings, three recordings. That R&B singer, what's his name? I'm playing on his new CD. Subbing with the Met—maternity leave. For her, not me."

When the tea cups were emptied and the gingerbread eaten, Rose pushed herself away from the table. "The taxi will be here any minute." She headed down the hall to gather her floral bag. They went out to the front step, Rose clapping the red hat on her head.

The two children next door bounded across their small patch of yard. "Miss Rose! Are you leaving?" the boy yelled.

"Any minute now," Rose answered. "Come and give me a hug!" The children did so, making her promise to send postcards from New York.

Down the street, a taxi rounded the corner. Heat prickled Amy's eyes. She blinked, vowing she wouldn't cry. Rose swept her into a hug that knocked the cherry red hat to the ground. "You have your art bag and your phone?"

"Yes." Amy nodded, her voice muffled as she hugged Rose back, her face buried in her shoulder.

"It's no good sitting home mourning. I know it hurts. But it's going to hurt less if you go do something you love and get this call over with."

"Yes," Amy said again. "I will."

"If your parents are awful, call me. Text me. Send me a long e-mail detailing every rotten thing they said, if you need to. But maybe you'll be surprised. And at least it'll be off your shoulders."

"I should get my things and go home with you," Amy said in a rush.

The taxi glided to a stop in front of Amy's house. She bit her lip as Rose leaned down to retrieve her hat. Hefting her floral bag and jamming the hat back on her head, Rose hugged Amy again, squeezing hard. "No, you shouldn't. You're right where you need to be. Call me, write, e-mail. I'm going to clear my schedule, and I'll be back in a month or two. You're going to have students by then, and paintings painted and songs written. And you're going to find out what you need to about Shawn and Niall to give you peace."

The taxi honked.

Rose kissed Amy on each cheek, squeezed her arm, and climbed into the cab. She rolled down the window to call, "Get your art bag and get going! I expect to hear from you soon!"

Standing on the curb, Amy smiled through the tears, waving as the cab pulled away. She wanted to go in her house, climb under the peach duvet, and hide from the world. Or grab her own suitcase and follow Rose to the airport and back to New York.

"Miss Amy?"

She started at the piping voice of the girl. "Hi. Elizabeth, right?"

The girl smiled. "Miss Rose told us if we make sure you go paint, you'll give us gingerbread when you get back."

"We love Miss Rose's gingerbread!" The boy looked up earnestly at her, his eyes pleading.

Amy laughed. "That Miss Rose knows how to get things done, doesn't she?" Rose knew she wouldn't disappoint two children. "All right, I assume you're two more of her new best friends and have her phone number?"

The girl nodded earnestly.

"Okay, I'm going to get my things. As soon as you see me walk out the door, you send her a text and tell her I'm on my way."

Stirling Castle, 1314

Shawn sighed in relief as Mass ended. He'd worked all night, after his riding lesson, provisioning Douglas's raiding party, while Niall slept, and come straight to Mass. *Yada, yada, yada,* on and on and on in Latin, forever. He scratched his ear, and rose from the pew, unsure whether dying under a medieval sword, or surviving only to have daily Mass inflicted on him was the worse fate. At least he'd gone in as Niall this morning, rather than as Brother Andrew.

"That itch must surely be gone by now." Niall, in the gray robe, the hood shrouding his face, appeared at his side, as they filed down the side aisle, past tall niches holding solemn-eyed statues.

"These shoes were made for walking, running, jumping," Shawn hissed back. "Anything but sitting still. I was not made for sitting still."

"You might try it sometimes. It does wonders for the soul."

"My soul is fine, thanks. Skibbedy-doo-doo-ba."

"What does that mean?" Niall asked in irritation.

"It's a kind of music." They exited the chapel, into the wider halls of Stirling castle. Shawn strained for a glimpse of the women. They'd be coming from the choir. There were a few in there well worth a second look, and a couple who seemed to enjoy getting second looks quite as much as he enjoyed giving them.

"We've weightier matters than music," Niall murmured. "Or eyeing the lasses. You're making me look bad. Come along, we must wait for the Laird."

"Has he talked to Bruce yet?"

"He was gone before I got up. I don't know. Until we hear from him, you'll continue with your tutoring."

"Geography, French, Latin?" Shawn complained. "How about Napping 101. I've been up half the night."

"After your Latin."

"It's my turn to teach you something." Irritation and exhaustion burned in Shawn's stomach. "How 'bout something useful, like swimming."

The hall had emptied. Niall stopped, tilting his head back just enough that Shawn could see him staring silently from the depths of the hood. The light and the hood cast gray shadows on his face. Deep creases appeared around his mouth.

"You've got a phobia," Shawn said. "I can help you."

Niall started walking.

Shawn strode after him. "Associate good things with water," he said. "And bit by bit, it won't bother you so much."

"You've no clue what you're on about." Niall picked up his pace to a very un-monklike stride. "We've work to do until the Laird brings news."

"The first step is admitting you have a problem," Shawn called after him. Niall didn't answer.

"*Ego postulo ut dormias!*" Shawn yelled down the hall at his gray-robed back. "There's your Latin! I need to sleep!"

Bannockburn, Present

Amy sat on her tree stump, so recently vacated by Miss Rose, overlooking Bannockburn. She glanced at her watch. She had plenty of time, before the bus came, to enjoy the peace. Plenty of time for her stomach to gnaw at her insides, worrying about her parents' reaction.

Birds twittered across the field, free now of mist. An ensemble of unseen sheep joined their stuttering ostinato to the morning symphony. The cool smell of dewy morning grass made it hard to dwell on the events that had happened at the field. Still, she saw the horse rearing, the sword slashing, even as the memory of Rose's arms comforted her. Rose was right. She was where she needed to be. She smiled, feeling peace settle on her shoulders with the warm sun.

"Coffee?"

Amy's head jerked up. A man stood above her, holding two paper cups. He wore jeans and a dark t-shirt. A blue knit cap covered his hair. "You Americans love your morning coffee and the wind is chilly." He cocked a crooked grin, noting her long sleeves. He sat down without waiting to be asked, and handed her a cup.

"Angus." He offered his free hand.

"Amy." She studied him, even after he released her hand from a solid shake. "You look familiar."

"Aye. We've met, though I dinna blame you for no minding it." He took off the cap, revealing short black curls.

"The hospital." A wall of caution crept up inside her. "You're one of the officers who came, when Ni—Shawn was brought in." And he'd been in Shawn's suite, in Inverness, standing back against the wall during the interrogations, and telling the older man it was time to go. Gratitude and unease formed a strange brew in her stomach.

"Aye." He sipped his coffee and nodded at hers, encouraging her.

"I've answered all the questions." She took a drink. "Mocha with hazelnut? You managed to pick my favorite."

The man smiled. He wrapped his hands around his coffee and stared over the field. "I'm visiting a friend. I'm not here to ask questions."

She gave a short laugh. "Thank goodness. Everyone thinks I'm crazy." She sipped her mocha and added, "No, they're nicer than that. They say I'm overstressed." She shook her head. "Overstressed."

"Well, I did have that one question," the man admitted.

"Am I crazy?"

"No, how are you holding up? Your orchestra's left and the police aren't looking for him anymore. He was your boyfriend, no?"

Amy nodded. No need to elaborate on the complex web of feelings surrounding Shawn's disappearance—or the personal detail that she'd broken up with him. Down the hill, across the hedgerows, sheep bleated, the sound carrying on the crisp morning air.

A breeze rustled the man's dark curls. "So how are you holding up?" he asked.

Amy's mouth twitched upward. She kept her eyes on a cluster of tiny daisies springing up joyfully where men had died. "As you say, I'm alone, my boyfriend has disappeared, I've quit a good job. Everyone who's read the police reports thinks I'm crazy, excuse me, overstressed. I have no idea what I hope to gain here, yet I can't leave." She sipped her coffee. "But I'm okay. I have a house down the road. I'll be teaching music lessons. I feel like I'm where I need to be. I'm okay. I shouldn't be." She smiled, thinking of Rose. "But I think I really am."

They sat in silence for several minutes before the cop asked, "Are you hoping to find him?"

Amy shrugged. "You've read the police reports." She couldn't look at him. "You took some of them yourself."

"Aye."

Relief brushed her cheek, that he said no more. "No, I won't find him. I guess I just want to be near where it happened."

"'Twas an odd thing, the battle," the cop said.

Amy's heart picked up a beat. She turned, searching his eyes for a clue, hoping. "What do you mean?"

He stared out over the field. A car twisted around the narrow road beyond the hedges, heading toward the little creek. Amy had walked down to it several times in the last week, a small and unprepossessing trickle of water she could wade across, shaded by trees that gave it a dark, secret feel, still and peaceful. It was hard to imagine men dying there. She wondered if Shawn had been near it, if Niall had chased the English over it. He'd worn little protection, compared to the English knights' armor, when she'd left him in the hills, and she worried about him, wondering how he'd fared.

"I dinna ken," Angus said. "The cops on the field, people there, they saw strange things. Someone said he saw two Bruces. Another swore he saw a man killed, but there was no body, of course. The police chief here says he heard singing on the field. And when it was over, and the Scots routed the English, well, I've spent my life studying Scottish history, and I kept feeling summat was very wrong, that that wasn't how it ended, though I've been taught that all my life." He turned his cup in his hands. "So it was odd when you said Kleiner...." He cleared his throat. "When you said he thought he had to save the Scots at Bannockburn, for clearly we *did* win there, and they'd not need saving. Perhaps the fever had not quite worn off?"

Amy sipped her coffee through the tiny hole in the plastic lid. A bit of its warmth pushed back against the heavy breeze chilling her through the long sleeves. She couldn't tell him she'd seen two times overlap. That sort of thing didn't happen. And she had no explanation for why she alone remembered that, until just weeks ago, history books had, as he said, recorded an English victory—until Niall threw himself back in time and suddenly, the battle changed, and history changed. It was too much to think about.

In the brief silence, fear swept over her like a heckling murder of crows. He was the police. He'd think she was crazy. He might see the crucifix or ring and demand she give them into police custody. She twisted her thumb under her palm, turning Bruce's ring around her finger so that only the gold band showed.

The cop interrupted her thoughts. "Mike says you're interested in the years after the battle. If it's information you're wanting, the library here has plenty of books, and there are some good web sites." He cocked his head. "But why?"

She bit her lip. "Research. Something to do. I thought I'd write a—a paper." Her words tumbled out, wanting to distract him from the why. "That museum in Inverness with the diorama, it...."

"What museum?" he asked.

"With the diorama. It's huge. It...." She stopped. She'd found it for Niall, when he'd been searching for the reason the Scots lost.

"I know of no such museum," he said.

The unpleasant feeling of impossibility crawled down her neck. Now he'd definitely think she was crazy. "Thanks for the coffee." She pushed herself blindly off the tree stump. "I, uh, I have a bus to catch."

"Aye." He climbed to his feet.

She crossed the tarmac, past the white Centre that she alone seemed to remember had not existed a few weeks ago. She turned once. The cop, coffee in one hand and blue knit cap in the other, stood under the fringe of trees, staring after her.

Stirling Castle, 1314

"Get up!" Entering the small room he shared with Shawn, Niall shook the frame of the tester bed. "The Laird will be here soon. You're to be up and dressed." He'd spent the hours since Mass supervising preparations for Douglas's excursion into northern England. It had left him trembling, and irritable with his own weakness. A dozen worries and MacDougall's threat against Allene didn't help his mood.

"No need to yell." Grumbling, Shawn emerged from the blue curtains. His white linen shirt hung to his knees. He stretched, yawned, and scratched his chest. "Damn, it's downright medieval, starting a day without coffee. What does Old MacDonald want?"

"He is *not* Old MacDonald." Niall dropped into a chair. "Show respect."

"Yeah, I'm trying." Shawn yanked on a pair of trews.

Niall glowered. He had become used to looking at his own face. Almost. It had become more disconcerting as both he and Shawn moved into good health, and dressed alike in order to make the switches that allowed each to rest. Allene had kept busy sewing duplicates of his clothing, explaining to the women observant enough to notice that Niall had once again torn a good garment. She had trimmed their hair identically. And the fact that Shawn was continually exhorted to adopt Niall's character had its effect, too. Niall wondered how much he'd come to see Shawn as an extension of himself, and how far it was fair to push him, for the sake of Scotland, to 'be' Niall down to the finest details. Or how much it was even possible.

Nevertheless, it had to be done. Niall lifted his foot, loosening the thongs that bound his leather boots. "You'd best watch yourself with the lasses," he said. "My Lord Edward begins to think he and I are two of a kind. He's just after inviting me to join him for a visit to the Robertson sisters. I didn't appreciate it. Nor could he understand why I'd take offense after he saw 'me' chatting up Lady Robertson just before Mass this morning."

"I was not *chatting her up*." Tossing aside the nightshirt, Shawn pulled a fresh *leine* over his head. "I was admiring the beauty of God's handwork." He dropped onto the other chair, pulling on his boots.

They were close to his own, Niall noted, but not identical. It couldn't be helped, but only prayed no one looked close enough to notice the different shade, the rougher grain of hide, or the farther spacing of eyelets for the laces. The Laird said he worried overmuch about details. Niall pointed out that was a habit he'd gotten from the Laird himself, and one never knew when the details might make the difference.

"This going to church every morning business." Shawn gave a sharp yank at his laces. "Aren't you the one who says praise God in all things?"

Niall glared. "Do not blaspheme."

"What?" Shawn threw up his hands. "He really made one beautiful woman there, and I was appreciating it."

"Character is where true beauty lies. Try appreciating that."

"Are you saying you want me to hit on the ugly ones, too?"

Niall ripped off the first boot and threw it viciously against the wall. "Are you daft! Have you no understanding of anything?"

Shawn shrugged. "I'm trying. You people are, uh, pardon me for saying it, but you don't exactly see the world in a normal way."

Niall snorted. "Normal! I've seen what you consider normal! God have mercy on your time! If you're trying, you might start by sitting still at Mass and listening. You might learn something."

"I sit perfectly still!"

"The only time you sit still, *Brother Andrew*, is when your eyes are glazed over staring at the choir, hoping for a glimpse of the women! You'll no longer go as Niall with your face uncovered."

Shawn swore. "That is *not* fair. I don't want to be in that robe all the time with my neck all bent over."

"Perhaps instead of complaining, you ought to consider why," Niall suggested.

"Because you're a selfish a—"

Niall straightened. His eyes hardened, daring Shawn to use the word.

"...pig who doesn't want to go as Brother Andrew."

"No!" Niall yanked off his other boot and threw it after the first. "Because I did not appreciate watching myself dig in my ear, pick at my fingernails, and scratch my oxters through the entire Mass, that's why! If you must sully a name, it can at least be that of a man who doesn't actually exist, but I'll not have my name ruined!"

"I did *not* scratch my armpits! And my ear itched."

"Offer it up," Niall barked. "Whatever you scratched, 'tis not the way I behave at chapel, and people are asking questions. 'Tis a blessing I've a couple of head wounds to excuse 'my' odd behavior at times."

"Okay, I'm trying!" Shawn laced up his second boot. "Why don't you try having the least bit of understanding what it's like to be tossed into a different time!"

Niall snorted. "Yes, I'd have no idea what that's like."

"My world's a little easier to get by in." Shawn dismissed Niall's sarcasm. "There's not exactly anything to do at Mass here. There are no hymnals to look at. See, if I'd been thrown into a time after the Gutenberg press, I could sit still. That's not my fault."

"I've no idea what this Good Berg press is. But there's plenty to do at Mass. Worship God, for instance. Praise God, for another. Thank God, for a third. Think on His blessings for a fourth."

"That's all pretty much the same thing isn't it?" Shawn asked. "Look, I, excuse me, *you*, are getting all the credit, which means you—oh, wait, that means me! *I* have work to do to make *you* look like Superman."

"Who is this Superman you keep nattering on about?" Niall tore his shirt off over his head, replacing it with his nightshirt.

"And what exactly do I have to thank God for, anyway?" Shawn waved his hands beside his head and put on a false grin. "Whoohoo, I'm stuck in a brutal time with barbaric weapons in the hands of an entire world full of homicidal maniacs! Thank you, God, *thank you!*"

Niall pushed aside the bed curtains, and climbed in. "You've no respect." He punched the pillows into shape. "Try thank you, God, I'm alive. I recovered from being sliced nearly in half. D' you not see what a miracle that is? Or thank you God the Laird believed me and didn't disembowel me first and hang me later."

"That's not physically possible." Shawn shoved a dirk into his boot.

"If he's angry enough, it is. Or thank you God I've good food to eat."

It was Shawn's turn to snort. "It ain't exactly McDonald's!"

"Of course not. MacDonald's cooks are at Glenmirril. Try thank you God for the Laird's trust and a warm roof over my head." Niall yanked the covers over his legs. "D' you know what it is to spend years in a rat-infested dungeon?"

"I can imagine," Shawn spoke dryly. He pulled his vest over his shirt, and tugged it into place.

"Yes, Allene told me about that." Niall fell silent; he turned away, staring out the open window where the sky had become gray and the hills purple, as dusk fell. He was grateful to Shawn for comforting her then, and also profoundly unhappy with the thought of him having held her, for any reason. He recognized he could not be pleased in this situation, and offered his own silent prayer to God for peace, for wisdom. "Be grateful to God the soldiers didn't find you that day," he said softly.

They stared at one another, and suddenly, Niall's anger drained. Shawn had been a womanizer, self-centered, wanton, and careless of other people's lives and feelings. Niall chewed his lip. He supposed it was too much to expect a man to change overnight, or even in a couple of months, and truly, Shawn had become a different man. His eye might wander, but he seemed to have been faithful to the apology he'd left Amy on the rock in Hugh's camp. There had been no complaints from any fathers, husbands, or brothers, no sign of a woman spurned, no unaccounted-for absences on Shawn's part. The man hadn't been to church in years, and being made to go every morning must certainly be a difficult adjustment.

"I suppose I must give you credit," Niall muttered. The words hurt, like something being ripped from inside him. It was his pride, he knew, being torn out. He'd believed he was the better man. He stared out the window, stiff against the pillows, his back half-turned to Shawn. It took a strong man to see his own failings and change them. Maybe that made Shawn his equal.

"Thank you." Shawn spoke with dignity, rather than his usual sarcasm. He pushed a dirk into his other boot, and practiced a couple of quick draws. "When's the Laird coming?"

"Soon." Niall switched to French. "Try the move I showed you last night. And who did Bruce's sisters marry?"

They passed the time with Shawn practicing fighting, and reviewing French verbs, until a knock on the door brought reprieve. "Thank God!" Shawn muttered.

"About time you did so," Niall replied.

Allene and the Laird came in, MacDonald with bags under his eyes, Allene with blue ribbons plaited through her coppery hair, holding the wildest of its flyaway curls from her face, and a green kirtle held in at the waist with a jeweled girdle, heavily embroidered with blue and thread-of-gold. Niall's spirits lightened at sight of her, even as the weight of concern settled more painfully on his shoulders. Shawn held a chair, keeping his eyes off her, Niall was pleased to note. And Niall wondered, as he often did when his eyes fell on Allene, what Amy had done with the crucifix. He touched his own throat, where it should have hung, and hoped she hadn't needed to sell it. He felt better thinking it was with her rather than a stranger.

Allene's eyes met his. His hand fell from his throat. He swallowed.

"I've word from His Grace." MacDonald settled himself into a chair at the scarred wooden table. "You leave at dawn tomorrow. He wants all possible information on Lame John and his kin, Duncan."

Niall looked again to Allene. "What of Allene? Do we let MacDougall think he has cowed us? How would we explain to His Grace my continued presence at dinner? Or do we have a plan to protect her?"

"How about we tell the Bruce what's going on?" Shawn suggested.

The Laird shook his head. "I've thought much on it, Shawn. The more men know a secret, the less 'tis a secret worth having. Even a king."

"He'd speak to his advisers," Niall said. "He would need to. And there are those like Edward Bruce who would not resist a wink or a jest now and then, thinking himself clever to be in on the secret and speaking so boldly yet obliquely in front of others. But eventually, a clever man will add up the clues. We mayn't like MacDougall, but let us never underestimate him."

They sat silently for a minute, looking each from one to another. Then Niall asked, "How are we to protect Allene? What has the Bruce to say about that?"

"He wants her back at Glenmirril," the Laird said. "My men and Hugh's, those who aren't going with the Douglas, will leave with her tomorrow morning."

They all turned to Shawn, leaning against the wall. Niall asked the question on every mind. "What of Shawn?"

The Laird sighed. "'Tis too much for an old man. He can't be seen here. Do we tell the men of MacDonald you are on Bruce's business, which they will accept and have him continue to Glenmirril as Brother Andrew, or have him travel with us as you?"

"Word might reach His Grace if Shawn travels as Niall to Glenmirril," Allene said. "So they must both disappear."

They all turned back to Shawn. His hand went to his ear. He looked at Niall, tightened his jaw, and let it fall. Niall couldn't stop the corner of his mouth quirking up. "Does your ear itch?" he asked.

Shawn cast him a dirty look.

"So we're agreed he must leave Stirling, and not be seen as Niall," MacDonald concluded. "That our entire company leaves together will perhaps set MacDougall's mind at ease that you're not going to Creagsmalan. We'll start together and have you leave on your own, Niall, when we approach Duncan's land."

"And Shawn will live in hiding at Glenmirril?" Allene asked.

"How about I go with Niall?" Shawn suggested. "Two heads are better than one, especially when they're this good-looking."

Niall's mouth quirked up again. The Laird appeared too lost in thought to have heard. Allene smiled a small, secret smile at Niall. He winked at her. She blushed and lowered her eyes.

"Think on it, Niall," said the Laird. "Would it serve to have him with you? Would it serve Scotland? Is there aught more helpful he could be doing, living as Brother Andrew for a wee bit? Now, Shawn, Niall's work to do yet. The Douglas and Edward Bruce leave tomorrow at dawn, and you must have their supplies in order. Niall, rest well. Allene, come along, lass." He pushed himself with the grunt of old age from his chair, and shuffled to the door with Allene and Shawn following him.

The loss of energy disturbed Niall. The Laird had ever been the strongest of men, in body and spirit. "My Lord...."

The Laird turned, waiting.

Niall swallowed. "'Tis naught. God go with you." As soon as the door closed behind them, he was out of bed, on his knees on the hard stones, the chill biting into his skin. A crucifix hung on the wall in this room, as it did in his own chambers at Glenmirril. He crossed himself, but had no words, so confused were his thoughts. His head hung, listening for God's voice.

But God was silent.

He glanced at the chest that held his father's sword, thinking of his father giving him the crucifix just before leaving forever. "My Lord Father in Heaven, I ask that You grant Allene safety," he said at last. "Guide the men who protect her and grant them safe passage." He fell silent for a time, before saying, "Might I pray for Amy, though she'll not be born for hundreds of years?" In his lifetime, she existed, in his own past. He bowed his head and whispered, "And please make me a better man tomorrow than I was today."

He'd said those words often, not thinking much on them. Tonight, he recognized his complete lack of humility in regards to Shawn. He'd done little but remonstrate with and criticize a man who was, after all, in an unenviable position. He'd been nobility of sorts in his world, and was now nothing, subject to every whim of the Laird and Niall himself, denied even his own identity, or credit for any of his hard work. And the worst he'd done was squirm at Mass and be friendlier to women than Niall would have been.

"Still," Niall told God, "he's harming my name." Even as he said it, shame filled him. There were bigger worries. He fell silent, sending out wordless pleas for God's protection over Scotland and King Robert, and all the rest.

Finally, he rose, climbed back between the thick hangings, and sank into the feather mattress and clouds of fur, thinking of his upcoming mission to Creagsmalan. Being caught there would mean the end of his days on earth. He thought with unease of the messengers already on their way to alert Duncan MacDougall. Rumor had it Duncan was not overly bright. But even he, with proper warning, stood half a chance of recognizing Niall.

Still, his king had commanded. Niall had no choice but to go. He added a prayer that something might prevent the messages reaching Duncan, and sank into fitful sleep.

The Trossachs, Present

The beauty of technology: I can make this awful call from the most beautiful, calming place on earth, high in the mountains beside a glittering blue loch, tall Douglas pines like castles around me, my paints beside me.

The tyranny of technology: Even here in this tall grass on the rocky shore, an osprey posing on a tree branch ten feet away, my stomach is in knots, as it has been for the whole bus ride, just having the phone in my hand. Even here on the shore, my pencil in hand, the osprey outlined on my sketch pad, I can't escape the fear of this call. They know I left Shawn in the tower.

My thoughts travel back to my first boyfriend. I liked him. But after spending that night talking with Shawn, going skating with him, seeing his humor and kindness, I fell in love with him, and I understood how little I'd really felt for Brian. When I found out Brian cheated, I didn't think twice about breaking up. But it still hurt. I called my mother in tears. Well, she said, you did spend an awful lot of time in that practice room. What did you expect?

I hadn't thought of it in a long time, but it came to me on the bus, and I understood suddenly what Rose meant when she said I need to understand why I accept so much blame. I didn't give Brian every minute, everything he wanted. It was my own fault he cheated, my mother hinted, not so delicately. I believed her, even though I was shocked and hurt when she said it. I blocked it out, refused to believe she meant what I heard. Because what mother would say such a thing to her daughter?

I find a little forgiveness for myself—understanding those words were burned deep in my soul—for giving Shawn everything he said he needed, because my own mother told me that's what I had to do. And with Shawn, his good side was so good, I loved every minute with him. I didn't want to lose that. So I gave everything, so no one could ever say—What did you expect?

I know what I expect when I call. Sketching the bandit's mask on the osprey doesn't stop my hands shaking. *Taking a deep breath and looking up to the clouds floating like Highland sheep in the blue pasture of the sky doesn't stop the shaking. Thinking of the dozen voice mails my parents have left makes the shaking worse. The only thing worse than making this phone call is putting it off even longer.*

I brace myself. She can't possibly blame me for him disappearing.

I hit Mom in my contacts.

Her voice comes over the line before the first ring. "Amy! Why in the world haven't you answered? Why haven't you called? What's happening there? Have they found him?"

I don't want to talk about any of it. I guess I know deep down she can blame me. And really—she's right. I shouldn't have left him. Shawn would change the subject, ignore her questions. "I'm out by a loch, painting," *I say.*

"Painting?" *Disapproval drips from her voice like sap sliding down a tree trunk in winter. I hear what she doesn't say. Why are you painting when Shawn is missing? What's wrong with you?*

I study the osprey's wings, deciding what color to use on them. Dark chestnut, maybe. "I thought it was time to paint again." *The sun splashes suddenly from behind one of the cotton-candy clouds, striking the bird's wing. It glints bronze, the same color as Shawn's hair when the sun hit it. It hurts, thinking of him.*

"Painting? What are you thinking? They're saying you left him in a tower and he got hurt. I just haven't known what to say to Karen and Ellie when we go golfing. What were you thinking?"

"He wouldn't listen." *I hear my voice slide up a third.* "He was being obnoxious and arrogant." *I try to believe I was justified. I can't tell her he cheated. She'll know I messed up again.*

"You can't just walk off and leave someone because you don't like what they said. He got hurt. Now he's disappeared."

Her accusation marches alongside years of accusations. I try to sketch the bandit's mask across the osprey's eyes. My hand trembles. I exchange the pencil for a brush.

"And why did you stay? Conrad was quite upset when he called."

"Conrad's always like that." *I touch the fine tip of the brush to the dark chestnut splotch of paint, wishing my hand would stop shaking.*

"But, Amy, he has to replace you. You've lost your job. You've caused so much uproar. You've...."

I sweep an arc of golden-brown, like Shawn's hair, across the wing, trying to tune out all the problems I've caused. She's right. I've made my problems everyone's. I should have....

I drop my hand, clutching the brush, to my knee. Rose wouldn't listen meekly to this. "I didn't call to talk about this." *I try to sound strong, I try to sound like Rose.*

My mother stops abruptly. "Well.... Oh. But...."

In the background, my father's voice booms, and she yells, "Amy's on the phone." *Everything echoes on the speaker phone.*

My father's voice bursts over the line. "Did they—find him?"

"No." *I glance from the bird on the branch to the bird on the sketch pad, putting off the moment of saying it. Guilt, the eternal guilt, crushes my heart in an iron fist. I shouldn't have told Shawn's mother before my own.*

"No news?" my father presses.

"No." There never will be, and I can't explain why I'm not anxiously awaiting news like the rest of the world. "It's just, well...." There's no way except to just say it. "I'm sort of—pregnant."

No sound comes over the line.

My heart pounds. I lift another paintbrush, dabbed in pale blue, trying to calm myself, and add a hint of light tap-dancing on the surface of the loch. The effect isn't bad. Why did I let Shawn's opinion affect mine? Drawing was one thing he couldn't do very well.

The silence stretches on the phone. Then my mother says, "But...." The word hangs, a full half rest. "How did this happen?"

The paintbrush falls to my knee. I let out a sound reminiscent of Shawn's snorts and Rose speaks through me. "Well, I think you know."

"Amy! I didn't mean! I mean, what I meant was, I thought—"

"I'm sorry, Mom." I squeeze my eyes shut, wanting the pain of their disappointment to stop. "I know what you meant." I make excuses. "You don't know what it's like out here. I thought the same thing. I thought marriage mattered, and I thought...." I stop. "I don't know anyone who isn't."

"He did this, didn't he," my father explodes. "Did he push you into this?"

I think, with a little irony, that it was my own mother who pushed me into it. She told me if a man cheats on me it's my fault. I think of Niall on the train, horrified that my father isn't here protecting me, I think of the difference between Allene's father and mine, and I'm not sure whose ways are right, but I think maybe my father could have been there more than he was, and maybe we'd be having a different conversation.

"We kept hearing he was like this," my father says.

"Don't you understand, Dad," I say, refusing to voice my true thoughts. "It's the whole world, not just him. It's hard to stand by a set of values when everyone tells you you're crazy and out of touch." I won't tell them Shawn hinted he'd leave me. I can't really blame him, not with the expectations of this world. Still, I made my own decision. Repeatedly.

"But he...."

"I know you worried about him," I interrupt. On the loch, a fish leaps and lands again with a plop, sending ripples out in widening circles. "But you loved him, too." He'd just put out another CD. They hadn't known what to expect from a 23-year-old star with high energy and a bad reputation, who, in just over a year, had turned a classical orchestra into a pop culture icon. Tears sting my eyes. "Remember how he was the day you met him at Aunt Carrie's house, so cheerful, so friendly, so funny? Remember how generous he was with Carrie's boys?"

My mother reprimands my father. "She's just lost someone she loves."

"But he...."

My mother talks over him. "Do you want me to come over, Amy?"

The day with Carrie shines brightly in my memory, Shawn playing football with my young cousins—the man I believed in, the man I kept staying for. It's hard to imagine that the man rolling in the grass with five boys did anything as hateful as cheat and lie, to me, to Celine. He was upset with me. Things were bad between us. I realize I'm making excuses for him —again.

"*Amy, do you want your mother to come over?*" My father speaks sharply, as if it's not the first time he's asked.

I pull myself from the sun-dappled memory, shaking my head, brushing at damp cheeks. It's the last thing I want. "*No. I'm fine.*"

"*But you're alone. You're pregnant. How are...?*"

I sniff, my hand under my nose, hating the way I sound. "*I'm fine. I'm happier than I've been in a long time.*" I realize, as the words fly out, how impossible they must sound to my parents who know nothing of my suspicions about Shawn's cheating. But it does no good to ruin what's left of Shawn's reputation. Especially when he's dead, and I'm not really sure, anyway, apart from Celine. "*I mean, I'm finding a lot of peace here. I'm happy being alone.*" Another heavy sniff comes out. Shawn walked with me through the dim woods after playing football with my cousins, held my hand, kissed me by a stream. I brush at tears.

"*If you're sure,*" my mother said. "*If you change your mind....*"

"*You need someone, Amy.*" That's my father.

"*No, really.*" I blow into a tissue. "*I'm fine.*" I say good-bye, close the phone, and turn my hand to study Bruce's ring. Almost immediately, the phone trills the opening measures of a Telemann sonata. I jump. I don't want to talk to my mother. But the number is unknown. With another swipe at my eyes, I answer to a burst of excited Scottish dialect.

"*I've a ten year old daughter now who couldn't believe her eyes when she saw you're available to teach lessons!*"

It takes me a second to realize what the woman is talking about.

"*Sinead's a handful that one,*" the woman warns. "*But she loves violin and she'll give you no trouble. She's that excited to have lessons, she is. Can she start soon?*"

I press fingers against tears still welling under my eyes but manage to put on a professional voice. We make arrangements and I hang up, pleased I've managed to appear quite sane. I've survived this awful phone call to my parents, I have a student. Things are looking up, but Shawn is still dead, and I'm still pregnant. I look around the peaceful wilderness, the loch slapping softly across the pebbly beach. I'm not sure if 'a handful' is exactly what I need to take my mind off things, or exactly what I don't need. I guess I'll find out, because money—that, I will need.

Stirling Castle, 1314

James Douglas, Edward Bruce, and their armies gathered in the misty gray before dawn. A few bright stars clung to the palette of night sky, twinkling over Stirling's parapets. Mist crawled across the ground, weaving in and out of the hooves and feet that packed the expansive courtyard. Shawn wheeled Lord Abernathy's horse around, having made sure it was re-shod. Stores of food waited for men to gather, food they would carry under their saddles. The Scots did not have England's power, but what they had, they used well. While England struggled to drag supply wagons through serrated hills, bumping them along the glens in between, the Scots rode or jogged, each man carrying what he needed.

The heavy smell of leather filled the courtyard. It creaked from saddles and belts and armor. Shawn's own studded vest, over a linen shirt, creaked with the rest. Thick beards were everywhere, interspersed with younger, fresher faces. Some looked grim, some excited. Men poured from the great hall, and their last hot meal before weeks of eating oatcakes.

James Douglas strode up to Shawn. "Let's have a look." He held out his hand.

Shawn gave him the supply list. They looked it over together, Douglas shuffling through the pages. "There you go, I knew young Ailde would need his dirk replaced," he said. "They've all got rations. Good. Long night, aye?"

"Aye," Shawn replied. He'd left the previous night's conversation with Niall, the Laird, and Allene, and come straight to work.

"Don't know how you do it," Douglas said, "working day and night."

Shawn smiled. "All for Scotland, My Lord."

"Good man." Douglas clapped him on the back. "Sign here."

Shawn lifted a quill presented to him by a boy carrying a writing case. He laid the sheet on the leather-covered surface and signed Niall's name. Despite Allene's efforts, it was a far cry from what Niall would have produced. But it would raise no questions, as his twenty-first century script would have. Underneath, he stroked the small insignia of a trombone with which he'd signed letters to Amy. He glanced up, his heart hammering with fear Douglas would notice the mark and question it. But Douglas was gripping the reins of a restless pony and shouting over his shoulder to Edward Bruce. The boy sprinkled fine sand on the ink to dry it, and sifted it off again.

A horse whinnied in Shawn's ear. It was closer to a pony, really, one of the hardy hobbins the Scots rode through their tough hills. To Shawn, it qualified as large. Several weeks ago, he would have jumped at the sound. Now, he reached into his pocket for an apple and held it over his shoulder. The animal snuffled, wet velvety lips grazing his fingers, and chomped the apple with large teeth. Shawn yanked his hand away, holding back a grimace Niall would not have felt.

"Good, then." Douglas raised an arm to a young man with a horn. A signal blared across the courtyard. A trumpeter on the ramparts picked up the sound, and sent another call out across the meadow far below. There, hundreds more men, just finishing breakfast, checking their gear and the straps on their horses, would mount and fall in behind their leaders.

Among them, Shawn knew, were the Laird, Hugh, and their men, preparing for their march to Glenmirril, to deliver Allene safely. The most recent gathering of lords had been uncomfortable, with MacDougall casting an evil eye and baring yellow teeth at him. In his previous existence, Shawn would have made an issue of it. Here—now—he held his peace, knowing Allene was on her way to safety.

The drawbridge lowered with a creaking of chains and groaning of wood. Harnesses jingled. Men laughed and called. Douglas cantered to the front of the group, raising his great sword in the gray dawn, shouting his war cry. "A Douglas!"

"A Douglas!" The call echoed back from hundreds of men. The drawbridge thumped into place on the far edge of the great moat. Douglas kicked his hobbin, and the shaggy animal jumped into a trot, leading the army out into the world.

Bannockburn, Present

Sinead appeared at Amy's front door promptly on Monday afternoon, looking every inch the handful her mother had promised. She looked up at Amy with jet black curls, freckles, and dark blue eyes sparkling with the same mischief Shawn's always had. "Did you really play in that American orchestra? Mam says they're the best. She says we're very lucky you moved here. Did you play with anyone famous?"

"Come in." Amy smiled, wondering how genuine her smile would be after forty-five minutes of such energy. "I'll answer three questions. Then you tell me three things about yourself, and we'll start. Deal?" She led the girl into the small living room, where a music stand and her own violin waited. White lace curtains cast dappled sunlight over the pale carpet and fawn-colored sofa.

Sinead chattered as she pulled out her violin. "Mam says you were with that orchestra that man disappeared from. Mam says don't ask you about it because it might upset you, so that's not one of my questions."

The corner of Amy's mouth quirked upward, at Sinead's innocent incomprehension of how she'd just defeated her mother's purpose.

The girl tucked her violin under her chin and skimmed up and down the G scale with ease. "Are you famous?"

"No. How about the D scale?" Though she said nothing, a thrill tingled through Amy, recognizing the girl's talent.

Sinead's bow flew across strings; her fingers danced. "Are you rich?"

"No," Amy said. "Lighter on the bow. You'll love the sound."

Sinead tried it, and grinned. "Aren't all Americans rich?"

"No." Amy's smile broadened. "That's your third question."

Sinead lowered the violin, pouting. "That's not fair, Miss Amy. I wanted to know if you had a cat."

"Two. They're with a friend. How about the A scale?"

"Easy." She flashed through it. "We've got kittens if you want one."

"I'd love to, but I can't have a cat right now. Tuning on the C sharp. Slow down and listen carefully." Amy demonstrated, humming the C sharp as she played. Sinead copied her. "Very nice," Amy said. "Not many students have such perfect intonation." She could teach this girl anything, she thought! "My turn. Do you live nearby?"

"Just around the block. My brother John taught me thirds, too. He says they're easy, but if you do them fast, people are impressed." She skipped up and down the strings in the familiar exercise.

"I *am* impressed." Amy's mind flashed to Shawn's assessment of *Blue Bells of Scotland. I just do it because it impresses people.* Her heart clenched in her chest, remembering him that last evening, lying in the grass in Glenmirril's deserted courtyard. She pushed her thoughts back to her student. "Very good. So you have a brother?"

"Two. John is seventeen, Joe is fourteen. Mam caught John smoking, and you should have heard her yelling!"

"I imagine," said Amy. "I'd yell, too. Since you can do thirds so well already, let's try alternating slurs and staccatos."

Mrs. Gordon was right, Amy thought, as she watched Sinead's bow bounce and slide on the strings, in thinking the girl might be a handful at school. But she clearly loved violin. "I practice two hours a day," she said proudly, lowering the instrument. "Joe says it's stupid but Johnny says I might play in the Symphony one day. Can you ever imagine living in a place like Glasgow?"

Amy laughed, and wrapped up the lesson after forty-five minutes that shot by as quickly as a Bach Invention. She waved as the girl skipped down the front walk. Closing the door, she rested a hand on her stomach. "We'll be fine, won't we? I think I'm looking forward to Mondays."

Stirling Castle, 1314

Watching the sea of men flow across the drawbridge, Shawn didn't notice Brother Andrew at his side until Niall touched his sleeve. "We've business with MacDougall."

"They're leaving," Shawn objected. He didn't add that he had no desire to have any business with MacDougall.

Niall waved away his concern. "It takes a wee bit of time to get so many men moving. This won't take long." He pulled Shawn through the crowd, into the great hall. Checking that it was empty, he put his mouth to Shawn's ear and whispered.

"MacDonald knows about this?" Shawn asked, dubiously.

Niall snorted. "Of course not. He's far too cautious. MacDougall will be here soon. 'Tis easy enough to get into his room. Just do as I've told you."

"We're dressed the same?" Shawn asked. Though he questioned the wisdom of the plan, he shared Niall's concern for Allene.

Niall looked him over and nodded, before disappearing up the stairs to the upper chambers. Shawn waited, beckoning a servant to bring food to one of the long tables running the length of the hall. He ate hot porridge, his boots scuffling the rush mats under his feet. His heart pounded; his insides turned watery. His initial unease with the plan grew, but it was too late. Niall would be in MacDougall's room. He finished his porridge and scratched the ears of a wolfhound nosing at his hand for food. His nerves stretched tauter with each second.

Finally, MacDougall entered, guffawing loudly. His men, an uncouth and grubby lot in black leather, surrounded him. He appeared, as usual, bigger and meaner than anyone around him. Shawn supposed it was as well to have him fighting for the Bruce and Scotland as against, but it did nothing to increase his liking of the man. He rose to his feet, tightening his muscles against nervous tremors.

MacDougall saw the meaning in his movement, and came to him, face to face. "What d' you want, you little pup?"

"A few words." Shawn's stomach did back flips. He forced himself to picture Peter, the elderly concertmaster, and slide a sneer into his voice.

"I'll give you a word, aw' right." MacDougall grinned at the men around him. They laughed at his witticism, showing various shades of their leader's yellow teeth.

"Let's take a walk," Shawn suggested, trying to keep the tremors of fear from his voice. This man could easily kill him. The first thing was to get him away from his posse. MacDougall hesitated, giving Shawn a shot of courage. "Surely you're not afraid to be alone with a little pup?" He lifted one sardonic eyebrow.

MacDougall grumbled, but jerked a head at his men, who scattered to the tables, shouting for food. Feeling more confident, Shawn led the way up the stairs, toward MacDougall's chambers. "'Tis a small man who threatens women." He felt his old bravado creeping up around him.

MacDougall's hand fell on the hilt of the dirk tucked in his belt.

"I'm not the only one saying so," Shawn added. "You pull that knife on me, it doesn't stop tongues wagging."

"What d' you want!" The man's hand slid from the dirk, but his demeanor did not improve.

"You're not the only one who hears things not meant for your ears. Things Bruce might like to hear." It was Niall's guess MacDougall had not immediately become Bruce's most loyal supporter. MacDougall's face turned brick red, suggesting Niall had guessed accurately.

"You may have heard stories." Shawn leaned close, warming to his role. "I'm everywhere. I do everything." He dropped his voice, almost whispering, "I move faster than you can imagine, and you'll never know where I am." Just to make sure the man understood, he said, "When you think I'm out in the meadow, I may be right behind you, hearing every word. And it's all stored safely in case anything happens to me. If anyone touches Allene, what I know goes straight to the Bruce. *Capisce?*"

MacDougall cocked his head at the foreign word.

"Understand?" Shawn snapped. He stopped outside MacDougall's room. "I suggest you make sure your secrets are safe where you left them." Given MacDougall's wide eyes, and the jolt of his body, Shawn suspected Niall had double-checked what had been a good guess anyway.

"Get outta here!" MacDougall wrenched the knife from his belt. Shawn turned—the most difficult back-turning he'd ever done—and walked away, his spine tingling in anticipation of a blade plunging between his vertebrae. All remained quiet behind him. Around the corner, he stopped, listening. There were several moments of silence; then the crash of the wooden door slamming against the wall.

Shawn strained to hear. He didn't envy Niall taking on the angrier half of this escapade, and hoped he was half as good with a knife as Shawn believed—or maybe, considering MacDougall's rage, twice as good. The door slammed shut. Shawn waited, knowing he was risking blowing their cover; knowing he couldn't go to Niall's aid if things went badly—and knowing Niall was not the only one who occasionally disregarded orders. His nerves started trembling again.

A girl in servant's clothing hurried down the hall, clutching a bundle of neatly folded linen. He recognized her, a girl he had smiled at too brightly, been too friendly with. Niall had objected strongly. She bobbed a curtsy. "My Lord Niall!" She smiled breathlessly, hoping for his previous attentions, if her suddenly rosy cheeks were anything to judge by. His insides warmed at sight of her; but he did his best imitation of Niall, inclining his head gravely, not cracking a smile. Her face fell. She hurried away.

Cursing the lost moment, Shawn strained his ears again, stretching toward the corner around which he dared not show himself. Niall was taking his sweet old time, he thought with irritation. It was another full minute before he was rewarded.

MacDougall's roar erupted suddenly through the stone walls. Shawn, used though he was to dealing with powerful and angry men, cringed. The angry men of his twenty-first century life hadn't carried deadly steel, and feared prison. MacDougall did first and not the second. A flood of medieval swearing exploded from the room, pummeling his ears. Then Niall's voice belted down the hall.

"I warned you," he bellowed. "If I don't meet my men before they ride, there are those who know to pass this to Bruce. Back away and it stays between us. You touch Allene, and you'll never know where I am and when my knife will slide between your ribs." The door slammed again; footsteps stormed out, the muted *pat-pat* of leather on stone, the swish of linen sleeves against leather vest ready for riding.

Niall stormed around the corner, almost slamming into Shawn. They stood a moment, two men looking in a mirror. Then Niall gripped his arm and hastened him down the hall to the stairs, up to the next floor. "Did I not tell you to get back to the room?"

Shawn shrugged Niall's hand off. "Did MacDonald not tell you to leave things be with MacDougall?" he spit back. "Get your hand off me. He could have killed you. You people seem to like that sort of thing. So how about 'thanks for waiting to see I got out alive?'"

Niall threw open their own door, and they pushed in together. Niall's eyes threw daggers.

"You're welcome!" Shawn slammed the door shut. "It was my pleasure to watch your back. Thanks for appreciating it. Glad you didn't need me, because you know, in my world, men who don't like you still don't pull knives on you. I like to think it took some guts on my part to stick around, just in case, knowing I could end up with a knife in any of my many parts I value!"

Niall's anger faded. The frown lightened, even as the gray sky outside the window brightened to pale blue. He smiled. Then he laughed. "It did. 'Tis only that I was still in the heat of the moment. And by the by, you've a better proper Highland accent when you're not deliberately mocking someone with it."

"My Highland accent is just fine. Did you forget I'm the best of Scotland? That means my accent is, too."

"Only with buxom women hanging all over you," Niall retorted. "I see none in this room."

Shawn dropped into a chair. The long night and the adrenaline rush of the last half hour crashed over him, making his head heavy. He heaved a big breath. "What happened?"

Niall chuckled. "What is it your people say? Two matching outfits, three pence, matching boots priceless, the look on his face, a hundred pounds!"

Shawn laughed out loud.

"What?" Niall demanded. "What's so funny?"

Shawn gripped his stomach, laughing harder, leaning forward in his chair. A long night, a dangerous escapade, and exhaustion all made Niall's mistake hysterical. "First, a hundred pounds is nothing."

"It is here—now." Irritation flashed across Niall's face.

"Okay, well, that's not how it goes anyway. 'Matching outfits, three pence, matching boots, a pound sterling, the look on his face—priceless!'"

"Aye," Niall agreed.

"By the way, that other one you keep misquoting, it's not, 'You're back in Toto,' it's 'I don't think we're in Kansas anymore, Toto.' Kansas is a state."

"Toto isn't a shire?" Niall asked.

"We have states, not shires. Same thing, I guess. Toto is a dog. Anywho. What happened?"

Niall hoisted himself onto the stone sill of the window. He propped one leather boot up against the wall. "MacDougall flung the door open in rage, slammed it shut, and raced for the wardrobe. He dug through his things like Toto digging for a bone."

"I think you have the wrong idea about Toto." Shawn rubbed tired eyes. His head hurt. "He's not like your wolfhounds. He's this little tiny dog like the size of a rat on steroids. Weak steroids at that. Nice try with the analogy, though. Good literary technique. I can see it all."

"Never mind," Niall said. "I'm just trying to make you feel at home in our world. So he dug through like a starving wolfhound after a bone. He pulled out the letters I had already found."

Shawn raised one eyebrow. "Keeping things from me? Aren't we each supposed to know everything the other does, so we don't make mistakes?"

Niall shrugged. "'Tis no matter. You know now. Nobody else knew, either, so no one would have noticed you didn't know you'd been in his things."

Shawn groaned. "I'm way too tired for this. What happened?"

"He threw himself down at the table, rifling through them, cursing and muttering."

"Where were you?"

Niall laughed. "Sitting in the window the whole time, just like I am now. He was far too angry to pay heed. And it underscored my—your—our—point, when he saw how little notice he'd taken."

MacDougall had torn through his correspondence a second time, Niall continued. Shawn blinked. His eyes drooped. MacDougall had muttered to himself that it was all there, and risen, pacing and demanding to know what the 'pup' really knew.

"It was then I swung my legs down off the windowsill," Niall said.

Shawn's eyes snapped open. He shook his head, wondering if he'd missed anything.

"I've not once seen MacDougall at a loss for words." Niall laughed. "His face fell. He turned white as a bone. He looked to the door, to me, to the door and said, ''Tis impossible, you just went....' Then he turned red and went for his knife."

"Why didn't he kill you?" Shawn asked.

"You didn't hear me? I told him others know the information and would pass it on. He was still in shock, still yelling about how I'd got in. I think we've made our point, aye?" He smiled. "Off to Glenmirril. Are you ready to ride?"

Shawn groaned, leaning back in his chair. For a moment, his head swam into sleep, swirling into black depths of unconsciousness. He jolted up with a start, to see Niall tossing him the robe of their alter ego. "Time to go, Brother Andrew."

Bannockburn, Present

Amy slid a pan of fish fillets into the oven for dinner and returned to the living room, energized by Sinead's lesson, to play her own violin. As her bow danced through a Telemann sonata, the phone rang.

"Rob!" she said in surprise, when she recognized his voice. She tucked her violin into its case.

"Hey!" His voice came over the phone with what sounded like forced cheer. "How are you?"

"Good." She polished the face of the violin. "Great."

"You barely e-mail me."

She paused, startled at his presumption, then found her voice. "I've been busy. I started teaching a student. I just finished." She laid the cloth over the face of the violin and snapped the case shut.

"What else are you up to?"

"I go to the field." When he didn't answer, she imagined he must be thinking it was unhealthy. "I go to church," she added. "I'm thinking about going to Iona."

"Iona? The island? Why?"

"I hear it's peaceful." She hadn't told Rob about Shawn's message. She decided not to tell him about meeting the cop or heeding his suggestion to search for Niall's fate on the internet.

"Yeah." He was silent a moment, then added, "We miss you here."

"Rob, I'm not gone forever." She moved down the narrow hall to the kitchen, set the phone on the counter on speaker, and pulled a head of lettuce from the refrigerator, shredding it into a bowl as she talked. "It's a year, that's all."

"I'm just saying...."

"Tell me what's going on there." She didn't want to argue with him. She listened while he talked of the weather, and Dana, and the summer concert series. When he paused, she took a breath. "You're not telling me what they did about Shawn."

"I didn't want to upset you." He cleared his throat. "Dan found a guy on trumpet. He's got Shawn's charisma, but not his way of attracting trouble. He and I are working up some duets."

She checked the fish—it was a warm golden brown, and its aroma filled the kitchen—and listened awhile longer. Rob saw himself as the new best friend of the new star. She encouraged him, applauded him, and, sliding the pan from the oven, told him she had to go. "Don't worry about upsetting me," she assured him. "They have to move on."

"Yeah." Rob cleared his throat. "What about you, Amy? How are you going to move on, going to that field all the time? I worry about you, all alone over there."

"I'm okay, Rob," she said, pleased to realize how true it was. Rose's visit had helped. Maybe time, and the painting and music on which Rose had insisted, were helping. "I really am."

There was a brief silence. She knew him well enough, she guessed he was swallowing, deciding whether to say more. "I could maybe...."

"I have to go, Rob," she interrupted. She didn't want him to offer to come over.

"Give me a call sometime, then," Rob said. "Drop me some e-mails, let me know you're okay. Okay?"

"I'll try." Amy ended the call. She sank down at the table, wondering if she should be doing more to move on, rather than sitting at the field every day, reliving Shawn's death, and running dozens of internet searches seeking Niall's fate. She was painting, and writing music, and teaching lessons, she reassured herself. She was moving on. But she wanted—no, needed—to know what had happened to Niall.

Trossachs, Scotland, 1314

The Laird's company traveled at the quick pace for which the Scots were renowned, covering sixty miles in a day. They alternately trotted, cantered, and walked, through forest hills, across passes, along streams. Niall took comfort in his father's sword thumping against his back, MacDonald and Hugh and their men around him, and Allene riding hard at his side. He found his eyes straying to her frequently. She caught his look. "What?" she asked.

"Your father said we'd be married as soon as we get to Glenmirril."

"Which means when you get back." Her eyes sparkled; a slow blush crept up her cheeks.

"I'll be back quickly." He grinned as her blush deepened. "Are you not tired?" he asked. "Your father will call a stop if you need to."

She shook her head. "We've no time to spare. Shawn has the worst of it. He was up all night."

Looking back to where the few monks traveled at the back of the group, he sympathized with the one sagging in his saddle. The man's hands gripped his pommel, and he jerked from sleep. "Aye, he's had a long day," he agreed. Niall was relieved for his sake when they stopped for the night, where the main party would leave for Glenmirril. He watched the robed monk drop into exhausted sleep, wrapped in a large plaid.

"He must eat," Allene fretted.

"Leave him." Niall rubbed the stubble of beard growing in after a day on the road. "He's a grown man." He led her to the edge of the clearing, by a towering fir, where they ate hard bannocks, under the Laird's watchful eye. She held his hand while the fire behind them drifted lower, till it was only embers, and night insects chirped and buzzed.

"You promised you'd be back quickly to marry me," she finally said, softly. "Take care."

He wrapped an arm around her shoulder and leaned close to kiss the side of her head, burying his face in her hair. "I always do." He doubted his trick with MacDougall qualified as taking care, but it would assure the man thought twice before touching her. "If MacDougall or his men try to harm you," he said, "tell them the information goes straight to Bruce."

She lifted her head off his shoulder, searching his eyes in the dim light. "What do you mean?"

"'Tis no matter," Niall said. "Tell them. Remind them."

"What have you done, Niall?" Her face was dark in the night, the shadows of fire flickering across it.

He smiled. "I've assured your safety. Trust me, aye?"

Chapter Seven

"Bannockburn, now we've plenty on that!" In the cool blue interior of the library, with summer sun pouring down from windows high in the walls, the gray-haired librarian helped Amy collect a stack of books on medieval history and deposit them on a table with her laptop. Amy added two books on Iona.

Dozens of Google searches on Bannockburn, Iona, and Columba had given her no ideas at all about Shawn's meaning or Niall's fate. It hadn't take long to realize that, like the museum, most sites skimmed over the years between the battle and the Declaration of Arbroath, so that the table she'd created on her laptop, with a cell for every month of every year between the two events, remained stubbornly austere except for the Laird's party staying at Stirling after Bannockburn, Angus Og's fleets fighting John of Lorn, and a few battles Edward Bruce fought in Ireland. Reading the professor's books in her small garden had turned up little more. Finally, having lost patience both with the internet and the sight of her own four walls, Amy had headed for the library, making a long walk of it in the warm August day.

Now, with books piled high on the table, she lost herself in stories, occasionally filling in cells on her chart. Bishop Lamberton had gone to London for peace talks that failed. Edward Bruce, Thomas Moray, and the Black Douglas had made lightning raids into Northern England that August.

Every twenty minutes, the librarian popped up with more books. "A little later than the time you're looking for." She squeezed a leather-bound tome onto a corner of the desk. "But you never know."

"Thank you." Amy fought back a smile. The woman meant to be helpful. Like the internet, each book led to a dozen more possibilities. She thumbed through another account of Randolph, Earl of Moray, fighting the English Sir Clifford on an escarpment. On her walk to the library, she had stopped to rest at a steep slope running down to a park, where children kicked a black and white ball. She wondered if that might be where the men had clashed, where Clifford had died on Scottish lances.

She slammed the book shut in irritation. None of it touched Niall.

The librarian, red-cheeked, bustled up to her elbow right on schedule, adding two books to the tottering pile. "These are about the Viking raids. Bruce's sister married the Norwegian king, so you might find something. We're closing for lunch. But we'll keep your books right here," she promised, "if you'd like to run down to the co-op for some food. Or they've lovely bridies at the deli. And if it's Bannockburn you're interested in, the burn itself is a lovely place to eat."

Amy thanked her, touched by her thoughtfulness, despite the growing pile of volumes with no connection whatsoever to Bannockburn. Her stomach once again swirled with yellow nausea. Thankfully, there'd been little morning sickness, and never at inopportune moments. But dry crackers and a pint of milk sounded good.

Scotland, 1314

Shawn jolted awake to find his hobbin jarring to a halt and the party, thankfully, stopping for the night. In the dark crevasses of a deep forested glen, men slid off their ponies, exhausted, rolling into huge woolen tartans, whispering in muted voices in the dark. Amidst the trees, a fire crackled to life. It was too far for warmth, but close enough for comfort in its tiny flickering light and wood scent.

Shawn, too, slid from his mount, grateful Niall had insisted on teaching him to ride. The animal whickered and nudged his elbow with a hard, bony nose. He edged away, wary of its teeth, but gave it a tentative pat on the neck. It had carried him while he slept, after all. Midges swarmed his face. He brushed half-heartedly, looking for Niall or Allene. It was a big party, and a dark night. Fir trees loomed above and around. They could be anywhere. Pine needles covered the beaten earth floor. The campfire, in the distance, sprang a little higher, and settled. Shawn bundled his tartan close, packed himself into the warm herd of men settling for the night, and slept.

Bannockburn, Present

"Miss Amy, Miss Amy!" Sinead hopped up and down in front of the dairy case at the back of the co-op, setting her black curls bouncing. Her cheeks flushed with excitement and she gripped another girl's hand. "Graine, this is Miss Amy, my violin teacher. She played with that American symphony! She's the best!"

Amused, Amy chatted briefly with the girls before buying a pint of milk, crackers, and a roast beef sandwich. Outside the store, she stopped short at the sight of her student leaning against the wall. "Sinead! You got out here fast!"

Sinead smiled wanly, but said nothing. Amy smiled uncertainly, waved goodbye, and headed down the street. Perhaps she'd had a disagreement with her friend.

Amy set off across a field toward the creek that had given its name to a battle. Two boys ran ahead, kicking a ball between them with no thought of the men who had fought, bled, and died there for them to be able to live freely on this beautiful day. Amy followed in their wake, enjoying their shouts and laughter. But she remembered the area as she'd seen it that day—acres of swampland swarming with foot soldiers, pike men, and war horses; hot sun bearing down on sweating bodies, stinking of blood, sounding with trumpets. She'd heard the chaotic roar and screams of battle; just for a few moments, she had seen and heard and smelled it all.

She stopped, squeezing her eyes shut. Shawn had been in the middle of the bloodshed and brutality. With a slow breath, she opened her eyes, bringing herself fully into the warm present. There was no chaos, no mayhem, only a warm summer day, fluffy white clouds, and tiny wildflowers dotting the field. She stooped, brushed her finger over the snow-white daisies waving in the breeze, and wondered, as Shawn had fallen, had there been daisies? Or had they all been crushed underfoot by then? She hoped, foolishly, that his last sight had been one of beauty. He'd put beauty into the world with his music, after all. He deserved that much. She stood abruptly, irritated, upset, needing to live in the present at least for a little bit.

She soon reached the bank of the little Bannock Burn. Trees arched overhead in a long, green bower, giving the winding stream a secret, hidden feel. She sat down to eat her lunch, trailing her fingers in the tree-shaded water. English soldiers had drowned trying to cross back over, the books said, pursued by swarms of furious Scots. She wondered if Niall had been among them, or if the stream had been deeper then. It was harmless now, just an ankle-high creek tumbling over rocks, perfect for splashing in on a hot day. She unwrapped the sandwich and opened the carton of milk. The sound of sheep lowing came to her, and a soft whisper. She looked around, but no one was there.

Go home, Sassenach!

Her heart skipped a beat, then pulsed more swiftly at the deep voice.

He's dead!

She cocked her head, listening to the murmur of shouts, calls, moans, far off, yet all around. She re-wrapped the sandwich with trembling fingers. But something held her another moment, listening for Shawn's voice, for Niall's. The babble of words rose and fell, a melody of distant echoes. Shawn's and Niall's voices were not among them. She gathered her lunch, scrambled to her feet, and hurried from the bower, her heart pounding.

Western Scotland, 1314

Niall woke to a dark forest. Ponies rustled under the trees. The fires had died to glowing embers, scattered forlornly through the forest. He stretched, and scratched his chest, yawning. After breathing deeply of fresh pine air, he gathered his tartan, pulling it around himself as a cloak, took his father's sword, and stepped gingerly over the sleeping men, across the stream, to the privacy of a large tree. He planted his sword in the earth to make a cross, and knelt before it in the dark, his head bowed.

My Lord, Father in Heaven, he prayed, *please protect Allene.* He looked back to the camp. He could see her by the crackling fire, her hair tumbled across the ground as she slept near her father and Hugh. He bit back a smile, thinking how different his world was from Amy's. He found it sad that Amy had no one to look after her, as the Laird guarded Allene, and wondered that Amy had not seemed to feel any lack.

He returned to his prayers, asking guidance for his upcoming mission. The MacDougalls would not be happy if they found him there; their dungeons would speak eloquently and painfully of their displeasure. He prayed for Scotland, for the Pope to recognize the righteousness of their cause, for Douglas, Bruce, Shawn, Amy, and a dozen others. He thanked God for the new day, for the victory at Bannockburn, and for whatever mysterious plans He had in mind, with the strange events of the past weeks.

"You must have Your reasons for leaving Shawn here," he said. "Though I confess they are beyond me." He bowed his head. He rather enjoyed Shawn's presence. And Shawn had made him a legend.

A hand fell on his shoulder. He looked up. MacDonald, a dark form in the pre-dawn, dropped stiffly to his old knees beside Niall, and together they said an *Ave*, a *Pater*, and a *Gloria*.

When they finished, the Laird spoke gruffly. "Good thing 'twas me, and not our enemy, Lad. Take heed next time. I'd talk a wee bit to you and

Shawn before we part. Where is he?"

"With the monks." Niall climbed to his feet.

MacDonald, too, hauled himself to his feet, gripping the nearby tree with a hand almost as gnarled as its trunk. "Wait here, Lad, lest his hood has fallen in his sleep and someone sees the two of you."

Niall waited among the dark trees, drinking cool water from the stream. Presently, the Laird stormed back, Hugh in his wake. "He is nowhere!"

"We've checked all the monks," Hugh added.

Niall scrambled to his feet, panic pounding at his heart. "What of the other men?"

Thunder blazed in MacDonald's eyes. "I've asked them all if they've seen you or Brother Andrew this morning and none has seen a you who seems to be him!"

Niall planted his hands on his hips, and arched his head back, staring up at the trees soaring high against the graying sky. He took a deep breath and looked back at the Laird. "I trust him. He'd not leave us deliberately."

"Then what's become of him?" MacDonald demanded.

"Did he get separated from us on the road?" suggested Hugh.

"'Twould not be possible," Niall said. "We're none so hard to see, a hundred strong tramping through the forest."

"He'd been up all night," said the Laird. "Could he have fallen asleep while he rode?"

"He did, but his hobbin followed us," said Niall. "I saw him."

"Perchance you mistook the wrong monk for him," suggested Hugh. "Maybe Shawn rolled into a ravine somewhere. He's none so skilled a rider."

"We must find him!" Niall said.

The Laird looked from Niall and Hugh, back to the camp where Allene slept. "You would endanger Allene by going back for him."

Niall knew it was true. He paused, his eyes closed, seeing Shawn's world, and Shawn, accustomed to buses and teeming cities, lost in this forest. "Shawn will die, if not from being set upon by bandits, then because he does not know how to survive in this." Niall waved his hand at the forest and eastern mountains, now etched in faint pink sunrise. "D' you understand in his time there are markets on every corner to buy food? He's no knowledge of hunting or finding berries, or what is safe to eat."

Allene appeared around the tree, startling them all. Sleep had rumpled her brown woolen traveling gown. Her freckles stood out against skin unusually pale in the dim forest. Her red hair jetted out around her face. "Shawn is missing?"

The four of them stood in a circle around Niall's sword. MacDonald, Hugh, and Niall said nothing. Their mouths tightened grimly. The morning's first bird let out a trill. Niall, hands on hips, turned away. He wanted to find Shawn. He didn't want it to be nearly so important to Allene.

"Allene, I'll not risk you," the Laird said fiercely.

"I'm surrounded by a hundred of your best men," Allene countered. "Niall has done naught to rouse MacDougall's anger yet. He believes Niall is returning to Glenmirril. Shawn, by contrast, Father, is alone in a wilderness. He's done all you've demanded of him. He saw me safely to Hugh and rescued Brother David from the English."

"She's the right of it, Malcolm." Hugh stared at the ground, his hands on his hips. "He did all that."

"Aye, I know all this!" The scar on the Laird's cheek turned white against his stormy face.

Allene was not to be stopped. "He fought valiantly at Bannockburn, and risked himself for a helpless child. And you'll not turn back for him?" Her hands went to her hips as well. Niall turned, amusement touching the corners of his mouth, at the likeness between father and daughter. "I'm ashamed to call you father, if that's how you repay such a man. You may as well join MacDougall, for you're of his ilk, if so be it."

A second bird joined the first, and a red squirrel darted from limb to limb, while she and MacDonald glared at one another. "How can I turn back?" he finally demanded. "Niall has orders from the Bruce, and you must be safely in Glenmirril lest MacDougall find out. You know he'll keep his word, Allene."

Allene looked to Niall, her eyebrows arched. He knew she was waiting for an explanation of his words the previous night. He shook his head, forbidding her to tell her father he'd taken matters into his own hands. "Niall is clever, Father," she said, finally. "MacDougall will not find out. And I am still surrounded by a hundred of your best men."

Grudgingly, Niall offered a solution. "I was to part company with you here, My Lord. I'll go as planned, while you take the company to search for Shawn." He pulled his father's sword from the ground, offering it to the Laird. "I can't take this with me if I wish to pass unnoticed in Dundolam. If I disappear and leave it behind, it will give you cause to search for me—him."

"How am I to explain that you were here but last night?" Flustered, MacDonald accepted the sword. "Or why I think you've gone east, rather than north?"

The four of them stared at one another, while the stream bubbled and more birds joined the morning chorus. Niall noted the decision had been made without the Laird admitting he'd given in.

"None have seen me yet this morning," Niall said.

"You must say he was captured in the night," said Hugh.

"Will they believe MacDougall took him back to Stirling?" Allene asked.

"'Twould be better if one of the men decides we must search to the east."

"Aye," agreed the Laird. "Fewer questions will be asked of us that way."

"All the men know of MacDougall's threat," Hugh reminded them. "Someone will think of it."

With the decision made, MacDonald crept through the trees for Niall's hobbin, while Niall, Allene, and Hugh stole into denser forest. It would not do to have one of the waking men come upon them and ruin the plan now, before it began.

Hugh clapped him on the back. "God go with you, Lad."

In minutes, MacDonald splashed back across the stream with the horse. He gripped Niall, hand to wrist, his face grim. "God go with you, Lad. You'll meet me back at Stirling in a fortnight, eh, with news for His Grace."

"Aye." Their hands dropped. Niall turned to Allene. She lowered her eyes, tears glinting in the corners. He pulled her into his embrace. Her fly-away hair tickled his nose. She smelled of forest pines, rich, damp earth bursting with life, cool morning air, and crisp, fresh dewdrops. "I'll be *okay*."

She laughed, the laughter of nervousness, her face buried in his chest.

"What is this *okay*?"

Niall smiled into her hair. "Shawn's word. It means aw' right. You're to pray for me morning and night, aye?" He thought again of MacDougall's messengers on their way to warn Duncan.

She nodded, reaching up to twist a strand of his hair around her finger. It flashed a deep chestnut copper in the weak morning sun. She touched the scruff on his neck.

"And do your best to find Shawn." He kissed the top of her head, powerfully aware of the Laird's watchful eye. He gave her a last, stronger squeeze, and drank in one last sight of her deep blue eyes, smiling his reassurance. "I'll be aw' right. And in a few weeks, you'll be my wife. Go with your father now, and spread the alarm." He mounted his hobbin, turned its nose west, where the sky was still deep blue, alight with stars, and slapped the animal's reins.

He stopped once, turned to see her watching him, Hugh at her side, her father tugging at her arm, but watching as well. She raised her hand in farewell, and turned suddenly into her father's chest. His pony tossed its head, eager to be running. Swallowing hard, Niall leaned over the animal's neck, urging it on, dodging trees, clambering a small rise, splashing through a stream, trying to outrun his thoughts. He was tired of sacrificing his hopes and dreams for this awful war that Scotland had never asked for.

He was supposed to have wed Allene months ago, but one thing after another had prevented it. And now, he was riding straight to his enemy's arms, Duncan already warned to watch for him; perhaps to die on a rack or gallows, never to see her again. A doe bolted from her drink by a creek. A branch scraped his sleeve. Minutes later, another snagged in his tartan, billowing out behind him. "I don't want to go," he murmured to God.

And I didn't want to die on a cross, came a whisper on the breeze.

Niall had no breath to answer, and no answer to give. The silent words were not the comforting promise of safety he'd wished to hear.

Bannockburn, Present

Back among the quiet safety of books, Amy had just opened her laptop when the librarian hurried up with pleasure. "See what I'm just after finding!" She held out a new volume.

A picture of a bearded medieval warrior adorned the front with *John Barbour* printed under the image, and in larger letters underneath, *The Brus and Other Works*. Amy stared at the man, as her thumb strayed under her palm to feel the warm gold of his ring.

"It's John Barbour's poem, *The Brus*," the woman piped in her ear.

Amy bit back a smile. She could imagine Shawn meeting the woman's eyes gravely and asking, "John Barbour the author? Is it about the Bruce?" But Amy was not Shawn. She thanked the woman and flipped it open.

Storys to rede are delatabill
Suppos that thai be nocht bot fabill
Than suld storys that suthfast wer
And thai war said on gude maner

She touched the words, understanding in a flash why Niall had asked her to read to him, and why it had taken him so long to get through the pages she'd printed off. It was hard to imagine her own modern English must have looked as strange to him as this did to her. Still, she thought, she could get used to it.

"Tis hard to work through medieval English," the librarian said. "So I found you one with translations on the facing page."

Amy met her eyes, touched. "Thank you." The woman couldn't know how important this was. "Does it talk about after Bannockburn?"

"Most folk want to know about the battle itself," the librarian replied. "Very few ask what happened after." She eased the book from Amy's hand, and turned to the table of contents. "See here." She pointed. "He talks about the days afterward. And here." She offered Amy a second book. "This one is in the style of Barbour, and talks a great deal about after the battle."

Amy thanked her again and settled down with the new book. With help from the footnotes, she waded through war in Ireland, famine, and the battle at Dundalk, typing notes now and again, wondering, after the tenth page, what she hoped to accomplish. She sighed, and turned the page half-heartedly, ready to quit. But her eyes lit on the word *Cambil*. Startled, she lifted the book closer.

Lord Cambil suffert a wound hidwys to see
Bot stunning the lords, coveryt he.
Then symt he to be everqher,
And never dyd he tyre.
He did fell ane hunder tree
And no respit tok he

Frowning, she scanned the modern translation. *Lord Campbell suffered a hideous wound but stunned the lords by recovering. Then he seemed to be everywhere, never tiring. He felled a hundred trees and took no rest.* And the next stanza, *He worked twenty hours a day without sleep, training great warriors for battle.*

There had been many Campbells, she knew, and there was no mention of these things on Glenmirril's website, so there was no reason to think it was Niall. Although, she thought, he *had* told her he trained Glenmirril's men. She turned back to the introduction. The book was not always historically accurate, it warned. It was a romance, borrowing heavily from reality, with elements of exaggeration. She re-read the stanzas. He felled a hundred trees and trained men twenty hours a day—after a hideous wound. It seemed unlikely, no matter who he was.

A glance at the clock showed it was closing time. The librarian smiled across the empty library. Amy rose. "The book is great. Can I check these out?"

She was soon heading home, carrying her backpack and books through clusters of row houses like her own, each with its patch of yard—or garden as it was called here—a lace curtain fluttering in the front window and the matching eyes of the bedroom windows upstairs, looking down. The day was warm. She was pregnant, tired, and hungry. Though she tried to let the fresh air energize her, her mind stuck on the disturbing thought of what hideous wound Niall might have sustained, and two questions: Was it even the right Lord Campbell? And if so, why? Why was he the lucky winner of the author's poetic license, turning him into a medieval superhero? The book stuck to the truth, tending toward embellishment and bias, rather than outright fiction, the introduction had said. So if it was Niall—why? What had he done, in truth, that the author had exaggerated in such a way?

Central Scotland, 1314

The Laird's men pounded the thick summer ferns far off the path for many miles, working their way back along the route toward Stirling. It had not taken long, talking amongst themselves, to decide Niall must have been carried off in the wee hours. It was a natural next step, as Hugh had hoped, for Ronan to mention MacDougall's threats. "You can't trust that man," he spit. "Here's our Niall going about his own business as MacDougall wanted, and he can't stop."

Allene stayed close by her father, the two of them occasionally breaking away from the men to hiss, "Shawn! Are you there, Shawn!" into the woods and underbrush.

The return trip, laced with searching every possible inch of the forest, took much longer than the journey out. Halfway back, they were forced to stop and make camp for the night.

"We'll not find him in the dark," MacDonald said. "We'll keep searching the moment the sun rises, all the way back to Stirling, if we must."

He settled in beside Allene for the night, his own concern for Shawn growing. It was true, as Allene had reminded him throughout the day, that Shawn had done all he was told, shown loyalty and courage. MacDonald grew in his own concern for a man who probably did not deserve whatever fate the forest held for a lone traveler, especially if MacDougall himself should decide to head home and find him first.

Bannockburn, Present

Amy's cell phone trilled its Telemann sonata as she dropped her books and backpack in the living room. She hit *talk* even as she headed to the kitchen and dug a battered pot from the cupboard. "Hello!" She set the pot on the small range and searched the cupboards for soup.

"Amy?" The voice echoed over the line as if from a distance.

She almost jumped at the sound of an American accent. "Rob!" She dropped the can of soup on the counter, clattering, before it settled flat. "What a surprise! How are you?"

"The question is, how are you? Your e-mails have slowed down."

She stifled a sigh. "Rob, I'm busy. I don't always have time."

"You have time now, don't you?"

"A little. I'm making dinner." She pushed a long black tendril of hair, damp with summer heat, behind her ear. "How's the new trumpet player?"

"Good. He's good. He and I have a brass quintet. We've got some gigs lined up, Canadian Brass type stuff. I'm doing the arranging."

She turned the phone to speaker and set it on the counter while she searched for the can opener. She missed arranging for the orchestra. "That's great, Rob. I always knew you'd be good at it." It had been lonely, writing the piece Rose demanded, without Shawn at her side. "What are you working on?"

"A 60s CD. The Righteous Brothers, that kind of thing."

The can was quickly opened and the soup emptied into the pot and heating. While he talked, she took a head of lettuce from the refrigerator. The word *lettuce* danced before her eyes as John Barbour might have spelled it. *Lytus, lettis, letys.* She smiled. *I ried twa mych Medyval Inglys toda.* Despite the losses, she hadn't been this happy since—she thought back—since the first year and a half with Shawn, since before the first lie, the first accidental discovery of a text from a woman. She pulled out a bag of shredded cheese and a bottle of French dressing.

"How about you?" he asked. "Have you seen a doctor?"

"I have an appointment set up." She told him about her students—four of them now, all on Monday so she could have the week free. Hating the feeling of hiding, and wanting someone to talk to, she told him about her research. She shook the lettuce dry, and reached for a knife. "I can e-mail it to you," she offered. "If you're interested."

"Uh. Okay." He hesitated. "I don't really get it. You know this Niall didn't really exist."

She bit her lip. Her glance fell on the ring. "Read my notes, Rob. He existed. Remember the day we brought—him—to the hospital and the cop told us Niall Campbell is mentioned on the castle's tour?"

"You know what I mean, Amy." She knew his habits so well, it was easy to picture him. He was without a doubt letting his eyes slide away, his head turning a fraction to one side, focusing his eyes elsewhere.

"Rob, I'm going to tell you something I haven't told anyone except Rose, Celine, and Aaron. I'm wearing a crucifix he gave me. When did Shawn ever wear a crucifix?"

"Shawn got hit hard in the head, Amy. You have to let go of this outlandish story. It's not healthy."

Amy snatched up the knife. "I shouldn't have said anything," she snapped. "I shouldn't say this. But I'm wearing a medieval ring on my finger. Shawn threw it to me that day." She smashed the knife down hard, shredding the lettuce. "Where did Shawn get a medieval ring? Explain that, Rob. I'm not crazy."

"Okay, okay. I'm sorry."

"No you're not." The knife paused in its silver sweep. She set it down, wiping her hands on a towel.

"Can't I be concerned for you? You're stressed."

"Can't you have a little faith in me? Look, forget it." She tossed the knife in the sink and pushed the shredded lettuce into a bowl, dousing it with dressing and sprinkling grated cheese over it. "I know this is crazy. I *know* that. But I need to know what happened to Niall Campbell."

"Okay, I really don't get it." Rob sounded angry. "Shawn disappears and you're tracking down some minor medieval figure. What gives?"

"You and the entire police force witnessed my humiliating re-telling of what he told me on the train." She heard herself yelling, and tried to rein in her anger. "You know what gives. I *believe* him. I'm wearing a ring and a crucifix from the 1200s. Shawn is not here, Rob. He died under the hooves of a medieval warhorse, and I know you'll never believe that, but I'm never going to find him here. I'm looking for both of them, any record. Maybe I'll find something to tell me where Shawn was buried. I don't know."

Rob didn't answer. She stirred the soup with more venom than it deserved, sloshing it, sizzling, onto the burner. "Rob?"

"Yeah. I'm here."

She poured the soup into a bowl, waiting, thinking with irritation it was his own long distance money he was wasting to give her the silent treatment. "Do you understand I need someone to talk to?" she finally asked. "Everyone thinks I'm the grieving girlfriend looking for him, that I'm a little bit crazy, researching this guy. I say I'm doing a paper. I say it takes my mind off him, if they really ask. I don't tell anyone the truth, and sometimes, I just need to be real with someone. You say you care. You want to be my friend. So be it."

From the phone on the counter came one word. "Yeah."

Amy threw a hand in the air. "*Yeah?* What does *that* mean? Yeah? Are you kidding me?" There was another awkward silence, in which she shuffled her dinner to the small table tucked in the corner of a kitchen that would have fit easily in her bedroom at home.

"Are you happy?" he asked.

"Yeah." She dropped onto the chair, chin in hand. "You know he spent most of this past year lying, keeping me off balance, and probably cheating. This has been really good. I love the country and the people are kind." When he didn't answer, she said, "Hey Rob, thanks for calling. I really am okay."

She sampled her dinner, her thoughts drifting to Shawn's insistence that the woman who texted him so frequently was an agent.

"Do you like that piece?"

"Sorry, what?" She poked at the salad. It looked less appetizing than it had. "Bad conn...." She stopped. She'd hated Shawn's lies. Even the little ones had hurt. "Sorry, Rob, my mind wandered."

"I can call back later." He sounded hurt.

"No, really. My mind was on other things. What piece?"

"*Pachelbel's Canon.* I want to dedicate the arrangement to you."

"Rob." She paused, unsure what to say. "Rob, that's kind."

"You know I don't want *kind* from you." His voice was husky.

She tried to keep the irritation from showing too blatantly. "And you know exactly where I stand. I love Pachelbel. I'd be honored, as long as you understand...." She stopped. There was no nice way to say, *As long as you understand it's not going to buy me.*

She heard a small sound over the line, and was sure his Adam's apple had just bobbed with a swallow, and he'd blinked his blue eyes hard. She smiled. It was so easy to see, even thousands of miles away. But tenderness wasn't the love he wanted from her.

"I understand," he said. "I didn't mean it like that. I just wanted to dedicate it. To someone. I thought I'd put the melody in the trombone. Would you like that? It wouldn't make you sad?"

"Rob," she whispered. Her heart softened a little. "I'm sorry if I sounded...you know, ungrateful. Yes, I'd like it."

Scotland, 1314

Shawn awoke bleary, rubbing dawn's cold mist from his eyes, squinting at the leather and mail-clad bodies rustling around him. He ran a hand through his hair, pushing it from his eyes. Some men still slept. Some sat up sleepily, while others moved, ghostly shapes through murky gloam, thrusting food over small fires or seeing to their horses in the gray pre-dawn.

Something was wrong. Shawn sat up, scratching his unshaven neck.

For a half second, he thought it was being in medieval Scotland's great Caledonian forest. He should be sliding from between red silk sheets in his king size bed. He shook his head, squinting at pines, men, and ponies. He'd long since quit expecting to wake to the twenty-first century. He'd expected a medieval forest with fourteenth-century warriors. So what was wrong?

They weren't English, were they? He peered through the forest, to men stirring and moving, in tunics, and breeks of sturdy woven fiber. They were definitely Scots, with tartans everywhere. He threw the robe off himself. In any direction, as far as he could see, men moved through trees, pushing among gray tendrils of mist and silvery gray pine needles and birch trunks. He scrambled to his feet, straining to see, listening.

The man beside him stirred and stretched. "Cold day," he said.

"Aye." Shawn scanned the forest once more. "Where's MacDonald?"

"MacDonald?"

Mounting unease crawled up Shawn's skin. He gathered his tartan, tossing it over his shoulder, and pushed through the growing number of wakeful men, among the small fires. The first five didn't know MacDonald. The sixth, rising from his fire and gulping an oatcake, said, "Warn't he goin' back to Glenmirril?"

"Aye, he was," Shawn said. He'd walked far enough, pushing tree limbs aside and brushing against other men in the forest, to see there were more than a hundred men here. There seemed no end to them, in fact, forever appearing out of the mist and from around trees. Then he came face to face with Lachlan, the younger man from Glenmirril. They stared at each other.

"Niall!" Lachlan broke into a broad grin. He slapped Shawn on the arm. "You've come with us. I thought you were going home."

Shawn stared, unable to think of a single word to say in response.

"Did Douglas ask you to come along?" The grin did not leave the other man's face.

"Uh, yes. No." Shawn tried furiously to think like Niall. What would Niall do? *Maybe I can get myself a bracelet,* he thought with irritation. *WWND.* Douglas had not asked Niall along, so he couldn't claim that. Niall would tell the truth. It was a unique thought, for Shawn. Falling asleep and letting his pony follow the wrong group was—stupid. A mess. Would make him a laughingstock. But it was the truth.

Douglas himself brushed through the mist at that moment. "Is that young Campbell I see?" he asked. For all his fierce reputation as a warrior, he was not a blustery or loud-spoken man. "I was told you'd other business. What brings you here?"

Another man beside him spoke. "This is Niall Campbell, is it, Jamie? This is yer man who was asleep on his horse the whole way."

"Aye, and no wonder," Douglas said. "He was up all night seeing we were ready to march at dawn. Did Bruce send you after us, Campbell?"

"I fell asleep." Shawn resisted the urge to mumble and stare at the ground. In another life, he'd have had a good laugh about the mistake. But mistakes in this world tended to have more serious consequences.

"Aye," said Douglas, "but what brings you to us?"

"I fell asleep on my horse, back at the castle," Shawn repeated, wishing the men would disperse. Instead, more appeared with every word. "It followed the wrong group."

A huge guffaw erupted from the back of the crowd, and spread quickly around the entire circle. Douglas's mouth quirked up, and Shawn thought again, what would Niall do? He wouldn't stand here like a thrashed puppy.

Shawn, too grinned. "The Laird'll not like this. Mayhap I'll just head back to Stirling now." He thought maybe, with the geography Niall had drilled into his head, he could ride north, and find someone to direct him to Glenmirril.

The Douglas, laughing as hard as any of his men, shook his head. "Niall, I've heard you were ever a prankster. You know bandits'll kill a man riding alone, and I can spare neither time nor men to escort you. You'll have to join us on our mission of mercy to free Northumbria's cattle and gold."

Shawn smiled, a frozen smile. He had a large scar running halfway around his body from his last experience with medieval warfare. He had no one, not Hugh, Niall, or MacDonald, to teach him more about fighting. "Aye, what a fine idea!" He grinned like he'd just won a Grammy. He felt sick to his stomach.

Men clapped him on the back, welcoming him.

"I'll just do that, then. Aye." He sighed, looking at the pony beside him, chomping grass with huge teeth, and wondered if he would survive the first day of this business.

Bannockburn, Present

Medieval spellings danced before Amy's eyes. On the tree stump beyond the Heritage Centre's parking lot, under the fringe of trees waving fresh green leaves overhead, she lifted her head from Barbour to stare down the slope stretching before her. Daisies sprinkled the grass; hedges hemmed in the field far below. At her side lay a copy of Andro of Wyntoun's *Orygynale Cronykil of Scotland*. She saw again, Shawn running, throwing the ring; the horse rising, sword slashing. She stared blankly at Barbour, open on her lap to the days after the battle.

"Beautiful day."

She spun on the stump, slamming the book. It toppled to the ground. She looked from the ruddy cheeks and curly black hair of the policeman, Angus, back to the leather cover, now dusted with dirt like powdered sugar. He leaned at the same time she did, to pick it up. The coffee in his hand sloshed in its paper cup. He set the other on the ground, to reach for the book. Their heads bumped.

"Ow!" She clapped a hand to her head.

"I'm sorry!" His ruddy cheeks turned a shade brighter. A self-conscious grin hovered on his mouth. "John Barbour, *The Brus*." He glanced at the book as he held it out to her. "Scotland's greatest moment."

"I took your advice and went to the library."

"'Tis unusual for an American to take such an interest." He tilted his head. His eyes pierced hers with unspoken questions.

A blush flew to her cheeks. She became suddenly conscious of the bottle green sleeveless shirt that set off her thick, black hair, and denim shorts revealing a great deal of her legs. She could hardly say, *my missing boyfriend was killed at the Battle of Bannockburn.* She shrugged. "As you say, the best of Scotland." She cringed to hear Shawn's slogan come out of her mouth. "I want to know more."

"About Niall Campbell?" He settled his large frame onto the ground beside her, crossing his legs. "It was mocha hazelnut you liked, aye?"

She smiled, bit her lip with a quick glance at the ground, and met his eyes again. "Thank you." She accepted the cup. "How did you know? I mean, about Niall?"

"Fascinating man, what's known of him. It's who...." He stopped.

"Who Shawn claimed to be. You were at the hospital that day, when I said Shawn called himself Niall Campbell."

"I'm sorry." He looked at the ground. "I shouldn't have said anything."

"It's okay." Amy's insides turned over heavily. She didn't know the man sitting beside her. The ugly truth of Shawn's womanizing and lying wasn't appropriate. She sipped her coffee, staring over the fields in the sudden silence. A sheep bleated, beyond the hedgerows at the bottom of the slope. A breeze brushed over the daisies, and they leaned down the hill, straining for a glimpse of the sheep.

The man cleared his throat. "I asked around about that museum."

"Oh, that," Amy said quickly. "I was mistaken."

At the same time, he said, "Nobody has heard of it."

"I was mistaken," she said again.

"But I can send you information on Niall Campbell, if you'd like."

She threw out words, hurling the conversation away from the missing museum. "You'd do that?" She thought of asking if he knew any connection between Niall or Glenmirril, and Iona. But he was the police.

"Of course. I love history. You'll not be able to shut me up, will be the real problem." A corner of his mouth turned up. The breeze ruffled his dark hair.

"I got the information on Glenmirril's website."

"There's more at Glenmirril itself. If you give me your e-mail, I'll send what I can find." He pulled out a small spiral notebook and pen. "I'll put your e-mail down right here with Inverness's most wanted."

She smiled. "I'd like that. I mean, the information about Niall. Not being with Inverness's most wanted. I mean, not that you thought." She laughed. "I'm making a fool of myself. I guess you know what I mean."

He smiled. "I think so."

West of Scotland, 1314

Niall drove his hobbin swiftly through the forest, aware of every sound. At the approach of men, he hid, knowing well the danger of bandits to a lone traveler. He banished all thought of Shawn and Allene. He had a mission, and spent the long ride planning and praying. Duncan MacDougall had not paid fealty to Bruce. Yet he continued to live on Scottish lands, a danger to Bruce and the struggling nation of Scotland. He had to be watched.

Niall entered Dundolam, the town below Creagsmalan, in the evening, pulling a hooded cowl over his head, even though the newly-grown beard would help hide his identity. It was no difficulty finding a small inn that served hot meals and gave him a bed for the night, lumpy and flea-ridden though it might be, not to mention already infested with a larger guest of the inn's paying variety. The other man snored loudly, sprawled across the bed. He'd thrown off the covers, despite the room's chill, and his hairy legs stuck out from under a nightshirt.

Niall returned to the inn's dining area, a dark room with a roaring fire, heavy wooden bar, and a scattering of booths and tables. It was filling quickly with a crowd of working men. Three barmaids in white blouses, bodices, and long woolen skirts swished through the room, bearing tankards of ale.

A coin on the table brought him a steak pie, a pitcher of ale and talkative companions. Men did not call it wagging their tongues, but it had the same effect, especially as the Bruce's money allowed Niall to be generous with the ale. He absorbed every bit of talk such as men might venture to spill: the laundress who trimmed men's hair and was free with more than her soap, the smith who'd had a brawl with a farmer, the lad and lass who'd sent up banns, Lord Duncan who foolishly thought his wife wouldn't notice his frequent trips to the kitchens or the comely scullery maid who worked there, the long absence of MacDougall at Stirling. Niall stored it all away, telling them he was Fionn of Bergen, a traveling minstrel, set upon in the hills, and his instrument stolen.

"We've a recorder," spoke up a skinny man scarred by pox. He came around the bar, wiping his hands on an apron. His few strands of hair hung, gray and sad as a wraith, around his ears. "Will you play for us?"

Niall smiled, amused at the man's assumption that one instrument was much like another. Still, Shawn's insistence on teaching Niall something had left him with a passing knowledge of recorder. He nodded, and almost immediately found the wooden instrument in his hand. The skinny man gripped a bodhran on his knee, beater ready. Niall ran up and down a scale, tapped his toe, and began, the drummer keeping a dull, but steady beat. The barmaids skipped a little more quickly, smiling now as they carried dinner to the crowd. Toes tapped all around the tavern, and a man got up to dance, reaching for a barmaid and swinging her around.

After several more tunes, feeling comfortable with the fingering, Niall tried a ballad. The drummer sang along in a clear tenor, more beautiful than any might have expected, given his homely looks. Niall smiled around the recorder's mouthpiece, and kept playing, moving into a slow folk song he'd often played on harp. Men joined their voices to his melody. A boy pushed the youngest barmaid forward. She sang the second verse alone, smiling at Niall, and the crowd came in again on the chorus.

Niall stopped, at last, thanking the man. "'Tis well made and a pleasure to play." He offered the instrument back.

"Take it," the man said. "My son played it, but he's long since dead, poor lad. He'd be happy to hear it sing again."

Niall tucked it in his belt, thanking the man for the gift, and returned to his meal. His talkative companions, having drunk the whole pitcher of ale while he played, were eager to tell more tales. He listened, volunteering nothing about himself, storing every bit away, and finally, pretending to stumble a little from ale he'd really consumed very little of, bid good night and climbed up to his room. He picked the covers up off the floor, squeezed in between his bed mate and the wall and fell into a deep sleep.

Bannockburn, Present

As Amy juggled a load of groceries and her bag of painting supplies with her house key, her phone trilled from inside her house. She managed to get through the front door, drop the groceries on the counter, and reach it before it stopped. The name on caller ID brought a smile to her face. "Rose! You're calling awfully late!" Amy switched the phone to speaker and set it on the counter, while she pulled groceries from bags.

"I just finished a concert." Rose's voice came from the counter. "I called before it started, but you didn't answer."

"I forgot my phone at home." Amy slid bread in the breadbox. "I had to get out. I was in danger of checking my e-mail every five minutes."

"What were you expecting?" Rose's voice lit up with hope. "Did you give that tour guide your e-mail?"

"No." Amy laughed. "I told I have no interest in getting involved with anyone. No, I was waiting for information about Niall." While she put away the milk, Amy recounted the story of meeting the cop at the Heritage Centre, and his offer to send information.

"Twice in a month?" Rose asked.

"He's visiting a friend." Even now, Amy was tempted to leave the groceries and run up to check the e-mail while she talked to Rose. "I was really excited to see what he found about Niall, but nothing came yesterday."

"If he's a policeman," Rose consoled, "he may be busy."

"I guess." But disappointment lingered in her heart. "He was probably just being nice when he offered. I bet he forgot as soon as I left the field."

"Better to get out, then. What did you do?"

"Practiced." Amy put a box of crackers in the cupboard. "Painted."

"My bird is done?"

"It's in my office waiting for you." She didn't try hiding the pride shining in her voice. "An osprey sat there like it was posing. It turned out great." She pulled an array of spices from a bag. "I saw the doctor yesterday. I heard the baby's heartbeat!" The glow of the moment rushed over her, the breathless flutter at hearing proof of the unseen child's existence. "It was amazing!"

"And yet," Rose said, "you sound sad."

Amy paused in the act of pulling a pan from the cupboard. The same sorrow she'd felt in the doctor's office rose in her again. "Can you really hear that over the phone," she asked softly, "or is it obvious why I would be?"

"Both," came Rose's voice from the counter. "Someone was missing."

"Yeah." Amy set the pan on the counter. She drew the back of her hand under her nose, blinking hard, before reaching for the chicken. "Yeah, I was angry at him for not being there. Although it's hardly his fault something impossible happened in that tower." Still, she'd spent the previous day angry, and the anger had brought the horse rearing back to life in her nightmares.

"He gave you reason to walk away, and if he'd listened, he'd be here," Rose said from the phone.

A chill touched Amy's spine as a thought occurred to her. "Or would we both have disappeared if I'd stayed there?" She slid the chicken into the pan, and washed her hands.

"I don't know," came the disembodied voice.

Amy shut off the water and tumbled fresh mushrooms and an onion onto a cutting board, slicing them wafer-thin the way Shawn liked them. "I don't hear you say that often."

"Hm." Rose sounded indignant. "I don't deal with time travel often. Of course, I've been doing some reading."

"That doesn't surprise me." Amy diced the onions swiftly.

"Don't be impertinent," Rose returned.

Amy laughed. "Yes, Miss Rose. What did you find out?" She sprinkled the vegetables over the chicken and slid it into the oven.

"Nothing," Rose said. "I've lived on the internet this week, in between rehearsals. I've searched every possible term related to Glenmirril, Iona, and Niall Campbell. And I'm still at a complete loss. What about you?"

"The same. I've run every search I can think of. I've spent hours reading every book I can find." Amy sliced a green pepper. "Nothing." She rinsed and shredded the romaine. "Mostly, all the reading makes me think what it must have been like for Shawn, caught in a time like that. But I've about given up on figuring out what he meant by Iona." Her fingers worked quickly through the last of the lettuce. "It really doesn't matter anymore, does it?"

"If it's still eating at you, then it matters," Rose said. "You need answers. Why don't you check that e-mail now? Maybe he sent something."

Amy needed little encouragement. There was plenty of time while the chicken baked. Taking the phone, she climbed the stairs to the office and opened her laptop.

As she did, Rose's voice came from the phone. "Amy, it's awfully late here. I'm dead tired. I called to tell you I'm coming back."

"You are?" Amy's smile grew.

"Yes," Rose said. "I forwarded the itinerary to you, and I'm pleased to hear this time, you sound happy about it, but not as if someone just threw you a lifeline."

Amy laughed, recognizing the truth of Rose's observation. "Because I *am* happy, and not so desperately in need. And it feels good. Like someone I used to know."

"Like someone you used to *be*," Rose said. "You did the right thing staying there. Now I have to get to bed, so I'll leave you to Mister I Just Come to Visit a Friend."

"Oh, come on," Amy protested. "You said the same thing about the tour guide." She pulled up her e-mail.

Rose sniffed. "I was right then, too. Let me know if he found anything."

"But Angus doesn't...."

"Enjoy your dinner! Good night!" The line clicked, leaving Amy alone in the office.

"Thanks for calling, Rose," Amy sighed. "Sleep well." She typed in her password with the anticipation of Christmas morning. The name Angus

MacLean jumped out at her. Her mouth quirked up in a smile, though why, she didn't know. She hardly knew the man. Rose was wrong. She was eager to learn Niall's fate, that was all.

Still, she saved it for last. She looked over Rose's itinerary and scanned Rob's usual expression of concern. Her fingers hovered over the keyboard. He didn't want to hear about her walks to the battlefield, her excursions onto the infidelity forum she'd found, or her research on Niall. *Things are great,* she typed. *The weather's chilly.* Lacking anything else to say, she added, *I hope you're well,* and hit send.

Then, with the same fluttering of nerves that accompanied every solo performance, she opened the e-mail from Angus. *How's the research going?* he asked, and gave her a few links. *My dad thinks Niall went to London with Lamberton shortly after the battle,* he added.

Amy pulled up her spreadsheet and added the information before reading further. *I've not had the time I'd hoped, but you'll find more information about him at the archives. I've friends who work there who can get you in, if you'd like.*

Amy became still. Memories of the castle engulfed her, the tower rising above her and mist swirling around her legs, climbing to her waist, as she shouted up at Shawn. She shook her head, pulling herself from the flashback. She didn't want to go to Glenmirril, though she wondered, could it be more traumatic than sitting at the battlefield, re-living his death, every day?

Still, she didn't want to see the place she'd spent the last hours with him. It would bring everything back, the argument, the tour guide saying a man protects his family, and her crushing sense of loss that day in the courtyard over the first baby. The look on Shawn's face came to her clearly. He'd been uncomfortable. That was unusual for him. It was the same look in the tower when she brought it up, before he got angry, before she got mad enough to leave. She felt sick. She shouldn't have left. He shouldn't have been so obtuse. She squeezed her eyes shut, willing herself out of the thoughts. With a deep breath and force of will, she opened them again on the present, to the e-mail before her.

What do you call a man whose career is in ruins? Angus asked. Dots trailed down the screen. Amy scrolled down to the answer.

A historian.

With a smile, she hit reply. *Thanks for taking the time to help me.* After a moment's hesitation, she typed, *I'll think about Glenmirril.* Then she added one of Shawn's few clean jokes: *Why did the trombonist cross the playground?* She hit a series of dots, smiling as she typed, *To get to the other slide,* and hit send.

Immediately, she changed her mind. She shouldn't have told a trombone joke. It dredged up Shawn's ghost. She sighed, sat back, and told herself it didn't matter. He was just a guy being friendly like everyone else here. He didn't care if she told a trombone joke. Maybe it was a little strange he'd been down twice in one month, from as far as Inverness. But he might have business or family. Maybe he liked Bannockburn. Maybe it was a girlfriend he was visiting. She was surprised to find the thought disappointed her.

The computer hummed into sleep as she shut it down. She ate a quiet dinner, the offer of Glenmirril nagging at her. She wanted to know what she'd find about Niall there, or maybe, by some miracle, even something about Shawn's death or burial. But she didn't want to go.

Finally, with the dishes cleaned, she went to bed, wearing Shawn's big, fluffy robe. She lay in the dark, with a sliver of white moon tangled in the tree limbs outside her window, smiling gently through the lace curtains; thinking of Shawn holding her through the night in Castle Tioram, and Niall's arm wrapped around her on the train, his cheek resting on her head, and missing all she'd lost. Niall would have prayed. She wrapped her hand around his crucifix.

God? Outside her window, the tree swayed, a silhouette black against the moon. In her room, all was quiet. She had a baby coming. She didn't need to go to a castle that filled her with anxiety. *God, should I go anyway?* He remained silent. Shawn was dead. Nothing she learned there would help her or this child.

She made her decision. She'd skip whatever scraps of information Glenmirril held. She rolled over, pulling Shawn's robe snugly around herself, smelling his aftershave on it, clutching Niall's crucifix, and fell asleep to dreams of the tower, of Shawn leaning over it, shouting for her to come back.

Dundolam, Western Scotland, 1314

Niall spent a week entertaining at the inn, in exchange for food and lodging. His Grace's gold would keep him well enough, but it wouldn't do to have questions asked around town why a man had no need to earn a living. He sought the town talk and mood like rare coins, formulated plans, and waited his chance. He needed to know if Duncan MacDougall would remain peaceful, or if Bruce must prepare for trouble in his western islands.

The townsfolk themselves cared little whether Bruce or a Plantagenet called himself king. Niall didn't blame them. Duncan MacDougall, lord of the lands, had greater impact on their daily lives by far than Bruce or Edward or any man hundreds of miles away calling himself king. Duncan decided when and for whom they would fight. He meted out justice, wove the aura of mercy and goodwill, or fear and terror, under which they lived, and wielded power over life and death.

The washer woman, Niall found, a girl called Joan, was not only free with her soap and wares, but with her tales. She eyed him up and down, smiling slowly from under half-lowered lashes, when he entered her yard, and he became conscious of his own broad shoulders, height, and thickening chestnut-copper beard.

He sat by her large washtubs, waiting while she scrubbed his spare linen shirt along with a dozen others, churning them with lye, and beating dirt from them with a large wooden cudgel. Sweat coated her flushed cheeks. She worked in short sleeves, revealing fleshy red arms that leapt and trembled with each thrash of the cudgel. Her mouth moved faster than her arms. "My Lord, now, merrit but these few years and already in trouble with his mistress, cattin' after women. That Bessie in the kitchens, now, she's comely, she is, but is she worth it, is she? And in the kitchens, I tell you! Where in the kitchens does the man find a dark corner for their doings?" A long tale and many details of various of Dundolam's citizenry followed. Niall saw the wealth of information on which he'd stumbled.

He found excuses to return the following days. It was easy enough, with a question or two wedged into her crush of words, to get almost any information he could think to ask. The woman rivaled the internet, Niall thought, with a smile. Amidst stories of the Lord and his trysts with Bessie, a heated catfight between two maids, and the goings-on of a dozen servants, whose names Niall filed away as quickly as she spewed them, he gained a clearer picture of the layout inside the castle each time he returned.

After several days, he dared ask for more specific information. "What of events at Stirling? Surely Milord Duncan...."

He had no need to say more. Indeed, he had no time to say more, for she was talking again. "Ah, that man! Can he make a wise decision even once in his life! No, he'll not swear fealty to the Bruce. But then, what d' ye expect of a man who doesn't appreciate a woman like Milady Christina? Beautiful, she is, is she not? And her clothes, oh my!" Niall soon knew every detail of Christina's wardrobe, her extensive collection of fine dresses and cloaks, even details of her undergarments he was sure the Lady Christina would not appreciate a wandering minstrel knowing.

"And Milord is a fool. 'Tis his own wife's maid's clothes he squeezes into, now, is it not, to disguise himself to run down to meet Bessie. Does he not think his own wife will notice her husband in her maid's clothes?"

"It must be a rather large maid," Niall ventured.

"Aye, the maid's a big lass, and Milord not overly so." She winked, making her meaning clear. Niall would have been shocked to hear such words from another girl's mouth. But Joan laughed out loud, flashing healthy, white teeth. A black curl tumbled over one eye. She pushed it away with the back of her wrist. "I'm sure ye've no problem with lasses saying such things about ye," she added with a wink.

The tips of Niall's ears grew hot. But Shawn's ways had worked well in London; surely they'd work here. He smiled easily, as Shawn would do. "I've had no complaints." Strictly speaking, it was true. But his real problem was steering the conversation back to MacDougall's intentions.

Joan's own intentions were becoming markedly clear, as she paused to fan herself with a hand, and lift her blouse off damp, sweating skin, peering at him from under thick lashes.

"Surely ye've a young man," Niall said. "In Milord's employ, perhaps?"

The question set her off on a long story of a false lover, a Norseman who had fought on the galleys of John of Lorn, Duncan's kin. She lifted the shirts from the wash, one by one, moving them to a tub of clear water.

"Has he many galleys?" Niall asked.

"Och, now, would I care? I only know my love went away, and when the ships come back one night, his brother comes and tells me Ranald has stayed in England with a lass, and posted his banns already, has he not?"

"These ships are big? How could MacDougall leave a man behind?"

She waved a hand. "There are plenty o' men to take his place."

Niall sighed. It wasn't much. If only she cared about armies and military strategy as fervently as she cared about Lady Christina's undergarments. He tried again. "He'll be needing men soon?"

Joan swirled her cudgel through the steaming cauldron. "Now, does Milord tell me his business?"

Niall imagined only a fool would.

"Though there was quite a to-do but a week ago." She lifted another shirt, dripping with gray lye water, held it high a moment, shedding as much as possible, and dropped it into the tub of clear water. Niall leaned forward. She dimpled at him, mistaking his interest, and leaned much farther over the lye tub than necessary, searching with the cudgel in the swirling gray streaks for another shirt. He wondered if she'd ever fallen entirely out of the blouse, for she threatened to do so now. She came up from her search, triumphant, flashing him a broad smile, as she hoisted her wares high in the air. The shirt dripped, and passed into the fresh rinsing water.

"There was a to-do," Niall reminded her. "Were men called up?"

"Men? I've no idea about men being called up, though the town does seem a wee bit quiet of late. No, I meant Milady Christina's festivities. There's quite a stramash, what with preparations. Workmen, my goodness, in and out of Creagsmalan, and all the lasses hoping for a glimpse of the nobles. Why, I'm washing for most all of them up at the castle, myself." She selected a fresh stick, and, hoisting a pot of bubbling water off the fire, poured it into the tub of rinsing water. Steam rose around her face, and through it came more details of clothing of all the gentry near and far. Niall recognized a few names, but he'd met none of them face to face.

"Oh, my, I'm that hot, I am!" Once again, Joan stopped stirring to fan herself and lift the white blouse, flapping its edge frantically atop her large breasts. "Goodness, sir, you must think me something awful!" She dimpled again, and Niall was sure she didn't fear it in the least.

"Not at all," he lied, hoping to find a confessor soon. She smiled coyly from under her eyelashes, and went back to stirring, once again leaning far over the tub. She chattered on about her friends and their new husbands while he assessed what he'd learned so far—more than he could have hoped for, and very little of it useful.

She began transferring shirts to a second rinsing tub, talking about the coming ball. There would be a hunt, of course, and days of feasting. Even now, the butcher and his apprentices were slaughtering cattle. Musicians were gathering. Surely he'd heard? She reached into the steaming water for a shirt to hang on a line, and soon a dozen similar bell-sleeved garments fluttered in a row.

Niall ventured one last attempt at military information. "Perhaps the festivities are a send-off for MacDougall's men?"

Joan shrugged. "I'd not know. Milord doesn't come here anymore, but Faolan, now, who plays the lute, he's here often for clean shirts, is he not? One of his musicians has taken ill, poor man, and he can find no one to take his place." She clipped the last shirt in place, and plumped down beside him, smelling of soap and sweat, and all smiles.

Irritation hummed through Niall. Faolan's problems were of no more interest to him than the Lady Christina's undergarments. He needed to know Duncan's plans. He needed a way into the castle.

She ran a hand down the length of his chestnut hair, to his shoulder, before letting her fingers trail across his beard.

Now, he thought, he had real problems.

Chapter Eight

Bannockburn, Present

Even from as far away as the tall pole bearing Scotland's blue and white Saltire, Amy recognized Angus's solid form under the red and gold trees fringing the Heritage Centre's parking lot. He stood there with Mike. She scuffed through leaves in leather boots that had reminded her of Niall's, and buried her hands in her new fall coat of soft, fawn-colored leather.

Instant comparisons between Shawn and Angus jumped to mind. It came, she thought, from having just left church. She'd sat through a good part of the morning, arms resting on the pew before her in the empty sanctuary, mulling over her reading on the infidelity forum. The more she sat in the quiet church these past weeks, under the colored beams of light jetting through stained glass, the more her thoughts steadied. Or maybe it was being free of the sticky web of Shawn's lies and smooth persuasion. But she'd admitted to herself that Shawn had likely had multiple affairs, despite what he'd told Celine, despite Rob claiming to have been with Caroline.

She wanted to believe he was the one who didn't follow the pattern she saw over and over on the infidelity forum. He was one of a kind, after all. But they'd reminded her on the board, *You saw what he was from the start.* The real question, she thought, was how she'd gotten so stupid, how she'd let him convince her that the sincere, loving man she saw in private was the real man, and the man she saw in public only the act.

Because, she defended herself, he'd shown her that good side for so long, never giving her reason to doubt, until the past year. The rage had returned, growing slowly and steadily, deep within, till she'd wanted to race home and smash his trombone, rip his shirts to shreds. A deep breath, and a fist clenched around Niall's crucifix had slowly calmed her. He'd apologized, he'd redeemed himself in giving his life for a child. And if he'd cheated, they reminded her on the forum, it was his own brokenness, not a fault in her. She had a good life, a talent she loved, a child on the way, and Rose's visit to look forward to.

Nonetheless, she'd resolved to walk home the long way, through the fallen leaves scattered over the battlefield, letting the cool fall air blow away the last of the hot rage. It had to be healthier than smashing things.

Angus lifted a hand as she approached. "Hello!"

Mike, too, greeted her with a wave. "Found more on our Niall?"

"Bits and pieces." She joined them under the trees.

They stood, their feet scuffling in red leaves, smiling at each other, before Angus asked, "Was the information I sent helpful?"

"Oh, very," Amy assured him.

"You're being kind." A corner of his mouth twitched upward. "I did tell you I'm an amateur historian. Most information is useless on its own. It's only when you get enough to form a big picture that it helps."

She blushed, glanced at the ground, and back up. He stared at her intently, his head cocked to one side, as if a question burned in his mind. His eyes were dark blue, almost black, and piercing. Her blush deepened. "Caught," she admitted. "But it's still one piece I didn't have before."

"It's important to know the whole history of the time," Angus said, "to really understand a person. It's chilly out here. If you've time for coffee, I know a fair bit of Glenmirril's history." He glanced at Mike.

Amy followed his look.

"Aye." Mike nodded vigorously. "He knows Glenmirril well. Verra interesting events up there. I think you'd like to hear it."

Amy rifled through a mental calendar. It didn't take long to review another commitment-free day. She'd already taken a long walk and visited the church. There was time to play her violin later. And Mike and Angus seemed pleasant company. "I'd love to," she said.

Smiles passed around the trio, like a theme from instrument to instrument, and as one, they turned to cross the parking lot, past the white stucco museum, and out to the main road. "Enjoy your bridies," Mike said, as a bus slid up to the stop. A golden leaf swirled from the tree above, danced around his face, and floated to the ground. He climbed up the step. "I'm off to a well-deserved rest in the twenty-first century."

"Have a good one." Angus waved.

Amy looked from Angus to the bus doors sliding shut behind Mike. "I thought he was coming."

Angus grinned. "I'm verra safe, but if I misled you and you don't want to go, I understand."

She bit her lip, hating the blush that warmed her face. "Just surprised, that's all. Of course I'll go."

Dundolam, 1314

Niall bolted up off the hewn log, jarring Joan's hand from his hair. As if the motion jolted something out of the very air, the idea dropped into his head. Faolan needed a musician, Niall needed a way into the castle, and his alter ego, Fionn, needed work.

"Now, then, did something sting you?" Joan asked in surprise.

"Not at all!" Niall's thoughts spun in excitement. He backed away from Joan's reaching hand. Faolan's musicians would be visible in the gallery for all to see. He shouldn't risk having someone recognize him. Especially not with Duncan already warned to watch for him.

But the idea had taken root.

"What is it, then?" Joan took another step toward him.

"'Tis only...." He looked for a reason he'd be backing away, his germ of an idea growing with his excitement. This feat, though only he and Allene would know, would be his own.

"'Tis only what, Fionn? You've such lovely hair."

There were ways, he thought, to make himself less recognizable. "No!" He took her hand as she reached for it again. "'Tis dirty and long." He almost smiled, thinking of Shawn's sweet smelling French shampoo. *Jhirmack.* But he kept his face grim. "I'm no fit company for a lass, since I took to the road."

"'Tis not too long," Joan objected.

"Very much too long," Niall insisted. "I'm wont to being clean-shaven."

"Now, if that's all," Joan said, "I can shave you and trim your hair."

"Could you?" Niall asked, his eyes wide. "Still, you being accustomed to a fine Norseman...." He sighed. "If only I had the fine golden hair you love."

A smile spread across Joan's fleshy face. "Why, Fionn, if it's golden hair you're wanting, I can do that, too."

"You wouldn't!" he said, and this time, let her grasp his hand.

"I would!" She twined her fingers in his. "Really, Fionn, 'twould be great fun!"

"What a grand idea! You're very clever!" he said. He didn't care to think of Allene's reaction, but there it was. Better Allene's displeasure than MacDougall's gallows.

"Verra! I'll get things ready, and we'll do it this afternoon!"

His mind jumped to the next problem. He couldn't return to the inn with his changed looks. "Joan, will Faolan be by again, d' you think?"

"He often comes in the evening."

"Will you introduce us?" Niall asked.

Joan smiled coyly. "I'd be pleased to do anything you like, Fionn."

♫

Niall knelt in the small kirk of Dundolam, praying Faolan would accept him as a musician, and that he would get the information Bruce needed. He prayed for his own safety, thinking of the messenger sent to Duncan, and Allene waiting at Glenmirril, and asked forgiveness for using an obviously lonely girl. He would have to ask his confessor, when he returned to Glenmirril, did the greater good of Scotland justify it, or should he have looked for a kinder way, even at risk to an entire nation, to get what Bruce needed? He wondered if Shawn would have dared further, giving Joan all she obviously wanted, and learned more.

With a glance at the sun climbing high outside the kirk's windows, he rose from his knees, feeling no more at peace than when he'd gone in. Intent on entering Duncan's castle as a musician, he threaded back to Joan's through the town's narrow streets, sidestepping bairns, horses, and garbage being tossed out windows.

His past experience with the MacDougalls really ought to have cured him of such recklessness, he thought, as to put himself on public view. But then, it was the very daring of placing himself under his enemy's nose, in plain sight, that appealed to him. He smiled, skirting a fishmonger's cart. They'd be talking about it for years, back at Glenmirril.

And this feat would be his own. It stung, knowing his reputation was largely Shawn's doing. *Forgive me,* he addressed God silently. *I remain a wee bit vain. 'Tis for Scotland and should not matter whose doing it is.* It could hardly sting less for Shawn, he supposed, knowing someone else reaped the glory for all his efforts.

Joan waited in the courtyard behind her mother's house. She giggled and blushed when he rounded the corner, thinking—well, he knew she imagined a great romance between them. She noticed very little, so fast did her mouth move. That he kept coming back, kept listening, and smiled now and again, had led her to see what she wished. Still, he didn't care to lead a lass on, even such a one as Joan.

"There ye are, Fionn!" she cried. "Come over here, now."

She seated him on a rough-hewn log, and pushed his head back over a tub of water. She leaned in close, her bosom in his face, talking and giggling. Niall tried to listen—one never knew what scrap of information might save one. But her fingers massaged his scalp, and she'd anointed herself with a delightful rose perfume. Against his will, he relaxed into the scent, the warm water, and the fingers working through his hair.

It would have taken her great effort to build the fire and have the water so pleasantly warm for him—her elderly mother couldn't have done it, and her father had died in the wars some time ago. Guilt gnawed. He tried to say an *Ave* for her, a dozen *Aves*, but the massaging fingers relaxed the words right out of his mind. The warm bosom in his face gave him need to swallow his natural impulses, ones that had not risen when that bosom had been at a greater distance. He wondered if Shawn had it right after all. What could it hurt? He snapped his eyes open, trying to pull himself from the pleasant trance, but the sight was too much, and he slammed his eyes shut again.

It would hurt Allene, he reminded himself sternly. It would break her trust in him. It would harm his faith in his own character. It would damage the respect between himself and the Laird. That's what it would hurt. He tried to think on his mission.

"Och, now, relax that jaw!" Joan purred. "Why are ye so tense? Does the warm water not feel good?" She poured something into his hair, the feel of it flowing in a slow drone under the quick tempo of her words, its flowery scent reminding him of Shawn's shampoo. She worked it in with strong fingers, murmuring, her words becoming softer.

He caught *Bessie* and knew they were back to her favorite subject, the Lord and his trysts with the kitchen maid. Insight flickered across his relaxed mind. Shawn would have seen it sooner. "He loved you once."

"Aye," Joan agreed on a sigh. "He came himself to get his shirts washed. He tossed me aside for her." Her voice took on a brittle edge. "I hate that man." She was silent a moment, before speaking more softly. "'Tis neither here nor there. He's a fool, not like you. So smart and handsome. 'Tis a wonder, sure, ye've no lass waitin' for you at home."

"Not to worry." Niall avoided an outright lie. Her fingers kneaded his skull. Guilt gnawed at him, for Allene, for Joan herself, as she poured warm pitchers of water, slowly, tauntingly, over his hair. Her blouse brushed his cheek, soft as a down pillow, and stayed there. Something else flowed through his hair, her fingers tugged and pulled, and her rose fragrance enveloped him.

Her fingers moved to his lip, working through his mustache, tugging down along the sides of his mouth. "There now, let it sit a wee bit. I'll shave that beard, and we'll have a fine Norseman. Hold still." The warmth lifted off his cheek, something cool slathered his chin. With each scrape of the blade, Niall felt himself shedding, becoming a new man. He wondered what he'd look like, wondered for the hundredth time what had become of Shawn and if they'd found him; how MacDonald would react to losing his secret twins. Of course, his hair and beard would grow out and he and Shawn would look alike again—assuming they found Shawn alive and well.

Joan droned on, a descant above his thoughts. She was back to Duncan, telling how he'd watched her wash shirts, how he'd spirited her away into the house while they soaked.

"Ye're no shocked now, are ye, Fionn?" she asked. "I know what they say, but really, I've not done such horrid things, no matter what they say. He said he loved me. He said Milady kept at him day and night, and knowing there was a gentle soul here, loving him, was all that kept him going." The blade scraped an ostinato beneath her story.

Guilt swam high in Niall's chest, along with the memory of Celine at the harp. For all Joan lacked the harpist's fragile, wide-eyed looks, with his eyes closed, he heard the trusting, wounded girl inside her, no different from Celine. He wanted to tell Joan men had used the same line for a thousand years, and would for a thousand to come. He consoled himself he'd used no false words. He'd only come back and listened. But then, he admitted with a stab of pain in his heart, he'd known that was all it would take to get what he wanted. *For Scotland, My Lord*, he prayed. *I'd not have hurt her for my own pleasure.*

"Then one day, after I'd given everything, thinkin' he loved me, he had Bessie drop off his shirts. I sent messages to him. He didn't answer. And one day he rode by on his big, black horse and looked down at me and told me I was to stay away from him and stop spreadin' stories, lest he have me whipped in the square."

The blade stopped. Niall opened his eyes. She stared down at him, the long blade hanging limply at her side, flecked with soap. Her eyes were dry and red. *What you did for the least of these, you did for Me.* She didn't look so rough and uncouth as she had that first day.

"I'm not so awful as all that, am I, Fionn?" she asked.

"No," he said. And he meant it.

"Hold still, while I rinse you off." She leaned forward, fingers stroking, warm water flowing, words caressing. His desire fled, leaving in its wake only compassion for her search for love. And anger at the younger MacDougall.

Bannockburn, Present

A strong breeze tugged at Amy's thick braid on the way to the coffee shop, but the brisk walk warmed her.

"The bridies here are not to be beat," Angus said, placing an order when they entered.

"It smells great." Amy slipped off her coat. The aroma of lattes mixed with the pleasant smells of meat and pastry and chocolate. She and Shawn had loved searching out new coffee shops. He would have liked this place.

Angus collected their food and coffee, and they chose a table just big enough for two. "Tell me about the States," he said. "I've always hoped to go."

"Which part? They're all different." She emptied a long, thin packet of sugar into her white ceramic mug.

"Where are you from?"

"New York, originally."

"Big place."

She stirred milk into her coffee. "You mean New York City? A lot of the state is farms and hills and small towns just like anywhere. Very beautiful."

"I hear lots of Scots settled there." He sipped his coffee black, watching her over the rim of the mug.

Amy frowned. "No, it was more the Dutch, really. New Amsterdam, you know."

"Are *you* of Scottish descent? I swear I see a bit of Scots in you."

She tasted her coffee. "Because of the black hair? That's Italian and a sixteenth Cherokee. The rest is German, Dutch, and a touch of Swede. No Scots at all."

He picked up his pastry, his head cocked to one side. "You're sure? I'm usually a good guess of these things."

She laughed. "Of course I'm sure."

He blushed. "Of course you are. That was foolish of me."

She studied her bridie, wondering how to eat it. Deciding Angus's method must be correct, and noting napkins aplenty in the holder, she picked it up. She could almost taste the pastry oils through her skin. Spices filled the meat, making her tongue tingle with the flavor. "I hope it's not a strike against me," she added.

"Not at all." He smiled. "Tell me about where you live now." He had a dozen questions about life in the Midwest, and being a symphony musician, adding, "I play bagpipes myself, with the police drum and pipe band."

Her eyes lit up. "You didn't tell me you were a fellow musician!"

He grinned, glancing at his food. "I'm not of your caliber now, am I?"

"You play with a group. I'm sure you're very good."

He waved the compliment off. "Just something I enjoy. But I promised to tell you more about Glenmirril."

She found herself once again comparing him to Shawn, as he talked. Shawn would have elaborated on any skill, embroidering it into great accomplishments regardless of facts.

"Records only start in the mid to late 1200s, but some excavation work on the foundation suggests there was a structure there much earlier." Angus spoke with the same animation that had always come over Shawn when he arranged. *A minor seventh there,* she could almost hear him saying, his eyes alight. *Then follow it right away with a thirteen chord. Listen! It's perfect!*

"The earlier structure would have been wood, so there's nothing left, but we can see the foundations." He leaned forward, his eyes intent. "A Pictish chief lived where Urquhart is now, in the time of Columba."

A customer entered, letting in cool air that swirled around Amy's leather boots. She sipped her coffee, enjoying its warmth, but sadly aware of Shawn's legacy on her life. Angus seemed nice. But Shawn had convinced her he was, too, and she found herself wondering who this cop really was, behind the pleasant mask and sincere eyes. She wondered if she'd ever trust another man.

"But if you really want to know about Niall Campbell, Glenmirril's the place." Angus swallowed the last of his coffee. "You said you'd think about it, in your e-mail."

Before Amy could answer, the waitress appeared at Angus's elbow, refilling his cup. She raised questioning eyebrows at Amy, and at her nod, poured her coffee, too. Amy added sugar and milk, stirring to cover the sudden quiet.

"They've a verra nice archives that's not open to the public." Angus leaned forward, his big hands wrapped around his newly-warmed cup. "But my mates would let you in."

She bit her lip. Everything associated with Glenmirril hung like a storm cloud around her—the argument with Shawn, dark, hovering feelings of anger and helplessness, worry and guilt the next morning, thinking he was hurt because of her. And guilt that she'd left him to disappear into a brutal time and get killed. "People were looking at me strangely there." It slipped out. It was the least of her concerns. She shook her head. "Of all that happened there, I don't know why I'm worried about that." She dared a glance up at Angus.

His eyebrows furrowed, as if puzzling over an ancient code. "Sometimes it's easier to focus on the small things. Who was looking at you strangely?"

Her hands scrambled, under the table, twisting Bruce's ring. "It's silly. Never mind."

"No, who?"

"One of the living history actors. The guy with the horses."

A thoughtful frown tugged down the corners of his mouth. "I imagine so," he murmured.

"What? What's that supposed to mean?" She forcibly stopped her fingers twisting the ring, placing her hands on the tabletop.

"Nothing." Angus stared at the crumbs on his plate.

Amy gave her coffee one last, unnecessary stir. The spoon clinked against the cup and dribbled a small mocha stain on the napkin as she set it down. She spoke with bravado she didn't feel. "Look, you know, it happened. I left him there and he disappeared."

Angus looked up, his black eyebrows knit.

"I mean, he came back strange and disappeared *later*. I can't expect everyone to pretend around me forever. The thought of going there makes me kind of uncomfortable."

He was silent only briefly before asking, "Did the Stirling police keep in touch with you? Do you hope to find him?"

Amy shrugged. "He's not coming back." Even before the words left her mouth, she felt herself diving after them, snatching at them, but they slipped between her fingers and hung in the air. Her lip trembled; tears stung her eyes. She swallowed. She'd lived too long with her own thoughts, forgetting the rest of the world knew a different story.

"He's missing," Angus said gently. "Missing people are often found."

Her hands crept back under the table, alternately twisting Bruce's ring and clenching one another, trying to stop the habit. "I just feel it." She gave a weak laugh. "Women's intuition, maybe." *Shut up,* she remonstrated with herself. *He's the police. He'll think you killed him.* She tried for a better explanation. "He had everything. I know he caused a lot of trouble, but one thing about Shawn, he loved life. He lived every minute to the fullest." *For better or worse,* she thought cynically. "He'd never willingly disappear."

Angus said nothing. She removed her hands from under the table, but found them still clutching one another, elbows on table, hands pressed against her lips. She forced herself to loosen her grip.

"You're absolutely sure he's not coming back?" Angus leaned forward. His dark eyes pierced hers.

She nodded, swallowing; avoiding his eyes. "It wouldn't be like him to disappear." She couldn't explain—really, Angus was just someone she barely knew—wouldn't tell him the whole truth about Shawn. She gulped the last of her milky coffee and stood abruptly, fumbling for her coat. "I have to go. I have, um, I really need to practice."

The look on his face told her he knew it was an excuse. He rose, a hand on her arm. "I understand about Glenmirril. I didn't think. Really, I didn't. But if you still want to research Niall Campbell, I've a friend at the archives in Edinburgh, if you'd like me to get you in there. This research seems to give you some peace."

Her discomfort settled. She was able to meet his eyes again. "Thanks." She hesitated. "You'd do that for me? I'm a stranger to you." A nervous laugh fluttered up from her stomach, thinking of Shawn's favorite line. *There are no strangers, only friends we haven't met.* She'd rolled her eyes at him often enough, hearing him say it to one of his backstage bimbos, her hands between both of his and his eyes burning holes in hers, lighting up the space between them. *It's all show,* he'd reassured her constantly. *We sell another twenty albums every time I do it, to her and all her friends. Don't worry.*

Amy's laugh died away. "If you would, yes, I'd like that."

Creagsmalan Castle, 1314

Up in the musicians' gallery, looking down into the great hall, Niall's fingers danced on the recorder. He thought with longing of the hundred strong orchestra in Inverness's twenty-first century. Faolan had been quick to take Niall on, and a days' practice with the trio had left Niall increasingly confident on the instrument, even with the distraction of the long, blonde mustache tickling his chin. Piping the simple melodies of folk songs, dances, and reels was easy enough, as was singing ballads to the accompaniment of Faolan's lute.

Candles glittered from wall sconces and chandeliers hanging from the high ceiling. Fires roared in great braziers at either end and either side of the hall. Men and women swirled in all the colors of a king's gems, bathed and powdered and jeweled for the occasion.

Christina was as beautiful as Joan had said, no more than twenty, with regal bearing, and finely sculpted cheeks. Black hair spilled from under her barbet, down her back in a heavy braid that reminded him of Amy's, but for the silver cord woven through it, punctuated with small jewels. A kirtle of deep blue, with sleeves drooping halfway to the floor, emphasized the color of her eyes. She moved among her guests with graciousness stamped on every graceful lift of her hand to a man's lips, every elegant incline of her neck in greeting a lord, every leaning in to an older woman to better hear her words.

"Lovely, is she not?" Faolan noted Niall's gaze. "There's not a man who's not enchanted by her. But though Milord has a wandering eye, he dislikes another man's eye on her. He has a jealous temper."

"Does he now?" Niall murmured. It explained why she was never in the company of a man for more than a moment, and always with one of her women close by her side.

Faolan lifted his lute, tapped his toe, and they started a lively strathspey. A man who must be Duncan MacDougall entered. Though shorter by many inches, he bore a startling resemblance to the MacDougall Niall knew, the hair as thick and dark, and sweeping back from a high forehead. The teeth were the same, strong and even, though not yet yellow. The nose was hooked and proud. He moved with the unmistakable air of the lord of the manor, and swept across to Lady Christina, taking her arm with a possessiveness that

Faolan's words suggested none but MacDougall himself would dare. He brushed through the crowd with her, to the center of the floor, swinging her into the strathspey. Niall piped, sweeping his eyes across the crowd, but always coming back to Christina. A smile sat in carved place on her features. She kept her eyes fixed on her husband's chin, swinging and spinning in excellent form, the smile never growing nor fading.

She was as unhappy as Joan, Niall thought, while his fingers danced. He gulped air and skipped through the next phrase, adding a little trill to the already lively tune. Christina's eyes lifted to his. Her smile quivered, and settled back to its frozen carving. Her gaze returned to MacDougall's thick, black beard. The bodhran beat out the last cadence, and Niall and Faolan skidded to an abrupt stop. The nobility stepped back, ladies pressing delicate white hands to their breasts, eyes alight with exertion, and lords smiling all around.

Christina's head bowed as she dropped a curtsy to her husband. Niall's eyes lingered on her. He had kept alert before the festivities, listening to servants and nobles alike, for clues to MacDougall's intentions. He'd heard no more than a passing scathing reference to Bruce. It might have reflected the speaker's feelings, or the lord's. It was not enough to raise Bruce's army. But Christina: if anyone would know, apart from MacDougall himself, it was Christina; or possibly Bessie, down in the kitchens.

Faolan tapped his toe, and they started a graceful piece, with the men and women executing mincing steps at a more stately tempo. Niall's eyes drifted back to Christina. Her smile had not changed. MacDougall gripped her delicate hand in his like dungeon irons. When the dance called for him to hand her off to another man, his eyes followed, hard and warning. Niall drifted up a step in the melody. Christina's gaze stayed low on her companion's chest, until he handed her back to her husband.

As Niall drew in air, his thoughts returned to Bessie. He knew only that she worked in the kitchens, a servant like his own new persona. Would a girl being wooed by the master of the castle be foolish enough to speak even to another servant? Would she know anything? Would Duncan be as jealous of his mistress as of his wife? No, he wouldn't, Niall decided. Bessie was indeed the safer path to try for information. But Christina was the surer.

The smell of cooking drifted up from the kitchens. Boys gathered at the far end of the hall, bearing great platters of food. Niall's stomach rumbled. It had been hours since the minstrels had been fed. He scanned the crowd again, and started, to find Christina's eyes on him, intensely blue across the room. She dropped her gaze at once. The bodhran sounded the end of the piece. Faolan turned to Niall. "Ye'd best hope," he warned, "that MacDougall does not notice his wife's eye on you."

Edinburgh, Present

The Edinburgh Archives stood at the head of Princes Street, a grand old building with wide stone steps soaring up to a portico edged by massive stone columns. Inside was a large center of scholarly study, dizzying in its many floors circling the entrance, spiraling up to the ceiling, all lined with endless shelves.

"It's like something out of a sci-fi movie." Amy craned her neck, staring up to the ceiling far above. Excitement and awe hummed side by side in her at the treasures of information waiting to be unearthed.

A morose and gaunt man, who looked as if he belonged in one of the archives' drawers himself, met them in the foyer and shook Angus's hand with an attempt at a smile. "Nice to see you, Inspector." He shook Amy's hand with even less enthusiasm, before leading them to a large, bright room full of tables and files. "Cameras watch everything," he warned. "What is it you're wanting?" He sighed. His long face fell, as if asking how she planned on doing him in.

Amy's mouth twitched in amusement, curious if her answer would provoke a deeper sigh of resignation. "Anything about Niall Campbell from Glenmirril. He was at Stirling Castle in 1314."

"Well, then." He did indeed seem resigned as he shuffled to wide marble stairs, and up to one of the floors circling the foyer. Row after row of shelves, papers, and old leather books filled the space. "Edward took many of Scotland's records about that time, you mind."

"Edward the Second, king of England during Bannockburn," Angus clarified. "He wanted to destroy Scotland's history and culture."

"*Many* were never *recovered*." The librarian eyed Amy sternly, as if she herself bore responsibility. "But these are the years you're wanting." He handed them each a pair of gloves. "Wear the gloves, mind." His tone left no doubt that he was sure her fingers were as sticky as a three year old's. She glanced up at Angus, covered a smile, and pulled them on.

The old man took a folder full of papers from a shelf, rifling through with long, bony fingers, and mumbling to himself. He pulled two more files before he was satisfied, and left them, checking carefully they hadn't smuggled in food or drinks.

Amy glanced at Angus again.

"'Tis his way." His mouth twitched and his eyes danced. "He means no harm. Shall we?"

Amy pulled a notebook from her purse. She and Angus sat side by side, rustling through their piles, silent but for the scratch of their pencils, noting all they found. After some time, she sighed. "Court records about who took whose pig. A comment on the damp season. There's not much." She pushed aside a photocopy of a page from an old book.

"It takes time," Angus said. "And a great deal of patience." They returned to silent reading, shuffling photocopies and older originals. Some time later, he spoke again. "To Robert, King of Scots, salutations." He edged a modern copy of an ancient document toward her, and his voice rose in excitement. "There's some that's cut off, then he tells how they've been through Durham."

"Where's that?" Amy set her papers down.

"Northern England. They raided there." Angus leaned in, squinting for a moment, before reading again. "We've captured many treasures to finance our fight against our oppressors. My Lord Niel Cambel." Angus stopped, turned to her, and raised his eyebrows significantly. "*Of Glenmirril.*" He smiled at her gasp of breath and finished. "Has been invaluable in his courage and quick thinking. I tell you, Your Grace, he is a man after your own heart, of great compassion and mercy."

Angus scanned the letter silently, while Amy's nerves grew taut with excitement. Compassion and mercy sounded like Niall. "Is there more?"

Angus shook his head. "No. It mentions a Ronan and two Williams—at least, I think it's two—and tells of their plans to head home." He handed the piece to her. She typed it, word for word, into her laptop, along with his summarized translation. It wasn't much. But then, her heart leapt—for it was everything! She checked the date. September, 1314. Niall had survived Bannockburn, despite a *hidwys wound,* and gone with the Black Douglas! She could trace a man like Douglas, and maybe learn more of Niall's fate.

Angus was scanning the next sheet. Amy leaned close. The scent of his soap caught her attention. She re-focused on the document he studied. "You can read that?" she asked.

"Minimally." A smile spread across his face, his eyes locked on the paper. "I picked up a bit of this and that, working on James' palace."

"What are you smiling at?"

He raised his head, meeting her eyes. He looked pleased with himself. "How much would it be worth to you to know?"

She laughed. "Not fair! You offered to help, and now you're withholding information."

"Ah, but this is very good information." His eyes twinkled.

"I'll buy lunch," Amy offered.

His smile grew. "This information is worth far more than lunch."

"Really?" Her eyes widened. Her heart fluttered. "Dinner?"

"I'll hold you to it." He grinned, tapping the parchment. "It seems your Niall was knighted by Bruce himself."

"*What?*" She leaned closer, scanning the words for any she recognized. She wanted to cheer for the man she'd known and half-loved, just months ago. And it left a glow, a bold streak of confidence she'd lost with Shawn, that a man who could earn knighthood from one of history's greats had felt something for her. Her smile grew so broad her face hurt. "He deserved it." She stopped herself saying, *He was kind.*

"I'm sure he did." Angus looked askance at her. "You speak as if you knew him."

Amy shook her head quickly. "Don't be ridiculous." Her heart gave a hard thump, and she bowed her head over the papers.

Angus cleared his throat. "We've only the few more things here. Then let's go celebrate his good news with a nice lunch."

They worked through the last documents, Amy with excitement over what they'd found. At the same time, with a lunch, just the two of them, it began to niggle at her that she should mention to Angus the little issue of pregnancy. But it wasn't as if he had any interest in her. He might take it wrong. By two, they'd covered everything, with no more mention of Niall. At lunch, she told herself, she'd just casually mention that she was pregnant.

"Well isn't that interesting?" Angus murmured.

"What?" Amy leaned close, but the ancient script told her nothing.

Angus slapped his notebook shut. "Lunch, aye?"

"Did you find something?" She reached for the notebook.

He snatched it back, holding it out of her reach, grinning. "Aye, I found I'm verra hungry."

Creagsmalan Castle, 1314

The festivities lasted for days, with the minstrels playing for dances, dinner entertainment, and in sunny courtyards on clear mornings. Niall found Christina's eyes on him more times than could be accounted for by chance. Though he loved playing, musicians were not men of stature, as in Shawn's day. They were servants. A lady would no more take note of a musician than of a baker. He thought uneasily of the messengers sent to Duncan. But it was impossible that Christina should recognize him.

Between rehearsals and performances, Niall wandered the castle, as much as he dared, talking to servants, and listening for bits of conversation that might prove useful. He heard a rumble of deep voices talking about repairs to the galleys. The men stopped when Niall rounded the corner, staring at him sullenly. It wasn't enough. Any man with half a brain kept his ships in order, with or without plans for war.

After playing for dinner, Niall wandered to the dim kitchens, and did his best impression of Shawn, flirting with the maids there. He quickly picked out Bessie, a slender girl, younger than Christina by several years, her dark hair tucked into a kerchief, safe from the flames roaring in the large hearth. She answered his questions in monosyllables, her eyes on her work. She looked to have been bonny once, but her face carried the mark of fear, lining it with worry all wrong for one so young. Regardless of who was safer, he was sure he'd get no information from her, even if she did know anything.

To the other girl, Ellen, several years' Bessie's senior, he hinted, "Things will settle down when the master takes his men away, no?"

"Oh, aye, one hopes." She looked him up and down, leaving no doubt she approved of his height, broad shoulders, and golden-blonde hair.

Buoyed by her appreciation, a smile spread under his drooping blonde mustache. It was easy to see why Shawn liked this sort of thing! "You'll be having plenty of free time, then, with less work."

"Oh, aye, there's always work to be done, sure." She was none so forthcoming as Joan, but downright talkative compared to Bessie. "But I could find time to get away even now."

His heart kicked up a beat as he took her meaning. "Faolan says the gardens are quite lovely. Would you want to show me?"

She studied his cropped golden hair, and smiled broadly. "Oh, aye, 'twould be lovely indeed. I'll be through here soon enough."

Taking his leave, he threaded through the dark hall, rising steadily back to the surface. He found the walled garden, quiet in the night, and paced among the flowering bushes and bowers, hands clenched in prayer, wary of where he was going. He'd charmed women in London with mere words. But he was pressing for specific information this time, alone, in a place of mortal danger. The lives of men and the survival of a nation outweighed false words, but he still didn't care for what he was about to do.

"Fionn?" The soft voice caressed his ear.

He spun, startled, and was immediately taken aback by her fair face. Moonlight shone on her thick, long curls, and cut a swath of silver along her cheek. She was much prettier, here in the garden, than he'd noticed in the kitchens lit by roaring fires. He swallowed. He was here to get information.

Clearing his throat, he led her to a bench, beating back his conscience.

He held her hand, thought of Allene, and spoke softly. "My Lady, you've captured my heart. I believe one could sooner dry up the sea than stop me loving you."

"You're having me on." She smiled up at him. "Is that not a song they sing in the north?"

"Aye, you've caught me." Niall grinned, while his mind scrambled to recover. He hadn't expected her to recognize the words. He spoke as he thought Shawn might, lowering his voice. "'Tis only that your lovely eyes addled my mind and made true poetry fly from my tongue, for how could a thought stay in a man's head in the presence of such beauty?" He hated himself and gloated all at once. Shawn could hardly have done better!

Allene would have kicked him good and hard. Or thrown a bucket of cold water on him. *That'll cool you down*, he could hear her saying. He smiled. Ellen dimpled, thinking it was for her. The night breeze rustled the bushes behind them; it was cool enough to give him an excuse to remove his cloak and drape it around her shoulders. He left his arm there. She laid her head on his shoulder.

Shawn would have been proud.

Niall himself felt small and mean. But Bruce must know what Duncan MacDougall planned. He swallowed his distaste for his methods. "'Tis a job, preparing for Milord's departure."

"Aye, we'll be drying beef and baking bannocks, day and night. Two thousand men, off to re-take Man, with his kin John of Lorn."

Niall's heart jumped. Bruce held the Isle of Man. This was what he needed, real evidence, at last, of MacDougall's plans. He forced his voice to casual interest. "Is His Lordship taking on men?"

"Aye, Fionn." She laughed, gazing up at him. Her eyes shone. "He's great need of a piper. Sure ye'll enchant his enemies."

"Sure my music can inspire Milord's men. The truth is," he confessed, "I've swung a sword in my day, and miss it. When does he leave? Might I yet sign on?"

"Time aplenty," she assured him. "Not till winter."

"Winter is a broad swath of time."

She shrugged. "'Tis neither here nor there." She lifted her face to him. The moonlight carved her features in ivory. She was bonny, out of the hot kitchens, with her hair flowing free—and waiting. His insides lurched. He'd managed not to be unfaithful to Allene in his prior attempts at charming information from women. But then, he'd never been alone inside the enemy's castle, pretending to be someone else.

And he'd never found those women attractive.

She touched his cheek, and spoke playfully. "Surely ye didn't ask me here to speak of war."

Options chased through his head in swift succession. His heart pounded a painful staccato, thinking of Allene. But there was no fury like a woman scorned, and a furious woman could mean the end of his days here on earth. He might never see Allene again.

Ellen pulled back, frowning. "Fionn?"

Wanting or not wanting had no bearing. He lowered his lips to hers. She was soft and willing, melting into his arms, her head upturned, her eyes closed, and her body warm against his. His pulse went double time as his hand sank into her thick hair.

Then again, if Joan heard of this, she'd be equally furious. And he liked kissing Ellen all too much. He hated discovering he could be so faithless. Maybe it was enough that Ellen wouldn't be furious. He pulled back. "I'd not take advantage. What would your da say?"

Ellen smiled, a sultry curve of her lips in the dark. "'Tis but a kiss. I'll keep quiet, if ye do. My da will never know."

"How quiet will ye keep?" He stalled, seeking a way out, wishing he had his crucifix. "If ye tell one person, the whole town is like to know by dawn." Meaning, Joan.

"I'll tell no one." She tilted her head. "D' ye not wish to kiss me?"

Then again, he'd be safe from Joan's fury once he got out of the castle. "Verra much." It was easy to say with half-lowered eyes, because it was true. Everything in him wanted her. She was attractive and soft, and kissing her turned his insides warm. She would mistake his husky whisper of guilt for one of desire. He swallowed his loathing at betraying Allene, and kissed her some more. MacDougall and Lame John would attack the Isle of Man. Niall must survive to tell Bruce. And to get back to Allene.

Edinburgh, Present

Angus took Amy to a small pub brimming with a lively lunch crowd of businessmen and tourists, and the rich, warm smells of meat, potatoes, and fish. "My treat," Angus insisted. "The fish pie is the best. Or maybe you'd like haggis?"

"I'd love haggis," Amy said. "I had it the first night the orchestra got here. Like meatloaf, only better."

"I'll not remind you what's in it." He laid down the menu.

She grinned. "I appreciate that. Now. What was so interesting?"

After he'd placed the order, he reached for her notebook. "First, let's see your notes. Sometimes when you read through again, connections jump out." He flipped through the book, paused at a page, and looked up, eyes wide.

"What?" Amy reached for the notebook.

He turned it, revealing her sketch of Peter bowed over his violin.

"Oh, that," she said.

"*Oh, that?*" He raised his eyebrows. "You've quite the gift."

Amy studied it, critically. "I guess it's okay." The pencil strokes were fluid and smooth, moving the shading subtly from light to dark. She'd caught the shadow on his sleeve and face, half lit by a spotlight. "Most people could do that, though."

Shawn had never actually criticized her drawing; only glanced, grunted acknowledgment, and turned the conversation to other things. His silence spoke volumes. Her work was no good. And he was too nice to say so.

Angus was scratching away in the notebook.

She leaned forward. "What are you doing?"

He held it up, showing a stick figure gripping a bulbous, out-of-proportion stringed instrument jammed up against what might be its nose. Rays poured from the spotlight in straight lines, like a kindergartener's sun, smacking the unfortunate stick figure in the head. "You're right." He beamed. "Mine is just as good."

Amy burst out laughing. "Really. You're joking."

He became serious, studying his work. "Yes, I am. Usually, my drawing is much worse, but you inspired me to greatness."

She bit her lip, trying not to laugh again. "Really," she insisted.

"Really." He shook his head sadly. "That's about the best I can do. D' you not recognize your own talent?"

Amy blinked down at her hands. Shawn's opinion shamed her. And it angered her, to see how he'd twisted her views—about reality, relationships, even herself. While practicing the previous week, she'd remembered what it was to like the sound of her own violin. She'd attended Juilliard—on a full scholarship. She'd won her first audition for a professional symphony. Peter had already hinted she would be concert mistress when he retired. Yet she doubted herself. She heard only Shawn's voice. *What was up with your playing tonight? A little off?*

Angus turned to another page in the notebook. A colt danced in a field with pine trees in the background.

"I haven't seen that in years," she murmured, touching the sheet. "This was with the things my mother sent over. I hadn't even looked." Even in charcoal, the morning dew twinkled on each blade of grass. She'd drawn it the weekend she and Shawn had helped his mother move into her new house. They'd wandered on a long, early morning walk, down a dirt road, to a field. Shawn had been perfect that day, that whole weekend—the man she kept believing was the real Shawn.

It never would have changed, she realized, because of those moments, and knew she still cherished a fantasy that the man who left the apology would have made it back to her, that they would have lived an endless life of morning walks and perfect weekends. Maybe he would even have looked at her drawings with admiration, as Angus did. She gave her head a sharp shake. It was foolish to put the dead on a pedestal. The living could never achieve the perfection of a fantasy.

"'Tis beautiful," Angus said.

She became aware of their fingers touching at the edge of the pad, and pulled her hand away. His dark eyes flickered to hers, boring into her soul, and returned to the notebook. He flipped the page. She let her breath out slowly, shocked at the flutter that shivered through her when their eyes met.

Angus cleared his throat. "Two horses shod; dispute between cartwright and blacksmith heard by William Hayes." He scanned the rest silently, before looking up in triumph. "Not much here!"

She pulled back. It stung of Shawn's criticisms. "You did say any little bit might fit with something we find later." Her words, *we* and *later,* jumped out at her. She hoped he didn't notice them, or the defensive tone that crept into her voice.

"I meant no criticism," Angus said hastily. "Only that I've a surprise!" He handed her his own small notebook. His eyes danced with excitement. "The physician's records from Stirling Castle, June and July of 1314."

The significance of the dates struck her. Her eyes widened. "That would be...." She stopped. It would be not only when Niall had been at Stirling, but when the dead and wounded had been carried off the battlefield. There was no way to ask if the records might, somehow, concern Shawn Kleiner, twenty-first century musician.

"Yes." He grinned. "When Niall was there."

She drew in a slow breath. Her words came out little more than a whisper. "You didn't...find a mention of him...did you?" She looked up at the sudden, warm, smell of haggis.

The waitress appeared, laughing over her shoulder and calling back to someone still in the kitchen. Balancing a heavy tray, she leaned over the table to set fish pie and a Guinness before Angus. Amy smiled, remembering the waitress at the hotel, pushing up against Niall, and the look on Niall's face.

"What's so funny?" Angus smiled back.

"Nothing." It was Niall's shock at such brazenness, at what Shawn would have loved, that made it funny. She could hardly explain.

The woman set Amy's haggis in front of her with a pleasant, "Enjoy your meal, then! I'll be right back with coffee!"

"What did you find?" Amy leaned forward.

"Read it." Angus indicated the notebook with a nod of his head.

She read, scanning the words a second, and a third time, before lifting her eyes to his. Her insides flipped and flopped, remembering each detail of sitting beside Niall at the computer for hours on end, his arm around her on the train, his shirt and trews smelling of heather, his chestnut hair bound back with a leather thong, and his gentle bass voice telling her about life in medieval Glenmirril.

"Seems our Niall's a bit of a mystery man." Angus leaned forward, his eyes alight with excitement.

Amy cocked her head, the steaming haggis forgotten. "It makes no sense. It says Niall Campbell from Glenmirril?"

"Aye, whoever wrote the records was quite clear on that."

Excitement grew in her. "I think this joust is mentioned in the books in my house! But not about the physician being called." She read it again, her finger running under as if to verify, then raised her eyes to Angus. "So first he gets knocked out cold and has to be carried off the field. According to the professor's book—if this is the same incident—he immediately sweeps out of his tent waving and blowing kisses to the ladies." *You are just like Shawn,* she'd said to him on the train. Maybe they were more alike than she'd realized.

"He's fine at dinner," Angus continued. "Chatting up lasses and playing his harp. Malcolm MacDonald—there's a song about him."

"There is?"

"Old MacDonald."

Amy groaned. "I thought we were being serious here."

"Aye, verra. Old Malcolm insists the physician must bleed Niall, though he's quite healthy at dinner. When the physician appears at the chambers, Niall himself answers, the picture of health, and says all is well and his services are not needed."

The smell of haggis drifted, tantalizing, to Amy's senses. She glanced down, thought of Niall praying before meals, and, even as she said an internal thanks, took a forkful.

"Good?" Angus asked.

"The best." Amy savored the taste.

"So what d' you think that was all about?"

"Well, it *is* strange," Amy said. "But you said records can get corrupted.

Could there be a mistake in the way it's been handed down?"

"This was one of the few originals from that time."

"A mistake in reading or translation?"

"I'm familiar enough with medieval English." He paused, blinked at his meal as if suddenly realizing it was there, and took a healthy bite.

"Maybe the Laird was just flat out wrong."

"Malcolm MacDonald was no fool." Angus stabbed at his fish pie. "Glenmirril's history says he was wise and level-headed, well-respected. Yet he insists a physician come for a perfectly healthy man?"

"Maybe the physician got it wrong," Amy suggested. "Maybe, with a battle just over, and lots of injured men, he was being pulled in ten different directions. I mean, there can't have been a lot of physicians in those days, right? Maybe someone else needed bleeding. He went to the wrong door, wondering why a healthy man needed bleeding, and sure enough, because he was wrong to begin with, a healthy Niall Campbell opens the door and says he's fine."

"This was weeks after Bannockburn." Angus washed down his pie with a swallow of frothing Guinness. "Things would have settled down by then."

Amy smiled. "You've got yourself a mustache."

Angus laughed self-consciously and wiped it away with a napkin. "And," he said, "I'd think he'd not make a mistake about Niall, for that's not the first thing he had to say about him."

"What else?" She leaned forward, every muscle taut.

The waitress appeared with coffee, smiling brightly. "There ye are, then. How's the haggis?"

"Great." Her insides churned at the delay, desperate to know what history said about Niall. "Thanks." Her feelings jumped like a drunken bow careening off staccatos, thinking of him, worrying about him, hoping Angus didn't see it in her face. But what she felt for Niall wasn't real, she reminded herself. She'd barely known him, and everything she'd felt for him was mixed up with having believed he was Shawn. Still, what she'd loved in him was the good she'd seen in Shawn—strength, tenderness, determination, love. That love was ultimately for Allene, and that fidelity was appealing.

"Amy?" Angus asked. "Would you like more cream and sugar?"

The waitress stared at her, waiting for an answer.

"Oh, yes, I'm sorry." Amy laughed, releasing the tension that had risen, thinking of Niall and her constant need to be on guard against saying the wrong thing. She lifted her fork. "What else did he say about Niall?"

"He was cut nearly in half at Bannockburn."

"No, that was...." Her fork clattered to the plate. She stopped, feeling the same blow to her gut she'd felt at the unexplained women's names in Shawn's cell phone. Something didn't fit.

"No need to panic," said Angus, and she became aware of the heightened pitch of her voice. "It was seven hundred years ago."

The sword slashed across her mind, clear as a big screen movie, swiping across Shawn's midsection. She felt sick. But Angus was talking about Niall. Her hands flew under the table, her right hand tightening around the Bruce's ring. "How?" It was impossible they'd both received such similar injuries. Her mind reeled. It must be the *hydwys wound* to which the book referred.

"The physician didn't say, except they didn't expect him to live, but sewed him together, all the same, at the Laird's insistence."

Amy covered her mouth with her hands, her elbows resting on the table, horrified at the thought of such an injury to Niall. In her mind, he was alive; healthy and strong as he had been behind the theater fighting Jimmy; on the train; and heading into the mountains, barely three months ago. "But he was jousting in July. And fighting with Douglas in August. Wouldn't an injury like that kill him or at least permanently cripple him?"

"More remarkable than jousting a month later, he was fine the day after Bannockburn, out riding, preparing to leave for London with Lamberton."

Amy shook her head. "That's not possible. The physician's report must be wrong." The answer came to her in a flash. The man must have treated Shawn on the battlefield, and later, seeing Niall, thought he'd witnessed a miracle recovery. She sighed in relief for Niall.

Angus shrugged. "It seems unlikely."

"Yes. Well." It was likely enough, knowing there were two men who looked alike. But she couldn't tell him that. She took a bite of her dinner. With thoughts of Niall swirling in her mind, of Barbour's wild reports of his accomplishments, jousting, battle injuries, fighting with James Douglas, and earning knighthood, she barely tasted her meal. The thought of Shawn being stitched together with the crude supplies of medieval Scotland made her feel ill. A quick death under a sword had been bad enough to contemplate. Imagining the drawn-out suffering of their attempts to save him was far worse.

"An arrow in the arse, cut in half at Bannockburn, and knocked out in jousting," Angus mused. "Let us hope the next year is better for poor Niall."

Amy took a deep breath, steadying her nerves. The up to the minute news of seven hundred years ago was turning today into a roller coaster ride she hadn't expected.

"You're looking verra strained." Angus laid down his fork. "How much time are you spending on this research?"

She looked up. "Honestly? Between the library and internet, I pretty much live in 1314."

He poked at his fish pie, looking down and back up. "The Highland Games are being held in Pitlochry in a week and seven hundred years, if you'd like to join me. It might do you good to visit the twenty-first century. It's not an altogether bad place." He spoke gently, a glimmer of humor in his eye.

It brought a smile to her face. "So I've heard. I did promise my dad I'd get to some Highland Games and send him pictures."

"Next Friday, then?"

She hesitated. She didn't even know where Pitlochry was.

"I could take you from there right back to the fourteenth century, if it would make you feel better."

"Really?" She tried to guess what he meant.

"We can leave the games early and go on to Creagsmalan in the west. It's got a great archives, too. You might learn more there."

More archives—it was too tempting to pass up. And Angus was right. She needed a break from Shawn and Niall. She found herself nodding, even as she wondered what she'd just agreed to.

A faint swirl of nausea rose in her stomach, and she remembered she'd never gotten around to mentioning the little matter of pregnancy.

Chapter Nine

Northumbria, England, 1314

Under cover of trees, atop a dark ridge surrounded by hundreds of silent, shadowy warriors, Shawn sat uneasily astride his garron. It tossed its restless head, eager for action. Shawn's heart pulsed in his throat.

Beside him, Douglas gave a short, sharp jerk on his reins, and his black stallion reared suddenly against gray clouds frosting a full moon. It let out an angry whinny, lips pulled back from massive teeth. Sweat glistened on its flanks, picked out in detail by the silver glow. "A Douglas!" Atop the beast, Douglas roared his war cry and thrust a blazing torch into the sky. All along the ridge, the cry of "Douglas! Douglas!" echoed back, and answering flames shot to life. The horse pawed the sky, and landed back on earth with a jarring thud.

"Five minutes, Campbell," Douglas barked. A man shouted in the town below. The thin wail of a child carried across the night air. Douglas kicked his mount and leaned into its neck, baring his teeth. All along the ridge, Scotsmen burst from the woods, thundering down the slope. The first torches reached the fields. Trails of fire streaked behind each rider. People ran from bothies, women and children screaming, men flinging up arms against the thundering garrons. Cries of "Douglas, Douglas!" carried up the slope. Douglas charged the gates of the town, sending the lone guard fleeing.

Around Shawn, Niall's men waited under the dark trees. Shawn sat his mount, trying to hide the burn in his thighs from two days' hard riding. He patted the animal uneasily, still unsure what it was Amy liked so much about horses. He counted the minutes, trying to still his thundering heart, shocked at the primeval adrenaline screaming through his own blood, trying to hold himself back. "What do your sisters do back at Glenmirril?" he asked Lachlan. Anything to pass time; just like waiting backstage for his entrance.

"Sew, tend the garden, help the midwife."

"You miss them?"

"Aye, and I miss Margaret."

"Is that your...betrothed?"

Lachlan smiled, his gaze drifting far away. "Aye." The one soft word, breathed out on a sigh, held a world of memories and hopes. Shawn turned away, feeling all he'd thrown away with Amy.

"Now?" asked Lachlan. His gray hobbin skipped a pace to the side, eager for action.

"A minute yet."

"Patience, Lachlan," spoke Will, the older man who had been in Hugh's camp. "There's time enough afore ye for this business."

"Straight for the kirk," Shawn reminded them. He was shocked Douglas had picked Niall, of all men, to deal with the church. "Naught is our concern, but the church's treasure." He couldn't believe he was going to raid a church. Not that he'd been asked his opinion. James Douglas had ordered. But his father, though not yet born, would surely be turning in his grave if he could.

His son—raiding a church! It must be done, Shawn reminded himself, if the Scots were to finance the war that would win peace.

The minutes counted, he rose suddenly in his stirrups. He managed to disguise the scream of pain ripping through his thighs as a war cry. "Douglas! Douglas!" He dropped back, trying to remember all Niall had taught him as the hobbin hurtled down the hill, jolting his every aching muscle. He leaned low, clinging for dear life, his hand wrapped in the mane while men and ponies swarmed alongside him, thundering toward the town. "Douglas! Douglas!" echoed before and behind and on every side. Townsfolk ran. Young girls with long hair and ghostly white nightdresses screamed. Clouds scudded across the sky, freeing the full moon's bright silver light over the macabre scene. Fires crackled and roared, children cried, Scots marauded everywhere, grabbing food, prodding cattle, taking treasures, rings, gold.

Shawn and his men—Niall's men—pounded through the city gates, down the cobbled main street, swinging knives at the few men brave enough to try to stop them. Hair streamed out behind them, tartans flapped in the wild night ride. Hobbins' hooves rolled like snare drums down cobble stones, toward the church with its huge arched door and spire reaching to Heaven for God's mercy. The ponies skidded to a halt, with a sick scraping of hooves on stone. Sweat and horseflesh stung Shawn's nose. Adrenaline drove him mindlessly. He threw himself from his horse, forgetting the pain in his thighs and stormed up the church stairs.

A frail old man in white robes raised his arms, barring the large wooden doors. "Please, sir!" His voice shook as badly as his arms. "'Tis a house of God. Spare the house of God, My Lord."

"When Edward gives us peace, your house of God will see us no more!" Shawn bellowed. Two of his men lifted the little abbot under his arms and set him aside. Lachlan tore keys from his belt. "Where is the church's treasure?" Shawn demanded. "Hand it over, and no one gets hurt." His father would be weeping. Lachlan dropped the keys, a jarring weight, in Shawn's waiting hand, and a moment later, pushing the pleading abbot before him, they entered the church. "Where?" Shawn yelled.

His voice echoed in the church. It dwarfed him, the ceiling soaring high over his head in arched panels. Thick columns marched the length of the nave, holding up the mighty roof. Gold leaf covered everything. Outside, ponies whickered, men yelled, women screamed, children cried. Inside was only peace and the weeping old abbot.

"Spread out!" Shawn's roar shattered the peace. "Break every door! The cellar, the belfry, everywhere!" Amy would be scandalized. He pushed his face into the abbot's. "Do you know what England has done to my people!" Anger ripped through him, anger at himself for what he was doing, anger at the English for forcing him to do it. "Do you know Edward's men have crucified our priests on their own church doors and burned our churches!" He pushed himself nose to nose with the quivering abbot. "Do you understand, Sassenach! *They've nailed our priests to the doors and burned the church around them!*"

The abbot shook his head frantically. "The people of Durham have done naught to you, sir!"

"Would you like to die by crucifixion, fire, or both?" Shawn replied.

The abbot turned as white as his robes. "No, My Lord, please no, sir, 'twas none of my doing."

Around them, the sacking raged, men pounding, men breaking, men searching. Cries of, "Over here!" and "I've found summat!" yanked the old abbot's head this way and that.

"Durham will not pay for our priests being crucified," Shawn whispered. The old man trembled. "But it will pay for us to make war against Edward until he treats for peace as we asked. Mind it: *we* sued for peace. Edward refused. *Your Edward.* Thank him for us being here tonight."

A young Scot led his pony into the church, laughing.

"Out!" Shawn wheeled on the man. Niall would not tolerate such desecration. And suddenly, he knew why Douglas had chosen Niall of all men to pillage the church. It was not the cruel irony it appeared. "Get the gold and we'll leave," he told the abbot.

To a Scot swinging a sword at a gold column, he barked, "That is not what we came for, Owen! You were ordered to find the treasure. Go!" He looked around, satisfied his men were doing their duty, before searching for his second interest. What part of this structure might last seven hundred years? He knew nothing of Durham in his own time, and history had changed, anyway.

There! He grabbed his dirk, striding to the altar. The influence of his father and Niall was strong. He made the sign of the cross as he fell to his knee. Here, near the front, on the stair. He dug in with powerful strokes of arms hardened by training for war, over and over and over, till he had three slashes carved deep. They weren't as refined as the usual elongated S. They didn't even connect—just a long center line with shorter ones above on the left and below on the right. But they were long, and they were deep. Short of removing the whole stone floor, this mark would be here in seven hundred years.

He rose, staring at the three deep scars. *What am I doing? She's back in the States, painting a nursery and buying a crib with Rob.* He shoved the dirk in his belt, his mouth tight. It didn't matter. He'd left the mark everywhere he could; he'd continue to do so. It gave him hope. Of what he didn't know.

The abbot stared at him, trembling against the altar. "The gold," Shawn said. "Your life will be spared, which is more than Edward's men did for our priests. Thank God for that."

The abbot crossed himself, and scurried into the sacristy. Shawn yelled for a man to follow. The old cleric pulled back a rush mat, revealing a ring flush in the wooden floor. Shawn yanked it as Owen joined them. A section of the floor lifted, revealing piles of coins, chalices, rings, and plates. Owen knelt, shoving it all into a large burlap sack.

"Now the rest," Shawn said to the priest. "Or we burn the church."

Before the night was over, he'd collected ten large sacks from the church, both what the abbot revealed and what his men found. They stripped rings and a crucifix and a large gold bracelet from the abbot himself and from a woman who seemed to be his housekeeper, trembling at the back of one room, when they swarmed his living quarters.

Shawn made the sign of the cross, genuflecting before the Blessed Sacrament—the men would expect it of Niall—and ordered his men out of the church. "Pray for our priests who were crucified," he told the trembling abbot. "Pray Edward gives us the peace we asked for. Otherwise, this time next year, aye?"

They gathered the stolen goods, mounted their hobbins, and thundered back down the middle of the town. Around them, things had quieted. All over, Scots poured from houses, sporrans and burlap sacks full of coins, jewelry, food, all the things they needed to continue the fight till Edward promised peace. "Go," Shawn told Lachlan. "Take them back to the ridge. I'll be right there." He slowed, letting his pony plod through the streets.

What Englishmen remained in town did not bother him. They cast fearful glances, or angry grimaces—brave, in the situation, Shawn thought— and hurried on their way. With medieval houses towering in above him on either side of the street, and just a narrow alley of stars shining down from above, he clopped through, seeing the occasional Scot running with a bag of loot. He heard no more clashes of steel; only the scream now and again of a woman. His heart sped up, realizing what he was hearing. He slid from the pony, as one of the men under Edward Bruce's command stumbled from a doorway, yanking his breeks up. From inside came the soft sounds of crying.

Shawn swallowed.

"Not to yer liking, Altar Boy?"

Shawn said nothing. Thoughts paralyzed him. *We're the good guys,* immediately chased by, *Not in my worst moments would I have done that.*

The Scotsman stepped close, face to face, reeking of sweat. "Not man enough, eh, Niall laddie? I've heard ye spend more time on yer knees in church than with women."

Again, Shawn said nothing. The sound of the woman whimpering came through the door. His own ugly words about Aaron, a lifetime ago, echoed in his mind. *Not man enough.* He'd even used that witty line: *altar boy.*

The Scotsman grunted, shoving him in the chest. He reached inside the door for his bag of loot, and ambled down the street. "Ye're no better'n me, Laddie!" he shouted back over his shoulder. "Wasn't it you sacked the church! You defiled the house of God, me only a wench!"

Shawn stood still, the pony's reins limp in his hand. The feeling of unreality exploded around him. This had all happened seven centuries before his own birth. It was the stuff of history books. He shook himself. He didn't have the luxury of thinking about it.

Halfway down the street, the man turned and shouted, "Don't put on airs! She's there for the taking. Just Sassenach scum."

Gray frosted the eastern sky now, the first warning of dawn. Shawn had maybe thirty minutes before he had to be out, back up the ridge with his men. What happened in that house—it was normal here. He'd been a long time without. Temptation curled its claws around his shoulders, gripped his arms, whispered its raspy voice in his ear.

Just then, a woman ran around the corner, looking behind her. She slammed full into him, turning, gasping, crying, fear carved on her face. With a glance at the gray creeping higher on the horizon, he grabbed her arm, pushed her through the door.

She screamed.

He clamped his hand over her mouth, glancing back at the door. "Sh!" He knew what Niall would do. He knew what he must do to retain himself in this place. "Be quiet for your own sake!" He pushed the door shut behind him. Immediately, there came a pounding from the other side, and harsh Highland voices. Shawn let go of the girl, hoping she had the sense to keep quiet. She darted away. He eased the door open, throwing all his anger at the man outside, snapping, "Leave a man in peace!"

"Seen a lassie run this way?" the man at the door demanded.

"Do I look like your guard?" Shawn shoved him roughly in the chest. "Get back to the ridge with your commander."

The Scot looked stunned.

"Where's your loot!" Shawn pressed his advantage. "Is that pathetic little bag all you have? How is the Bruce supposed to fund this war if you spend your time chasing women—being outrun by a lass!" He spit venom into the street for good measure. "Instead of doing your job. We're here for money, not women!" He slammed the door in the man's face, and leaned against it, his heart thumping, hoping, praying, the man would leave.

You have no cause to ask God for anything!

Still, he made the sign of the cross. It seemed to work for Niall, and maybe God would take pity on him for Niall's sake. For the women's sake. He opened his eyes. The two women—the original occupant and the one he'd pulled in—huddled in a dark corner, clutching one another, watching him with eyes big enough to shine even in the dim interior of the house.

"I won't hurt you," he said. "I'm sorry."

They said nothing, only stared. A shudder escaped one of them.

"I'm sorry," he said again. "We only want peace from England."

One of the women spat at his feet.

He swallowed, and let himself out. On the hobbin, with a loud *hiya!* he charged out of the town, across the dark charred fields, and back to his men in the hills, trying to outrun it all. The pony was not fast enough.

Bannockburn, Present

The weather had lost its short stint of warmth by late September, and Amy found herself bundled in a warm sweater with a pair of thin gloves tucked in her purse, ready for her trip to the Games and museum with Angus. She'd braided her hair down her back. Her jeans still fit, and if she appeared any larger, sweaters would hide it for some time, still. She touched her stomach. It would be obvious soon enough. *It's not like people care so much anymore*, she thought, heading down the hall to the kitchen. It was a different world out there. "It's just not a different world in my head," she murmured to her unborn child.

Her phone rang while she cleaned her breakfast dishes. She hesitated, seeing Rob's name on the caller ID, but hit *talk*.

"Hey, what's up?" His voice came brightly from the phone.

He had no claim on her, she thought irritably, so she had no reason to feel such guilt. It was time to stop leaving pieces out. "You called just on time!" The false brightness ringing in her voice irritated her. "I'm heading out to see some Highland Games and a castle."

He jumped on it. "How are you getting there?"

"A friend is driving." She felt only a little guilt for toying with him, for making him ask. But it wasn't as if they'd ever gone out. She'd never so much as kissed him.

He resisted a full second longer than she would have guessed him capable. "What friend?"

"Remember the cop at the hospital when Ni—Shawn was brought in? Angus, who knew so much about Glenmirril? He's taking me."

"Doesn't the guy live up in Inverness?"

"He has a friend he visits down here. Sometimes I run into him." She hit the speaker button and set the phone on the counter.

"He's been to your house?"

Amy sighed, putting the bread in the breadbox. "No, Rob. We're not seeing each other or—anything—if that's what you're worried about. For that matter, neither are you and I. You have no reason to quiz me."

She could picture him swallowing and turning red, his eyes blinking hard. "I'm not quizzing you. I'm concerned, that's all."

She pushed the garbage can to the edge of the table with her toe, and used a cloth to brush crumbs off the table into it. "I know you better than that, Rob."

He said nothing while she ran hot water in the sink, throwing in a dash of electric green detergent. "Can you blame me?" he finally asked. "You're all alone. I don't want this guy taking advantage of you."

She plunged her arms into the soapy water. "How's he going to do that, Rob? It's not like I have money for him to con me out of. It's not like he'd want to sleep with me, pregnant with another man's child."

"Okay, that was blunt." Rob's voice echoed, loud and tinny. "Ouch."

"Well, what did you expect?" Amy snapped. "There are only so many ways to take advantage of women." She swished a cloth over the mug, saucer, plate, and fork, and put them on the drain board. "And I'm not that wealthy."

"You don't know men very well if you think he's not going to be attracted because—well, you know."

"Yeah, I know. Well, if it makes you feel better, he's shown absolutely no romantic interest in me."

"Just how much time have you spent with him?" Rob asked.

She told him, as she dried the last dish, and the list suddenly sounded long.

Rob cleared his throat. "Chances are you're the only *friend* he's driving down to see, Amy. Do you know how far Inverness is?"

"It was a long train ride, but by car...."

"Nearly two hundred miles, Amy! The guy has a full time job two hundred miles away and he's driving down every week. Maybe he's waiting because you just lost someone. But that's showing interest. I wouldn't drive that far every week to see my best friend."

Nervousness welled in Amy's stomach. He saw what Rose did. With the butter stowed in the refrigerator, she took the phone to the front room, checking that things were in place. She felt her face flush, and was glad Rob couldn't see it. "You're wrong, Rob. He hasn't done anything."

"Just wait," Rob said ominously. "It's coming. Have fun at the castle." His well-wishes sounded more like a petulant child than genuine regards. "I would have stayed there with you. I would have driven you."

Irritation boiled in her. "Rob, don't do this to yourself. He's a nice guy, and it's not like you had any claim on me. I have to go."

She ended the call, pressing the phone to her lips. Of course Angus wasn't just being friendly to a bereaved and potentially crazy American. It *was* a long drive and gas was expensive.

She liked him. She looked forward to his e-mails with jokes at the end. There had been two more, sending information and finalizing plans for the Games. The thought of kissing him had crept gently up on her last night, the way her cats did when she lay in bed in the dark, nudging and demanding attention. But it was too soon, too complicated, and hardly fair to Angus, with her obsession with tracking Niall, or her feelings for Shawn snapping back and forth like a pennant in every breeze.

Or being pregnant.

She wondered when her affections had become so...erratic. She'd once believed herself loyal and faithful. But her self-accusation was unfair, she told herself. She'd thought Niall was Shawn. With Rob, she'd been surprised another man was interested in her—Shawn had often enough hinted no one else would be—and foolishly allowed him to hug her. But she'd never felt anything for him. And Angus—he was just a friend. Looking forward to his e-mails meant nothing.

She sank to the stair, feeling drained, and wondering again if she *had* fallen in love with Niall, or if she only hoped to find something of Shawn through him. Her feelings weren't an open book even to herself, but swirling Scottish gloam, obscuring every intention. Some days, she grieved Shawn, holding tight to the image of him carving an apology, hour after hour through the cold night, in danger of Hugh catching him in the act of disfiguring the treasured Heart of the camp. Other times, anger raged through her. An apology carved on a Heart was the least he owed her.

The doorbell rang.

The sound jolted Amy. She jumped to her feet, pulling on the knit hat, a match to the white gloves from the pound store. They made a nice contrast to her complexion and black hair, and self consciousness washed over her. She'd known it when she bought them. But now, she didn't want to appear as if she'd gone out of her way to look good for him.

Her hand shook as she opened the door. Rob's words flooded over her, turning her giddy as she stared at Angus in the doorway, seeing him suddenly through Rob's eyes. Rob would be jealous. Angus was tall and broad, with ruddy cheeks and dark blue eyes, heavy lashes, and coarse black hair cropped short. "The ladies love the curls," he'd joked at the pub in Edinburgh. "But I don't care for being told how cute they are. Or adorable!" he'd warned with a mock glare.

He filled her doorway now. "You look bonnie!" He said it as a brother might, barely glancing at the Highland cardigan in hunter green, the soft leather knee-high boots like Niall's, or her black hair braided in a thick plait to her waist. A warm glow touched her cheeks, regardless of whether he meant it as a brother or otherwise. In the last year, Shawn had been miserly with compliments, and hearing them from any man pleased her, especially a man she'd just noticed was very pleasing himself.

Angus held out a large yellow envelope. "My mate who works at Stirling found these. Probably all the wrong centuries, but who knows."

"Thanks." Amy glanced inside at a thick sheaf of papers, before tucking the envelope in the backpack holding her laptop. "I packed lunch." She turned down the narrow hall toward the kitchen, forcibly removing her mind from his looks and piercing eyes.

"Ah now, I'd have taken you for lunch."

"Please," she called over her shoulder. "You've done so much for me. Let me do something for you."

"You already have," he said softly.

She spun. "What?"

His eyes widened. "Excuse me?"

"What did you say?" She waited in the kitchen doorway for his answer.

"I didn't say a word. Should I have?"

She bit her lip, smiling. "Don't try that on me. I'm a musician. My hearing is very good."

He smiled, too. A dimple appeared in one cheek.

She turned quickly for the cooler, her heart fluttering. Guilt crept into her throat, over Rob's hurt, over thinking about another man with Shawn so newly gone, over not telling Angus everything.

"Let me help you." He took one end, and they bumped down the narrow hall with it, smiling self-consciously at one another.

She had to tell him she was pregnant, if this was what Rob and Rose said it was. And she knew it was. She wondered she couldn't believe it till two people pointed it out. But then, she'd spent the past year with Shawn turning reality on its head, making her mistrust her own judgment. A flame of anger licked through the guilt and burned it away as they pushed the cooler into the back of his green mini. She'd enjoy the day, with another man. There was not a thing she could do for Shawn now.

But she had to tell Angus. He'd certainly lose interest when he knew she was pregnant. It wasn't fair, withholding that while he spent time and money on her, not knowing the whole truth. But his smile made her wish, vehemently, to continue withholding anything that might drive him away.

Creagsmalan, 1314

Faolan approached Niall in the cramped room the musicians shared. "Ye've been summoned to play for Milady." Faolan placed a hand on Niall's shoulder, unsmiling. "Take care, Fionn. MacDougall watches her like a hawk. Like the rest of us, he'll wonder why she summoned you alone."

The words sank like a stone in Niall's gut. He had what he needed. No one had looked twice at him. He'd even crossed paths with Duncan himself, leaving the kitchens the previous night. The Lord was a fool indeed, thinking a change of cloak and eye patch would fool anyone.

But he'd been summoned by the lady. He might anger MacDougall by ignoring her summons, as well as by accepting them. And maybe he'd find out more. Regardless, he had little choice. A musician did not ignore a lady.

He polished the recorder till the wood shone, and when he could no longer put off the inevitable, tucked it under his arm. A servant led him. Niall watched each twist and turn of the hall, memorizing.

It couldn't go wrong, he assured himself. Nobody at the castle knew him. Even if they had, the drooping mustache hid the shape of his jaw, and the golden hair and recorder both would keep anyone from thinking of Niall Campbell. He'd play for Christina and her ladies, he'd keep his eyes off her, and MacDougall would have no cause for anger.

The servant ushered him into a large antechamber. Tapestries hung over gray stonework. Warm sunlight poured through heavy leaded glass in large windows. On settees, women pushed dainty silver needles through altar linens. They bowed over their work, their long hair spilling in all shades from under coifs and caps, and the barbets under their chins gave them a faintly nunnish air. The unmarried girls were easy to spot for their bolder glances and bare heads.

Christina sat apart, in a shadowed corner, before an easel. She laid down her charcoal. "Come, Fionn of Bergen." Her voice was low and husky. Her eyes held his. Shadows fell across her cheek, but the smile reached her eyes this time, and glowed around her mouth. She held out a thin, white hand. He dropped to one knee and kissed her fingertips. "I hope you'll not be distressed to know my women find you fair and wish to hear you play." A tittering sounded behind hands. Heads bowed, two dozen blue eyes glancing up shyly from all around the linen.

He smiled, rose to his feet, and bowed low. "I'd be distressed to know otherwise. 'Tis my pleasure. Ballads, dances?"

"As you wish. Fionn." She emphasized the name. She lowered her eyes, picked up her charcoal, and continued sketching.

He lifted the recorder to his lips, playing a ballad, his nerves dancing. "Sing for us, Isobel," Christina said. A girl left her place to join Niall. She sang in sweet tones of her love for a shepherd boy, while Niall piped. Soon, one of the women rose and, curtsying to her lady, left the room. After another song, a servant knocked, summoning away a small group. They left with giggles and whispers. Isobel kept singing; Niall kept playing; Christina kept drawing. But as more women found excuses to leave, his fingers grew clammy on the smooth wood of the instrument.

To the last, Christina spoke. "My husband is on the hunt. See if he's sent word of his return. Tell the cooks when dinner must be served."

The woman looked from Niall to Christina. Isobel sang, Niall played, as if neither noticed the emptying room. "Now, Marjory," Christina said gently. "You'll be back quickly, aye?"

Marjory bobbed a curtsy. "Aye, Milady. Right quickly."

Niall's insides tumbled like an eel in a trap. She'd planned it. He hoped Duncan had been led far away by the fastest stag. She rose, her scarlet kirtle swishing over the mats covering the gray stone floor. "Come, Fionn. Isobel, keep singing, please."

Niall liked the woman all the more when he heard the word *please* come from her mouth. She led him to the window. Scotland glittered like a green jewel, fresh from a morning shower, beyond the leaded glass. Fine mist hung over the trees, several furlongs away, across a broad stretch of grass. In the sunlight, close up, he saw a yellow bruise along her cheek, that powder had covered while she sat in the shadows.

"I hear you're a great favorite with the lasses." Her melodic voice drew his attention from the bruise.

"I'm flattered if lasses think so," he replied cautiously.

"I've heard you're kind."

"I hope 'tis true." He spoke with his heart. He didn't feel kind to any of them, not to Joan, not to Ellen, and certainly not to Allene.

"I believe it is. I see it in your eyes." She lifted her face to him, her blue eyes startling in their depth. Isobel's song drifted over them, high and sweet. Christina lowered her voice. "I am selfish enough that did I not fear for your life, I would dare find out what it is to be kissed by a kind man, regardless of how many you've favored with such kindness."

He swallowed, wondering how much the statement was sad truth, how much reprimand, and how much warning. He changed the subject. "I've heard your husband is a noble warrior."

"Aye, and courageous. Especially against women." She looked him up and down. "And poorly armed minstrels. His father arrives tonight."

Niall's heart pounded. This time there was no doubt it was a warning. "What mean you, Milady?" She couldn't possibly know. He'd never met her.

Turning her back to Isobel, Christina slid a scrap of parchment onto the windowsill. She smiled, a kind and gentle smile, and took a seat, this time on the settee. The first woman returned, giggling and curtsying, taking her place at the altar linen beside Christina. Niall slid the parchment into a pocket. He resumed his spot, and began a slow pavane, while her women returned in twos and threes.

Christina bowed her head over the altar linen, her kirtle a blood-red jewel against the white. When the last of the women had returned, she raised her eyes, not quite to his. "I thank you, Fionn of Bergen. You are looking quite pale. If you are unwell, Faolan would excuse you from playing tonight. You must speak to him."

He took her meaning and her dismissal, and, with another kiss of the cool fingertips, and a bow to the women, let himself out.

Pitlochry, Scotland, Present

Angus recounted Scotland's history as they rode to the Highland Games. Some of it she knew, though there were multiple versions, centuries later, and some of it was new. Some was lore, and some fact. But all of it took her mind off Rob's dire warnings about Angus's intentions, and the car flashing around sharp bends on roads that didn't deserve to be called two-laned.

At regular intervals, they came upon cars speeding equally at them, and Angus swerved, a foot on the brakes, into one of the many pullouts, or waited while the on-coming car did so, and they passed safely.

"It's a wonder you don't have more fatalities here!" Amy gasped, after the third one.

Angus grinned, worrying her even more as his eyes came off the twisting road. "We've our share of that. But don't worry," he added, "I'm trained to drive like a mad man in the safest possible way."

She leaned back on the seat. She couldn't remember a man going so out of his way, ever, only for friendship. Rob was right. He did a lot of driving down from Inverness to visit 'a friend'—a friend who was never named, and with whom he couldn't possibly spend much time, considering he'd been with her. Yet he had done nothing beyond mere friendship.

Still, something inside her glowed.

Music came from the car speakers, the nasal sounds of an oboe carrying the melody in a woodwind ensemble. She opened her eyes to see him smiling at her. "You'll like this station. Classical."

"Would you be surprised to know I love playing it," she said, "but don't actually listen to it much?"

"Oh." His face fell. He reached for the buttons.

She touched his arm. "I like it. I just meant, don't feel we have to listen to classical because that's my job. I know not everyone loves it."

His smile returned. "I find it peaceful."

She smiled, and relaxed again. "Okay, as long as you really like it."

The woodwind ensemble ended. Strains of medieval music took its place. It was easy to imagine women bending like reeds over lutes, shawms, and harps, in elaborate headdresses with girdles sweeping in elegant points down from their waists, and long sleeves brushing the floor. She saw them, before a fireplace in Glenmirril's great hall where she had walked herself, but with rush mats on the floor and long wooden tables and dogs dashing among the servants' legs as Niall had described. And one of the women had red hair, a hot temper, and a laughing eye turned to Niall, eating at the head table with the lords, in a fine tunic with golden brown hair spilling over his shoulders.

She swallowed, and opened her eyes, pulling herself from the fourteenth century back to the twenty-first, to hills and trees flashing by, and one of Scotland's many rocky-bedded streams running alongside them, and now and again a garden of the ever-present shaggy Highland cattle.

"You'll not have seen Highland games before, then?" he asked. "The *maide leisg*, now there's an interesting story." And he gave her a history of the games, fascinating in its details.

"You were born to be a storyteller," she said. "You make it so interesting."

"Aye." He eased the car around a curve. "Because I find it interesting, myself. I'd like to be a tour guide at one of the castles one day and work with the children. You'll not tell the other cops, now, will you?" He flashed a smile that made her think she could cope with her grief over a man who had cheated on her.

Creagsmalan, 1314

In his chamber, Niall slid the note from his pocket. His heart pounded furiously; his mind scrambled to guess how Christina knew. The messengers had been sent to Duncan, and Christina herself had never laid eyes on him. He smoothed the parchment on his cot and read the spidery flow of words: *25 ships, 2,000 men, Isle of Man, leaving January. If you are the kind man I believe you to be, take Bessie. He is on the hunt. Leave immediately.*

Immediately was underlined. Three times.

It was exactly what he'd come for. But her request did nothing to calm his racing pulse. Men took mistresses. Did she think removing Bessie would solve that problem for her? It made his departure more difficult and significantly more dangerous, if rumors of Duncan's temper were credible. He believed they were. Like father, like son, and he suspected he'd seen the evidence, in the bruise on her cheek.

He surveyed the room. There was nothing to take but his cloak. It was a stall while he considered what he was about to do. There was nothing for it but to just go to the kitchens and get the girl. Christina had risked herself to give him all he needed, and asked a favor in return. A man of honor granted a lady's favor. After shredding the parchment and pushing the pieces deep in the ashes of the room's small grate, he donned his cloak, and left.

Bessie was heaving a pot onto the fire as he entered. Ellen's face lit up. His heart sank to his stomach, but he beamed. She threw her arms around him. He looked over her shoulder, motioning to Bessie, pleading with his eyes, mouthing, *Come with me.*

Ellen stepped back, rubbed her nose against his in glee, and whispered, "Will ye meet me in the garden after the feast?"

He grinned, motioning all the while to Bessie, who stared with wide eyes, and trembling mouth. And he told one of the few lies of his life. "Aye, Ellen, I cannot stay away from you." If all was as he pretended, if he had no prior commitments, it would be true enough. He stepped back, giving her a wink, and said, "I've been sent to fetch Bessie."

Bessie shrank into a corner, shaking her head.

"Please, Bessie," he urged. "You'll be glad, truly, lass."

"Oh, go on with ye, Bessie," Ellen chided. "Ye can trust Fionn. He's a good heart." She put a hand on the girl's shoulder, pushing her forward. Niall begged her, with silent eyes, to trust him and make this easy. Bessie moved reluctantly from the chamber, and Ellen took the moment to stretch on tiptoe and whisper in Niall's ear, "She used to be lively, before Milord took a fancy to her. Now he's always here, whisking her away. Milady plays the jealous wife, trying to protect the girl. Treat her kind."

"Is that the way of it?" Niall wanted to kiss Ellen, for her kind heart shining in her concern for Bessie. He did, his hands on either side of her face, his eyes locked on hers, his lips touching hers swiftly. "Everything I do...." He stopped, not knowing how to finish. "Trust me," he said, instead.

"Bring her back quickly," Ellen replied. "We've a great deal of work."

"Aye." He turned. Christina had said immediately. An ugly picture was forming of the real situation. Bessie waited in the hall, rigid. "Come along," he said. "Have you a cloak?"

She nodded. Her feet made no sound on the packed dirt floor. He gripped her hand, hurrying her along. He turned to speak to her. "Get it and meet me in the garden under the yew tree." He rounded a corner, and slammed into something hard.

It was Duncan MacDougall, dressed for the hunt.

Pitlochry, Scotland, Present

The games were all Angus had promised: sports, dancing, music, crafts, a fair, competitions and nationalistic bragging all rolled into one among the green hills of Pitlochry. Angus bought burgers from a white food wagon, and they ate while watching the hammer throw. Afterward, they strolled around the grassy meadow where the games took place, watching pipers perform for judges, Amy snapping dozens of pictures.

In a dim tent, she studied the intricate artwork adorning the blades of the *sgian dubhs*, and ran her fingertip over handles of horn and wood. The smell of leather sheaths permeated the booth. She touched one, much like the one Niall had carried. "*Sgian dubh?*" she asked. "What does it mean?"

"*Dubh* is black," Angus answered.

The craftsman offered her a dirk. "It can mean the actual color of the wood, or have a more metaphorical meaning." He raised shaggy white eyebrows. "You never knew who your enemies were, so you hid knives in your boot or under your arm when you left your other weapons at the door."

Niall's discomfort at being made to leave his dirk in his room came back to her.

"Come now, the massed pipe band is about to come in." Angus touched her shoulder, leading her out of the tent, and let his hand fall again. They walked side by side, past a stage with highland dancing in full swing to the sound of yet another piper. Amy stopped at the sight of black curls bobbing over a red checked dress.

"It's Sinead!" she said. "My violin student." Angus stopped beside her. They watched the girl's feet fly, her arms arced over her head gracefully, and her skirt bouncing to the sound of the pipes. The music ended, and the dancers filed off the stage.

"Hi, how are you?" Amy greeted Sinead as she passed. "You never told me you dance. You're very good."

The girl smiled her familiar gap-toothed smile. "Thank you. I practice two hours a day." The other dancers hurried by, laughing. Sinead darted after them.

Amy turned to Angus. "What a talented girl! She plays violin like a prodigy, too! Although she's usually friendlier."

Angus shrugged. "It takes a lot of energy, the dancing, and she's with her friends. The pipe band is coming. That's something you don't see every day in the States, aye?"

As the announcer called for attention, they found a seat among the crowds on the hill. Then came the blood-stirring beat of the bodhran and the skirling of dozens of pipes. Dozens of men marched in, backs straight, kilts swishing over bare knees and woolen socks. Their pipes reached for the sky, all of them singing together. The bass drummers swung their sticks, swirling them in circles above their heads and striking their drums again.

A smile spread across Amy's face. Angus grinned. "It's something, is it not? Can you imagine it in the days when it led men to war?"

Amy nodded. She could imagine many things, in the last three months, that she'd hardly thought of before.

"'Twould have been a bit after the time you're looking at," Angus said. "The Jacobites and Covenanters."

"I love it," she said in enthusiasm. Men with full gray beards and men younger than herself marched with a thousand years of pride stiffening their backs and lifting their chins. All around, the same pride glowed on thousands more faces. The band came to a stop, with the official competitors for the Highland games marching in their wake. A clan chief struck his shield, an eighteenth century cannon fired a noisy blast of smoke, the crowd cheered, and the games began.

"We can head on to the museum," Angus offered.

"Angus, this was a dirty trick!" She turned to him, her cheeks bright with excitement. "This is definitely a whole day sort of thing."

He grinned. "It could be." The pipe band marched off the field and the announcer called out the name of the first competitor as Angus added, "'Twas not so much a dirty trick as thinking you could use a wee break from the things weighing you down."

She tilted her head. Her right thumb crossed under her palm, feeling the gold of Bruce's ring. "Do I seem weighed down?" She'd found a peace in recent months she hadn't known with Shawn.

"How could you not be?" he asked. "Someone you love disappeared." A burly man in a red kilt and black t-shirt, with sturdy tennis shoes on his feet and long hair, strode to the field, waving.

Amy bowed her head, unsure what to say.

"I'm sorry," he murmured. "'Tis none of my business."

"It must seem crazy, in light of the circumstances, to be researching someone who lived seven hundred years ago."

The competitor heaved a massive log, at least twice his own height, up into his cupped hands so that it pointed straight to the sun.

"We all deal with grief in our own way." Angus seemed unconcerned by her choice of coping. "Is it because Shawn claimed to be him?" When she didn't answer, he said, "Whatever the reason, if it helps, why not?"

Amy rubbed her thumb along the bottom curve of the ring. The man on the field flexed his arms and heaved, sending the log flying. It landed with a bump and skip, and settled on the grass.

"Och, verra nice!" Angus thumped his big hands enthusiastically. All around them, applause broke out, and men cheered.

"It didn't go very far," Amy said, doubtfully.

"'Tis not the point of caber tossing. You want it to point at noon, see? Not to one side or the other." They watched as the man tossed the caber a second time, and his competitor a third, to applause and shouts from the crowd, before Angus turned to her and said, "I'll tell you what. Have you time for a weekend? I can stay the night with Mike, and we'll do the castle tomorrow. I'll take you for a nice dinner tonight to make it up."

Amy laughed. "There's nothing to make up. I'd love to spend the day here."

"And Creagsmalan tomorrow?"

She nodded, and settled in for a day of Highland Games, crowned with a dinner of beef pie at a noisy pub, forgetting Niall and Shawn for a few happy hours.

Creagsmalan, 1314

"My wife's favorite minstrel with my favorite little kitchen maid."

Duncan MacDougall stood before them, clothed in black leather armor. He was shorter than Niall by six inches, and slighter.

In a fair fight, Niall judged, he'd be fine. But a fight with the lord of the castle would not be fair. Guards would come. And Bessie shrank behind him, clinging to his hand behind his back with so much strength, he doubted he'd be able to shake her off even to protect her.

"Milord." Niall spoke calmly over the pounding of his heart. If only Duncan hadn't heard his last words. *Please, My Lord God, please.* He grabbed the first explanation that leapt to mind. "I was told to bring her to the upper kitchens."

"By whom?" In the underground hallway, torchlight flickered across Duncan's leather and glinted off the black sheen of his beard. His teeth and eyes flashed white in the gloom.

"Your wife, Milord." He hated himself for saying it, but Christina was the only one who could give him any excuse for his action. His heart pounded. Duncan was supposed to be on a hunt. He desperately hoped Christina had a quick wit, and that this would not result in more bruises for her. He took it as a good sign Duncan had not said anything about his plans to meet Bessie in the garden.

"We'll have a talk with her about that, aye?" Duncan replied. "Did my wife also tell you to hold the girl's hand?"

"She was scared in the dark, sir. I sought only to reassure her and encourage her to hurry." Behind his back, Niall tried to wiggle his hand out of Bessie's grip.

Duncan shoved Niall aside, grabbing Bessie's arm. "Did My Lady summon you to the upper kitchens?"

The girl's face went bone white in the torchlight. Her eyes grew twice as big. Sweat stood out on her forehead, glinting in the weak light. *Say aye,* Niall prayed. As if she heard his thoughts, she nodded mutely.

"What for, girl?"

Niall opened his mouth to speak. Duncan thumped a fist in his chest. "Is your name girl?" he roared. "I didn't speak to you, Minstrel Boy." He gave Bessie's arm a rough shake. "I'm waiting."

She opened her mouth, tried once, tried twice, and finally got the words out, her voice quivering. "I don't know, Milord. He only just came. He is sweet on Ellen, Milord." Niall could feel her trembling beside him, and suspected the few words were, for her, the equivalent of leaping raging rivers and facing armies.

Duncan looked from one to the other. His resemblance to his father was uncanny. "Come." He gripped a shoulder of each, pushing them through the narrow hall ahead of him, while Niall's mind raced. His only hope was if the man had not heard him tell Bessie to meet him in the garden.

West of Scotland, Present

They spent the early morning drive, through fertile fields and misty glens, trading stories. "Me da was a cop," Angus said. "It seemed the thing to do. Still, I love it and I'd miss it if I had to quit." He glanced at her. "D' you miss your orchestra?"

"A lot." She looked beyond the hills outside, to memories. "And I miss my cats, and my piano. Other than that, I could stay here forever. I love Edinburgh. It has some really nice antique stores."

"You like antiques?" He took his gaze briefly from the road.

"I always have." Amy gave a soft laugh. "At least, if you count from the age of three as always."

"Three?" he queried. "What makes a three year old love antiques?"

"It's when I met Rose, my violin teacher."

"She must be remarkable if you remember that far back."

"She is remarkable." Amy smiled. "She's coming back for another visit in a few days." She leaned back against her seat. "My first memory of her apartment is the smell of cinnamon and apples. But what I remember most, is when she played at my parents' Christmas party. She saw me on the stairs, and smiled and kept playing, and every once in awhile, she'd smile again."

Angus chuckled. "Was that so unusual it stands out? Your parents never looked at you and smiled?"

"My mother says I was difficult."

"When you were *three?*" The smile fled Angus's face.

"I suppose I was." Amy shrugged. "They were busy."

"Too busy to smile at their daughter," Angus mused. The car slowed as a shaggy Highland cow ambled onto the road, swinging its big head to study Amy, its nose almost touching her window. Sun glinted off its bronze coat, as bright as Shawn's hair when the sun hit it.

"It's not like they're bad people," Amy objected. Although the window was closed, she drew back from the long horns.

"Of course not." Angus grinned. "Just busy. They're harmless. The cows, I mean. Though I'm sure your mum and dad are, too."

The animal wandered in front of the car, forcing Angus to stop completely. Amy's breathing constricted. She should have chosen her words more carefully. She'd given a bad impression of her parents.

"What were they so busy with?" Angus asked.

"The usual. Meetings for my dad. Business trips. How long do these cows block the road?"

"As long as they like. Your mum?"

"Shopping. Nails. Hair." She leaned forward, watching with interest as the cow ambled another few feet up the road before tripping into the pasture on the other side.

"Verra important." Angus touched the gas, and the car moved again.

"She did a lot of charity work." Amy watched the shaggy red cow munching grass. It seemed mild enough. "She had to look respectable."

Angus shook his head with energy. "Oh, now, I'm not criticizing. I'm a wreck if I don't have my nails and hair just right."

"Stop it!" But Amy found herself laughing, her tension draining. "You are so criticizing. Really, she's a good person. She does a lot of charity work."

"A good person with great nails," Angus said. "And verra busy. No time to look at her child and smile."

"I shouldn't have said that." Amy gazed out the window.

"Why not, if it's the truth?"

"I didn't mean to make them look bad."

"Tell me about Miss Rose," Angus replied. "Cinnamon and apples."

"And lace." Amy was glad to leave the subject of her parents. "Maroon. Velvet. Old-fashioned portraits and sepia prints. A dozen violins hanging on the walls. It was a nineteenth century brownstone in New York City." To a child raised in a modern home on acreage, it was another world, and Miss Rose the fairy princess who presided over its treasures. "We had gingerbread and tea after my lessons. She served from a china teapot with red roses, in china cups."

"To a three year old?"

Amy laughed. "Yes, to a three year old. And later to a five year old, and a ten year old. I took lessons with her until I left for Juilliard."

"She taught you well."

"Yes." The word came out as a sigh. "Sometimes she took me out in the city, and we'd listen to the rhythms of cars and trains or horns honking, or foreign languages, and go back and write music based on those rhythms. Sometimes after my lesson, she'd take me to her rehearsals."

"Your mother didn't mind?"

"I guess not." The question gave Amy pause. "It's just the way it was."

"Your mother's nails must have taken a lot of doing," Angus said.

"You're not saying...?" Amy's heart pounded out a quick staccato. "My lessons were an hour long. Nail appointments...."

Angus shrugged. "I'm not saying anything. Only, it sounds as if you spent a lot of time with her." Before she could respond, he said, "So you like art, and antiques, and you went to Juilliard. You must have had plenty of boyfriends." His eyes slid off the road toward her.

She blushed. But she was grateful once again to leave the subject of her parents. "Not really." Rob's warning came back to her.

"How's that possible?" His eyes drifted over her face and the heavy braid hanging over her shoulder.

Amy shrugged. "I lived in a practice room. I only had one boyfriend before Shawn."

His name brought silence to the car.

The mini hummed past another rocky stream, that opened into a loch with another rocky shore. Amy cleared her throat. "You can ask, you know."

He stared straight ahead. "I figured you'd say when you're ready."

"I feel like a fraud," Amy said. "What do you know about him?"

Angus's hands tightened on the wheel. "You couldn't help but hear things. The hotel in Edinburgh, for one."

"That!" Amy rolled her eyes. "He outdid himself there. That kind of thing made the news." She stopped. There was no reason to tell the ugly details. Apart from Celine, it was nothing but unsubstantiated suspicions, anyway. She stared out the window at the hills flashing by. "It doesn't matter. He apologized. There's no reason to smear someone's name when they're gone, is there? Or when they've apologized."

Angus shook his head. "I guess not."

"But it isn't quite what everyone thinks. I broke up with him, before he was...." She stopped again. Nobody knew he'd been killed. "The night before he disappeared." She saw her mistake immediately. Angus believed Shawn had disappeared at the battle, after being alone in the wilderness for days beforehand. She raced on, giving him no chance to question the timing of the breakup. "I feel wrong getting all this sympathy. But I don't want to air dirty laundry. Know what I mean?"

"I do."

The car climbed higher into hills covered in the brown remains of heather. Her heart pulsed too quickly, and she cast him a sideways glance, hoping he wouldn't question when she'd broken up with Shawn. The loch trailed away into a river.

"Life doesn't hand us neat packages to work with, does it?" he asked.

She gave a short laugh, and sank back against her seat. He hadn't caught the discrepancy. "Understatement of the year." She gazed out the window at the river. Exhilarating high altitude freshness reached through the closed windows. "I thought when I met my first boyfriend it was all smooth sailing. I really thought, when I won the audition for the orchestra, that my life was set, no more worries."

He took his eyes off the narrow twisting road long enough to wink at her. "Aye, I was once young and foolish, too."

She laughed. "When Shawn showed up at my door and I saw that good side of him, I really believed the rest was show, and I thought I'd lucked out, and had it all—a great boyfriend, a great job. It was perfect for more than a year. Then he started...well, the things he did. Just a little at first, then more, and always showing me enough of the good side to keep me believing in him."

"And you still do," Angus pointed out. "You said he apologized. Such men apologize a thousand times. Why was this time any different?"

Amy twisted uncomfortably. "Circumstances," she evaded. "It was an apology he didn't have to make, under circumstances that—well, he took a serious chance." Her hands clenched over the Bruce's ring. "He had to have meant it to take a chance like that."

Once again, his eyes came off the road, studying her quizzically. A car roared around a bend, shooting straight toward them. Amy gasped. Angus slammed on the brakes and slid the mini neatly into a pullout. The other car flashed past. Angus stayed in the pullout. "I've just become The Police to you, haven't I?" he asked softly.

Creagsmalan, 1314

Christina sat demurely at her needlework, her needle flashing in and out of an angel's silver wing. Her eyes flickered calmly over Niall and back to her husband. Around her, the women bent their heads, not looking up. Caught in Duncan's other hand, bare of his hunting gloves, Bessie's head drooped. Her entire body leaned away from him, though she did not pull.

"Aye, My Lord," Christina acknowledged. "I sent for her to be brought to the upper kitchens. I've heard wonders of her skill, and thought 'twas time she had a better position. 'Tis no good for a young girl to be shut up in those dark kitchens underground all day."

Duncan glared at Bessie. "Girl, you're happy in the lower kitchens, aye?" She nodded, staring at the floor. Duncan shoved her toward the door. "Back to your work. I'll be down in a bit." Bessie stumbled, and, shaking, ran for the door. Duncan turned on Christina. "You'll leave the kitchen staff alone."

Christina licked her lips. "Yes, My Lord."

"I'll be back up to deal with you. Clear these women out."

"Yes, My Lord." She spoke calmly. But the color drained from her face.

"My Lord, 'twas none of her doing!" Niall spoke frantically, his heart pounding. Fear leapt to Christina's eyes. She gave a short shake of her head.

"You'll be quiet until spoken to, Minstrel Boy," Duncan roared, giving Niall a hard shake; then, with Niall in his iron grip, Duncan charged for the door, dragging him back through the labyrinth of stone hallways. Niall kept his head, over the thundering of his heart, replaying the route in his mind, matching it up to all he knew of the castle.

They were going back to the lower kitchens, he realized. Ellen would verify it was she in whom he was interested. He thanked God, noting the irony, that he'd broken his own moral code and kissed her.

Duncan dragged him into the hallway, the light from outside dying quickly as they moved deeper in and down the first dank flight of stairs. At the bottom, he pushed Niall up against the damp wall, hand on his throat. "My wife told you to meet the girl in the garden in her cloak?"

Niall swallowed. "Only that it was cold, sir." It was a poor answer.

"D' you take me for a fool!" Duncan roared. He shoved Niall off the wall, to the next flight of steps. Niall stumbled on the last stair, catching himself on a landing, and turned the corner, down the next flight. Duncan was surely going to ask Ellen; she would tell him they'd been in the garden, that he had no interest in Bessie. Duncan pushed him again, grabbed the back of his neck, and thrust him through the kitchen door. The kitchen girls paused in their work, eyes wide.

"Nobody leaves this kitchen with any wandering minstrels, d' you hear? Bessie, come with us." The girl came forward, every inch of her shaking. "You," Duncan bellowed at Ellen, "Tell Martainn he's needed in the dungeons."

Chapter Ten

Creagsmalan, Present

I've just become The Police to you.

Angus's words thundered in her ears.

He waited, watching her, for an answer.

"Yes." She gave the ring a sharp twist. The car hummed. "I mean, no." The thought flashed across her mind: Shawn was right. She imagined things. Angus *was* the police. Maybe he was only being friendly to get information about Shawn's disappearance. She shook her head, refusing to believe it.

"Amy?"

"I'm sorry. I hate speaking in riddles. There's nothing I hate more, after Shawn's stories. But you'd think I'm crazy."

"I'd never think that," Angus said.

Amy smiled ruefully. "There may come a day you're put to the test."

Angus's shoulders relaxed, and the tension in the car melted away. "'Twill be an easy test." Giving a quick grin, Angus shifted the car into gear and pulled back onto the road.

Amy relaxed against the seat. She would simply not talk about Shawn anymore, she decided. If Angus was showing attention to get information, he didn't deserve it. And if he really was interested in her, he didn't want to hear about Shawn, anyway. With the decision made, her mood and her worries lightened by the time they reached the castle.

♫

Creagsmalan proved to be a well-restored fourteenth century castle, clinging to Scotland's west coast. Its stark walls stretched high against the gray sky. As Angus and Amy climbed from the mini, the clouds above opened up with a drizzle, turning the castle's black walls shiny and slick.

"Iona's out this way, isn't it?" Amy asked, the realization hitting her. "How far is it?"

"Iona?" Angus's umbrella opened with a pop. He stared at her. She wondered if she'd said something wrong. Then his face relaxed in a grin. He beckoned her under the umbrella, and they crunched over the damp path of shell and stone to the castle. "Fifty miles. We'd have to take a ferry, cross Mull, and catch another ferry from Fionnphort. Are you interested in it?"

Amy shrugged. "No. Just curious. Creagsmalan is beautiful."

"Some call it the most romantic castle in Scotland." Angus flashed his Historic Scotland pass at the gate.

Amy couldn't resist poking fun at his pride. "I've noticed a number of castles are called 'the most romantic in Scotland.'"

"And it's true in every case." He spoke without irony as he ushered her along a dirt path turning muddy in the fall rain. To the west, the sea stretched out steely-gray under a heavy cloud of mist.

As they approached the heavy wooden doors of the gatehouse, Amy raised her eyes to the centuries-old etching deep in a stone at the top of the entry. "MacDougall. I know that name."

"If it's Niall Campbell you're after," said Angus, "the MacDougalls and MacDonalds of Glenmirril had a bit of bad blood between them. That's why I thought Creagsmalan might interest you."

Amy frowned. Niall's enemy lived here, near Iona. She wondered if she was seeing ghosts around every corner, or if there was, in fact, some obvious connection she was missing. But Shawn couldn't have known that within his first days there, to leave it carved on the rock.

Huddled under the umbrella together, they passed through the arch, to the inner close. The castle walls rose around them. "In fact," said Angus, "'twas MacDougall who shot Niall Campbell in the arse on one of the cattle raids between the two."

"Those were the MacDonalds' cattle," Amy said.

Angus cocked his head. "And where would you have read that?"

"I don't remember." Amy changed the subject. "Where to, first?" She looked around the courtyard, at the entrances into the towers at each corner of the castle. "You said these lead to the ramparts, private chambers, kitchens, and dungeons."

"And the wine cellars." But Angus was not so easily distracted. "Nobody knows whose they originally were, seven hundred years later."

In the drizzle, Amy tugged her hat down over her ears. "I just heard it somewhere. You think there could be something about Niall here?"

"'Twould be a stroke of luck, indeed. He's not likely ever to have been here, as he was their enemy. But it'll give you a clearer picture of the times and the people he knew." Angus seemed happy to search every corner of the castle in detail, reading every word on every display with her, although she guessed, with his passion, he knew it quite well already. Indeed, he stabbed a finger at a placard and said, "The younger MacDougall died before 1317."

"How do you know?" Amy asked.

"It happened at Glenmirril. I stumbled across it while I was looking for information to send you." He harrumphed. "They didn't do their research so well, unless it's a typo."

She studied him, trying to read his intentions even as he returned to reading placards.

He looked up from another display, pointing to the card. "There was more to the story. It had been a verra wet summer, or none of that would have happened." He straightened. "There's more upstairs." They explored the airy halls of the second and third floors, and large empty rooms that had once been chambers and antechambers. She dug her camera from her purse to click pictures out through stone apertures to impressionist-painting views of water and drizzly rocky hills. She ran her hand along the stone walls, letting every rough bit of the surface graze her fingertips, trying to feel the people who had lived here.

Maybe this had been the room of the very MacDougall who had shot Niall. It was easy to imagine him, in a white linen nightshirt in a giant four poster bed like Shawn had had at the hotel. Her mind filled in the details, down to the carving of the hunt scene on the footboard. His servant called him; he rolled over, shaking his wife's shoulder.

But no, he'd been cruel.

He'd no doubt been with a mistress, not his wife. It was easy to imagine

him roused from sleep, alerted to the disappearance of the cattle he himself
had stolen, throwing on his gear, yelling for his men, storming into the bailey
below calling for his horse. She peered out the window, down to the cobbled
courtyard. Had the rain drizzled that night, as it did now, full of ghostly mist
as Glenmirril had been, or had it been a clear, moonlit night? She wondered
if he'd known where he hit Niall; if he'd come back gloating. She touched the
walls, as if they might tell her what had been said here. No doubt they'd
spoken of Niall in these very rooms.

The pitter-patter of raindrops slowed and stilled outside, and a ray of
sunshine shot suddenly through the windows. "The chapel's the original
from the late 1200s," Angus said, cheerfully. "Come and see it."

They twisted down a flight of stairs and across the courtyard by the
stables, damp with the early drizzle. "'Tis not morning in Scotland without a
little rain," Angus said, as Amy skipped over a puddle.

They entered the chapel, deep and dark. Its center aisle stretched like a
runway toward a distant altar. Stone walls soared two stories high to a
restored roof. "Typical medieval English," Angus said. "It doesn't surprise
me, as the MacDougalls sided with England time and again."

"What's English about it?" Amy raised her camera to snap a picture.

"The length of the aisle. The way the transepts project." He pointed
with his umbrella as he spoke, to wings stretching perpendicular to the main
body of the church. "And the windows are tall and narrow." She raised her
camera to zoom in on one of the five stone casements high above, each
reaching to an elegant pointed arch. Light poured down.

"It's beautiful," she said. "A very stark beauty."

"'Twould have been something else again when MacDougall used it.
Religion meant a great deal in medieval times." He led her halfway down the
side aisle, past half a dozen side shrines set in recesses. "The chapel would
have been a work of art. Stained glass, gold, tapestries, vestments. Close
your eyes and imagine it."

She stopped between the pews and stone wall, doing so. His words
painted pictures to life behind her eyelids. The altar would have been under
the circular opening that gazed, empty-eyed, from above. A rose window
would have poured down jewel-colored shards of light, sparkling off a gold
chalice raised high in the priest's hands. She saw his gold-threaded
vestments, his face lifted in prayer; an altar cloth embroidered with grapes
and wheat and silver-winged angels. Men would chant from the choir, a
ghostly rise and fall of a *Gloria* or *Sanctus* echoing throughout the great
cathedral cavern. A whisper of voices brushed her ear, a low throaty woman's
voice, like the low register of a clarinet, musical and amused.

...respect the privacy of the chapel.

Her eyes flew open. Her heart raced. She peered at the dark walls, the
columns rising to the roof high above.

"This would have been the confessional." Angus indicated another deep
recess in the wall. "There'd have been dividers inside, walls and a door." He
stopped. "Are you aw' right? You look rather pale." He touched her arm.

She drew in a breath. There were no voices. "I'm fine. What would the
tapestries have been like?" Anything to take his mind off her, to keep him
from noticing the tremors running up and down her arms. She touched the
wall, pretending interest in what might have hung there. It helped stop the

faint trembling. She inspected the gray stones, cool under her fingertips, while he talked about tapestries, symbolism, purity, Christ, flowers. His words washed over her, barely heard.

Her eyes fell on an imperfection, visible even against the rough texture of the walls. She moved closer, kneeling and squinting. "Angus, look."

The story of the tapestry stopped. "What have you found?" He squatted beside her, studying the scratches. "Medieval graffiti," he announced. "Someone passed the time carving. In Linlithgow, you can still see where Margaret sat in the bower, carving by the hour."

Amy ran her finger over it, moving her head to let the light catch it at a different angle, until she was able to trace the shape. She frowned, tracing it again. She pulled out her camera, took pictures, and ripped a sheet of paper from her notebook, placing it over the marks and rubbing with a pencil. It showed clearly that the carving was exactly what she thought. The trembling resumed, and grew. She wished Rose were here already, to look at it, to give her some ideas.

"Just someone carving." Angus's dark eyebrows knit together.

The woman's throaty voice whispered, *And hang you instead.*

Amy's hand jolted off the wall. The notebook and pencil clattered to the floor. She shot to her feet, looking around, her breath coming in quick sharp jerks.

"Amy?" His voice rose in alarm. He leapt up, too, reaching for her.

She drew a deep breath. "I'm fine!" She gave a nervous laugh. It echoed in the empty church. "Is this place haunted?"

"Plenty of castles are." He spoke matter-of-factly.

She laughed. "I'm joking. It was just a draft. It's a nice chapel. It's great." She gathered up her notebook, the rubbing, and fallen pencil, with a last glance at the carving. "How about that picnic?" She resisted the urge to run from the woman's ghostly voice, and from the carving—a carving that could only mean Niall himself had been here.

Creagsmalan Castle, 1314

The kitchen girls paled. Ellen wrung her hands and sucked in her lips. "Oh, no, Milord, he was only...."

Duncan backhanded her.

She crumpled to the floor, hand to face. A whimper came from her lips. Niall strained forward, reaching for her. Duncan yanked him back, yelling for another girl to go. "Lead the way, girl," he bellowed at Bessie.

She did so, visibly shaking, taking them further down the dark hall, with Duncan's fingers digging into the back of Niall's neck the whole way. Niall considered taking on the man. It was too far to call for guards. He might have to kill Duncan outright. Several people would thank him.

"Go quietly," Duncan hissed in his ear, "and Christina will fare better."

Niall sucked in a breath. The sense of having his mind read ran like winter chill down his spine. All thought of fighting drained away. A guard was already on his way. He couldn't win this one.

They turned a dark corner into a darker hall, and stopped in front of a heavy wooden door with iron bars set at eye level. Duncan kicked it open, and shoved Niall inside. Niall stumbled, landing against the opposite wall.

The door closed, the lock clicked. Niall scrambled to his feet, searching the cell in the dim light filtering from the high grating.

In all things be grateful. The verse jumped into his mind, mocking him. He ran his hands along the walls. They were solid stone, no weaknesses, no gaps. He looked up to the bars set in the opposite wall. They were too high to reach, except with his fingertips. From the dark hall came the sound of another cell door slamming.

Niall paused. It seemed odd to lock up Bessie. He looked up again to the window. He could be grateful for light and air, if only a little. It could be worse. Duncan didn't know who he was. That would be far worse.

From down the hall, he heard Bessie. "No! No, Milord, please no."

He stooped instinctively for the knife in his boot. He glanced down at it, surprised. It was another thing to be grateful for. Duncan had always been rumored to be duller than a sword after battle. He had not even thought to look for weapons.

Niall went to the door, peering out, his heart hammering. Duncan was nowhere to be seen. But his voice could be heard, rumbling, and then sounds Niall didn't want to hear, punctuated by Bessie's cries.

It could be worse. He could be Bessie. He said *Ave* after *Ave* as he felt every inch of the door, searching for any weakness. There was none.

Creagsmalan Castle, Present

Angus retrieved a heavy blanket and the cooler from his mini. With an eye to the brightening skies, they carried it between them to the rocks overlooking the sea. Angus shook the blanket out, letting it fly up and land neatly over a mossy black rock spangled with lichen, and the patch of scrubby grass surrounding it. Amy spread out the lunch, her mind still reeling from the voice in the chapel, and spinning at the implications of the carving.

"Verra American." Angus helped her remove ham sandwiches and sodas from the cooler. "Not a bridie in sight."

"It's only fair." Amy handed him an apple. "You've shown me so much of Scottish culture. Although Cokes and castles hardly compare." Her mind strayed back to the voice, and the carving outside the confessional.

"I'll pack the next one, and bring Irn-Bru. You've not lived till you've had one." Angus bit into an apple and wiped his mouth. "Why Niall Campbell? Is it because that's who Shawn thought he was, when he awoke?"

"Mmhm." She bit into her sandwich, stalling, wishing he hadn't asked about Shawn. It resurrected her worry about his intentions, when she'd relaxed in his company these last hours. But he'd offered her the best possible explanation, apart from an impossible truth. She sipped her Coke. "I don't know if you remember, but I saw the tapestry at Glenmirril, and commented to Shawn that the man in it—who was Niall—looked like him. The more I learn, it seems the likeness was uncanny."

Angus lowered his apple. "You've found actual likenesses? Very few paintings survive from that time."

Amy closed her right fist around her thumb, feeling Bruce's ring inside the palm of her hand. "Um, descriptions. He was a fascinating man. Very religious." She spoke heedlessly, quickly, looking for anything to say, to move him away from the question of likenesses. He was right. There was no way she could know what a man from the fourteenth century had looked like. "When he was young, he was caught kissing the Laird's daughter behind an oven and whipped for it. Then the Laird took him under his wing, gave him tutors, and so on."

"Where did you learn all this?" Angus studied her with furrowed brows, his apple momentarily forgotten. "I've never heard that story."

"Um...." She took a hasty gulp of her Coke. "I'll have to check my notes. I just remember the story. They say there were lots of Viking raids on the coast here."

"Mm." Angus pointed out to sea. "They'd've come from there, in the 1200s. That's why we've so many castles on the coast, guarding the water inroads to Scotland." He resumed eating, finishing his apple and two ham sandwiches while he told tales of Viking attacks.

Twelve hundreds would have been recent history to Niall, she thought. His grandparents may have remembered those days. But then, Niall had barely known his own father. Perhaps he'd never met his grandparents at all. She resisted the urge to pull out her notebook and jot a note to look into his genealogy. Not that it would tell her anything about Niall himself. Nor would it explain eerie voices whispering of hanging, or the carving that could only have been made by Niall.

The sky brightened while they ate, till a rainbow smudged a faint pastel arch across the watery sky, dipping into the far reaches of mountain and water. With the cooler and blanket stowed back in the car, they returned to the castle. "'Tis a shame to leave this sunny day for the dungeons," Angus said, "but it's the last thing before we meet the director of the archives."

"Lead on," she said with more bravado than she felt. If the carving proved Niall had been here, in his enemy's castle, the dungeons were exactly where she should look. The thought stirred uneasiness deep in her. "We'll appreciate the sun all the more when we come up for air."

Her words proved quickly prophetic. She missed the sun long before they reached the dungeons. The dirt floor inched downward, first with sun beams filtering in from the courtyard, glistening in puddles left from the rain; then with the way growing increasingly dark. A narrow flight of stone stairs opened before them, gaping in the half-light with evil promises. She didn't want to go down; didn't want to imagine men—possibly Niall—hauled down these stairs against their will, and left in the dark below for months or years. Forever.

Angus offered his arm. "We don't have to go."

"Do I look that scared?" She grimaced. But the carving propelled her onward. "I'm fine. But I'll apologize right now if I hang onto you."

He hesitated, then tucked her hand in his elbow, and led the way, edging down rough, narrow stone stairs. Damp walls closed in. She became grateful for the few electric lights mounted on the walls, and the rope handrail journeying beside them.

The stairs opened, finally, into a large room with windows far up at the top, and a huge round brazier in the middle. "These were the kitchens," Angus said. "They'd've done the heavy cooking here, roasting full carcasses." With light falling in thin sheets from the windows above, Amy let go of Angus's arm to search the walls, the brazier, any place a mark might have been left. She found nothing. And the moment of heading back into the dark could not be delayed. If Niall had been down here, it wouldn't have been in the kitchens.

Angus tucked her hand in his arm again, and they returned to the dank, narrow hall. Distantly spaced lights, faint smudges of yellow in the gloom, lit the way. Under each was a placard, telling of life in the dungeon, for guards and prisoners. "Tell me there weren't torture chambers," Amy whispered. The ghosts of the long-dead walked beside her, trailing chilly fingers down her arms, through her sleeves, down the length of her hair.

"There were always torture chambers," Angus said. "'Twas a brutal time." He stopped at a wooden door with bars in the window at the top. It hung open. Amy stepped in. There was little to see: an empty stone-walled cell large enough for a man to lie down on its packed-earth floor. High in the wall, if Angus stretched up, he could have reached the three-barred grate that let in a striped square of light. She ran her fingers along the walls, and, squinting, made out the faint and softened letters FB, and a long series of short strokes carved on one wall.

"A prisoner counting the days, most likely." Angus stood close beside her in the gloom.

"I wonder if he left by low road or high at the end of those marks." She trailed her fingers to the end of the long stretch of vertical lines.

"I'd say most didn't go on to a happy life," Angus answered.

Amy backed out of the cell, a shiver crawling down her spine. The carving had been in the chapel. Surely there was no reason a prisoner would be taken to church, so maybe Niall hadn't been in the dungeon, despite the bad blood between himself and the MacDougalls. Still, as they walked down the narrow hall, pressed close together, she searched the remaining cells. She was relieved to find the mark was in none of them.

They followed the hall to a large room with chains hanging on the walls, glinting in the dull sheen of electric light. She didn't want to read the placards. The gruesome depictions she could see from here were enough. It was all too easy to imagine anything and everything that might have happened. Nausea bloomed in her stomach. "Can we go?"

"Aye. Not the prettier part of the medieval world." Angus followed her as she hurried out of the torture room, down the musty hall to the kitchens, and up into the light of day, where the last ghostly fingers slid from her back. Her stomach churned the whole way.

In the old prison guardhouse, she bolted for the restroom, slamming to her knees in front of the toilet barely on time to vomit. She hovered there, holding her braid up off the floor with one hand.

The mark could be coincidence, she told herself. Maybe Niall hadn't been in the dungeons. She closed her eyes, breathing deeply to calm herself. Finally, satisfied she'd flushed the nausea from her system, she left the stall. She stared into the mirror as she washed her hands. Her face was pale. She re-braided her hair, and doused her face with cold water, hoping her agitation didn't show.

Angus turned from his study of a claymore in a glass case when she emerged from the bathroom. A frown creased his forehead. "Are you aw' right? You took off like there were marauding Vikings after you."

"Fine. I just—I'm fine, thanks."

The frown deepened. But he only asked, "Ready for dinner?"

"I feel guilty," Amy said. "I didn't find anything, and here you're spending so much time and money on me. Thank you."

"I've not been here for years," Angus said. "'Tis I should be thanking you. Although I talked with the director, and he's been called away. There's a nice hostel in town. I'll get you a room, and he'll show us the archives tomorrow."

Amy nodded, her mind still caught fast on the chapel wall. It couldn't be coincidence. Someone in this castle had carved the exact same symbol with which Shawn had signed his letters to her: the flattened, elongated S that doubled as a sketch of a trombone. With Shawn dead, it left only Niall who knew that mark.

Northumbria, England, 1314

Shawn's days dragged on, with endless marches, looting, pillaging, sacking.

Raping.

He made his thoughts on that clear to his small group of men. They seemed willing to accept his commands. He sat with the other commanders in the evenings, discussing strategy and routes, and brought it up. One of the men spit into the fire. "Go on and say yer prayers, Niall, and leave the men alone." He picked at his teeth with a rough, yellow nail.

Douglas looked around the crackling fire. "We're here to fund a war and convince the English to give us peace. Tell your men to stop." He turned his meat over the fire. "William, how much farther is safe?"

"We've pushed a good ways in." De Soules unrolled a map. The men, one of them shooting Shawn an ugly look, crowded over it. Firelight flickered over the parchment. De Soules stabbed at their location. "Appleby is two hundred miles from Stirling. We've done well, aye? We've a king's ransom already, cattle slowing us and a long way home. 'Tis time to turn back."

"I say push on." Edward Bruce's voice burst from the other side of the campfire, with the intensity and discretion of a charging bull. "We've got them cowering and on the run. Push on to London and force peace."

"A messenger came from Randolph today," James said. "He fears he can't safely guard our back much longer."

"Bah!" Edward spat. "A hundred Englishmen will run from two Scots. And he wants us to withdraw."

Shawn roasted his own beef over the fire, while the argument raged around him. The smell of burned fields and the pall of black smoke rising from the town hung over their evening meal. He was amazed it still affected him; he'd smelled it often enough these past days. It seemed not to bother the other men at all. But then, this had been their lives, from earliest days. Among his 'men' were two boys who could not legally drink a beer or buy a pack of cigarettes in his own time. They should be playing in a marching band or shooting hoops or fishing with their fathers. Here, they terrified the English, burned, looted, and swilled ale.

"Home, then," James said.

Edward Bruce shot from his seat across the fire, voicing his opinion in colorful terms, stomping around the campfire. Some men muttered with him. Others looked nervous. He was still the king's brother, after all. They didn't care to be on his bad side.

Douglas stood firm. "Thomas can no longer hold our back. It does Scotland no good for us to reach too far, get killed, and lose what we've gained." He rose, glaring at the commanders, quelling further discussion. "Tell your men. We head north at dawn. Campbell!"

Shawn's head snapped up. Fear washed over him, wondering if someone had seen him leave his mark. He'd been repeatedly assigned to the churches, and had left the three slashes every time, sometimes in several places. He didn't know why anyone should care, but then, this world remained foreign to him. "My Lord?" he queried, trying to keep his voice even.

"The church as usual. The twa lads with you herd the cattle. Armstrong, your three lads, and Owen, you'll lead them." He ripped off a chunk of meat with his teeth, and disappeared, calling orders into the rising gloam. The commanders around the campfire, too, dispersed. Shawn found Lachlan and his men around their own fire, and relayed the orders.

"I'm more'n ready." Taran, one of the boys he'd helped train at Stirling, wiped his knife on his trews and pushed it into his boot.

His left arm, Shawn noted, stayed closed to his body. "You wash that arm like I told you to?" he asked.

"'Tis aw' right." Taran didn't meet Shawn's eyes.

Shawn shook his head. "'Tis not aw' right. Let's go." He yanked the protesting boy to his feet.

"Do what he says." By the fire, Taran's one-eyed father paused in eating his meat to reprimand his son.

Shawn held back what he wanted to say: *Your mother almost died giving birth to you. You are not going to throw it all away for an infection that doesn't have to happen.* He grimaced, thinking how the girls storming the stage, a lifetime ago, would react to such fatherly words coming from the mouth of Shawn Kleiner.

Nonetheless, he pulled Taran to the nearby stream, making him remove his shirt and scrub the angry raw gash on his upper arm. A burly villager had sliced the boy on the raid two days ago. Shawn wished he knew anything about herbs that might take the place of modern antibiotics. *Boil the water* was all he remembered. With a sigh for the sleep he was losing, he shouted for Lachlan and a pot, and with Taran's father, oversaw further cleaning. Finally, with fresh English beef filling his stomach, washed down with a good sopping of ale, with Taran's arm thoroughly cleaned, he burrowed into his tartan near the fire.

"Think he'll be aw' right?" Lachlan, lying near him in the dark, kept his voice low.

Shawn gazed up at the few stars sparkling through the dark canopy of trees towering over them. "I hope." He couldn't say why the thought of Taran dying burned so deeply. In reality, the boy had died hundreds of years before Shawn's own birth. When and how should hardly matter to him.

But it did.

He closed his eyes briefly and opened them again, focusing on what might be the North Star or Venus, so brightly did it shine. All his modern knowledge of millennia-long burning gases only encouraged the fanciful wish that somewhere, sometime, Amy might be looking at the same stars.

"You think much about Margaret?" he asked Lachlan.

"Every minute." Red shadows flickered over the man's scanty black beard; flames crackled and popped softly. Midges swarmed.

It was hopeless. Amy would be back in the States, preparing for a concert, maybe, donning her long black skirt and the black blouse with the billowing sleeves, brushing her thick hair to a high sheen. "I never told her how beautiful she is," he whispered.

"We're heading home and you can tell her," replied Lachlan.

Shawn fell silent, wondering who the orchestra had gotten to replace him. Maybe that up and coming kid just out of college with the trumpet, who had been making headlines of his own. He wondered if Amy had a nursery ready for the baby, if Rob had asked her to marry him yet. With her love of old-fashioned things and old-fashioned ways, she would value that, being married before she had a baby. He imagined them making plans around the kitchen table, maybe touring a hospital together, buying sheets for the crib, and stuffed animals to tuck in its corners, waiting.

It wasn't self pity, he told himself. You couldn't really pity yourself when you deserved to have lost it all. But he thought of her hair, hanging thick and black to her waist. He'd never told her how beautiful he found it. Or how much he loved her creamy complexion, perfect and smooth as a child's. Or the way her smile broke out at unexpected moments.

He knew why he'd never told her. If she'd known how easily she could find someone better than him, he would have had to change his ways.

And he'd liked life just fine the way it was.

He rolled over, his back to Lachlan, yanking the tartan over his shoulder, and scowled at the fire. Caroline, yep, she'd been fun for a whole night. It hadn't been worth it. The marks were stupid. Amy was back home, not here looking for three slashed lines that didn't even look like the symbol he'd used to sign her letters, anyway. There must be thousands of castles in England, she would presume he'd died, and she would almost certainly be glad to be done with the nightmare their relationship must have been for her.

He sniffed, and cleared his throat. Self pity had no place here. He'd gotten trapped by doing a good deed. Maybe it only proved he'd been right all along, to turn his back on his father's ways. Then again, considering how badly he'd messed up with Amy, maybe it was just as well he hadn't gotten back.

He could only worry now about Niall and MacDonald. And he didn't exactly have a cell phone to call and tell them what had happened. Once again, there was nothing he could do, except what Douglas told him, and hope it all worked out—somehow—when he got back. He understood why they prayed. There was nothing else to do.

Creagsmalan, Present

The knock at the door jarred Amy from a heavy sleep. She rubbed bleary eyes, pushing her legs over the edge of the bed.

"Amy?" Angus spoke softly through the door.

"I'm up." She stumbled to the door. A dozen worries had kept her up through the night, chasing away sleep until the window in her small room turned gray with dawn. There was the puzzle of Shawn's mark in

Creagsmalan's chapel, the nagging worry over Angus's intentions, the pressing need to tell him she was pregnant, and the questions swirling around the disturbing words, the low throaty woman's voice in the chapel. *And hang you instead.* Along with the these, she worried that the lack of sleep would harm the baby.

Clutching Shawn's thick white robe over her pajamas, she opened the door. In the hall, Angus beamed in a thick wool sweater, his cheeks ruddy from the cool morning. He held two paper cups and a bulging paper bag. "You ordered hazelnut mocha?"

A smile spread across her face. If he was showering her with attention to get information, he put on a good act. He looked genuinely pleased to see her. She accepted the mocha, taking a long sip. "Mmm."

"I've bread, jam, and bacon," he said. "It'll be ready in ten minutes."

Amy showered and dressed quickly in jeans, a long, thick-knit cardigan in kelly green, and her leather boots, and braided her hair down her back. An hour later, revived by coffee and breakfast, she was wide awake when a short man with a round belly let them into a back room of Creagsmalan's museum.

"Amy, me mate, Brian." Angus introduced them.

Brian grinned, shook her hand, and presented them each with a pair of crisp, white gloves. "To keep the oils off," he explained.

Excitement gripped Amy, raising the hairs on her arms. The smell of history and mystery hung in the air, even after he flicked on the lights and scattered the shadows to the far corners. A long black-topped table lay before them with stools set out. Equipment she couldn't identify lined more tables along the walls, and sat on acres of shelves and cabinets.

Brian bustled to the tables, reminding her of a munchkin both in his shape and child-like enthusiasm. "I've spent three days pulling all I could find from that time," he said. "It's all here on the table, but you're free to look farther. Just let me know. Sometimes, a person may be mentioned in a letter written many years later, so you could go through ten years of documents with no mention of the man you want, and in the eleventh year, you might find a reference to him that makes sense of all that was said before, d' you see? No food or drink. We can't risk that. Imagine something surviving seven centuries of war and mayhem, only to be destroyed by a latte!" He laughed, a delightfully innocent piping sound. He rattled off a few more rules, before adding, "Our break room is just outside. You're welcome to the coffee and bickies there." And he left them.

Amy pulled off her coat. "It feels like Christmas!" She scanned the neat piles of documents and copies spread across the table as she tugged on her gloves. "I want to start on all of it at once."

Angus donned his own gloves. "It always hits me like this! Ah, now, when I helped at King James' castle...." His eyes shone. "I woke up every morning before dawn, wishing they'd all not sleep in so, I wanted to get back to work that badly!"

Amy smiled. "That's how Shawn was about trombone." She stopped abruptly. She'd promised herself she wouldn't talk about Shawn.

"And?" Angus pressed.

What did it matter, she asked herself. The moment was easy, relaxed, and Angus was waiting. It was hardly classified information. "He couldn't wait to play, never wanted to take a break, couldn't understand why other people wanted to quit after a few hours' rehearsal." She laughed. "He used to get people mad on tour because he would practice in the bathroom till all hours of the night. He said it had great acoustics."

"Aye." Angus's voice was soft. He didn't look or sound like a cop, and her thoughts swung back to believing Rob and Rose. "You can see it when someone has a calling." He moved to the far right of the table. Amy followed. The loss of Shawn, and all the things she'd loved about him suddenly, viciously, shoved away the anger at the rest. They'd gone to a carnival once. He'd been like a child, enthusiastic and warm, not the cynical, worldly man the orchestra saw.

She wanted to tell Angus to look for any reference to Shawn, but even if she could tell him such a thing, there was no reason Shawn would be mentioned here. He'd died under hooves and steel at Bannockburn. The Creagsmalan archives would not record that fact.

She blinked hard, and sniffed once, short and sharp, as she set up her laptop on the far left of the table. Angus glanced at her, but said nothing. When he did speak, his voice was gentle. "I'll start at this end. You'll understand the medieval spelling?"

"Reading Barbour for a week straight got me pretty acclimated." She picked up the first document. "But you'd still be much more familiar with it than I am."

They lapsed into silence, but for the shuffling of plastic-protected documents, the tapping of Amy's keyboard, the scratch of Angus's pencil in his notebook, or the occasional hushed exclamation between them. A medieval world of births and deaths marched through Amy's fingers into her laptop, receipts for bundles of hay, a scribbled note about attending a council, another scrap that appeared, with some squinting at faded spidery script, to be a love letter.

She pushed them away finally.

"Not giving up, are you?" Angus paused in his own search.

"No." She stretched her arms over her head, fingers laced, palms upward, and arched her back. A flutter inside made her smile, almost laugh. Angus looked at her quizzically, and she thought he really needed to be told. Soon. "It's nothing," she said. "It's just, looking at these, I see how right Brian is. Look at this love letter, or whatever it is. It says *meet in my room*. But there are no names. Only the year, 1314, no date. Is it a love letter, or two men plotting against MacDougall? What if I set this aside and forget it, when it's just what I need?"

"Ah, there's the trick of it. I believe my historical research has helped me on the police force. Take down the information, review your notes, and if there's something there, it'll click with the next bit of information you find. If not, it's interesting on its own, aye?"

"It is." She pointed to another scrap. "There was some disturbance here in October 1314, but this is too far gone to tell me much."

They bent back to their work, immersed again in a world of turnips and wagon wheels and horses shod and men outfitted for war. Very little of it was surviving documents, but rather later copies of records, old articles referencing pieces that had since been lost, manuscripts telling of past events, genealogies, and academic treatises on Clan MacDougall.

A gentle rapping brought their heads up, and Brian's bubbling energy burst in. "It's past two! Have you not had a break yet!"

"Past two!" Amy said in surprise. "We just got here!"

"I've bridies for you. Come outside. Walk around the grounds a bit, stretch out, and come back fresh."

They took his advice, joining him for an entertaining lunch break. "Niall Campbell, now." Brian stuffed half a bridie in his mouth, talking around it. "He was from Glenmirril. The MacDonalds and MacDougalls were ever at the knag and widdie."

"At loggerheads," Angus clarified for Amy.

"Aye, that they were. So if Niall Campbell was ever here, sure 'twould be to steal their cattle."

"Those were the MacDonalds' cattle," said Angus.

"And where would you be hearing that?"

Angus jerked his head at Amy. "She's become quite the expert on Niall Campbell. Somewhere in her studies she found it."

"Well, now, I'm a particular fan of the MacDougalls. I'd not believe it of them." He chuckled. "Did you hear about the time MacDougall shot one of the thieving MacDonalds in the arse?"

Amy bristled. "That was Niall, and he almost died!"

Angus touched her arm. "'Twas seven hundred years ago. 'Tis no matter now."

She felt her lips purse. But there was no rational explanation for taking it so personally. "Sorry," she mumbled. "I'm afraid it's all become very real to me."

"Aye, I understand," Brian said. "When I first came here, I spent so much time with the MacDougalls, I told my girlfriend Eoin had broken his leg, and such did I say it that she wanted to know why I'd not mentioned my friend Eoin to her before. 'Twas a wee shock to pull myself from the fifteen hundreds and realize the poor man had been dead these many years."

"When I helped at James's castle," Angus said, "I woke up feeling I was going to see a friend. 'Twas at times disorienting to remember he'd not be there himself."

Amy took another bite of her bridie, torn between hunger and mild nausea. "What are the most interesting stories of the MacDougalls?" She sipped the citrus-flavored Irn-Bru Brian offered.

"Well, of the time you're looking at, that particular MacDougall had a younger son, Duncan, who didn't much make the history books. He had a wife, and he had a mistress, a young girl who worked in the kitchens. He used to go down there dressed as a maid himself, to spend time with her." The story wound through his escapades donning various disguises to be with his true love, of his angry wife appearing in the kitchens and the weaving apartments and stables, inspecting the maids and young women, to see which of them might be her husband in disguise.

"He eventually got smart and started hiding his face under a hood. Once, he blackened a tooth, and put on an eye patch. He tried to walk right past her to the kitchens, but she was suspicious, and followed. He kept going, hearing her every step of the way, down into the dungeons."

"We went there yesterday." Amy finished her bridie. "I can't imagine what it was like then. It's bad enough with electric lights."

"Aye, that it is. Well he kept going, turning a corner."

Amy thought she knew the exact corner.

Brian warmed to his story. "And reached the guard, and they say his wife came in screaming now she'd got him, and out stepped the man in the hood and eye patch from a cell, and fell at her knees begging forgiveness, and pulling her right out of there as fast as he could go. Apparently, she didn't forgive him, for the next day, the jailer found him dazed and locked right back in the cell. How she did it was anyone's guess."

"Maybe the story's been corrupted over the years and lost all truth in the re-telling," Angus suggested.

Brian nodded. "That happens. Well, the guard seems to have brought MacDougall's wrath on himself, and not lived much longer. 'Twas unhealthy to displease the lord, in those days." He chuckled at his own understatement.

Amy felt vindicated in her judgment of MacDougall. She had little sympathy for his younger son, Duncan. Maybe a night in a rat-infested cell had cured him of his wandering eye. Although, she admitted, it might not have done much for Shawn. Then again, she'd often wondered what he'd endured in his brief stay in the fourteenth century—he may well have encountered rats—and how those events had influenced the apology he'd left.

"That Christina," Brian added. "A temper like a Valkyrie, sneaking, lying, conniving, helping his enemies against him, and finally ran off with another man."

"*He* cheated on *her*," Amy objected.

"Men had mistresses in those days." Brian shrugged. "She drove him to it with her nagging and screaming."

Amy's eyes narrowed.

"Time for a walk, eh?" Angus clapped his hands together.

"Good idea." Amy shot Brian another pointed glower as they packed the remains of the lunch.

With a quick walk around the grounds, they returned to the archives and donned their white gloves. There was little sense of time in the windowless room, but it seemed only a moment later that Angus broke into her perusal of documents. "Here's a transcription of a letter to MacDougall, 1314, about prisoners. William stole his neighbor's sheep. Rabbie punched his father. There's a third prisoner here, unnamed. It seems to be asking whether to torture him."

"Ouch! No names? No response?"

Angus shuffled through the few things remaining in his pile. He shook his head. "There's no more about that."

Amy scanned the last of her own pile, a will bequeathing all earthly goods to 'my daughter Iona.' She stared at the name.

"What is it?" Angus asked.

"The name, Iona." But he didn't know Shawn had carved it on the rock in Hugh's camp. She tried to think how to ask what she needed, and settled for, "Could this Iona have any connection to Glenmirril, or Niall?"

Angus pulled the parchment over, studying it. He shook his head. "I'd not think so. Why d' you ask?"

"No reason."

"'Tis a strange thing to ask." His eyebrows dipped into a deep frown. "For no reason."

"No, really, nothing." She tapped a last note in her laptop, and snapped it shut. She'd hoped to find some mention of the symbol or Niall, maybe a note telling how Niall had relayed the story of Shawn's death and where he was buried. She dropped her head on her hands with a sigh. It had been an unrealistic hope, ridiculous, even.

"Come now!" Angus patted her back. "This is the life of a researcher. Don't be discouraged. Let's take his advice and look in future years." Crossing to the cabinet, he began thumbing through. "1315, looks like cattle, purchases of weapons, payment of a dowry." He lifted a pile out carefully, laying it on the table.

"How far do we look?" Amy gave the pile a dubious eye.

"We'll go through these and decide then." He pulled half the documents to himself and started going through.

Amy did likewise. She worked in silence, reading photocopies and fragile originals, her white-gloved finger running along under the words. "You know I'm skimming things I can barely read," she finally said. "Just hoping to see the name Niall Campbell."

"Pass me anything you find in Gaelic," he replied.

"I should have thought of that. I must be getting too tired to do this." She dropped her gaze to the parchment in front of her. *Damhair 1314. Tog na croiche. Niel Cambeul.* She stared at the name. Her heart thumped hard. Excitement lurched high in her chest. She touched Angus's arm. "I found something!" Her left hand closed over her right, feeling the sharp stone of Bruce's ring against her palm.

Angus pulled the parchment over. His eyes darted side to side.

"It's our Niall, isn't it?" Her voice rose a major third.

"I hope not." He lifted his eyes to hers.

"Why?" She realized she was squeezing his arm. "What does it say?"

"He's been in their dungeon for over a month. They're building gallows to hang him."

Borderlands, 1314

Shawn's pony trotted toward Scotland's border, over rolling hills. Lachlan and Owen rode on either side, and all around him were his men, Will and the boy Taran and Taran's father, the armies of Douglas, de Soules, and Edward Bruce, and hundreds of head of cattle. Ahead of him, Douglas's blue and white banner snapped in the breeze. Relief and trepidation tumbled together inside him, two bear cubs fighting. The burning, the sacking, the looting, were over. For a time, at least, he'd have relief from the screams of women, and roar of flames and the heavy smell of smoke on the air.

Lachlan looked as worn as Shawn felt. "Taran's arm is well?" he asked.

"The infection's nearly gone," Shawn answered. "Though he was none too happy with me making him wash it yet again." They rode in comfortable silence for another ten minutes before Shawn added, "Long days in the saddle are almost over." In his former life, he would have scorned such an obvious statement. Here, it passed the time, and knit a web of camaraderie with a man who might one day guard his back.

Owen gave a weak chuckle. "First thing I'm doing at Stirling is eat summat other than bannocks and oats. Beautiful women will bring it to me. I'll sit at a real table."

"What a treat not to have to slaughter the cow myself." Shawn grinned. "First thing for me—a hot bath. Wash my hair." It hung past his shoulders in shades of chestnut and filth. "Maybe a shave." He rubbed his hand over his thick auburn beard. Nobody back home would recognize him.

"A roof over our heads," Lachlan added. "A day closer to Margaret."

As Niall Campbell, thought Shawn, he'd have not only a roof, but his own room and a bed. He felt a little guilt for his men—Niall's men—who would be lucky to get a piece of floor in the great hall. Otherwise, they'd continue to bivouac in the open air.

"Sure an you'll be marrying Milady as soon as we get back," said Owen.

"Sure an I will." Shawn smiled, trying to look like an eager bridegroom rather than Shawn Kleiner, Lothario, going home to an empty bed, and tried to think brighter thoughts. A few days where he didn't wonder if today would be his last would be the best of all. But an uncertain future awaited him at Stirling. There was that little problem of his original mistake, drifting off to sleep and going where Niall wasn't supposed to go. He had no idea of his next move, whether he should ask after the Laird, try to explain to Bruce that he needed to head to Glenmirril, or await further developments.

He wondered if—no, he corrected himself, he wondered *how* angry the Laird would be, or Niall for that matter. Mistakes were not easily laughed off here. And this one may have cost the Laird his plans for having secret look-alikes. He wasn't sure the Laird had entirely trusted him, anyway, and this wouldn't help. And what if he had to explain to Bruce why Niall Campbell had been in England?

He rubbed his bearded neck, feeling a phantom rope, feeling the burn and the jolt. He'd heard it wasn't so bad if the hanging snapped your neck. It was when it didn't, when you strangled slowly, that it got a little unpleasant. "I'd give anything for a cell phone and Niall's number," he muttered.

"What's that?" asked Lachlan.

"'Twas naught," Shawn said. *Note to self*, he thought, *don't mutter about cell phones.* The pony jolted under him. Leather creaked, harnesses jingled, cattle lowed. The smell of men and animals filled the air. He wondered if he'd ever get used to it.

Ahead, sunlight flashed off metal. A cry rose from the ranks. A ways ahead, under the blue and white banner, Douglas raised a hand, shielding his eyes and squinting northward. He pointed. A small group burst forward, kicking their hobbins. A buzz of voices rose from the tired men, news traveling back among them. Some reached for their knives. Leaders shouted instructions. As quickly as it had risen, the murmur died. Military order rippled over the group, spreading an eerie quiet, as they looked north, waiting to see who approached.

Shawn's jaw tightened. The shadow of death was supposed to leave him alone for a little bit, now that they were leaving England, and yet here was a possible enemy ahead, ending it all, for him, for Douglas, for Scotland. The Bruce needed the wealth they carried.

And he thought of Amy, as he so often did, counting and recounting the days of her pregnancy, thinking of what could have been. He could see the little house she and Rob might live in together, laughing in front of a fireplace in the evenings. He'd buy her an older home, with the woodwork and paneling of bygone eras she loved; maybe a stained glass transom over a door, or leaded glass in a little window looking in on a turn in the stairway.

She'd put lace at the windows and on the table. She liked lace, and he wondered why he thought of it now. He'd teased her about her love of old things, and he realized with a start she hadn't asked to go in an antique shop for months. He swallowed. She'd hidden herself and who she was from him, as much as he'd hidden the other women from her. But he'd made her do it. He'd made her ashamed of who she was.

"They're coming back." Lachlan's hand tightened on his sword. Ahead, a group of horsemen thundered down on them.

Shawn squinted. A banner of red and gold unfurled in the distance. As recognition dawned, he laughed with relief, and sent up a whoop. "'Tis our king!" he shouted. The men around him took up the shout, spreading the word back. The ponies caught the excitement. Their ears perked up, and they lifted their feet higher. Electric joy danced among the men, giving energy to their trot. Bags of gold jingled and clattered from every saddle. The men began talking again. Ahead, as the flag neared, its field of gold became Bruce's rearing lion. All around Shawn, men cheered.

"Onward!" Douglas shouted, and they moved from a trot to a canter. Men whooped with relief and hope. "To the king!" Hooves struck the hard grass under them. They were still in England, but their king was here! They were as good as home.

Shawn charged with them, wondering if he was as good as home, or as good as dead.

West of Scotland, Present

Laughter, talk and cheerful chaos filled the roadside pub. Amy and Angus climbed over a herd of backpacks left in the entry by the crowd of hikers who filled the place. While Angus went for a pitcher of ale, Amy found the last empty table, in front of a large stone fireplace, between a particularly rowdy group of college students in colorful fleeces and a gaunt old man with sunken cheeks and eyes, and enough last holdouts of white hair standing almost straight up, that he couldn't be called bald. He lifted his half-empty mug of ale in greeting.

She nodded with a polite smile, and with the warmth from the fire, pulled off her coat. The place was peaceful compared to the questions storming her mind with the ferocity of Douglas's raiders. Why had Niall been at Creagsmalan? It couldn't have been willingly. Why had he been in the chapel? Last rites? Most importantly, had he escaped hanging?

She pressed her fingertips to her temples, trying to sort through what the voice in the chapel meant. *And hang you instead.* She couldn't have imagined the words, as she hadn't known until afterward that they'd built gallows for Niall. Maybe it was coincidence. Surely hundreds of men had been hanged at Creagsmalan. Maybe she *had* imagined it. Maybe she was more overstressed than she believed.

But the voice had been so strong, so clear, that she could almost see the woman's eyebrow lift in wry admonishment. Had Niall been hanged instead of someone else? Who and why?

At a shout from the next table, Amy looked up. Angus pushed his way through a pack of giggling girls, a pitcher and two mugs held over his head.

"You found a place by the fire!" He set the mugs down and lifted the pitcher high, cascading a waterfall of ale into her mug. "Got a headache?" he asked.

She shook her head. "Just trying to sort it out. Niall was a prisoner there." She leaned forward, the questions burning on her mind too hot for subtlety. "Would they have taken him to the chapel?"

"Possibly." Angus set down the frothing pitcher. "Depending on the rank and situation, prisoners were sometimes held in comfortable rooms until they were ransomed. Niall was sufficiently noble to escape the dungeon. But then there was bad blood between them to begin with."

A waitress appeared, setting fish and chips before each of them. Amy thanked her and turned to Angus. "How would he have gotten to the chapel?"

"What makes you think he was there at all?" He seated himself.

Amy hesitated, hating the evasions. It was impossible to tell the truth, but maybe she could put a rational spin on it.

"Amy?" His fork poised over his fish.

She bit her lip and made her decision. Rummaging in her purse, she found her notebook, and pulled out the rubbing of Shawn's symbol. She pushed it across the wooden table. "This was carved on the chapel wall."

Angus touched it. "That's what upset you?"

Again, she hesitated. She couldn't explain being upset. Shawn would have changed the subject. "I read about it. Niall used this as a mark." So much for honesty, she thought. Her thumb strayed under her palm to Bruce's ring.

"Where are you finding this information?" Angus's fork hovered over his forgotten meal.

She stabbed at her own golden fish, pushed it around her plate, and took a quick bite, searching for a story. "I, uh, I found it—well, I'd have to check my notes." Another lie. Under the table, her free hand fell on her stomach, growing taut against her jeans. She owed him the truth on many issues. She was as bad as Shawn.

But he accepted her explanation. Guilt gnawed inside her at his enthusiastic grin. He slapped his hands together. "Well, then, you're an amazing detective, you are, and I can't wait to follow this trail! It's quite the mystery why Niall Campbell was a guest of MacDougall's son."

The elderly man at the next table turned to them. "Is it Clan MacDougall you're talkin' aboot?" Words oozed from his sunken mouth. "Now my da worked for them, and my guid-sir." He scratched his chest through a tattered, dirty shirt of blue-gray and scooted his chair closer to their table, inviting himself.

"Can I buy you a Guinness?" Angus asked, completing the invitation.

"It's Niall Campbell, actually," Amy clarified.

As Angus left for the bar, the man reached back to his own table for his dinner. Words slurred through the gap where teeth should have been. "Niall Campbell, aye, I mind the name."

Amy doubted it with the entire force of her being. She doubted the man minded his own name most days. Body odor wafted off him, mingling with the smell of fish and chips. Her stomach stirred.

"The Lord o' the Castle, MacDougall hisself, he hated that man." He chuckled and spooned in a mouthful of meat pie. Sauce trickled down his beard. He grinned, licked it up with his tongue, and started the story.

"MacDougall, he was a guid man, he was. Treated my ancestors fair. But Campbell now, he was at Stirling with MacDougall. Threatening him, telling him watch his back. MacDougall, there he was, goin' to his own room, and Campbell appears outta the blue with his threats. 'I'm everywhere,' he says. 'Ye'll watch yer back every moment, aye?' And Campbell, away he walks down the hall.

"And MacDougall, he shrugs it off and opens his door and into his room he walks, and there's Campbell on his bed. 'Did I noo tell you, watch your step,' Campbell says, 'for ye'll never know where I am.' And he walks right through the wall, he does, and away."

"The Niall I'm talking about was seven hundred years ago," Amy said, doubtfully.

"Aye." The man swiped his sleeve across his mouth. "Tha's the one." Angus returned to the table with a tall Guinness, frothing and spilling down the sides, and set it in front of the old man.

Amy leaned forward. "Did MacDougall hang him?"

"Hang who?" The man hefted his mug toward Angus. "*Slainte!*"

"Niall Campbell. Did MacDougall hang him?"

Their new companion took a long draft of his drink. "Hang him?" He ran his hand over his lip, removing an ale mustache. A bead of Guinness remained, winking in his beard. "Aye, for witchcraft, if he did. A man ought not walk through walls." He stabbed at his fish, wolfed down a mouthful, and said, "Campbell charmed men. With his music."

Amy glanced at Angus, listening intently as he drank his own ale, and resigned herself to getting no straight answers.

The old man gulped another mouthful of his drink, this time failing to wipe his chin. "He lulled them to sleep, he did, and conquered whole castles. A devious one, he was." He continued his tales of MacDougall and Niall, one wilder than the next, as he helped himself to more ale from Angus's pitcher. Given the dearth of real information on Niall, Amy thought it unlikely so many stories had come down orally.

At last, having consumed more than half the Guinness, the man veered drunkenly toward the college students at the next table. "Is it Gordon Fraser I hear ye talkin' aboot? He walked through walls. He charmed fairies with his music."

Amy smiled, shaking her head. "Rose is going to get a kick out of this story. I hope you can meet her when she's here."

Angus gave a broad grin. "I dinna wish to disappoint you, but many of his stories sound suspiciously like tales of Fionn mac Cumhaill. Fionn fought a fire-breathing fairy named Aillen who charmed the men of Tara to sleep with his music before burning their castles to the ground."

Amy feigned disappointment. "So Niall never walked through walls?"

Angus winked. "I wasn't there. But I'm guessing not." The smile fled his face, and he studied her with eyebrows drawn together.

"What?" She touched her hair, glanced down at her turtleneck. Niall's crucifix hung, dark against the black. She resisted tucking it back in. Maybe Angus hadn't seen it.

Angus reached out a hand and lifted it. "Medieval? Where did you get such a thing?"

Borderlands, 1314

The Bruce held court on the border, standing under a silken awning of crimson and gold, on a hastily-constructed dais with his queen, Elizabeth, beside him.

"Beautiful woman, aye?" Lachlan, beside Shawn, patted his hobbin's neck, settling it down.

"Aye." Shawn stared. Her hair shimmered down her back in blonde waves. She had beautiful eyes, full and warm. When she turned them on her husband, they glowed with love. Shawn's stomach tightened. Amy had looked at him that way their first year and a half.

"She's only just now come from Carlisle. She and Marjory and Bishop Wishart were exchanged for Hereford."

"Marjory?" Shawn asked.

Lachlan frowned. "Bruce's daughter?"

"Of course," Shawn said quickly. He touched his head, reminding Lachlan of his injuries, and returned to his study of Elizabeth. The queen carried herself with a regal bearing that belied her eight years in near-solitary isolation, barely ended. The sight made Shawn sit up a little straighter. If this slender woman could be so strong, certainly he need not slump in defeat because a few things were not going right. Beside him, Lachlan and several others straightened on their hobbins, too.

They waited. Their ponies flicked their tails, while Edward Bruce and Douglas strode forward, leaning low over the king's hand. The minutes ticked by as the sun beat down, hot on his heavy leather and chain mail. Ponies rustled, or leaned down to chomp at the grass. Wind blew cold on exposed skin.

The men waited silently. Shawn scanned Bruce's army, searching for Niall. Not seeing him, Shawn's eyes settled on the king, with his long auburn beard and hair, and face lined from years of hard living. A silent comparison of how he and Bruce had spent their time marched through his brain. It did not flatter Shawn. It was some consolation that he'd heard the man had been hot-headed and reckless in his own youth. His brother, Edward, still was.

On the dais now, some of that temper displayed itself, with the faces of all three men—Douglas, Edward in his black armor, and Bruce—drawn in dark irritation. Edward slapped his gloves against his thigh. His voice rose just enough to carry to the men, though not loud enough to make out words. Bruce drew himself taller, and even at this distance, his face showed his displeasure. Edward bowed stiffly, first to Bruce and then, with a softening and a lifting of her hand to his lips, to Elizabeth, and marched to the back of the dais.

Bruce and Douglas looked out, over the waiting men. Douglas's eyes fell on Shawn. Shawn drew back, sitting up straighter, surprised, and startling his pony, who yanked its head from lunch and danced back a step or two, bumping into the garron behind him. The last thing Shawn wanted was to be noticed. Maybe Niall was here, in a tent, or had just seen Bruce off from Stirling. Douglas raised his hand, beckoning.

Shaking, Shawn threw his leg over the animal's rump, to the ground. The distance to the dais, between ranks of men, suddenly lengthened. His head filled with heaviness, his view narrowing to the path ahead of him, the grass under his feet, the dais—and denunciation. He considered running; bolting through this mass of thousands of men and ponies and cattle. He could make it, get away! Darkness closed in on the edges of his vision.

Then he looked at the queen and her regal bearing. He would do no less. And he wouldn't escape this crowd, anyway. With force of will alone, he pushed back the darkness, pulled himself tall against the shaking in his legs, and fixed his eyes on Douglas. *I'm satisfied with the man I showed myself to be.* His father had once said those words to him. Taran clapped him on the shoulder as he passed. *No matter how people repaid me.* Shawn's father had been murdered when he'd tried to help an aimless, abused boy.

Lachlan reached out and shook his hand. And Shawn's deeds of the past weeks strengthened him and carried him forward. He'd helped MacDonald. He passed a pony's rump. He'd helped Niall in his last effort to protect Allene. He patted the pony's neck. He'd worked his hardest for Douglas and done everything he was asked. He stepped past a foot soldier. He'd protected women from rape. He took another step, his vision lightening. He'd pulled a child out of the way, into the shelter of the church, protecting him from thundering raiders. He walked past three more ponies.

Taran's father clapped his shoulder. He'd insisted on cleaning Taran's arm properly, maybe saved his life. His chin came up. He'd made his men to do their job without hurting women or children.

He reached the foot of the dais. Douglas's black, unsmiling eyes lit on him, holding him. Half a dozen ladies in cotehardies and kirtles and long fluttering sleeves and red lips splashed color on the palette.

I'm a fraud. Shawn's unwilling legs climbed the dais, shaking. *That's beyond my control.* He stopped before Bruce. *But everything in my control I've done well, I've done right.* He would die with dignity. He considered throwing himself at the king's feet, confessing the whole story and relying on his famed mercy. But he held himself straight, though his breath came short and shallow, leaving his head spinning and fuzzy.

Douglas spoke, a gentle voice for so fierce and deadly a warrior. "I present to your Grace, Niall Campbell of Glenmirril."

Robert's eyes met and held Shawn's, unsmiling. "'Tis the minstrel of Bannockburn, the man who inspired men to victory."

Shawn swallowed, inclining his head low over Bruce's raised hand, touching his lips to his large ring. He did the same with Elizabeth's hand, her fingers cool and dry in his. He met her eyes, dusky blue against her china complexion, and every part of him lurched in desire. He lowered his gaze quickly, noting the twitch of her mouth as he did so. She'd seen. He'd never be immune to a beautiful woman or beautiful eyes.

Bruce spoke. "I believe I received a letter from you, Douglas, about this man. I was particularly surprised to hear *he* was in your company."

Shawn lifted his chin. He would not meet his death sentence staring at the ground. He almost blurted, *I can explain.*

"I believe, Campbell, you had other business?"

"A mistake, Your Grace." Shawn steeled his muscles against the awful trembling. Sweat broke out across his forehead. He prayed Bruce at least didn't practice the drawing and quartering part of this whole execution business. "I'd been up all night. I fell asleep. My horse followed the wrong group."

Bruce's face remained stern. "A sad mistake for a soldier in my service. A serious one. I need that information."

"Your Grace," Shawn faltered, debating only briefly how to say it. "I believe I can get that information almost as quickly as if this hadn't happened." He hoped, he prayed, that Niall had gone ahead with the mission. He hoped, he prayed, that Niall would be back at Stirling, that they would somehow meet up with no one noticing two Nialls. He searched for a story to tell this hardened, world-wise man, about how he could get that information so quickly. Cell phones would not be a suitable explanation.

"I have heard of your ingeniousness," Bruce said. "Walking through walls?" He raised his eyebrows.

Shawn's heart pounded, unsure what Bruce thought of that.

"As I conveyed in the letter," Douglas said, and Shawn's legs weakened. He tightened his muscles, standing strong. "Campbell has distinguished himself in all his actions."

Shawn stared, tightening his jaw so it wouldn't gape, at Douglas. He waited, hoping it wasn't a cruel trick leading to a *but*....

"He has followed every order, gone above duty, shown the qualities of mercy and restraint against our enemies which you so value. He has led his men well and with courage, and shown quick wit in the face of attacks. Your Grace, I have personally seen him pull women and children to safety, at grave risk to himself."

"Indeed, a man after my own heart," Bruce agreed. "What do you ask of me, Sir James?"

"Knighthood. He has shown every virtue of a true Christian knight and well earned the title."

Shawn's knees trembled. His arms shook. The darkness closed in on his vision again. His breathing became shallow and tight. He reeled in the shock of finding not only reprieve from hanging, but honors.

"Kneel," Bruce commanded.

Shawn sank to his knees, hoping the slacking muscles that dropped him with a thud to the wooden dais would be mistaken for deliberate action. *I'm going to live!* He bowed his head, hiding the rush of blood that came from the flood of emotions, and the tight swallowing in his throat he couldn't seem to stop. He saw the hem of Bruce's tunic before him, and leather boots; he heard the hiss of steel as Bruce drew his sword. The heavy blade landed on first one shoulder, then another, thumping him into the dais each time. Bruce spoke grave words that roared through Shawn's ears unheard.

I'm going to live!

"Rise, Sir Niall."

He clambered to his knees, stunned, dazed, trying to draw in enough air to fight back the gray dizziness in his head. The wind had dropped, leaving heat on his shoulders from the sun, and the glare of it in his eyes. Douglas beamed, Bruce beamed. Elizabeth smiled a small, proud smile.

A man beside Bruce raised his voice, the sound ripping out over thousands of men. "I present Sir Niall Campbell, Knight!"

A roar went up from the men, loudest from his own, spreading back to the farthest stretches. The hobbins danced side to side under the roar, lifting their heads from munching; their ears perked. A young woman, several years his junior, stepped forward, a swirl of blues and whites and jet black hair, kissing him on each cheek. Another pressed a bunch of daisies into his hand and dropped in a low curtsy, a swish of green clothes and dark copper hair. Names rushed through his ears; a meaningless garble. Bruce offered his hand for another kiss of the ring. Shawn dropped to his knee, touching his lips to it again, and to Elizabeth's cool fingertips, stretched out a second time, and somehow, he was back, on shaking legs, by his pony, dazed.

I'm going to live!

Chapter Eleven

Amy's last student, a high school boy with stooped shoulders, long brown hair and a great deal of talent, nestled his violin into its red velvet, flashing one of his shy smiles. "Eighths at one-sixty! You're killing me, Miss Amy!"

"Use the metronome," she said. "You'll have it in no time."

"Promise?"

"I promise. Then we'll start on sixteenths!"

He groaned.

She laughed. She enjoyed teaching him each week. Lessons gave her a respite from Shawn and Niall. Now, the worries about Niall crept right back in the door as Colin left, along with the new worry about Angus. The memory was fresh in her mind, of the doubt in his eyes, just last evening at the pub, when she'd made up a story about the crucifix.

Colin flashed another shy grin at her door and scuffled down her front path, through red and gold leaves. With a sigh, she retreated into her house, cozy and warm with a fire crackling in the hearth. Rose would be here soon, taking a taxi from the airport, bringing with her wisdom and comfort.

Amy started dinner—one of Shawn's meatloaf recipes. It brought with it, as everything did, memories. He had made it after they had gone ice skating one snowy night, with the city lights shining on the rink outside the concert hall, and Christmas music playing. A man had tried to snap their picture. She had backed away. "I told you, Shawn, just you and me."

He'd placed himself between her and the camera.

"Just one? I'm a reporter, come on, you two look great together."

Shawn turned to her, questioning. She stared him down. "If you drag my life into your headlines I'll never go out with you again."

Shawn turned to the man. "All the pictures you want of me, but leave her alone." He smiled. "And I'll leave your camera alone."

He let her into his new house after skating, beaming. Moving boxes lined the walls of the two-story great room, beside a floor to ceiling fireplace with a pair of soaring windows on either side. "Sorry about the mess," he said. "I just got the keys two days ago. You like it?"

"Like it! It's incredible. And you're only twenty-two."

He threw his head back, laughing. "Amazing what you can buy with a couple CDs and a few appearances on talk shows. Want the grand tour?"

She hung back, hoping he wasn't going to be so predictable as to offer to show her the bedroom.

He turned left, past the great room. "You should see the kitchen!"

Surprised, she followed him. The kitchen opened up, acres of granite counters and slick silver appliances. "It's beautiful!" She ran a hand over the shining surfaces.

He threw the doors of the refrigerator open. "Deep freezer, extra wide shelves. Check out this oven!"

She stared in amazement as he grabbed a roll of ground beef from the refrigerator.

"What?" He stopped, staring at her.

"You," she said. "Excuse me for saying so, but you don't seem like the type to get excited over a kitchen."

"Because you never imagined I was the type who liked to cook."

She raised her eyebrows. "Seriously? This isn't going to lead to one of your obnoxious puns?"

He shook his head, already tearing into the beef. "Open the cupboard. I picked up my secret spices. You can chop onions. The right kind of onion makes all the difference. And an egg, crushed cornflakes, barbecue sauce."

She stared in disbelief.

He grinned. "Don't believe everything you hear. Give me a chance. At least you'll get a really good meatloaf out of it."

She had laughed, then, and opened the cupboard, bare but for a dozen brand new bottles of spices. He had delivered on his promise of the best meatloaf she'd ever tasted, followed by a game of Monopoly and a ride home, keeping his hands to himself.

And now, cracking an egg into her own meatloaf in her own small house in Scotland, the pain hit her fresh: Shawn was dead.

Trying to shake the memories away, she pushed the meatloaf into the oven and returned to the front room for her violin. Her bow flashed up and down minor scales. Her mind bounced, as fast as the bow's bright staccatos, from the doubt in Angus's eyes as he held her crucifix in his hand, to the weekend at Creagsmalan to Niall and the gallows. She shifted to the Paganini caprice that had won her the scholarship to Juilliard, even as she did a mental review of all she'd learned about Niall. She sighed, as her bow flew smoothly up a run of sixteenths. There was little to show for all the research. He'd spent time at Stirling after the battle, and gained a reputation for amazing feats, and for some reason gone to Creagsmalan—where he'd possibly died. She slid through a pair of octave jumps, winced at a scratchy tone, and abruptly laid the violin back in its case. Practice was worthless when she was so agitated about Niall's possible death.

Moments later, she was up in the professor's office, studying her notes and touching the rubbing of Shawn's mark. Niall had to have made it. She ran a few searches on Niall Campbell and Creagsmalan, made a timeline of all she knew, and printed it out, taping it to the wall in a long, horizontal line. She secured the rubbing from Creagsmalan's chapel above it. It told her nothing.

She considered checking her e-mail. But the doubt, the sorrow in Angus's eyes, when she'd lied to him, haunted her. She didn't want to open her account and find there was nothing from him. He was at work, she told herself. If her inbox was empty, it might only be that he was busy. Still, she didn't want to see. It did nothing to help her frustration over not knowing Niall's fate.

Outside, the neighbor children shouted in the street. Their dog barked. Streetlights winked on against the graying sky. Downstairs, the front door burst open, and Rose called, "I'm home!"

Amy pushed herself away from the fruitless search, rushing for the stairs. "Rose, thank goodness! I have so much to tell you!"

♫

It took Amy only minutes to fill Rose in on the weekend at Creagsmalan, trying to keep the agitation from her voice as she carried Rose's suitcase up the stairs. "The more I read of medieval history, the less likely it seems he escaped hanging, with the gallows already being built." Depression settled on her shoulders, thinking of the man who had leaned over a magazine trying to read modern English, who had walked beside her on the River Ness. "It hurts to think of him dying like that," she said. "It hurts to think of Allene left without him. They loved each other."

In her bedroom, Rose heaved her suitcase onto her bed. "What have you done so far to try to find out what happened to him?"

"Apart from asking a drunk old man with a head full of Irish fairy tales?" Amy watched while Rose unpacked. "I was up until all hours last night, and bright and early again this morning running every search I could think of on every possible combination of MacDougall, MacDonald, Campbell; Niall in every possible medieval spelling, hanging, Glenmirril." She sighed. "I searched his name with 1315, 1316, 1317, seeing if I could find any reference to him in later years. Nothing. Absolutely nothing. Come and see."

Hanging her last skirt in the closet, Rose followed Amy down the short hall to the office, where she studied the timeline on the wall. The smell of meatloaf drifted up the stairs. "Shall I get that out of the oven?" Rose asked.

Amy glanced at the clock. "A little longer." She studied the timeline, taking a step back and moving in again. "It doesn't help," she said.

"What are you trying to do?" Hands on hips, Rose watched her efforts.

Amy lifted her hands in resignation. "Figure out—anything. Anything I've missed. A date after October 1314 that would prove he didn't hang."

Rose crossed the room and ran her finger under the dates. "There isn't one," she said. "No amount of looking is going to change that. So ask another question and maybe we'll find answers from a different angle."

"Okay." Amy tapped the rubbing. "Why is he using Shawn's mark?"

The smell of meatloaf grew stronger. "We need to get that," Rose said.

Frustrated at her lack of ideas, at the emptiness in her head that spun around the question like candy floss, leaving only fluff, Amy followed Rose down to the kitchen, and snapped on the burner under the kettle, while Rose pulled dinner from the oven. It turned her stomach.

"You don't look well," Rose commented.

"I don't feel well." Amy took lettuce from the refrigerator.

"Morning sickness?"

Amy shook her head. "Shawn is dead. I can't stop thinking about Niall." She shredded lettuce into a bowl. "What I keep coming back to is, he knew the symbol meant something to me."

"Do you think he was trying to leave you a message?" Rose slid two plates onto the table.

Amy sprinkled cheese on her salad, considering. The kettle screeched. She jumped, then let out a breath. The thought of a noose around Niall's neck, his hands tied behind his back, and his body jolting to a sharp stop at the end of a rope, had haunted her since Angus had spoken the words, fraying her nerves ever more steadily as she searched for evidence that he'd survived. She snatched the kettle off the burner and sloshed steaming water over a tea bag into Shawn's black mug. It splashed, burning her hand.

"Cold water!" Rose turned on the faucet.

Amy set the kettle down with a clatter. Tears pricked the corners of her eyes. "He was at Creagsmalan." She pushed her hand under the icy stream. "Near Iona, relatively speaking, and left a mark he knew meant something to me. And Shawn carved Iona on the rock."

"But Niall was at Creagsmalan *after* Shawn carved Iona," Rose reminded her. "Was Niall possibly on his way there because *he* knew what Shawn meant?"

"I don't know." With the sting abating in her hand, Amy shut off the water. "I keep trying to follow this through." She dried her hand. "Niall could have stayed here living Shawn's life. Instead, he went back for Allene and his country." She poured milk into the tea. "Niall was practical at heart. It would serve no purpose to send me a message. Especially one so unlikely I'd ever find, and impossible to figure out if I did." She stirred in sugar.

"So that isn't his purpose," Rose concluded.

"In fact, one mark doesn't mean he's using it." Amy sighed. "Maybe it was just a one-time thing. Maybe, as Angus said, just killing time."

"You sound disappointed." Rose dished meatloaf onto her plate.

"A little," Amy admitted. "He was kind. He seemed to see good in me."

"Which I'm sure restored something in you after Shawn."

"I guess that's it." Amy sipped her tea, breathing in oolong. "I guess I'd *like* to believe he was thinking of me."

Meatloaf and salad sat side by side on her plate, untouched. Amy stared at them, her appetite gone. Shawn, who had gone ice skating and shielded her from the cameras and loved to cook, was dead. A gallows had been built for Niall. She had lied to Angus about the crucifix and seen the doubt flash across his face. She pressed the palms of her hands against her eyes, promising herself she wouldn't cry. She broke her promise as easily as Shawn had always broken his.

Stirling Castle, 1314

Douglas's army entered Stirling to blaring trumpets, sun flashing off thousands of weapons, and dozens of banners snapping in the autumn breeze. Shawn rode tall. His muscles had grown strong with the endless riding of a Scottish border raider. He'd proven himself in battle. He'd been commended to a king. He wore a heavy gold chain around his neck, the mark of knighthood. *He was a knight!* Ragged and dirty though he may be, he was a knight, honored by the greatest king in Scottish history, the Bruce himself.

And still he felt the shadow of a rope on his neck, not knowing where the Laird might be, or how he might have taken Shawn's disappearance.

They rode in to cheers and throngs, washing away his fears in their tidal embrace. The old cockiness returned, all the old feelings of women cheering him onstage, and his old grin came back, raising his hand like the other soldiers. A girl met his eyes, lowered her gaze quickly, blushing, and raised her gaze back to his. He blew her a kiss.

And there, just beyond her, stood Allene. His face froze. His hand stopped mid-air. His fears and loneliness and everything crashed in on him, his months-long habit of being Niall, his weeks dodging the English and living in Hugh's camp with her, his need to know where he stood. His leg was over the pony of its own accord. He threw the reins to Lachlan, and all but Allene fled his mind. Nothing would stop Niall flying to her! He pushed through the crowd, past the girl to whom he'd blown the kiss, wrapping Allene in his embrace. His heart stampeded; he held her close in what would appear to anyone the embrace of the man who should already be her husband. "I fell asleep," he whispered furiously, needing her to understand. "The horse followed Douglas. Is your father going to hang me?"

She clung tightly. "Shawn, I thank our Lord and Savior you're safe! We looked everywhere for you. I've prayed these many weeks for your safety."

"He's not going to kill me?" A great sigh of air rushed from Shawn's lungs.

"You've proved yourself to him."

"What would Niall do now?" he whispered. "Do I get back in there?"

"Do what they do." She gripped his arm, turning him around. Some of the men had boosted their wives on their horses with them. He pulled back with a wide smile to the crowd. It was easy to fake, in the relief of knowing, after weeks of worrying, how things stood with the Laird. They cheered. Men slapped his shoulder. He pushed back through their midst, mounted the pony, and pulled Allene up behind him.

She clung to his waist, playing the part to perfection, leaning on his shoulder, her hair tickling his cheek. "Niall went to Creagsmalan," she breathed in his ear. "We told the men he disappeared in the night, and searched all the way back for him." She, too, smiled at the crowd, with shy eyes and blushes. "'Twas our hope, when we couldn't find you, that you'd somehow ended up with Sir James. We sent the men ahead to Glenmirril. We've yet to think how to explain that you were with us one night, yet ended up with Douglas."

"We'll think of something." Shawn's heartbeat slowed, bit by bit, absorbing it all. *I'm going to live!* It was becoming a disturbingly frequent chorus in his life, compared to the given it had once been. He waved to the shouting throngs. Lachlan grinned at him, and he grinned back. "I found Allene," he shouted over the yelling in the narrow street, the jingling harnesses, clopping hooves, and creaking leather.

He twisted his head to smile at her, and saw a pretty blush climb up her cheek. Her body pressed warmly against his back; her arms wrapped around his waist. His old life and feelings tackled him with vengeance, and he reminded himself he did not want Niall or MacDonald as his enemy. He craned his head back, instead, to whisper, "Niall's a knight now."

She squeezed him, pressed against his back. His senses danced. "Well done, Shawn!"

The ponies crowded close as they approached the arch leading to the armory and stables, leaving the last of the shouting crowd. Shawn paused long enough to let Allene slide to the ground. She gripped his hand, gazing into his eyes. Wrinkles creased her forehead. "I'll see you in the Great Hall. Niall. Hurry."

He watched her, with yearning he no longer wanted to feel, and relief at her departure. When she'd disappeared, he guided his horse through the cool dimness of the arch, into the sunshine of another courtyard and the controlled chaos of hundreds of men dismounting, shouting for boys to fetch and carry. He shook the heather scent of Allene's hair from his nose, wishing he could as easily shake his loneliness. Breathing deeply of horseflesh and leather and mud to dislodge her scent, he leaned to the task of caring for his pony.

A moment later, his hands stilled on the saddle. In his excitement at hearing he would live, he'd barely noticed the deep lines of tension around her mouth. Regardless of her assurance, something was wrong. His hand went to his neck, once again worrying.

Inverness, Present

Angus tapped his pen, steady as a metronome, on his desk, his chin resting on his fist. The weekend and his conversations with Amy played through his mind repeatedly. She'd broken up with Shawn. He should be happy. But whatever it was she wasn't saying left him uneasy.

Clive's hand clapped down on the pen, pinning it to the desk. "You've been tapping the damn thing for ten minutes straight," he grumbled. "Want to talk about it?"

"No."

Clive scooted his chair the short distance between their desks and plunked his arms on Angus's, sending two envelopes and a sales receipt fluttering to the floor. "A weekend away already. What could be wrong?"

"It wasn't a 'weekend away.' Not like that."

"Something happen?"

Angus yanked the pen from under Clive's hand and stabbed it in the Rangers mug on his desk. "We looked at Creagsmalan. Had a picnic."

"Tapping your pen is what you do when you're investigating and an answer won't come. You've wrapped up all your cases, so it must be her."

"Did I say I want to talk about it? I've work to do." Angus tugged a paper caught under Clive's arm.

Clive waited, solid as Gibraltar. "You're *not* working. You're stuck on whatever it is. Tell me, and we'll work it out together as we always have."

Angus sighed. "She broke up with him the night before he disappeared."

"That's good, right?" Clive asked. "If-when he shows up, she'll not go back to him."

Angus shook his head. "She knows something she's not saying."

"About his disappearance?" Clive straightened. "What?"

Angus gave a tight smile. "Now, wasn't it you told me we've no business —I stress the word business—talking to her? Wasn't it you warned me watch my step because we've no more questions for her?"

"Maybe we do."

"But I was talking to her as a friend, not as an officer on the case."

"Did I not say all along she's hiding something?" Clive asked. "What did she say?"

Angus sighed. "It's what she doesn't say—a nervous manner, twisting her ring, not looking me in the eye." He picked up a pen and tapped it three times. Clive slapped a hand on it. "She speaks of him in the past tense," Angus said, softly. "She said he's not coming back."

"Well, he's been missing for months. People think that means dead."

Angus sat up abruptly, reaching for his computer. His fingers clicked over the keyboard.

"Are you bringing up the case?" Clive asked.

"You know me well," Angus murmured. Files flashed onto the screen, with the name SHAWN KLEINER in bold. Clive leaned in beside him. They read in silence for a time.

Finally, Angus shoved the keyboard back under the desk, and kicked his feet up where it had been. He laced his fingers behind his head, staring at the ceiling. "This arrogant piece of shite comes to Scotland with a whole orchestra in tow. He's all over her when the cameras catch him at the airport. Causes a ruckus in Edinburgh. Throws a big party up here, gambles away his livelihood like the eejit he is, pawns her ring to buy it back, passes on some counterfeits he's unlucky enough to be given, and sneaks her into Glenmirril the most difficult possible way."

"Certainly he knew he could just walk right in," Clive said.

"I'm sure he did. He wasn't one to take the easy way. She leaves him in the castle overnight—you'd only do that if you were quite angry, aye?—feels guilty and races back in the morning. He's been hit in the head, shot. With an arrow. Doesn't know how or by who. He's raging with infection."

"And he came back a different man, according to everyone in the orchestra," Clive added. "Obsessed with the Battle of Bannockburn."

"She said he apologized." Angus cocked his head. "Which would be a different man indeed." He leaned forward. "Things get better between them, and *then* she breaks up with him before the re-enactment?"

"Which she didn't mention when we questioned her."

"She said there's no point destroying a man's reputation when he's gone. Maybe she thought it had no bearing. And we didn't think to ask."

"Now how would we think to ask such a thing?" Clive demanded.

"I don't know!" Angus swung his feet to the ground. "She leaves him in the tower when she's angry, but breaks up with him *after* he's apologized, *after* he's come back much improved? It makes no sense." Angus stood abruptly, turning in the cramped office to the filing cabinet. "It was the apology where she started evading." He rifled through the files. "Said he took a big chance. What's so risky about apologizing?" He lifted a folder out, glanced at its name, and jabbed it back in. "She said she didn't like speaking in riddles. She wears a medieval crucifix. She started evading again when I asked...here!" He yanked Shawn's file triumphantly, scattering its contents over his desk, digging through them, to the medical report. He tapped a scrawled note, and pushed it to Clive. "Read that."

Clive leaned close. "Scars on back appear old."

"Any idea what kind of scars Shawn Kleiner had on his back?"

"Now how would I know such a thing?" Clive asked. "Your new girlfriend would be the one to ask."

Angus frowned. "She's not exactly my girlfriend. She's recently lost someone. I can't think there's an appropriate way to ask such a thing." He shook his head. "No, that's a question for the police. And I was told we've no more questions for her." He picked up a pen, snapped it once on the edge of the desk, glanced at Clive, and thrust it into the mug with its predecessor. "He came back a different man, they all said. From a blow to the head."

"It happens." Clive pulled the report closer, scanning it.

"She's now verra interested in Bannockburn, herself. Though she wants to know only about the days afterward, and Niall Campbell. She knows a great deal about him I've never heard elsewhere. She tells me she can't remember where she heard it, says she'll check her notes. So far, she hasn't." He frowned hard at the wilted fern on the filing cabinet. "She was verra upset to hear Niall Campbell was hanged. She turned pale, looked as shocked as if she'd been told a dear friend had been killed."

"She's been under a great deal of stress." Clive scratched his chin. "'Tis an odd thing, to have your boyfriend go missing...."

"Ex-boyfriend." Angus rose from his seat, and snapped a dead leaf off the fern.

"...and start researching a medieval Highlander." Clive ran his finger under a line of writing, not looking up. "Why Niall Campbell?"

"Remember when they found Kleiner at Glenmirril, he called himself Niall Campbell?" Angus tossed the leaf at the garbage. It landed on the floor.

Clive looked up from the reports. "So he saw the tapestry, heard the name, got a blow to the head and serious infection, got mixed up with whatever dream he had while he was out, woke up confused. Does she think finding out about Niall Campbell will tell her something about her missing boyfriend?"

"She broke up with him. He wasn't—isn't—technically her boyfriend."

"But what we must come back to is, she knows something she's not telling. You don't think she killed him?" Clive chuckled. "The things I've heard about him, no one would blame her. She might even get a medal."

Angus shook his head. "No. Even if I thought she were capable, a thousand witnesses saw him at the battle. She was there with her own people and the chief of police holding her arm. Then he was just gone."

"So why won't she tell what she knows?"

"Why would she break up with him later, when things had been good between them?" Angus picked up the pen, rapping it sharply, *vivace,* on the edge of the desk. "She said I'd think she's crazy."

Bannockburn, Present

In lieu of dinner, Amy returned to her office, and weaving through a labyrinth of sites on Creagsmalan, Glenmirril, MacDougalls, and Campbells. Creagsmalan's site offered e-mail addresses, including Brian's. She tapped the edge of her laptop, wondering how quickly he'd call Angus if she asked questions about Niall. He'd already told her what he knew, she decided, and moved on to two forums on medieval and MacDougall history, where she asked for information on the death of Niall Campbell of Glenmirril.

Through it all, Angus worried at her mind. She had lied to him about the crucifix. She'd seen the doubt in his eyes. She avoided her e-mail, still dreading finding it empty of any word from him.

Rose appeared in the doorway with a cup of tea and a plate of apple slices. "You have to eat," she said.

Amy stared in frustration at the screen.

"Getting nowhere?" Rose squeezed her arm. "What you need is a good night's sleep."

Amy glanced at the clock. She'd spent hours lost in the web of useless information. "In a few minutes," she promised. "You go on."

"Are you sure?"

Amy nodded. She noted the faint circles under Rose's eyes. "You've just spent all day traveling. I promise just one more quick check and I'll go to bed."

"As long as you promise." Rose hugged her. "It's going to get better. You'll see." With good-nights said, she disappeared down the hall.

Amy heaved a sigh, frowning at the lace curtains. She stood, and paced the small room, trying to think where else she could look. She checked the forums, but no answers had come. Her stomach rumbled, but the thought of food nauseated her. She would warm up her tea, she decided. She rose from the chair, and nearly tripped, her toe caught in the strap of the backpack. The papers Angus had given her from Stirling jutted out of the top.

She stared at them, torn between a flicker of hope and the constant disappointments at every turn. But there was nothing else to try. Warning herself not to get her hopes up, she pulled them out slowly, and rifled through. "At least look," she whispered to herself. "It can't hurt."

With a sigh and a prayer, she took them downstairs. The living room still smelled of wood smoke. After stirring up the embers and adding another log, she snapped on a small lamp on the wall and curled up in the armchair in the soft glow of light to shuffle through printed lists, articles, and photocopies of older, handwritten documents, reading while the fire crackled and threw a flickering glow over her.

The first ten sheets offered nothing helpful. There was a dispute over a cow. Robert Bruce commended a man named Ronan. She looked at the date. A note in modern handwriting said *circa 1315*. Ronan may have been at Stirling in 1316, or in 1314 with Niall. The hairs prickled on her arm. Niall may have known Ronan. Ronan might have been at the battle. He might have been one of the thousands of nameless men who had swarmed around and in and amongst the re-enactors that day. She may have seen him herself. He may have been the one to carry Shawn's body from the field.

The tenuous thread broke.

He may have been or done any or all of that.

Or none of it.

The next five sheets had a note attached to them: *List of the dead carried off the field at Bannockburn.* She became still, not daring to hope. It was exactly what she'd wanted. She scanned the rest of the note. *Very incomplete; many of the dead were unknown to those doing the work; also, original document partially destroyed.*

She slid the note to the back, under its paper clip. Her finger moved, shaking, from name to name, through all five sheets. There was Alexander of Mar, David the Smith, Watt of Annandale. She found Adam of Glenmirril and wondered if he'd been a friend of Niall's. A young man, an old man? Had Niall mourned him? She rubbed her thumb along the bottom of Bruce's ring. There were two more names from Glenmirril. She marked them. But no mention of Shawn. There couldn't be, she knew. Unless Niall had identified the body, they would have had no name to record. Defeated, she shuffled the five page list, the very thing she had hoped for, to the back of the pile.

It had been no help at all.

She sat for a long time, staring up at the ceiling, arguing with herself. It was a fruitless search. And it changed nothing. *Accept it, Niall died,* she ordered herself. *They're both dead. You have to move on.* She wanted to look at the last page. And she didn't want to be disappointed again. Finally, chiding herself that it made sense to at least look, she pulled it out.

It was a photocopy of an ancient document. *Lucked out with this one,* was hand scrawled in blue ink on a yellow sticky note. *Some newb xeroxed this years ago—got canned, but now we can photocopy the photocopy. LOL.*

She lifted the yellow sheet off, and began reading. It appeared to be a supply list for James Douglas's army—weapons, armor, and food—dated August, 1314. A military supply list wouldn't tell her anything about Niall. Still, she leaned forward, entranced by the glimpse into history. Niall would have been there. Firelight flickered over the paper.

And there, at the bottom, she saw it: *Niall Campbell,* in flowing, oddly familiar script. She touched the letters, suddenly missing him, missing the way he'd looked into her eyes over candlelight at lunch, and kissed her backstage after the concert, his eyes shining. She missed his kindness.

She reached up, adjusting the lamp. And now, in the bright light, she saw it: the faint flattened and elongated S under his name, the impression of a trombone. Shawn's mark.

Creagsmalan Dungeon, 1314

His hair had grown longer, he'd grown thinner, and it was October, by the marks Niall had scratched on the wall, before MacDougall himself came down. As dull as the guard's company was, and the rats' social overtures downright repulsive, Niall had hoped for nothing more interesting.

Ellen had brought him food once a day, her face strained with worry, her cheeks streaked with tears, but the guard rarely allowed her more than to hand the scant meals through the door. She had managed to sneak a heavy cloak in to him, in addition to the one he'd been wearing, and a message hinting that Christina was doing what she could. He feared what Christina's face might look like, if she tried too hard.

He'd passed the endless solitary hours in the cell sharpening his knife on the stone walls, and repeatedly shaving away the tell-tale auburn beard that would give lie to the golden hair Joan had given him. He drew the sharp blade carefully over his jaw, telling himself he'd see the light of day again, Shawn would be found, all would be well once more, and Shawn wouldn't appreciate having to inflict matching scars on his own face. He smeared straw and dirt from the cell floor into his hair to disguise the dark roots that must be growing in; recoiling at the smell, he smeared it on his face to make sure he didn't look like an heir to a furlong of land, let alone Glenmirril.

As to Bessie, he heard her fate, several times a week, in the adjoining cell, while he closed his eyes with revulsion at Duncan's treatment of her, and prayed silently on his knees through each incident, for her, and for himself, that he might leave this dungeon alive and marry Allene as he'd been promised. He would take Bessie with him, he promised God, if He would just get him home to Allene. His eyes lifted to the dank dungeon ceiling, striving to see a life beyond it; he fought despair in the constant isolation of his small cell, day after day, feeling increasingly more abandoned by man and God.

He'd barely risen from his knees, after hearing Duncan leave, when MacDougall himself filled the cell's small door, with his familiar large nose and yellow teeth, dressed in black. Torchlight flickered over his ebony beard. "What have we here?" he asked. "A minstrel boy decides to steal my son's favorite kitchen maid. Not overly smart."

With his heart pounding erratically at MacDougall's unexpected appearance, Niall edged back into the shadows, away from the weak light spilling through the tiny grating above. He dared not speak. The noose was as good as around his neck, if MacDougall recognized his voice.

MacDougall raised a torch. Niall shielded his eyes against the glare, conveniently covering half his face, too. "You were spoken to, Minstrel!"

Niall lowered his hand only a little, and forced out a hoarse whisper. "My apologies, Milord, I've had but little to drink." He was filthy, gaunt, and had blonde hair. He prayed he looked nothing like the Niall Campbell MacDougall knew.

"Why would you sneak off with a kitchen maid?"

Niall forced out the scratchy voice. "Milady asked me to...."

"Bah!" MacDougall stepped into the cell. Niall shrank back, more in fear of being recognized than anything else. "Duncan is not overly bright, but his hearing is fine. Regardless of what Christina said, *you* told her to bring her cloak and meet you in the garden."

Niall hung his head, hoping to appear abashed. "Milord," he whispered, "my deepest apologies. 'Twas a moment of foolishness. She's a comely lass."

"I've asked around, and it seems you find no limit to the number of comely lasses. The washerwoman cannot stop blathering about you. One of those scullery maids seems to think she's caught your fancy."

"Aye," Niall confessed in his hoarse whisper. "I do have trouble restraining myself. I'd no idea the kitchen maid was Milord's, else I'd not have displeased him."

MacDougall grunted. "You should have admitted the truth to Duncan. He doesn't care overmuch for liars or being made a fool of to his face." He stepped closer, looming over Niall. "He didn't especially care to hear you were asked to play for his wife, either."

"My apologies, Milord." Niall hung his head.

"Look at me, Minstrel."

Niall's heart hammered. He closed his eyes in silent prayer that the changes Joan had wrought, the weight loss, and the filth, were enough, and lifted his face to the torchlight, avoiding MacDougall's eyes. Cold sweat slicked his arms and forehead, and it wasn't from the October chill coming through the grates. *Aves* marched through his head, an army begging Heaven for help. MacDougall played the torchlight over his face.

"You've a familiar look."

"I play in many castles, Milord." He hoped he imagined the shakiness in his own voice. "Ye may well have seen me. Were ye at Stirling?"

MacDougall nodded, lowering the torch. "I was." In the long silence, Niall kept his face raised, studying MacDougall and deciding whether to go for his knife if the man recognized him. The guard would not stand for it, but then MacDougall himself would block the guard from entering the cell to help him. On the other hand, the guard would raise the alarm before Niall could stop him.

Finally, MacDougall spoke. "Looking past the filth, I see why the lasses go for you, Minstrel. Perhaps time in the dungeon has taught you to be more careful which lasses *you* go for."

"Aye," Niall agreed heartily, and immediately lowered his voice back to the hoarse whisper. "I'd not have willingly displeased Milord."

"I understand an eye for fine lassies." MacDougall chuckled, lowered the torch, and backed from the room. "Duncan has recovered from his pique. Give me a day or so, and I'll have you out. But you'll leave Creagsmalan and Dundolam and never come back." Niall nodded, and MacDougall left. Niall immediately crossed himself, thanking his prayer-winged warriors.

Bannockburn, Present

A chill shot up Amy's arms. She leaned in, studying the mark more carefully. It was Shawn's. There was the lift of the upper line where the bell of a trombone would curve upward. It reached out to her like a hand from the grave. She swallowed hard, and gripped Bruce's ring, the smooth gold warm on her fingers, twisting even as questions twisted through her mind. Twice was not coincidence or passing the time.

There was no reason he'd try to leave her a message. Yet she was the only one he knew to whom the mark had significance. Did it have anything to do with the gallows? She pressed her hand to her temple, where a headache was starting. No, because this mark had been made in summer, before he went to Creagsmalan.

She needed more information, anything that might tell her why he'd claimed the mark as his own. She needed to know if he'd escaped the gallows. The answers, if they existed, were at Glenmirril.

But she didn't want to go.

She twisted Bruce's ring one last time and rose from the wing chair, pacing the small living room. The flames had died to embers. She picked up her phone and scrolled through to Celine's number. It would be morning in the States. There was no answer. She tried Aaron next. Apart from Rose, whom she didn't want to wake, they were the only ones who knew this crazy story. Aaron's phone rang five times before his voice mail answered.

"Hey, Aaron." Even to herself, her voice sounded demoralized and flat. "I found something strange. I wanted to talk to you or Celine."

She ended the call, wondering who else she could talk to. Dana didn't know the truth. But maybe it would help just to talk with her. She dialed, smiling when Dana answered.

"Amy!" she squealed. "Did you get the box I sent? Did you get the cards? How are you feeling? What have you been up to?

Amy laughed. "I'm feeling fine. I love the blanket. Thank you." She told Dana about the games and the castle, touching the statue of Bruce on the mantelpiece as she talked, her mind still on Shawn and Niall.

"Oh, *fun!* It's so quiet here without you and Shawn. Every week, it feels like something's missing, without Shawn's barbecues and parties."

"He didn't have them every week." Amy stooped, pushing a few twigs into the fireplace.

"Oh, I know it wasn't *every* week. I'm just saying, it feels so empty."

"Yeah." Amy's mind spun into a dark morass of memories, the past becoming real. She headed down the hall, to the kitchen. "I can't believe he's..." She caught herself on the word *dead*. "It all feels so unreal, like my life with him was all a dream." She lit the burner under the kettle.

"Are you sure you did the right thing, staying there, Amy? You were part of something big here. We're getting more and more publicity, we're doing another soundtrack." She paused for breath. "Conrad wants you back."

Amy looked around, at chipped linoleum in the small kitchen, in a small town, in a small country. It was a sharp contrast to Shawn's mansion on twenty acres. The unreality struck her anew. She gave a short laugh of disbelief. "And I'm crazy for not jumping at it. I have a degree from Juilliard and I'm teaching violin to students who might never play again after high school." It wasn't only Shawn, but her way of life, that had died.

"Do you miss it?" Dana pressed.

Amy pulled down the teabags. "I miss Celine, Peter, you. Everyone in the orchestra. I miss playing." She opened the refrigerator under the counter for milk. "But I'm happy here."

"You can't be."

Amy was silent for a beat. "Yes, Dana," she said softly, "I can be. I *am.*"

"I can't see how," Dana insisted. "I'd go crazy without the playing and the parties. Remember when Shawn's combo used to play at the club? Remember the night Trevor came?"

"Yeah, that was a good night." She let Dana slip her into a world of happy memories while the kettle whistled, while she poured water and sipped her hot drink. She laughed until tears ran down her cheeks. "I miss him so much," she whispered. Maybe, she thought, she could think about the good things, but remember the bad things just enough to stop the pain? Enough to learn from her own mistakes with him?

"What are the police doing?" Dana asked. "They have to find him."

"Yeah. Well." Amy brushed at her wet cheeks. There wasn't much to say. The horse and the sword slashing down and the question of why Niall was using Shawn's mark burned like a branding iron on her mind. "They've got other things to deal with."

"But why aren't you...?"

"They'll call me when they know something." She couldn't tell Dana there was no reason to push the police to find a man who had died in a medieval battle. "Hey, Dana, I've got to go." She searched for an excuse, but every one that presented itself was a lie. "I just need to go, okay? It was good talking to you."

She hit *end* before Dana could press for a reason. She tapped the phone against her mouth, wondering why calls with Dana left her so uneasy. They never had before. On an impulse, she turned off the ringer. She dropped into the rickety chair at the kitchen table, remembering a day in an inflatable castle. Another good day. She smiled, missing that part of him, wanting to polish off each good memory of him one last time, but it was time to pack them away, not have them out in the open all the time.

Maybe she could write stories about Shawn for their child, who would want to know some day. Maybe she could turn his robe into a blanket for the baby, something of his for the child, but not quite the constant reminder it was now. She would have to stop wearing it to bed, she decided.

Her thoughts turned back to the reason she'd called Dana. She'd hoped for some calming of her thoughts to decide about Glenmirril. But there was no one with whom to talk it over.

Putting away the milk, she climbed the stairs to the office. She stared for some time at the computer screen. There were no more searches left to run, no answers coming in at the forums. There was nothing to do but check her e-mail, and she was afraid to find out she'd driven away Angus, the one person here who had come to feel like a friend.

Finally, she decided it was no good wondering. She opened her account. *Angus MacLean* stood out in bold at the top of the inbox. A weight lifting off her shoulders, she opened it.

I enjoyed the weekend, he wrote. *Thank you.* She smiled, thinking of sitting by the dark water with him, the sun warm on the rocks and the wind cool on her cheek. Angus had been funny—a quiet humor that crept up on her, surprising her. His eyes were dark and intense, seeming to pierce her soul.

I hope you're having a good time with your Miss Rose. What do you call a midget clairvoyant who escaped from prison?

She scrolled down to the answer: *A small medium at large.*

Her smile broadened. She hit reply and typed. *Thank you for a great weekend. I loved the games, the castle, the archives, everything. Rose got here this evening. Maybe you can meet her.*

She stopped, thinking of her real reason for writing. The memory of leaving Shawn, of pushing through the mist in Glenmirril's courtyard, shouting up at him, was strong. She didn't want to go. She could hit *send* now. But Glenmirril held the best hope of answers. Shawn's carving in Creagsmalan's chapel wrapped around her, clinging to her like cold Highland mist. And the image of Niall jolting to a sharp, deadly stop at the end of a rope haunted her.

She typed quickly. *It's been wonderful having Rose back. She's already planned a trip to the Orkneys with Ina.* She hesitated. She needed to go to Glenmirril. The revulsion of the place was strong. She argued with herself silently, till she couldn't stand the voices in her head. But her fingers refused to type the words.

She added another of Shawn's jokes. *C, E-flat and G go into a bar. The bartender says....*

She typed a series of dots leading down the page to the punchline: '*Sorry, we don't serve minors.*'

She hit *send*, smiling, and sat back in her chair. A sound in the doorway caught her ear. She looked up to see Rose.

"You've been pacing in the living room, making tea, on the phone, up and down the stairs," Rose said. "What's going on?"

Amy bit her lip. "I was trying not to wake you up."

"Well, I'm awake, so what's going on?"

Guilt welled up in her stomach at having woken Rose. But gratitude at having her to talk to won out. And Rose was waiting. "Come downstairs," Amy said. In the living room, she handed Rose the sheaf of papers. "The one on top." She pointed. "The symbol at the bottom. It's Shawn's mark, under Niall's name."

"Hm." Rose stared at it while the seconds ticked by. "Twice is not a coincidence or killing time. You need to find out more if you can."

Amy bowed her head.

"Glenmirril is the most likely place for answers, isn't it?" Rose said.

"And the one place you haven't gone back."

"I don't want to go." Amy sank into the arm chair.

Rose seated herself on the couch, knee to knee with Amy. "You're tormenting yourself with the questions. You have a child who's going to ask one day. For both your sakes, you need to do this."

Amy shook her head. "Maybe I'm wrong. I mean, this whole thing is impossible." She gave a sudden laugh. "There's no way he's leaving me messages. Maybe it isn't even him. It must be something else."

"It must be that you doubt your instincts too much and you still feel guilt about leaving Shawn."

Amy stared at her hands, clutched between her knees. "I *shouldn't* have left him. I was mad, just because he said...."

Rose stood. "I was reading up on a fascinating place. Hermitage Castle. It's said to be quite haunted by the voices of the past. Horrible things happened there, and the cries of the Bad Lord Soulis's victims are still heard. I think we'll pay it a visit."

Chapter Twelve

"Fell asleep?" MacDonald's roar ripped into Shawn's eardrums with more fury than a squad of timpanists on steroids, only seconds after the door shut them into a bed chamber. *"Fell asleep?"*

"You should not have fallen asleep!" Hugh echoed. His eyebrows knit in one angry line swooping down over his nose. His big form blocked half the light that might have come in the window.

"You said he's not angry," Shawn muttered to Allene, daring move no further into the room.

"I said he'll not hang you," she corrected. "And he's *not* angry."

"He fell asleep!" Thunder rumbled in MacDonald's chest. The scar whitened on his cheek.

"He looks angry to me." Behind his back, Shawn felt for the doorknob. He wondered if this was what had caused her tension, back in the streets.

"I most certainly am angry!" MacDonald snapped at Allene.

She crossed the room, twitching her skirt up from the stone floor, and took his arm. "You're not angry. You're frantic and scared, as am I."

"Oh, is that all?" The tension sagged out of Shawn. "Hey, I'm touched, but I'm back safe and sound!" Reassured, he strode into the room and plunked himself down on a chair. "No more need to be frantic and scared." He lifted his foot, working at the ties on his boot. "Allene, could you help me with this? You might want to hold your nose."

MacDonald twitched his arm away from Allene. "'Twas not *you* for whom we were frantic." He shot a hooded glower at Allene. "And I am *not* scared. I'll kill MacDougall."

"We don't *know*," she said.

"We don't know *what?*" Shawn lowered his foot, hearing the catch in her breath. He glanced around the room, a horrible thought occurring to him. "Where's Niall?"

Allene's hands flew to her face; she spun into Hugh's arms, her body shaking. He wrapped her in a bear hug, his hand pressed in her hair.

His boot half-untied, Shawn rose, looking from Hugh to MacDonald. His voice dropped a third, feeling frantic, himself. "Where's Niall?"

"We don't know," MacDonald said. "We expected him back by now."

"Maybe he went to Glenmirril," Shawn said. "It's closer."

"We've had no message from there." MacDonald strode back and forth across the room, stopping at the window to stare out, his shoulders tense.

"News travels slow." Shawn's heart stepped up its pace. He didn't want to be left alone in this world without Niall.

"Still, he may have been found out." MacDonald spun from the window. "And here's where you come in."

Shawn's impulse was to groan and point out he'd just been through hell and back, and a few days' rest would be nice. But he couldn't pretend, even for the sake of a few days' rest, that he didn't understand the threat to Niall.

"What can I possibly do?"

"You're going to Creagsmalan."

"The lion's den?" His heart pounded more loudly still.

"No, Creagsmalan. Do you not listen, Lad? Duncan MacDougall's castle."

Hermitage Castle, Present

"We lucked out with such beautiful weather!" Amy and Rose rode two sedate mares over the moor toward the castle ruin. The smell of leather, the strength of the horse, the greens of trees and grass, a lace-sleeved top in royal blue, and the sun shining down on her helmet all felt good.

"Yes, I wouldn't have expected this in October." Rose had traded her flowing skirts for taupe jodhpurs reminiscent of the more romantic era in which she resided. A ribbon strung with cheerfully jangling coins belted a billowing blouse at the waist. Her boots gleamed black. Her frizz of hair spread in a soft reddish halo from under her helmet. "We've been talking so much about Niall, I haven't even asked about your weekend away with Angus," she mused.

Amy stared straight ahead, thinking of the doubt on Angus's face. "Rose, you see what you want to. It wasn't a weekend away. Not like that. He loves history and I need to know what happened to Niall."

"Is that all it's about?" Rose arched one slender auburn eyebrow. "Tracking Niall's fate? Who's this friend Angus is always visiting?"

Amy's horse tossed its head. She patted its shoulder. "I think he meant Mike at the Heritage Centre."

"Hm. I think you're naïve. Too much time in a practice room?"

Heat climbed up Amy's cheeks. "Really, Rose, he's shown absolutely no interest in me—that way."

"Does he know you're pregnant?"

The flush deepened. "There hasn't been a good time."

"He'll figure it out soon enough, if you don't tell him. Why haven't you?"

"I'm sort of embarrassed." Amy looked out across the moor, avoiding Rose's eyes. "This was never how I planned to live my life."

"Embarrassed. Hm. What's he like?"

"Upfront. Honest." The leather saddles creaked pleasantly. "Funny." She was surprised to hear her voice drop to a sigh. Her lips tightened. "Look, Rose, it doesn't matter. He's just someone I met, you know, and besides, he's definitely not going to be interested when he knows I'm pregnant."

"You don't know that," Rose said.

"It's not just about being pregnant," Amy countered. "Look what I have to offer him. Another man's child and this insane story. Do you know how many times I've hedged and flat out lied to him?" The agitation that had been simmering for two days boiled to the surface. "He saw the crucifix at the pub. I made up a stupid story. He *knew* I was lying."

"Which is not entirely your fault," Rose pointed out.

"Doesn't matter. Do you know how awful it felt to see the doubt in his eyes and know I was the one who put it there?" She knew all too well, from her last year with Shawn, how it gnawed in the gut.

They rode silently for several minutes, to the cheerful jingling of Rose's belt, before Rose said, "But you like him."

"Rose," Amy said, seeing the situation clearly even as she spoke the words, "there's no future when I have to lie. He'll eventually hate me for it. I hated myself."

"I get the feeling you've hated yourself a lot in the last year with Shawn." Rose looked up to a hawk circling lazily in the sky.

"I get the feeling I have." Amy stroked her horse's mane. "Maybe I don't want to get involved with anyone else because I made so many mistakes with Shawn. I've hated myself for giving in to everything he wanted, changing for him, being turned upside down by him. Since he's been gone, I can see he almost without a doubt was cheating on me, and I still can't believe I misjudged so badly, even when the facts are staring me in the face."

"I understand," Rose assured her. "I've been there, and it's so at odds with the face they show us. But why did you give in for him in the first place? Why did you change for him?"

"Because I doubted myself," Amy said. "He was so persuasive, he and Dana both, telling me over and over that my beliefs weren't practical or reasonable."

"Has Angus ever made you feel that way?"

"No. I feel good when I'm with him."

"Then what's holding you back?"

"Apart from this secret I can't tell him? Apart from being pregnant?"

"Pfft!" Rose dismissed it all with a wave of her hand. "Details!"

"Minor ones," Amy said dryly. "Has any mountain ever stood in your way?"

"They don't even try," Rose said. "So what's holding you back?"

"Okay, when you come right down to it, I just don't believe he's interested. Shawn always said I saw things that weren't there."

"And why," Rose asked, "have you always trusted Shawn over yourself? Or over me, for that matter?"

Amy shrugged. "I've asked myself that. I don't know. It just seems so ingrained."

Rose arched one eyebrow at Amy. Ahead, the castle came into view, a fortress blocking out a chunk of summer sky. "Have you read about it?" Rose asked.

"Not much." As with the violin, Amy trusted Rose would return to the point in her own good time. There were no answers to the problem with Angus, anyway. "It has quite a colorful past, but that's par for the course with medieval castles."

"It was here in Niall's time. One of its early owners was called Bad Lord Soulis. He practiced witchcraft and spirited away local children." The horses trotted along in the autumn sun, at odds with Rose's tale of the screams of Lord Soulis's victims, which local lore said could still be heard. "I do think," she added, "that the past hangs on in ways we can't fathom."

Amy gave her teacher a sidelong glance as their mounts shuffled to a stop. "Centuries past?" She threw her leg over the animal, and released the strap on her helmet.

"Our own pasts. They haunt us the same way the past haunts these old places." Rose flowed off her own horse.

Tying the animals, they headed toward the castle. "Obviously you think my past is haunting me." Amy was adept, after more than twenty years with

Rose, at guessing her meanings. "But why? I have a perfectly normal past."

Rose stopped in the arch of the castle entrance, soaring above her head like the arches of Lincoln Center. "We may or may not see the ghosts here that others have. Sometimes, we just have to see for ourselves to know what we believe. Shall we go in and find out?"

Dundolam, 1314

Shawn arrived in Dundolam on an early morning in late October.

He'd pressed the Laird, back at Stirling, to be sure of his facts first, and MacDonald had sent Hugh racing for Glenmirril, seeking news. Awaiting word, Allene had paced Shawn's room, wringing her hands. "Duncan can't have found him! Niall's far too clever."

The Laird had shuffled to the window, staring out at the blaze of gold and red leaves across the countryside. "Duncan is none too bright. How would he possibly figure it out?"

When word reached them that Niall had not returned to Glenmirril, they'd left Stirling with the remainder of MacDonald's men, and galloped west across the country, in a nightmare dream of icy winds blowing down between the hills that soared high around them with dying heather, and trees fiery with oranges, reds, and yellows, to Dundolam.

MacDonald and Allene took themselves to an inn, keeping out of sight, while Shawn, with his hood up, and the men with commoner's tunics hiding their chain mail, moved through the town, seeking information.

When Shawn cautiously lowered his hood in the town pub, men greeted him like an old friend, bursting from dark booths and dim corners, shaking his hand, and calling him Fionn. A skinny man with pock marks strode from behind the bar, wiping his hands on his apron. "Now how did that recorder work? Playin' at the castle on my son's recorder, imagine!" He beamed. "I made it myself."

Shawn tried to sort that out, while nodding and assuring the man it had gone great and the recorder was a fine instrument. He resisted his impulse to embellish the story with just how great, and searched instead, for ways to lead the discussion. "Seems like just yesterday, going to the castle."

"Aye, time does fly," the innkeeper agreed. "What's it been, now?" He turned to the three barmaids.

"Two months, maybe three," one of them said. "How Joan frets, sayin' as how ye never came back."

"Poor Joan," Shawn sympathized. He was grateful Allene wasn't around to hear about Joan's concern. "Will you take me to her?"

"Oh, aye." The girl looked around, and Shawn remembered a single woman in these days wouldn't go alone in the company of a man. "Jamie," she called to a boy. "Take Fionn down to the washerwoman's now, aye?"

The boy wore an oversized, grubby taupe tunic with a cowl hood, and brown hose tucked into curly-toed shoes. He looked up from under a mop of dark hair, and nodded. Shawn wondered about tipping here. He felt in his pocket for a small coin, while following the boy's quick trot out of the dim tavern, into bright sunshine. They traveled a maze of cobblestone streets, reeking with garbage and human waste. He stepped around a particularly noxious flow. It was no surprise people weren't bursting to move to the urban areas in this time, he thought. The boy led him down a narrow street. On the other end was a house with a large open yard. The boy pounded on the door, shouting, "Mistress Joan! Fionn is back!"

Shawn slipped the coin into his hand and waved him away. The fewer the better, as far as witnesses to him improvising his way blind through meeting a woman he supposedly knew—and well, by the sounds of it. The boy skipped away seconds before the door flew open, and a busty, red-cheeked girl launched herself like a missile into his arms, smothering him with kisses all over his face. "Oh, Fionn, ye've come back! Oh, Fionn, I was so worried, they said ye'd been thrown in the dungeon! Oh, Fionn, I knew sure it must be true if ye didn't come back to me. I just knew ye wouldn't leave without saying good-bye at least!"

How she managed to sprinkle his face with kisses and crush the life from him and still have breath to speak so quickly, he couldn't guess. Circular breathing, he decided. It was the only answer, which raised her talking to the level of a master musician.

He put a smile on his face, gathered the strength of months of hard living, and gripped her fleshy arms, pushing her away. "Aye, it's me, Fionn!" he said. "I'm back!"

Hermitage Castle, Present

It was easy to believe there were ghosts here, Amy thought, moments later as she stood in the middle of the castle ruin. Stone walls rose high, with lifeless, empty casements staring down, and autumn sun pouring through where once there had been a roof. In the same instant, Rose's comments, just minutes ago outside the castle, called Angus's questions about her parents to mind. She turned to Rose, leaning over her backpack. "Rose, I need to ask you something."

"Ask away." Rose's coin belt gave a cheerful jingle as she pulled a blanket from her backpack, and billowed it out in a cheerful rose-pink puff, letting it settle over the flagstone floor. She patted it, and they sat down.

Amy took a thermos and mugs from her own backpack. "I was telling Angus how you took me to rehearsals with you and we had gingerbread and tea after my lessons."

Rose smiled into a faraway time. "Those are some of my fondest memories."

"Mine, too." Pushing her braid back over her shoulder, Amy poured tea from the thermos. "But Angus thought it was odd. I never thought how strange that is, to spend so much time with your student."

Rose stared up a half-ruined flight of stairs. "You and I were close."

"When I was three?" Amy handed a mug to Rose.

"You turned four soon after you started lessons." Rose sipped her coffee, her eyes locked on a raven perched high atop a wall.

"That doesn't change anything." Amy watched the raven, too, not wanting to hear it, yet knowing she needed to. "My mother didn't come back for me, did she?"

The bird strutted along the wall, pecked at something too small to see, then shrieked, flapped its wings, and flew away. "Amy." Rose turned to her. "I loved every minute of our time together. I was proud to take you with me.

You were a beautiful child, well-behaved and polite, and my friends loved seeing you. Remember when you used to pull out your little violin and play for them?"

"Rose." The tightness grew in Amy's chest, till she felt she couldn't breathe. "Shawn lied to me. I suspect people in the orchestra knew things, and lied, too. No one wanted to hurt me. I understand you don't, either, but I need the truth. My mother dumped me, didn't she?"

Miss Rose sighed, not meeting Amy's eyes. "Your mother was a busy woman, Amy."

"Who's too busy to come back for their child?" Amy had been sure of the truth since Angus had spoken the words. But hearing it out loud made it real. Pain shot through her heart.

"It wasn't quite like that," Rose said. "I came to understand she would be gone for hours. We came to an arrangement."

"Meaning what?" Amy asked. "She paid you to babysit?"

Rose sighed. "Amy, I was young. I was shocked the first time she did it —angry. I told her my price was the same, as long as you were there. At first, I was fine with that. My husband had left me. I needed money badly. I knew I'd probably never have a child of my own, and here she was, foolish enough to pay me quite well to be a mother for a little bit each week, to have tea parties and play my violin for a perfect child. After awhile, I looked at you, sitting there, four years old, and all I could think was, here's a child whose mother didn't come back for her, a neglected child."

"Neglected?" Amy breathed the word. "I was well-fed. I had a beautiful bedroom, nice clothes."

"There are different kinds of neglect." Miss Rose spoke sharply, the first time Amy had ever heard her do so. "Deep down, I knew how you'd feel, if this day ever came. Amy, your mother would have done the same no matter what I did. I hoped the cost would make her pay some attention to you. When it didn't, I figured you and I had a lot to give each other."

"But he was right. She just didn't pick me up."

"No, she just didn't," Rose agreed. "I hoped it would never dawn on you. But now that it has, you have to see your mother had problems. You were a child any mother should have been grateful for. A prodigy, intelligent, beautiful and impeccable manners even at three. Fun to talk to. I've never had so much fun as the times we went to Coney Island and Central Park."

"But she needed to get away from me." Amy's hands clamped together, pressed against her lips. Heat prickled the corners of her eyes.

"No, Amy," Rose said forcefully. "*You* needed to get away from *her*. She filled your head with nonsense. She was an unhappy woman looking for someone to blame. Thank God you had that time away from her." She drew in a breath, and said quickly, "I'm sorry. I shouldn't talk like that about your mother. But don't ever think this says anything about you."

"No. No, okay, I won't." But the sun, shining down over the stark walls, swam around Amy's head. Her own voice came to her from far away. She stumbled to her feet, upsetting the coffee mug. It tumbled, spreading a brown stain across the blanket and flagstones. She crossed the courtyard, through an arch to a flight of stone stairs. Her mother had foisted her off on a violin teacher, for hours each week, for years on end. She tried to make sense of it. She'd been a difficult child. Her mother had always said so. She'd been demanding and rude. She'd spilled milk and broken a lamp and caused problems. Like leaving Shawn in a tower. Rose said just the opposite. But certainly a mother knew her own child?

Creagsmalan, 1314

Morning sun stretched one thin finger through the grates high above, turning a small square of fresh straw to gold, in the middle of the gloomy cell. The jailer had thrown it in shortly after MacDougall's visit, now that Niall was almost redeemed and forgiven. "Fionn!" hissed a voice from above. Niall swatted a rat twitching its nose against his, and jumped to his feet, stretching on his toes to see the small patch of the outside world visible to him. Ellen crouched at the grate. "Milord and Lady have convinced Milord to let you go. Milady has personally chosen the guards to escort you out of town, to be sure naught goes wrong."

His heart leapt, hardly daring believe. "When?" He reached up to her.

She stretched fingers through the grate to touch his. "Soon. God bless you, Fionn! I wish you didn't have to go."

"Thank you," he whispered. Allene filled his thoughts. He would live!

When she had hurried away, he crossed to the cell door, eager for any sight of guards coming to free him. The torch in the hall flickered pale light over the guard sleeping in the dark passage and sent a red glow into his cell. Thanks be to God, he was leaving, going home to marry Allene! Nothing would stop him. No more delays.

He dropped to his knees between the torchlight and sunlight and crossed himself, trying to steady his heart against the joy at his reprieve, and think solemnly on the Lord God. *I thank You, My Lord and Savior, Father in Heaven,* he began. The words *I'm going to live!* danced a sprightly jig in his mind. He turned his thoughts sternly back to prayer. *I thank You that MacDougall himself will not be back.* The less contact with him, the safer. He'd been accused of overconfidence. Even he did not wish to test himself that far.

I'm going to live! The thought shivered in delight through his soul. Prayer, he reminded himself, and bowed his head lower still. *I thank You with my whole heart and soul, my Father, my Savior, for setting me free.* It was fewer who left a dungeon alive than otherwise. *I thank You....*

A shadow fell across him, blocking the torchlight flickering from the hall. He lifted his head. MacDougall, the elder, stared in through the grates.

The man's silence unnerved him more than any bellowing could have done. MacDougall knew Niall's reputation for prayer.

How ironic, thought Niall, with the first tremors of fear rippling through him. Philandering had saved him; praying would be his death.

"I did indeed see ye at Stirling," MacDougall said slowly.

Still Niall hoped. He climbed to his knees and stood where he was, unwilling to step into the light. "I played for the Bruce, after Bannockburn." he said hoarsely.

"Aye, on harp, Campbell." MacDougall's voice turned low and ominous. "I believe I warned ye to stay away from me and mine, and now look what's in Duncan's cell."

Niall stared, his mind working furiously, hoping it came across as confusion. He could remind MacDougall of his threat back in Stirling. But he was safer not admitting to being Niall Campbell. Better to keep MacDougall off balance. Suddenly, he grinned, seeing the answer. "Ye dinna mean Campbell, the Highlander who was cut near in half at Bannockburn?" He laughed out loud. "What makes ye think such a thing?"

"I hear that washerwoman's daughter can do wonders with hair." MacDougall snorted. "Not to mention in bed, but that wouldn't interest a holy man like you, eh?"

"Aye, she cut my hair," Niall admitted.

"And without the mustache and filth, with dark hair, that's the face of Niall Campbell. We are not all such fools as Duncan. Of course, with his own wife conspiring to hide the messages I sent him to watch for you, it's no wonder he'd no clue."

Niall's heart sank. So that was how Christina had some inkling. But he still had his ace. "My Lord, I imagine being cut near in half left a noticeable scar on Campbell. Feel free to look."

Doubt flickered across MacDougall's face. Then he yelled for the guard, and threw the door open, holding the torch high, examining Niall's face closely, grabbing his chin, and turning his head to every angle. He thrust the keys at the guard and bellowed, "Show me!"

"Where?" Niall pretended ignorance. "Where was he wounded?"

"I saw it myself," MacDougall roared. "Lift your shirt. Across the waist."

Niall complied, lifting the vest and shirt high. MacDougall examined him, the torch flickering so close, Niall feared he'd burn to death saving himself from hanging. MacDougall's brow grew darker. "'Tis impossible," he breathed. "Guard, look. D' ye see a scar? Could it have healed?"

The guard, too, examined Niall, listening to MacDougall's description of the battle injury and the resulting scar, just months ago. "Such a thing could not disappear," the guard agreed.

Niall hovered between gloating and revulsion, holding the shirt high to make sure they saw every bit of untouched skin. If they heard his heart pounding like battle drums in his chest, they would count it as normal for any prisoner accused of being the Lord's mortal enemy.

MacDougall grunted, and stepped back. Niall breathed with relief to have the flames away from his clothing. "Keep him a bit," MacDougall said to the guard, and stalked out.

The guard shoved Niall backwards, up against the rough stone, and stepped out. The door swung shut, the key clicked.

Once again, Niall's future looked bleak.

Hermitage Castle, Present

"Ready for some company?" The sun had fallen, leaving Lord Soulis's home darker and colder, before Rose climbed the stairs.

Amy sat on a small landing, her arms wrapped around her knees, staring down over a broken wall into an empty courtyard. She nodded, her eyes locked on the blue lace of her long sleeves.

"Children believe everything's about them." Rose slid her arm around Amy's shoulder. "But it never is. It was about a father too busy with work, too wrapped up in himself, and a mother who was neglected and lonely, maybe a little self-centered and feeling sorry for herself. But it was never about you."

"Funny how it feels like it is." Amy lifted her gaze to the broken wall. "I feel like an idiot, running away. It's not like there's anywhere to go here."

Rose squeezed her shoulders. "Don't feel like an idiot. It's a shock to realize life isn't what we thought."

"I thought I could get to the ramparts." Amy's eyes traveled up stark, sheer walls, their ramparts long gone. "It should have been obvious I couldn't. Sometimes, I just don't see clearly."

Rose heaved a breath.

"Like Shawn," Amy continued. "We were talking about my mother, but all I've thought about, sitting here, is Shawn. Things should be so obvious. I know what I'd say if anyone else told me the story, but I *know* Shawn, I just can't believe it of him. He said it was an agent calling. And another one, just a girl who got his number and wouldn't leave him alone."

Rose patted Amy's knee. "There are things you wouldn't remember."

"Like?"

"You were a smart child. Perceptive. The first time your mother was late, you said so. She denied it. You told her what time it was. She turned her back to you, and I saw her change the time on her watch."

Amy frowned. "I do remember that day. I was wearing a green dress. I remember the confusion more than anything, because I had just looked at your clock. It was digital, but she said I didn't know how to tell time with an analog clock, and I was even more confused, because I didn't know what digital and analog meant. I thought she was saying I could read her watch, but not your clock. It was overwhelming."

"And she whisked you out before you could look at my clock again. Amy, I didn't know what to do. It wasn't my place to tell a child her mother had lied. I just hoped it was a one time thing."

Amy shook her head, denying. Sickness rose in her stomach. "What was she doing? Was she having an affair?"

"Nothing so dramatic, I don't think," Rose said. "An old school friend your father didn't like? More shopping than he cared for? Or maybe he just thought she belonged at home? I think he neglected her, and she was lonely and unhappy."

"I remember another time." Amy wrapped her arms more tightly around herself. A cloud scudded across the sun, dropping shadows over the home of Evil Lord Soulis. "We were riding the train home. I was ten. I said she smelled like the bakery you and I went to sometimes, remember the one with all the coffees and teas? She laughed and said I'd never had much of a sense of smell, and she'd been at the salon like always."

"I guarantee you were right," Rose said.

"Why would she want to hide a thing like that?"

Rose shrugged. "Why doesn't matter. Why won't help you now. What matters is, she did it over and over, she trained you to doubt your own senses, and you need to forgive yourself for not seeing clearly with Shawn. It's no wonder you didn't trust yourself after years of being told you were wrong."

"Yes." The word escaped, pale as a wraith. "No wonder." She noticed, suddenly, how dark the sky had grown, and the cold shadows in the courtyard below. She gave a nervous laugh. "They say the victims of Lord Soulis can still be heard here. I like to think I don't believe in ghosts, but this place is kind of eerie. If they exist, I don't want to see them."

"Oh, they exist," Rose assured her. "And it's good to make their acquaintance. Sometimes, we need to hear their stories." She rose, offering her hand to Amy. "But I think you've heard enough."

Dundolam, 1314

"Yer hair has grown out!" It took a good quarter hour of chatter before Joan noticed.

"Uh, yes, yes it has," Shawn agreed. "Did you like it best as it was?"

"Oh, aye!" Her gaze slid coyly to the ground, and back up, peering out under half-lowered lids.

Shawn tried to imagine what the pure and holy Niall could have done to bring this on. Surely he hadn't....

"Ye made a *verra* handsome Viking, Fionn. Oh, how the barmaids were jealous of me! Though Fionulla, mind ye, wanted me to bleach her hair, too."

"I imagine! Yes, bleached hair. Blondes do have more fun. How did you do that?" He resisted the urge to add *There ain't exactly a Wal-Mart selling hair dye in this town.* But the intricacies of medieval hair dye were not on his list of concerns.

He'd judged her talkative nature right, and another quarter hour of her detailed account of cutting, dyeing and shaving, heavily mixed with her own, easily evaded questions about Bessie—whoever that was—and the Lady and Lord, gave him a good idea why Niall had spent time with Joan. She plied him with ale and buttered bread, and waved to the grizzled, toothless woman who peered out the window to holler, "Keep at that washin,' Joan!"

With Shawn solidly plunked on a bench hewn from a log, pinned down by his meal, she went back to pounding laundry, moving back and forth between large tubs of steaming water. It took another hour, even with her quick and agile tongue, more fluent than Paganini on a violin, but he got a good idea of what had happened. Niall—or Fionn—had gone to the castle as a minstrel to play for Lady Christina's festivities. He'd been caught by the Lord, trying to sneak into the gardens with that Bessie. "But ye'd not do that, would ye now?" Joan asked. "I told ye how it broke my heart when the Lord threw me over for that chit, and I just knew ye'd not do the same. I knew ye to be kind and true. I saw it in yer eyes."

"No, *I* didn't throw you over for Bessie," Shawn assured her. But why Niall would want to spirit away the Lord's mistress, he couldn't guess.

While she heaved shirts from a tub, Joan continued the tale of Lady Christina chasing her husband down to the kitchens. She told it with an ease that suggested long practice on this particular piece. She told it like Amy played her favorite Telemann sonata, punctuating the story with staccatoed harrumphs and legato sighs; her voice rose and fell with precise dynamics, making it a masterpiece. Shawn wished Joan's talent could be turned to earning a better living than sloshing in boiling, lye-filled water all day. The steam reddened her round face, and tendrils of black hair curled around her cheeks, dripping condensation back into the tubs. Shawn listened, gathering what he could of the castle and what had happened there.

"So the kitchens are on the way to the dungeons?"

"Ye'd know best," Joan said, and he realized he must not underestimate her, solely because she talked without discretion. "That Ellen, now, she brought laundry one day, and she was all in tears about ye bein' in the dungeon, told how ye but came to fetch Bessie at Her Ladyship's command, and next thing Milord had ye marchin' back past the kitchens and ye never came up again. Ye'd'a thought, from her tears, that she'd reason to mourn ye." She snorted. "I told her how it was wi' ye and me. Tell me true, now, ye didn't kiss her in the gardens, did ye?"

"Oh, no," Shawn said. "I couldn't even tell you what she looks like." A bar of *Run Around Sue* ran around his head. Joan, Ellen, Bessie! Niall had become quite the player. Shawn hoped none of these stories reached Allene. He hoped Niall had gotten the information he needed.

Joan smirked. "I told her as much. I told her ye were a gentleman wi' courtly manners and would never make so bold. Unless perhaps ye'd no *respect* for a lass." She tossed her head, an accented final note to the melody.

"Oh, aye!" Shawn heartily agreed.

Joan pounded the water with a particularly forceful series of jabs, jolting the wooden tub. "She didn't like that at all!" Joan moved to the other tub, stirred with a cudgel, and lifted a shirt out. "Mind ye, some men can be *too* respectful. Some women might see a kiss as a sign o' love, not disrespect." She met his gaze forcefully. Her mother chose that moment to stick her head out the window and holler about the laundry again. Shawn breathed a sigh of relief.

"Aye, Mither," Joan yelled back, and the woman disappeared.

Shawn deliberately softened his eyes, not liking where he was going. "Oh, aye," he lowered his voice. "Might I come back later?" He angled his head toward the window. "Or meet you somewhere else?" He would have to discuss this with MacDonald and determine the best way to proceed. Joan was a wealth of information, but he needed to figure out how to use what she'd given him. Niall was, to all appearances, still in the dungeon, and he saw no way of breaking him out. At least not without more information.

Joan's face lit up. She shook the water from her arms, and launched herself around the tubs, gripping him in another loving death hug, and this time, she kissed him full on the lips. He did his best to wrap his arms around her like he meant it, but as quickly as possible, pulled back. "Your mother," he warned.

"Her!" Joan snorted. "She doesn't remember what it is to be in *love!*" She swiped her hand across one eye. "I thought ye were as good as dead, Fionn, and my heart was breakin' for all that was cut short atween us. They say they're even now buildin' your gallows in Creagsmalan's courtyard."

Train to Inverness, Present

The train clicked and clacked its way north.

On returning from the Hermitage, Amy had stared for some time at her computer screen, thinking of all the times she had been right, despite her mother's denials, despite Shawn's. Strength had grown in her. She was right about Glenmirril. She had to go.

With her jaw clamped tight against lingering doubt, she'd sent Angus an e-mail saying she'd visit Glenmirril. He had responded quickly, offering to drive down to get her and Rose. He'd book a hostel, he said, or his parents would be happy to have them. She'd smiled. This was Rob's great romance— a room in a hostel.

Still, Rob's warning lingered. Angus seemed to be offering to pay. She didn't want to feel obligated, and he was offering based on partial knowledge. She'd booked a room, bought train tickets, and sent him their arrival time. Rose had let her know that as soon as she met Angus, she'd be joining Ina in the Orkney Islands.

For the first hour on the train, while Rose read, Amy rested. Memories flickered behind her eyelids, as the rhythm of the train lulled her into relaxation. She'd ridden a train to Mallaig with Shawn, when they'd come alone to plan the orchestra's tour. He'd talked of the future, of building a stable on his property, even getting a horse, although he hated them himself.

She'd ridden this same train with Niall, thinking as she got on in Inverness that he was Shawn, and knowing, as they left in Stirling that he was Niall; listening to stories of his mother, tall, slender, and gracious; memories of his father laughing and carrying him into the great hall, of Lord Morrison's mischievous twin daughters. She smiled. Maybe she'd find something about them in the Glenmirril archives. They felt like old friends.

She pictured Allene as Niall had described her, reaching his shoulder, red-gold curls falling to her waist, and a sprinkle of freckles. Somehow, Shawn had managed the journey through the wilderness with her. Amy wondered what it had been like for him, where they'd slept along the way, if he'd complained endlessly as he was—had been—prone to do, when things didn't go his way, if he'd encountered the enemies Niall had said would be hunting him.

The train whistle sounded. The train slowed, chugging into the station. People swarmed the aisle, men in suits and women with children in tow, greetings being called, a child fussing. Amy checked her watch.

Rose lowered her book. "An hour until Inverness."

"I think I'll look over my notes." Amy slid her laptop and notebook from the backpack. "Angus said connections sometimes jump out later."

"You need to tell him the whole truth," Rose said.

Amy heaved a sigh. "I'll tell him I'm pregnant. I will. But I can't tell him this."

Rose, too, sighed, and lifted her book. Amy pulled up the history chart, barely noticing the train slide out of the station, into an autumn world of green-brown patchwork fields and red-gold trees, as she disappeared into medieval Scotland, Edward Bruce's foray into Ireland, the mighty galleys of Angus Og, and Douglas's raids in Northern England.

She opened her small notepad, and flipped through, searching for notes she hadn't yet entered into the computer. There. She tapped the pencil on the words. Niall had been in Creagsmalan's dungeon from roughly August until October 1314. She positioned the cursor, ready to type, and her eyes fell on the words already in the cell. She frowned, her fingers hovering over the keyboard. "Rose," she said. "Look at this."

Rose laid the book on her lap, leaning to study the computer screen. "Well," she said, "that's impossible, isn't it?"

Chapter Thirteen

"Lucky it's unseasonably warm, or we couldn't eat out here." Angus ushered Rose to the small outdoor dining area of one of his favorite restaurants.

"It's delightful!" Rose removed her sunglasses to scan the four round tables, each with two chairs, the potted plant, and the cheerful string of lights wrapped around the rail, before crossing the small balcony to look down to the silver-blue waters of the River Ness.

"Perfect for the glass of wine you need after the long train ride." Angus leaned his arms on the rail beside her. He saw why Amy liked Rose, from her red-blonde fluff of hair and the lacy white shawl she carried, to the fluttering silk scarf around her neck and her long skirt rippling in the breeze, to the alibis she didn't even try to disguise as sincere.

"Really, I'm exhausted," Rose protested.

Angus grinned. "Amy didn't believe you for a second and after watching you charge through the streets of Inverness, neither do I. How did she feel about being sent off?" They'd left her only moments before at the door of the restaurant, Rose pressing money into her hand, begging her to go buy a few things for her trip with Ina, and promising to meet her in half an hour.

Turning from her perusal of the water, Rose winked. "She told me not to embarrass you."

Angus chuckled. "I don't embarrass easily."

"So either you have no shame, or you have nothing to be embarrassed about. Tell me about yourself."

A breeze lifted off the river. Angus zipped up his windbreaker. "I think you're about to give me the father interrogation."

"Her father won't do it," Rose sniffed. "He's too busy."

"Are you ready for drinks?" They turned at the sound of the waitress's voice.

"What can I get you?" Angus asked Rose.

"Chablis." Rose settled her sunglasses back on her nose and seated herself in the metal framed chair. When Angus had ordered her drink and his Guinness, she asked, "How long have you been on the force?"

"Eight years." Angus joined her at the table, glad to answer her questions, glad to see she cared enough about Amy to ask them. "Before that, I did rescue work."

"What do you like about police work?" Rose pulled her shawl around her shoulders.

"I make a difference. My life matters."

Her eyebrows rose above the dark glasses. "I would think a life in rescue work matters a great deal."

He shrugged. "It was time for a change."

"Why?" Rose asked.

Angus sighed, not wanting to go into the whole story. "It was too close to things I preferred not to see every day."

Rose leaned forward. "What was her name?"

"You're awfully nosy, now." Angus couldn't help grinning. She was awfully perceptive, he thought.

"So I've been told." Rose smiled, but added more gravely, "In truth, I'm awfully concerned about Amy. Had she told me what Shawn was up to, I'd've flown out and had words with him."

Angus laughed. "Perhaps that's why she didn't tell you."

Rose chuckled. "Possibly. So tell me about her."

Angus sighed. "Her name was Julia. She was on the rescue team, as was the man she married." He stopped as the waitress came out on the deck with a tall, sweating Guinness and a Chablis, setting them on the white tablecloth. "Thanks," Angus murmured.

Rose, too, thanked her, and when she'd left, said to Angus, "You seem too sensible to run away over unrequited love. What's the rest of the story?"

"It was requited for a time." Angus stared out at the spires of St. Mary's across the river. He'd thought to one day marry Julia there. "Unfortunately, it pained her to tell me she'd stopped requiting."

"She cheated," Rose summarized. "Why didn't you just say so?"

Angus returned his eyes to Rose. "I prefer to see good in people."

"You and Amy are two of a kind in that sense." Rose twisted the stem of her wine glass, staring into the swirling white Chablis. "I'm not sure it served her well with Shawn."

"I'd have to agree." Angus tasted his beer, relishing the cool, smooth flow of it. "Yet it's a good quality."

"It's a double-edged sword is what it is." As the breeze grew, Rose inched the shawl higher on her shoulders. "Because there *was* good in Shawn. Lots of it. I reminded her of it myself, because she felt foolish mourning him after all the bad things."

Angus considered Amy's evasions. "Is that why she believes his apology means something?"

Rose tilted her head. "What did she tell you about that apology?"

"Not much. She said he took a big chance, making it, and I'm at a loss as to what she meant."

Rose sipped her wine. Voices rose from the street below. A horn honked. "I suspect she'll always see the good in him."

Angus studied her. The breeze ruffled her cloud of hair. It didn't go over his head that she had slid gracefully away from the issue of the apology. He suspected trying to get an answer from her would be like trying to catch the darting silver fish in the loch. He changed course, deciding it was the only way he'd get any answers. "Why do you think that is?"

"She needs to believe her judgment was right, after years of being told by her parents that it was off." She spoke without hesitation.

"Is that what it's about?" Angus's eyebrows knit in thought, his mind darting back to Amy's comments about her mother.

"In part," Rose said. "There's never one, simple explanation for who we are."

"Verra true," Angus agreed. "But doesn't that make it a wee bit of a catch-22? If she admits he's no good, she loses faith in herself. If she keeps her faith in herself, she stays with someone who's no good for her." He lifted his beer.

"On the contrary," Rose said. "It's quite safe."

He lowered the beer, untasted. "How so?"

She leaned forward, closing the subject as surely as she brought taxis screeching to halts. "Are you sorry you left rescue work?"

His eyebrows drew together, watching her in the bright sun.

She touched his hand. "Amy will tell you sooner or later. Are you sorry you left rescue work?"

"No." His face relaxed minimally. If Rose said Amy would tell him, he believed it. "It's hard on the heart. We don't save everyone."

"You care for people." Rose regarded him thoughtfully.

"There's really no other value in life, is there?" A boy shouted to his friend in the street below. A woman pushed a pram down the sidewalk by the river.

"Wealth, fame," Rose suggested. "Pursuing goals."

"Aye, there's that. My goal, though, is to leave good when I'm gone."

"I want that for Amy." Rose sighed, running a finger down the condensation of her wine glass. "Someone who cares about putting good in the world. In *her* world. I worry about her. She needs—someone."

"Needs?" Angus's eyebrows lifted. "She's got talent, skills, she's able to care for herself."

Rose shook her fluff of red hair. "You're more perceptive than that."

"I think I am," Angus agreed. "But perhaps you and I perceive different things. I'd like to hear your thoughts."

"She needs love. Amy's a bit naïve. And I'm partly to blame for that."

"How is that?" Angus's head tilted in curiosity, noting the sorrow that had crept into Rose's face.

"Our time together was something apart from the world." Rose leaned back in her chair, smiling up into the white clouds. "I think we lived a bit of a fantasy together. I pretended I had a daughter, and she pretended she had a mother who wanted nothing more than to be with her. I was an adult. I saw things in her parents she couldn't, and I tried to shield her from that. We dreamed and built beautiful futures for her together." Rose brought her gaze down from the clouds. "She trusted Shawn too much and herself too little, and her parents are partly to blame for that. But so am I."

"You?" he asked in surprise. "I'm getting the idea you were the strongest thing in her life."

"Yes, I was," Rose said bluntly. "But I taught her to look for something beautiful and romantic around every corner."

"Isn't that a good thing?" He lifted his Guinness again.

Rose shook her head. "I went too far. I taught her life would be a fairy tale. I didn't *want* dragons in her world, so I didn't warn her about them."

"Would that be a dragon named Shawn?"

"It would be dragons named Lies and Deceit." Rose leaned forward abruptly, arms on the table, piercing him with her electric blue gaze. "I failed to teach her that sometimes dragons manage to squeeze themselves into shining armor long enough to fool people. Maybe I feel I need to protect her from what I myself caused. Tell me, are you honest?"

"As opposed to Shawn?" Angus laughed. "You're smart enough to know both the dragon and the knight will answer that question the same way.

There's no way to prove which I am, but for time."

"Hm." Rose settled back. "You're honest enough to admit that." She lifted her wineglass, swirled it, and sipped, before asking, "Is your interest in her personal or professional?"

Angus stiffened. "Professional as in showering her with attention to get information about the Kleiner case? I'd not abuse her or my job that way. It's strictly personal."

"Why?" Rose asked. "What is it about her that draws you?"

Angus relaxed, smiling at his memories. "She's gentle, kind and compassionate. She's good. You can feel it." He stared over the balcony at the autumn sun glittering on the Ness. "I suppose some wouldn't care for that, but I do. I love her hair and her eyes. I tell jokes just to see her smile. I even like the shape of her ears. But really, Rose." He returned his gaze to her. "No scientist or theologian has ever been able to explain why one person is drawn to another." He swirled his glass, watching the beer twist in lazy, golden circles, thinking about the picture on his phone.

Rose removed her glasses, tapping them on the table until he looked at her. "It bothers me to feel you're holding back about something. I don't want another Shawn in her life."

"Make me a promise." He made the decision in a heartbeat. He'd never shown the picture to anyone. But the intuition that had never failed him told him it was time.

"If I can do it without compromising Amy."

"I think you can." Angus pulled out his phone and clicked through to the picture of the woman. "Promise you'll let me show her this in my own time." He waited for her nod before handing her the phone.

Rose studied the picture for a full minute, before asking, "Where did you get this?"

"It was found at Glenmirril seventy years ago." Angus's eyebrows puckered together as he watched her looking at the picture. Not a flicker of surprise crossed her face, only the mildest curiosity.

She lowered the phone. "Why are you staring at me like that?"

"Like what?" His certainty grew that he'd been correct in showing her.

"As if you're about to throw me in the squad car."

"You're very perceptive, Rose," he said. "But so am I. That the picture is seventy years old ought to surprise you. No, shock you. What is it *you're* not saying?"

Brakes squealed in the street below. Rose's lips tightened.

"You're from New York City," Angus pressed. "Yet your lack of surprise tells me you know something that I don't about a picture found seventy years ago in my own Highland castle. What is it?"

"You and Amy have a lot to talk about," she said in lieu of answering his question. "Maybe you could ease into it by asking what she found out on the train."

"The train?" Angus asked in confusion.

Rose took a hasty sip of wine and set the glass down with a clatter. "And I hope you know us both well enough to believe we're level-headed, logical, and very, very sane."

Excitement fluttered in Angus's stomach, the feeling he got when another clue snapped into place, even though he had no idea what it meant.

"This isn't the first time one of you has voiced a concern over sanity," he said.

Rose thrust the phone at him as if it had suddenly become red hot. "If you expect anything more than a flash in the pan romance—and I don't want you playing games like that with her...."

"My intentions are far more than that," he said firmly.

She raised one eyebrow. "How much more?"

"A great deal more." He stowed the phone in his pocket and matched her steady gaze. "I hope she'll feel the same. But there's a little issue of a missing boyfriend, is there not? An only-barely-ex-boyfriend, who *could* show up at any time."

"Is that what's held you back?" Rose lifted her glass and took an undignified gulp.

"Is he coming back?" The certainty grew in him that she knew something. "Is he dead?"

She didn't answer.

"I've been racking my brain," he said, "to think what an honest woman like Amy would cover up for him. She said she didn't want to ruin his name. Was it drugs? That might have gotten him killed."

Rose's nervousness evaporated in the afternoon sun. She laughed. "Inspector MacLean, I read up on you on the internet. They say you're a very good detective. But you clearly didn't investigate *Shawn himself.*"

Angus bristled. "He's all over the media. Everyone knows everything about him."

Rose shook her head. "No. There are things Shawn never told. His father was killed because he wouldn't give a boy money for drugs. Shawn hated drugs even more than he loved women. No, it wasn't drugs."

"You're speaking of him in the past tense," Angus said. "So does Amy. He's dead, isn't he?"

Rose looked at her watch. "It's time to meet Amy." She rose from the table and turned. Her skirt twisted like a cat around her legs.

"Rose."

She stopped.

"I'm asking not as a police officer," Angus said softly, "but as one who has resisted getting involved because he might return."

Rose turned back to him, planted her hands on the table, leaning almost nose to nose with him. The scarf around her neck fluttered in the breeze. "Think outside the box." Excitement shimmered in her voice. "What's the wildest thing you can possibly imagine? What could possibly make Amy and I both worry you'd question our very sanity?"

"That Kleiner was telling the truth when he said he's Niall Campbell." Angus laughed. "But he has a past. Clearly he's not a time-traveling medieval warrior living in two centuries." But something fluttered inside him, warning him not to laugh after all.

Rose smiled. "Get involved." Humor danced in her blue eyes. "You're in for the ride of your life." Before he could ask questions, she turned on her Victorian heel and left.

Dundolam, 1314

"*Gallows!*" Shawn whispered fiercely in the privacy of the Laird's room.

Allene paled, and reached for her father's hand. There was no time to spare her the truth.

"Fionn of Bergen, traveling musician, is to be hanged in two days. That's Niall, just in case we're not clear." Candlelight flickered on the small matchstick table between them. They had pulled the shutters tight against the October cold and prying ears.

MacDonald rose in agitation, lifting Niall's sword from the corner where it stood, touching its blade, as if it might be his last glimpse of Niall himself.

"Hanging him on what grounds?" Allene demanded.

"On the grounds he technically did trespass where he was told not to," Shawn snapped. "On the grounds MacDougall is lord and master and can do as he likes." He gave MacDonald a glare. "As has been made clear to me. I kind of get the impression no one really needs grounds in your time."

Allene touched her throat. "We've only the few men. Is there a way into the dungeon?"

"I don't even know a way into the castle at this point," Shawn said. "But we have one thing on our side."

The Laird set Niall's sword down. "We've ever been good at using what one thing we have, aye, Allene?" His voice came out a croak. His brows drew tightly over the bridge of his nose. He patted her hand. "Don't fash yourself, lass. It's two days yet."

"Well, really, we've got a few things," Shawn amended. "One, me, Niall's look-alike. Maybe we can use that. Create confusion, I don't know. Convince them they've got the wrong man."

"By showing them your face?" Allene said in disbelief. "Then you'd hang in his place."

"I'm flattered you care," Shawn said dryly. "Yes, that's a problem, but there's got to be some way to use it without that happening. Can we have them see me from a distance? Close enough they see Niall clearly, far enough for me to run like the coward I am at heart?"

The Laird snorted. "Cowardice didn't get Niall knighted, Lad."

"Yeah, times force things on us we'd rather not. I always felt I had a longer life expectancy when I was left to be a coward in peace." He must keep his voice down, Shawn reminded himself, as the Laird glanced at the door.

"What else?" the older man asked.

"The Lady Christina. I've managed to get reports from Ellen by way of Joan. Close your ears, Allene." But he didn't have time to spare her feelings. "Ellen feels—mistakenly, obviously—that she and Niall are, well, close."

"Why would she think such a thing!" Even in the dim light, color could be seen flashing up Allene's cheeks.

"There's a country at war here," Shawn snapped. "I told you to close your ears." He turned back to MacDonald. "There should be confusion at the castle. Joan has made sure everyone within ten miles knows Fionn is all over town, not down in the dungeon. She's better than e-mail."

"What's this *e-mail*?" asked Allene. "And why does the hussy think...?"

"What about the Lady Christina?" MacDonald interrupted.

"Joan says she's been trying to get Niall out. She sent him away to begin with, but asked him to take the kitchen maid." At Allene's insistence, Shawn explained that, letting his impatience show.

"We must meet with her," the Laird said.

"She's watched like a hawk. She's forbidden to leave the castle."

"Then I must get in."

"You can't, MacDougall will...."

MacDonald brushed aside Shawn's protest. "MacDougall will hang you in an instant. He's more likely to recognize me than one of my men, but I can't leave a meeting with Christina to them. Niall's life hangs on this."

Shawn did not voice his thought. *Bad choice of words.* He also did not voice the ramifications to himself. If Niall died, would he be expected to take over Niall's life for the next forty years, or however long people managed to survive in these barbaric times? He stuck to more practical issues. "You're assuming you *can* set up a meeting with her and get in."

MacDonald straightened. "We'll make a way." He glanced at Allene, and seemed to conclude, as Shawn had, that there was no time for delicacy. "The laundress can get a message in for us, aye?"

Shawn nodded. "She or Ellen, but we can't count on Ellen coming out."

"Joan must tell Christina where to meet us," the Laird said.

"First we need a way in," Shawn pointed out. He didn't relish walking into MacDougall's lair himself. Even less did he like the Laird doing it.

"The laundry must go back in, eh?" A crafty twinkle lit MacDonald's eye. "Arrange it with Joan. Now, where might Christina find a moment's privacy?"

"I doubt she'll agree to meet any of us in the toilet," Shawn said.

MacDonald smiled. "'Tis not what we think of first, in our time, when we seek privacy."

Glenmirril Castle, Present

"I used to have picnics back here all the time." Carrying a backpack full of food, Angus led Amy down the pebbly path to the shore behind Glenmirril, with the big rock and willowy alder. Its branches were bare. Angus looked out over choppy waters lapping almost to their feet, and grinned. "Maybe there's good reason I never did it in October. Will we go back?"

Huddled in a long, blue coat, Amy tugged her white scarf around her neck, trying to banish the chill. She'd sat with Shawn, and later Rob, on the same rock. As deeply as *MacDonald* was chiseled over Glenmirril's entrance, every detail of that sunny day was chiseled in her memory—blue sky, water, and spinning to see—Shawn. Naturally she'd seen Shawn. Who could have imagined he wasn't exactly who he looked like, right there where she'd left him? But it had been Niall, raising his knife, warding her off when she reached to touch his injured temple. She wondered, now, how he'd felt, finding his castle half ruined and strangers in bizarre clothing on his shore, the whole time burning up with fever.

She burrowed into her coat, fighting the ugly image of him twisting on the end of a rope. She wanted to stay here, near the memories, where Shawn and Niall both felt alive again. She wanted to be here, where so much had begun and ended. But she nodded. "It's gotten too breezy."

With the wind whipping her long hair, they climbed the path back to the water gate. It had been repaired and freshly painted since Niall had kicked it down last June. A new padlock clung to the small clasp. She smiled, remembering Niall's reaction to the gate. "What would it have been like in medieval times?" she asked.

Angus climbed over and reached for her hand. "It would have filled the arch; strong wood, reinforced with beams, studded with metal knobs to dull the axes of attackers." He helped her over.

Her heart fluttered at the touch of his hand. Her fears about him had dissipated with Rose's whispered approval at the door of the restaurant.

"This little gate would look weak and ridiculous to Niall," Angus added.

She started. It was as if he'd read her mind.

"Cold?" he asked.

She gave a short laugh. "Just surprised. I don't know why. It's no wonder Niall is on both our minds." She ducked her chin into her scarf. An idea occurred to her, and she asked, "Would he have been returned here?" The words were barely out before she thought if he'd been buried here, Angus would have known and said so.

"He'd be in the chapel crypts if he was. I don't recall seeing his name there. But if he died at Creagsmalan, he'd have had no burial at all."

She glanced up. "What...." Her voice came out shaky. She cleared her throat, trying to sound nonchalant. "What would they have done with him?"

His eyebrows puckered. "Come now, do you really want to know?" His frown deepened before he added, "His hanging seems to disturb you a great deal."

It was only her imagination, she told herself, that he saw past her words. She forced a laugh. "Yeah, they've become too real to me. Never mind." Bruce's brothers and William Wallace had been quartered, and their limbs displayed on castle walls. Her stomach turned at the thought of such a fate befalling Niall. She forced her mind from the gruesome image. "Where should we eat?" The tower hovered on her right. She hoped he wouldn't suggest it.

He hesitated long enough that she suspected it had been his first thought. "The dovecot will be warm." He led her through the crumbling wall dividing the baileys, to the broken-down half of Glenmirril.

"It's like a secret garden," Amy said, as they entered. When she'd come last June with Shawn, the lawn had been a neat green carpet. Now, rain had turned it into a lush jungle. Gardens lay in empty furrows of chocolate-brown earth. Tangles of skeletal vines lined either side of a cobbled walk winding past a round stone building two stories high. A crowd of barren rose bushes huddled against it, seeking warmth.

"I've always loved this half." Angus hefted the backpack on his shoulder as they crossed the courtyard through grass still damp with the last rain. They ducked into the dovecot's dim interior. In close quarters, out of the wind, warmth enveloped them. Small openings high up let in shafts of sunbeams that cast down ethereal, hazy light.

"They kept doves here?" Amy wondered if Niall had come to this bailey. It had been the realm of the blacksmith, gardener, and tanner. The northern half had been home to the Laird and nobles. But he might have come here, sometimes. She touched the wall, seeking his presence.

"Pigeons, actually." Angus pulled a plaid blanket from his backpack and shook it out over the dirt floor. "Up to two thousand."

Amy pulled her gaze from the dusty light pouring through the high openings. "That's a lot of pigeon pie."

"You know about pigeon pie in the States?"

She helped straighten the blanket. "I had some last June. It was good." Niall had ordered it, in his brief time here.

Angus paused, a bundle of plastic knives and forks suspended above the blanket. Shawn's ghost hovered between them. He knew—at least he thought he knew—who she'd been with last June. Then he smiled. "I've not tried it, myself. But in medieval times, pigeons might be the only fresh meat they had all winter." He reached in the backpack, pulling out ham sandwiches, apples, and chocolate cake with a flourish that left her waiting for a white rabbit.

She knelt down on the blanket, glancing up at him. A touch of shyness crept over her. "How was your drink with Rose?"

"Fine."

Amy laughed, the shyness fluttering away as quickly as it had come. "No. Nothing with Miss Rose is fine. Loud, exciting, fun, interesting. But never just fine."

Angus grinned. "She needed a rest after a long train ride, that's all."

Amy shook her head in mock despair. "I had started to believe you were honest. Rose could have walked all the way from Bannockburn and not needed a rest. What did she really want?"

Angus's smile broadened. "Ah, well, 'twas worth a try. She's a delightful character, your Miss Rose. I see why you love her. And I imagine you know what she wanted."

"I imagine so." Amy grimaced. "She was grilling you, wasn't she?"

"She wanted to know if I'm honest," Angus replied. A heartbeat of silence pulsed between them, before his voice dropped, and he said, "She suggested you and I have a great deal to discuss."

Amy lowered her eyes. "Such as?"

Angus didn't answer.

She looked up. He stared at his hands. Relived he didn't seem anxious to pursue it, she reached into the backpack with a faint tremble in her fingers. Rose wouldn't have told him. If she had, he certainly would have met her, after their drink, with *Are you crazy?* rather than a warm smile. "You both seemed happy when I got back, so I'll assume it went well." She pulled out another plastic tub, changing the subject. "You brought salad. I love salad."

"And carrots and cucumbers," he said. "How was the train ride?"

She noted he didn't ask what Rose thought they had to talk about. Her shoulders relaxed. "Here in Niall Campbell's home seems like the place to tell you." She helped him unwrap the vegetables.

He lifted a sandwich from a plastic tub. "What's the Stirling train to do with Niall Campbell?"

More than you could possibly imagine, she wanted to say. But she gave the rational answer. Well, first, I should tell you what I found in the papers your friend gave you."

"You found something?" Angus lowered the sandwich.

"The mark in Creagsmalan's chapel—there's a supply list for James Douglas's army, signed by Niall, with the same symbol underneath." She was grateful to finally have a source she could tell him about.

"Is there now?" Angus's words came out little more than a breath, his eyes wide. "Incredible! But how did you know, back at Creagsmalan....?"

"But there's more." Amy rushed into the middle of his sentence, having no answer for his question. "I reviewed my notes on the way. Creagsmalan says Niall was there in September and October 1314."

"Yes, but the mark...."

"Remember when he was knighted?" Amy raced on.

"After the raids in Northumbria. But...."

"On the borders. October, 1314."

Angus seemed to hover, for a moment, between his questions and the new mystery. Then a smile quirked the corner of his mouth; his dark eyes shone in the dim light. "Ah, there's the fun of it. Could he have gotten a reprieve and hightailed it over to Douglas?" He took a hearty bite of his sandwich.

"Douglas's letter to Bruce seemed to say he'd been with Niall from August onward. And Creagsmalan's records were from late October."

"There was a different Niall Campbell, then. Yet neither could have been Bruce's brother-in-law. So there must be a third. 'Tis possible. There were several men at the time named Robert Bruce."

Amy tilted her head, trying to remember. "I got the impression—I thought...." She stopped, unsure now. "Didn't they both say Niall Campbell of Glenmirril?" She reached for a ham and cheese sandwich.

"The one who was knighted, yes," Angus said. "At Creagsmalan, I'm not sure now. It can't be, if he was with Douglas. Which means, hopefully, our Niall wasn't hanged, after all. It could be," Angus added, "one of them was dated wrong in the original document. Or mis-copied. We'll ask tomorrow at the archives." He dug into his sandwich again.

Amy picked at the crust of hers. Niall had been at Creagsmalan. Shawn's mark proved it. But she didn't want to remind him of the mark and his questions.

"Busy man, our Niall," Angus commented. "In MacDougall's dungeon, fighting with Douglas, and playing concerts in modern Inverness."

Amy jolted, the nerves shooting up and down her arms.

"I'm sorry." The humor dropped abruptly from his voice. "I shouldn't joke about that." He handed her a drink. "But my mates in the archives are dying to know where you've learned so much about Niall. Like about this mark. They're always looking for new sources."

Chapter Fourteen

Glenmirril Archives, Present

Early the next morning, Amy studied the archives, taking in the long, raised tables, rows of file cabinets, and sleek modern equipment she couldn't name. Nerves trembled in her stomach, hoping Angus and his friends had forgotten the matter of sources. Asking if they'd ever seen anything of Shawn's mark in the ancient documents seemed a sure way to remind them, and here in an archives, there was already enough danger of them asking questions she couldn't answer.

But Angus's friend, Jack, spread his arms, encompassing the array of equipment and cabinets. "Impressed?" He beamed as if he'd built the place himself. "Temperature controlled, all the latest equipment."

"It's beautiful!" Amy's words came out on a sigh of relief. He hadn't asked about her sources. The ache in her stomach relaxed.

He handed them each a pair of white gloves. "The years you're interested in are at the end. There's not much left from then." He clapped Angus on the back. "Marjory remembers a book that might be just what you want. We can't find it, but we'll keep looking." He strode to the door.

Amy's shoulders sagged in relief.

Jack stopped, his hand on the knob, snapped his fingers, and turned to her. "Angus says you have some great sources on Niall Campbell."

The icy fist sank back into Amy's stomach. "Oh, um, yes, I guess I found a couple things Angus hadn't heard." She avoided Angus's eyes. "Just stuff on the internet. The professor's books."

"Do you have those sites, or the names of the books?" Jack asked.

What would Shawn do, she thought frantically. She patted the backpack holding her laptop and smiled, as Shawn would have. "It's all in here. This thing takes forever to boot up, but I'll look."

"Great, then! I'll see if I can't turn up that book." Beaming, Jack left.

Amy turned to Angus. He frowned. "Ready?" she asked brightly. "Where should we start?" She realized she was twisting Bruce's ring. Forcing herself to stop, she strode to the cabinets Jack had indicated, her heart hammering, hoping Angus wouldn't press the matter.

He joined her at the filing cabinet with another curious glance, but said nothing as they took folders full of documents to the tables. Amy battled within herself about asking him to look for the mark, for anything that would explain why Niall had used it. But she couldn't face his questions. She assured herself he'd tell her anything he found about Niall. He recognized the mark. He'd mention it if he found it.

For the next two hours, they searched with gentle fingers through fragile parchments, Amy praying he'd forget about her sources, while she searched for any sign of the flattened S and entered his translations of Gaelic documents into her laptop.

"Shawn spoke Gaelic." The words slipped out without thought. "I'm sorry," she said. "I'm sure you don't want to hear about him."

"No, you can talk about him." Angus looked up from the vellum he'd been studying. "You should. He was a big part of your life, no?"

She stretched her back, taking a break from the parchments spread before her. "Three years. Two and a half we were seeing each other." She studied Angus. She was coming to like her time with him more and more. But it seemed doomed if she had to keep lying. It was a tragic irony that the very things that brought them together—Shawn's disappearance and their mutual interest in Glenmirril's history—forced her to tell the lies that would drive him away.

"You're frowning." Angus's stool was close enough that the hairs on his arm tickled hers. "You don't like what you see?" he teased.

She blushed. "No. I mean yes, I mean, I don't normally stick my foot in my mouth so much. My mind wandered. Yes, he was a big part of my life. We did arrangements together. His CDs, I helped arrange the music." She didn't know why she said it, except she felt, these weeks researching with Angus, much as she'd felt working side by side with Shawn. Close.

"Did you now!" His eyes opened wide. "You can do so many things!"

The words *It was nothing, just some chords,* popped into her head. She stopped herself. It wasn't nothing. "Thank you," she said.

"How did he come to speak Gaelic? Not many Americans do."

"His grandmother was from Skye. And his dad was in a re-enacting group that spoke it." She leaned over, studying the smooth script of the document in front of Angus. "Beyond *mo gradh,* I don't recognize a word."

"'Tis not quite modern Gaelic, even if you did read it." Angus pushed the parchment over, pointing with his white glove. "It's about a cattle raid in 1313. Two men injured, and see here, *ech*—our modern Gaelic is *eich,* almost the same—a horse was injured, too."

She barely had time to wonder if Niall had been on that raid, before Angus started reading the next piece. She tapped on her laptop, entering as he translated. It wasn't much. A few names, Roland, Alexander, James; a few dates. "Here's one in English." Angus slid a torn piece of parchment across the table. It appeared to be a receipt.

She typed in the information about a pair of boots made in October 1314. The cordwainer groused about the haste. His grumbling came through the centuries-old ink, complaining he couldn't do his best work when rushed so.

"It's like being in a different world," Amy breathed. One that Shawn had lived in, if only briefly. The thought filled her with wonder.

"Exactly what I love." Angus lifted his eyes, staring at the ceiling as if he saw beyond it, smiling. "Imagine if a man could actually experience it. What wouldn't I give for such a chance!"

Amy's head shot up. Her heart thumped hard.

He lowered his gaze back to the papers before him. "One more."

She let out her breath, reassured he hadn't meant anything by it, and leaned in with him over a yellowed and stained fragment. The scent of his soap filled her nostrils. He read aloud, in his gruff voice, "I saw the stone cross in the archers slot...I believe the cross...will be here."

"Interesting," she said. "But whoever it is just saw the cross. It's already there. It makes no sense."

"None. 'Tis half the fun, guessing what it might have meant." Angus pushed himself back from the table, his stool scraping the floor, and grinned at her. "Speaking of guessing, I've a surprise! A little something Glenmirril likes to keep quiet, because we've no explanation and would like not to be a laughing stock. But it's intrigued academics and historians for years." He stretched his back, and crossed the room. "'Tis someone's idea of a joke, sure," he said over his shoulder. "What's perplexed researchers is who could have found ancient parchment and made authentic medieval ink."

"It was dated?" Amy followed him.

"It dates to medieval times." Angus led her to a long table set against the far wall, on which lay the parchments. "Judge for yourself."

Amy stared at the sketches. "Skyscrapers." She sank onto a stool. "Cars." She knew, as if she'd watched it happen.

Angus frowned. "You don't sound verra surprised."

"I am," she assured him, but her words sounded flat and lifeless—not at all surprised—even to herself. Niall was honest. Did someone see two of 'him' on the field? Did he have to explain to the Laird? He'd have told the truth. The Laird was no fool. He'd have demanded proof, asked questions. And Niall drew the pictures.

"Humph," Angus grunted.

She barely heard him, staring at the sketches. Her gloved finger touched the ink Niall's hands had laid on the parchment.

"Look at this." Angus slid another one over for her inspection. "See the splotches?" He pointed. "'Twas likely done by someone unfamiliar with a quill, as of course few people today are."

Amy touched the drawings. Maybe Niall had done it while still suffering from his injury. There was no mistaking the airplane—a side view of sorts, and one as though seen from the bottom. The skyscrapers clustered together, a group of three. She leaned closer, studying one of them. "It looks a little like the Foshay Tower."

"And what would that be?"

"One of the first skyscrapers in Minneapolis."

"Where's that?"

She blinked. "Minnesota. Where Shawn's from."

He frowned. "Well, that wouldn't be possible, would it now?"

"Of course not," she said.

"Unless our hoaxster is from there. It would seem a great coincidence." He continued to study it, his head tilted, his frown deepening. Then abruptly, he cleared his throat. "We're done here. Your laptop's booted. Can you find those sources?"

"Oh." She cleared her own throat, stalling, and forced her hand to stay off the ring. "Sure." She prayed something would spring to mind. She could make something up, claim the information had been in the professor's books. Her insides twisted like a coiled snake. She'd hated Shawn's lies. She crossed the room, Angus following her, and tapped the keys. Maybe she could make the computer freeze up. Angus stood behind her, watching, silent. She scrolled up and down the list on the start menu. "Sorry," she said. "I'm just trying to remember where it is." She tapped some more, her nerves jumping, selected the *Documents* folder, and scanned it, trying to guess which one she might pass off as sources on Niall.

The door flew open. With her nerves already stretched taut, Amy leapt half off her stool, slamming the laptop shut.

"It's just me!" Jack stood at the door, looking a bit alarmed.

"Sorry." Amy gave a nervous laugh. "You scared me."

"I'm sorry. I do have a bad habit of bursting in." He turned to Angus, his face aglow. "The book! Marjory found it with a book doctor. She's working on getting it back."

"Thank goodness!" Amy breathed.

"The sources," Angus reminded her.

"Angus, it's late," she protested. "I'm sorry, I shut the laptop and it'll take forever to reboot. Let's go see Glenmirril. Please."

Dundolam, 1314

The ride inside the clean laundry was less than comfortable. It could be worse, Shawn thought, as he bounced in the dark under a load of bleached linens. At least Niall hadn't struck up a friendship with the local peat-digger. He'd hidden in the innermost basket of the group Joan and her mother had loaded on their small pony cart, climbing in when her mother disappeared into the house for another basket. Joan covered him over, warning him to be still, especially when the wagon slowed at the castle gates.

He lay on his side in the dark, curled tightly, pulling stuffy air through the woven sides of the basket. He'd convinced MacDonald to let him go, making him see that he, of all of them, was in the best position to show Christina what they had to work with. It had taken no time to convince Joan, eager for excitement, eager to be part of Fionn's life, and persuaded with a few kisses. Compared to Niall hanging, or himself being left alone in this world without the closest thing he had to a friend, Shawn felt little guilt for his tactics, and promised himself he'd make it up to her, if he could.

As the wagon slowed, his heart raced. A gruff voice demanded Joan's business. She answered in muffled words. The pony's hooves began their clop-clopping, jolting him inside the basket. The cart bumped along, jarring him over every cobblestone, while the ache grew in his legs and back. Finally, the cart jerked to a halt. Joan rapped the basket and immediately, the weight on him lightened as she hoisted the linens off, whispering, "Hurry now!"

He climbed out, tumbling the basket on its side, into a small, sheltered courtyard, and yanked the hood of his robe over his head.

"The chapel is across the courtyard," she said.

He hurried to the church, as fast as he could go without raising eyebrows over a charging friar. There, he grabbed his knife, looking around as always for the thing that would most likely stand for seven centuries. With extra time, and the privacy of a silent church at dawn, he carved this one carefully, connecting the lines precisely, edging up the lip of the bell. He carved into it a second, a third, a fourth time, before slipping into the confessional.

He had only minutes to wait, uneasy in such close proximity to God, before he heard voices. A low and throaty woman's voice said, "My Lord would surely allow you to respect the privacy of the confessional. Wait by the back door. You'll see the whole church from there, and I've shown myself to be a good captive, have I not?" He heard the note of humor in her voice, and believed he liked this woman without ever having seen her.

The door of the adjoining booth opened, clicked shut again, and the tiny door slid aside, leaving a lattice work grill for them to peer through. Shawn verified the thick black hair he'd been told of, and deep blue eyes, before pulling his hood back. She looked hard, then spoke, a barely audible whisper. "Tell me why I should trust you."

Shawn whispered, his lips pressed to the grill. "I'm here with the Laird of Glenmirril and his daughter, Niall's betrothed. I want Niall out even more than you do, and right now neither you nor I has anyone else to trust. He's already scheduled to be hanged. How can I possibly make that worse?"

"My husband will gladly hang me beside him," she said. "Though 'tis perhaps not an unkind fate, compared to living with Duncan."

"Look closely at my face," Shawn whispered.

She peered at him through the lattice work and dim light.

With an oath, Shawn used his knife to slice through the delicate wood, and lifted the whole grill away. She gasped at the blasphemy.

"Save it. We don't have time for delicacy," Shawn hissed. "Look! I have Niall's face." As they studied one another, he saw her beauty was stained by a large bruise on the jaw. "Nobody knows this but MacDonald, his daughter, Niall, and me. And now you. I can walk through the streets like this so MacDougall will let 'Fionn' go."

"And hang you instead," Christina whispered.

"Yes, well, we're looking for a solution to that problem. Just an idea. Or Joan will cut and dye my hair to look like Fionn, if we can think of a way to use that. You know the castle, you know the players. Tell us what to do, and we'll do it. We have a dozen men with us. It's not much."

Christina studied him, long and hard. "I've a thought," she said, slowly. "My father-in-law is a lecher."

"A man after my own heart," Shawn said. "But how does that help Niall?"

She smiled the slow, sweet smile of an angel, and leaned through the place where the latticework grill had been, whispering her plan.

"You'll come with us?" Shawn said. "We could kidnap you."

"Then who will get the keys to Bessie? No, MacDougall will not know I was involved. He'll not hang me. First, we get Niall and Bessie out."

"But...." Shawn stopped, searching his mind for an answer.

"Milady," a deep voice called directly outside the confessional. "Surely your sins are not so great. Come out!"

Panic flitted across Christina's face, and settled quickly into a mask of calm. She raised her voice. "Anon, sir. Might I receive absolution?"

"Aye, but be quick. Milord will have my head."

"Do exactly as I've said," she whispered to Shawn. "We'll solve the rest later."

He reached for her hand through the opening. "I'm honored to know you," he said, and kissed her fingertips, with a sincerity he'd never felt in his life. She slipped her fingers from his and almost ran from the confessional.

Glenmirril, Present

It should have been a pleasant day, Amy thought, with Rose's reassurance about Angus's intentions. But his pressing for her sources took over where the worry about his intentions left off. It haunted her, as much as the ghosts of Shawn and Niall, through the halls of Glenmirril as she searched every placard and display for any mention of Niall; as she searched the walls for any sign of Shawn's mark carved as it had been at Creagsmalan.

It would have been worse, she consoled herself, had the October sun not shone down so brightly, had laughing tourists not filled the place. A group of children in little doublets and flowing dresses and coned hats followed a costumed tour guide, hanging on his every word, now and again turning to one another to admire their medieval clothing and giggle.

Still, the hallways she'd walked with Shawn called him forth—the sound of his voice, the one eyebrow cocked in amusement, the warmth of his hand. The gray-haired tour guide, who had led them so many months ago, passed with a group of camera-wielding tourists, giving the same speech about Robert the Bruce.

Amy glanced at Angus, as he led her through the stone hallways, with high arched windows open to the autumn sky. Niall's room pulled the breath from her lungs. She stood before the tapestry of Niall on horseback, laughing over his shoulder. It hurt to think of him dead.

"He must have been quite the character, aye?" Angus stood behind her, his presence a physical sensation though he didn't touch her. "Mooning MacDougall—'tis my favorite image of him."

Amy glanced at him, her heart fluttering. His words resurrected her fear that somehow, he knew, and was baiting her. He'd taken the police reports himself, after all. He knew the doctor insisted 'Shawn' had an arrow injury. He'd heard her re-tell the story, even though she'd stated it only as what 'Shawn' claimed. And he wanted to know how she knew what she knew. Rose couldn't have possibly told him. He wouldn't believe her even if she had. Still trying to settle her spinning thoughts, Amy ran her fingers down the red hangings on the bed.

The MacDougalls wair red; the MacDonalds wair blue. Niall's voice had frothed with indignation, that first day behind the castle, at the thought of wearing red. His hangings would have been blue. But she couldn't explain to the historical society why they should change the bed curtains. She saw him onstage in Inverness, telling a crowd of thousands, *I am Niall Campbell, born in 1290, heir to Glenmirril.* Having been on Shawn's case, Angus must have watched Niall speak those words on stage. There was no way he could believe it, she reassured herself. But he wanted her sources. And she had none to give.

She swallowed, shut her eyes, with the velvet of the red hangings soft under her fingers. *Yes, he was quite a character all right.* He'd died seven hundred years ago, possibly on MacDougall's gallows. She felt ill.

"Are you all right, Amy?" Angus's voice, deep and gruff, came out gently. She opened her eyes. "Fine, thanks."

"We've covered the whole castle," Angus said.

"Every placard," Amy agreed. She'd read every word of every display and searched the walls, but found nothing to explain his use of the mark or tell her if he'd left Creagsmalan alive.

"Except the tower."

Of all the sprawling complex of Glenmirril, the tower was the one place she absolutely didn't want to go. But if Niall's use of Shawn's mark had anything to do with her, the tower might be exactly the place he'd think she'd return to; exactly the place he might leave it.

Creagsmalan, 1314

Niall's small cell became busy. MacDougall and Duncan appeared twice each at the door, staring through the bars and grunting. Niall avoided praying on his knees, pacing the cell restlessly instead, and fighting his rage at God that he was going to die without having married Allene, without even seeing her one last time.

It only fanned his anger that praying, of all things, had condemned him!

Ellen appeared at the grate looking down from the street in the morning. "Milord's father is raging over rumors you've been seen in town!" she hissed. "What is amiss, Fionn!"

Niall rose on his toes, stretching his fingers up to her. He didn't know what it meant or what would come of it, but if people had seen him in town, Shawn was near. "I walk through walls!" he said, hope lightening his heart.

"You think this cause for jest?" Her fingers clutched his, the very tips he could stretch up to her. Her touch was warm after weeks of no human contact. "D' ye know Milord's father says you are someone else and talks of hanging you?"

"That's why he's been looking in on me," Niall said.

"Aye, most likely. He talks of magic, Fionn. Surely not."

"Surely not." Niall's jaw hardened. The man would find a reason to hang him, one way or another. He hoped the lack of a scar had at least bought Shawn the time he needed to stop it.

"Someone is coming!" She dropped a bundle through the grate. Her feet scuffed away, a soft brush of leather on the cobblestones above. As heavy boots sounded in the street, Niall scrambled to the floor, and found a kerchief tied around bannocks.

He'd barely finished eating them, when the key turned in the lock and MacDougall burst in, flinging the door wide before the jailer could remove the keys. They clanked angrily in the lock, a rough ostinato to MacDougall's rage. A look of maniacal glee accompanied his stream of invective. "I don't know what you've done, Campbell, but you'll not play me for a fool again. Have you got that chit lying for you, saying she's seen you in town? Or is she mad?"

A steady, muffled thumping began outside. MacDougall grabbed Niall's chin, yanking his face this way and that. "I don't know why you've no scar, but I know Niall Campbell's face and voice, here in my son's castle where Bruce told you to be. That's the sound of your gallows being built. You swing tomorrow, and a not a day too soon!" And he stormed out again, leaving Niall's heart pounding faster than the hammers outside. He wanted one more sight of Allene.

He returned to pacing the small space and praying, his words falling into a steady rhythm with the hammering in the courtyard. As the sun once again waned, he prayed and paced until his legs ached, unable to sit still with the pounding. It was late evening before the sound finally stopped. Shortly after, another voice whispered at the grate, a woman's voice low and sultry. "Bessie will free you just past dawn. Be ready to flee."

She stretched long, white fingers through the bars high above. He reached up, desperate for a human touch. "He's hanging me tomorrow!" He wanted to have faith in Shawn, in MacDonald, in Christina, but tomorrow sounded uncomfortably close.

"Not till noon," Christina said calmly. "When she comes, do exactly as she says, move fast, and above all, give the lass courage. I've only barely convinced her her lot cannot be worse. The poor thing has been shaking with fear these past hours."

"Tell me your plan," Niall pleaded. "Fear will drive it from her head."

She told him quickly. "And make her go with you. It should work if you do as I've said."

Should. He wished for a stronger word.

Her fingers slid from his. Her hooded form disappeared, leaving him once more alone in the dark, but for a rat snuffling at his toe. He slid down the damp wall, felt for his carved notches, and made another one. He still had his knife. He could fight the guards when they came. He clung to that hope.

After a moment, he forced himself to his knees in the straw. "Give them wisdom," he prayed. "Give Bessie courage. My Lord and Savior, work a miracle and give that frightened mouse courage." *If you have faith the size of a mustard seed, mountains will move.* That seemed more likely than Bessie finding some pluck. "I pray for absolution," he said. "I pray I've lived a life worthy to meet You at noon tomorrow, if I must, and that You'll watch over Shawn and Allene all the same."

He sank down, after two hours of prayer, into fitful sleep, curled in his cloak and the one Ellen had given him, the sound of hammers pulsing through his dreams.

Glenmirril, Present

Amy's dread mounted as they left the living quarters and crossed the courtyard, through a stiff breeze, to the northern tower. But her reluctance would be hard to explain to Angus. He believed Shawn had disappeared at the re-enactment, not from the tower. And she needed—wanted—to look for the mark.

"Cold?" Angus glanced down at her.

"The wind has picked up." She tugged her long blue coat close. The tower rose ahead, a massive block of gray stones, spewing memories and fanciful images. The mist had been thick that night, snaking around her in the courtyard as she'd shouted up to him. In her dreams, the fog twisted into ghostly shapes of men and horses, the past coming to life around her. She wondered again if she would have disappeared, too, had she stayed. The thought scared her. She wanted nothing to do with Niall's brutal world.

A teenage girl brushed against her, looking back with a laugh and quick apology and rushed to catch up with a gangly boy, and Amy realized Angus was staring at her. "The tower bothers you," he said.

She nodded. There was no way to explain, without sounding crazy.

"We don't have to go. Though I think 'tis the best part of Glenmirril."

She forced a laugh. "It's got a beautiful view. I'm being ridiculous."

"No, it's where you went...."

"With Shawn," she finished. "It's okay." A group of tourists chattering in German pushed toward the tower, engulfing them for a moment, and squeezing in twos and threes into the arched opening at the bottom of the tower stairs. She'd just follow them. She gave Angus a bright smile. "Come on. Last one there...." Shawn had always said *is an out of tune oboe.*

Angus grinned, his dark eyes shining with pleasure, and they ran the last twenty feet to the door. It was just a tower, she told herself, as its shadow swallowed her.

The chill of the day cut through her coat, crept in around the white scarf. Her foot landed on the flagstones at the bottom of the tower stairs. Angus swooped in behind her, laughing, saying, "You won!" just as the costumed tour guide burst up the stairs from the lower level. Schoolchildren in tunics and leggings and tall coned princess hats with fluttering veils swarmed around him, chatting and laughing, and carrying her in their wake up the curving stone stairs. She'd just do a quick search for the carved symbol and it would be fine.

Angus's hand fell on the small of her back. Two steps. A chill clutched her arms. Another step. Children flooded the small space, a boy squeezing by and scampering ahead of her. Iciness prickled her scalp. Another three steps, children shouting about the basement storeroom, and Angus saying something she couldn't hear.

Her lungs tightened. She drew in air, pulling in hard against the iron band shutting off her breathing. Something had happened in this tower, some strange magic. She'd abandoned Shawn and he'd been sucked into a brutal world that had killed him. She drew in another breath, but it flew back out in short, sharp puffs of air. Children pushed from behind. Pressure grew at her temples. Her leg muscles seized up. "I can't." It came out as a weak rasp, like sand paper on skin. She vaguely noted the arched window with the stone cross set in it, felt the stone wall pressing against her back. The children's laughter turned to a dull roar like ocean waves; their bright colors blurred into a kaleidoscope swirl brushing past her.

A man in a medieval hood stared at her. She yanked back, her heart pounding furiously.

"Amy, Amy, let's go down now." It was Angus's voice.

She must appear insane to him. She struggled for air. The chill deepened in her arms. The children swept away up the uneven slate stairs, and he was pulling her down, his grip strong on her arm, pulling her back to reality, pushing against a knot of middle-aged English women going up.

They emerged into the sunshine and stiff breeze of a clear October day, laughter and smiles in the courtyard, no mist, no ghosts.

And no way to explain to him why this tower should upset her so.

Creagsmalan, 1314

Christina waited in the stables. The sun silhouetted the eastern hills, a glorious burst of blood-red rising behind them. She wore a riding gown of her favorite sapphire blue, a basket clutched in her slender hands, praying for God's blessing on the venture, and for forgiveness of anything she might do to free Niall and Bessie. She'd loved Duncan. He was rich, handsome with his black hair, and kind when he wished—as he had, before marriage—romantic, witty, courtly, flattering. She'd been hurt at the news of the first woman, but such was marriage. She just hadn't expected it so quickly.

She'd swallowed the pain and continued to be a good wife. She'd been more hurt at rumors of the second, and shocked at his first rage when he threw her against a wall. She'd been disappointed in him the day she rode to the washerwoman's, and heard Joan's tale of his cruelty. But she knew him well enough by then to believe he could be so callous. She'd given Joan a coin, held her hand, and listened.

Back at the castle, she'd opened her ears and asked careful questions, and learned that Bessie, at first flattered and giddy, had quickly been disillusioned, and soon frightened, by the Lord's attentions. So began the jealous wife act. When she could, she sat with Bessie, clutching hands with one another before the Blessed Sacrament, unable to answer the girl's question: *Why?* "Courage, Bessie," she'd soothed time after time over many months. "Something will bring this to an end. We must pray."

MacDougall appeared now, filling the doorway of the stable. She lifted her chin, pulling herself from the past and willing the chill of fear away. MacDougall liked to believe he was more honorable than he was, or at least that others saw him as such. It was her only hope, that he would keep his end of the bargain. She reached for the reins of the big bay. He put his hand on hers, stopping her, and lowered his lips to hers. Every nerve shook. The image of the yellow teeth repulsed her. She forced herself to wait, before pulling away. "My Lord." She used the calm voice she'd perfected with Duncan. "You gave me your word."

"And I'll honor it," he whispered against her cheek. His breath smelled of venison and ale. "Before or after."

She didn't want to cut it any closer. The man, Shawn, would be waiting. "I want to get the food to the widows early." She hoped he interpreted that as a promise. "It means a great deal to me."

"Duncan does complain that you wish to give away the whole castle."

She lowered her eyes to the stable floor. "They've but little, My Lord. Duncan throws more to the dogs each night than what I ask for his people in a week."

"Why now?" he asked. "What changed your mind? 'Tis unlike you."

Her nerves kicked up a notch. He was a lecherous old man. She must not mistake that for slow wit. "I crave kindness." With trembling fingers, she lifted her skirt over the top of her short riding boot. She lifted her eyes to his, and saw what she'd hoped for, as he stared down at the ugly, puckered skin left from the poker Duncan had pressed into her leg the night Niall had tried to take Bessie away.

He swallowed. "My son did that?"

"Aye." She dropped the skirt, satisfied he believed her motives. "He was angry I spoke to Bessie. My Lord, the girl is young. I understand 'tis the way of men, and meant him no harm, but only to comfort her." The quivering in her arms grew, fearing he'd spot a hole in her story she had not foreseen. *Stick as close to the truth as you can,* Shawn had told her. "You've been kind to me, My Lord," she continued. That, too, was true. He'd been kind hoping for repayment, but it *was* true. "You've no idea...." She let the sentence hang. He was a soldier. He had ideas aplenty. "I crave the companionship of one to share my love for these people, sir." She knew MacDougall had agreed to the outing only to spend time alone with her, hoping it would lead to what he really wanted.

"I thought you were angry with me for ordering the hanging."

She lowered her eyes. "I've been foolish, My Lord. Forgive me. I was blinded by my ladies giggling over his fair looks. I've since heard how he tried to take advantage of Bessie, how he tried to take her to the gardens when I called for her to be sent to the upper kitchens." She let anger flash on her face and blaze in the depths of her blue eyes. "Has the girl not suffered enough!" She judged it sufficient anger for now. Shawn would add fuel to her supposed ire. Her heart pounded, willing MacDougall to mount his horse. She felt no braver than Bessie, fearing to find that what she thought was a skillful weaving of truth and lies would prove less sturdy than she hoped.

He bowed low over her hand, kissing her white fingertips. "You've a kind heart, My Lady. My son is a fool." She inclined her head in humble acknowledgment of the compliment, hoping Duncan had gotten at least a little of his foolishness from his father. With laced fingers, MacDougall boosted her onto the bay. She pulled on her leather gloves, and took the reins, waiting. He placed a boot in his own stirrup and mounted.

"My Lord." She stopped him as he twitched the reins. "Speaking of the prisoner, I've had reports the guard is drinking on duty and lax. You'll look into it when we return?"

He nodded, his face darkening. And taking the basket from her, they set off to feed the poor.

Glenmirril, Present

Demoralized by her failure, Amy stood silently before the life-sized crucifix. She'd wandered the chapel, searching half-heartedly for Niall's— Shawn's—mark, before stopping at the cross. Even hanging in a side shrine, it dominated Glenmirril's chapel. The wood was deep amber, with the bright sheen of old age. Christ stared up to Heaven. "I shouldn't touch it," she said.

Angus chuckled. "It has that effect. Go ahead. Touch it."

She put her hand on the leg. Wooden flesh shimmered, warm under her fingers, satin grown in a long-ago forest and aged to perfection. She closed her eyes, letting the sensation of honey-smooth wood sink into her fingers.

"Something else, aye?"

She opened her eyes, turning to him, but unwilling to take her hand from the wood.

"It's centuries old." Angus stood alongside her, touching the knee of the carved figure, just above her hand. "Nobody knows where it came from. It was found in a cave under the castle in the sixteenth century and brought up. Though the chapel itself has been in use continuously since the 1200s."

Amy looked around the chapel. Silver-gray stones lifted a restored roof a story and a half over their heads. Great crossbeam timbers arced above, matching the shape of the windows. A dozen wooden pews faced the raised stone altar, and one stained glass window shone down candy-colored bits of light through a shepherd holding a lamb. She wondered if, at this very moment seven centuries ago, Niall or Allene stood in the chapel with them, maybe in their last moments together before he ended up in MacDougall's dungeon, on MacDougall's gallows. Hairs rose on her arms, imagining them beside her, smelling the same candles, wax and incense, seeing the same sunlight shooting, a translucent bolt, through colored glass. She wondered if he'd touched the leg of Christ, too, if even now, his hand lay beside hers separated only by the thin veil of centuries. She wished the crucifix could speak to her, tell her what it had seen so many years ago, what had become of Niall, why he'd used Shawn's symbol.

But the cross had only been found in the sixteenth century.

She shook away the fanciful thoughts.

Angus touched her shoulder. "Will we sit down? You look pale."

Amy nodded. "I'm sorry. I'm a mess today." She followed him to the pew, breathing in the scent of wood polish.

"It often helps to talk about it," Angus said. Their arms touched, side by side on the hard bench.

She gave a short bark of a laugh. "I *can't* talk about it."

"Because I'm the police?"

"Because you'd think I'm crazy."

After a silence, he said, "That's where you left him. In the tower."

She nodded. "I'm sorry. It shouldn't...I shouldn't...." She reminded herself he thought Shawn had disappeared at Bannockburn.

"The best way to overcome fears is to face them."

"I left him. I have nightmares about that tower." They sat while the angle of the sunbeam lengthened.

"He attracted trouble," Angus said. "He got the wrong sort angry. It was him, not the tower."

Silence fell between them, as warm and full of life as the honey-colored sheen of wood before her. Her thoughts drifted back to Niall. "It's amazing to think he probably sat right here in this chapel," she said. "Probably hundreds of times."

"Aye." Angus followed her thoughts. "It's what I like about these old places. Feeling they're still here, all around me. I feel I'm soaking up the wisdom of their lives." After a minute, he added, "Let's look around a bit, and try the tower later. If you don't want to, we won't, but I think you'll feel better if you do."

Angus was right. Even apart from the search for Shawn's symbol, she had to face her fears. She stared at the tiny candle flames flickering under the crucifix. "Maybe when it's not so crowded?"

"We'll come after it closes," he promised.

She thought of the climb up the bramble-covered path with Shawn the previous June, scaling the crumbling wall and the drop down to the other side. It wasn't something to be doing when she was pregnant. But it was the only time the place would be deserted. "Okay." She nodded. "After it closes."

The Glen Beyond Creagsmalan, 1314

Shawn waited in the cover of forest just past the last hut. Niall's sword hung at his side, ready to use. Lachlan and Owen flanked him, a bow and arrow apiece dangling in relaxed, deadly hands. A glen stretched north before them, toward the castle, full of soft mist, hills rising on either side, purple in the rising sun. Smoke drifted from the chimney of the little hut a furlong away. Christina's plan was simple and elegant, with a brutal willingness to take advantage of MacDougall's Achilles' heel. "He desires me," she'd stated bluntly, forgoing the blush that would blaze up most women's faces in this era at the statement.

"You can't do that," Shawn had objected.

"Whisht!" she'd said derisively. "I'll find a way out of it."

The horse danced under him—a big and powerful stallion this time, ready to carry him far out of MacDougall's reach, should the man give chase. The archers at his side made that improbable. He missed his own small hobbin.

His head felt light, even bare, with the shoulder length hair cut short, and the beard removed under Joan's skillful hands. She'd exclaimed again over how quickly it had grown, and he'd reminded her to cut it not quite so short, maybe an inch longer than last time. She'd dyed it, leaning him over the tub, rinsing with hot water and impressive views that left no doubt what she wanted in exchange. He'd held her hand, torn, and settled for kissing her fingers and touching her cheek with a heartfelt thank you. And now, he worried again he'd followed Christina's directions poorly, was waiting on the wrong side of the hill, or at the wrong hut.

Lachlan nudged Shawn. "Niall, over there."

Christina and MacDougall rode into the far end of the glen, coming around the foot of a hill, tiny at this distance, her riding habit a flash of blue.

Adrenaline shot through Shawn. The time had come. He could die in this venture. Niall could die.

He watched silently, fighting the quiver of nerves. The far-away couple reached the first hut and dismounted. Their horses waited, heads down, while they disappeared inside. Shawn's own horse pawed, restless, and let out a whinny. It settled again, with a pat of his hand. Lachlan's horse sidestepped and danced back, nudging the other animal's nose, and returned to grazing in the dewy grass.

At last, with Shawn's nerves keyed high, MacDougall and Christina came out, mounted, and rode toward the small group under the trees. Lachlan and Owen pulled their hoods up, shielding their faces. Shawn stroked his horse's neck, trying to calm his own adrenaline rush.

Glenmirril, Present

"You're kidding." Amy stared at Glenmirril's modern sidewalk, curving from a small, unlocked gate down across a broad lawn. An arched bridge crossed the grassy ditch that had once been a moat. Floodlights lit the massive walls, a powerful fortress etched against the dark blue of the eastern sky. The moon hung there, a silver orb in the dusk. "It's not even locked," she said in disbelief, as Angus opened the gate and walked through.

"Well, we'll have to climb over the other." Twenty feet on, a second gate, no more than a waist-high pair of beams with two diagonal crossbars, secured with a small chain and padlock, blocked their entrance.

"Shawn must have known this." She felt her irritation with him grow.

"I imagine so." Angus stepped up on the gate, swinging a leg over.

"So climbing a bracken-covered hill and scaling a stone wall was totally unnecessary?" She shook her head in disgust. "Typical of him, having to throw in a little feel of danger and forbidden trespassing."

"There are no no-trespass laws in Scotland," Angus said. "And no police here. Except me, of course." He offered his hand, helping her over the gate.

She smiled, liking his quiet humor. His touch sent electricity shooting up her wrist. "I feel really stupid, not going up before." She tried to ignore the tingles as she clambered over the gate. He dropped her hand as she landed on the other side. "I'm not usually like this."

"You've been through a trauma," he said. "You're sure you don't want to talk about it?"

She hesitated. But her gut and Rose both told her he was a friend, not a cop. She lowered her head. "He wouldn't listen. He was so arrogant." They ambled down the sidewalk, across the lawn. "Something just snapped in me." She fell silent, walking to the bridge, thinking how strange this modern sidewalk must have looked to Niall. "I felt if I didn't stand up for myself *finally*, he'd grind me into dust."

They crossed the bridge, into Glenmirril's courtyard. The tower rose ahead on their left. Tendrils of mist floated, ankle high in the evening shadows, as they crossed the bailey, past the kirk. She spoke softly. "I really felt I'd disappear, just cease to be at all, if I let him push me one more time."

"Then something good happened here." Angus stopped in the arch leading into the tower, the open air of the courtyard behind them, the cool, dim interior and the stairs, smooth and sunken in the middle of each tread with centuries of use, before them.

She shook her head, clutching her arms around herself. The tower had taken her child's father. It wasn't good; it was terrible.

Angus touched her arm for only a second. "Nothing that happened is your fault. Can you do this?"

She nodded. They climbed past the window with the stone cross in its aperture. The stairs darkened, as they had that night. At the top, evening light poured over the parapets. Far below, the last rays of the western sun sparkled off the water.

Amy wandered the ten by ten square tower, running her hand over the stone walls in search of Shawn's mark. As she touched each wall, as each rough stone grazed her fingertips, she felt she could see everything at once, herself and Shawn and Allene and Niall, and all the tension. She closed her eyes, and felt an irrational rush of gratitude that she hadn't brought bluebells, as if they were to blame. She wondered who, seven centuries past, might be in the tower with her and Angus. She wondered if Niall came up sometimes. Did he—had he—ever come up after getting back to his own time? Or did he avoid the tower, not wanting to disappear into another century again?

Because there was no mark.

"Is it all right now?" Angus asked. "I've always loved it up here. Look at the sun on the water and the mountains."

She did so, feeling she could see exactly where Niall had lain with his cloak that night, irritated with Allene. Same place Shawn must have slept, probably after drinking all the beer and whiskey in the basket. But she felt no danger this time. Just two angry women storming away, two irritated men throwing themselves in the corner to sleep. They just woke up in the wrong times, that was all.

"You shouldn't feel so much guilt," Angus said. "'Tis unfortunate, but when people live recklessly, things tend to happen. You can't blame yourself." His voice was low, gravelly, close to her ear. He stood so close she could feel the warmth of his body, though he didn't touch her.

Her insides melted the way they had with Shawn.

The guilt melted away with it. She had done nothing wrong here.

Angus cleared his throat and stepped back. "Shall we go for dinner?"

She nodded numbly, sad and relieved the moment had passed. Her mind skipped from the lack of Shawn's symbol to her other problem. She had to tell him she was pregnant. At dinner, she promised herself. She had to tell him she was pregnant. At dinner, she promised herself.

Creagsmalan, 1314

Christina fought her fears as they left the hut, only a few minutes' ride from the castle. Shawn may not have found the place; MacDougall might give chase, catch him, and put an end to it all right there. The test would come in the next moments.

MacDougall boosted her into her saddle, smiling promises into her eyes. "Are you cold?" he asked. "You're trembling."

"There's a chill in the air." She tugged her cloak tight, reviewing her lines, reminding herself she was outraged at 'Fionn,' at the guard. She told herself the story, as MacDougall mounted his horse, convincing herself, feeling the anger. She smiled at MacDougall. He snapped his reins, and they rode, their knees touching, toward the wooded southern end of the glen.

She couldn't see them. Her heart pounded. If this plan failed, she'd need to think up another to save Niall, and there was no time. The horses' hooves plunked softly in the misty grass, now and again striking a rock in the soil. Smoke curled up from the second hut. They were close now, so close. She couldn't see him!

And then her heart pounded harder, faster, and fear shot up her arms. A great bay pranced out from under the trees, tossing its head. Niall—no, Fionn —no, Shawn—the likeness was uncanny!—sat boldly astride it in a forest green tunic. He lifted his chin arrogantly, grinning.

"MacDougall!" His voice rang down the glen. He threw his head back and laughed. "Give my thanks to your drunken guard."

MacDougall's face darkened. He made to kick his horse, but in that instant, two glistening chestnut stallions pranced from the wood, each with an archer astride, faces in the shadows of their hoods, arrows nocked, ready to fly. MacDougall's spurs fell, impotent.

"Make my day, MacDougall," the man Shawn yelled. "A step closer, and you've two arrows through the heart." He motioned with his head at the archers, and the three of them backed up, step by step, watching MacDougall, back under the fringe of oaks. "Let your dolt of a son know I've got Bessie!"

"You bring her back!" Christina shouted. "Milord, stop him!"

Shades of rage thundered across her father-in-law's face, above the heavy beard. He bared his yellow teeth. "Get back here, Campbell! Fight me like a man!"

"Campbell? My name is Fionn." Shawn grinned. "Milady, tell your husband his mistress already thinks I'm more man than he ever was! Shame I couldn't show you, too."

Christina gasped. She rose in her saddle, screaming at MacDougall. "Will you let him insult me so! And bite his thumb at you? Turn now for your men! They can't go far!"

MacDougall turned in a spinning flash of horse beyond her greatest hopes, leaning low over the animal's neck, whipping it, screaming for guards long before they rounded the hill out of the glen. Christina egged him on, bent over her speeding horse. "Did I not say the guard was lax! Get him up from the dungeon!" Her cloak whipped behind her. The horses snorted and frothed. She clung to her animal's mane. Wind bit her face. "Bessie is paying the price for his drunkenness!" She threw every rage she'd ever felt at Duncan into the act. "The guard! I want the guard!" They galloped into town, hooves striking cobblestones with sharp reports.

"To arms!" MacDougall roared.

"Every man!" Christina screamed.

Men streamed from inns and taverns. Women yanked children from before the thundering horses. MacDougall's soldiers poured from a pub, pulling on gloves as he bellowed instructions, still riding hard. "Give chase! South through the glen!" he shouted over his shoulder.

MacDougall and Christina blasted through the castle portcullis, neck and neck, throwing themselves to the ground as the horses whinnied and skidded and pulled up short, snorting and stamping in the shadow of the gallows. "Bring me the jailer!" MacDougall hollered. Blood flushed his face.

A man scurried to do their bidding, his curly toed shoes slipping on smooth stone, grabbing a wall to right himself, and running in fear, yelling. She grabbed MacDougall's arm. She must keep him moving, keep his anger high, lest he think. "He's let the poor girl into the hands of a villain!" She spun him around, his back to the dungeon stairs. "What will Duncan say!" Morning sun burst over the parapets.

Men hauled the guard up the stairs from the dungeons, thrusting him into the shadow of the gallows. Christina stepped forward, keeping the drama high, keeping every eye on herself—MacDougall, the guard, the men who had brought him up. She slapped the jailer. "You fool!" Her hands trembled as she grabbed the keys at his waist, hoping, praying, and tore with all her might. They came free with a satisfying rip of the belt, more than she'd hoped for. She flung them with all her strength, as if she didn't know they skidded toward the dungeon stairs, rattling down a step or two. She blazed blue-eyed fire into his face, giving no one time to think. "Do you know what you've done!"

"No, Milady." He was bleary-eyed from night duty. Red rimmed his eyes. He looked confused. His breath stank from last night's meal, and she suspected his clothes had not so distantly been in a tavern, giving him enough smell to make it believable.

"Look at his eyes!" She swirled the skirt of her riding habit, stomped in a circle around the cowering man. She dragged him around the corner of the gallows so when MacDougall stormed forward, gripping his chin and peering into his eyes, he saw nothing of the stairs. Christina prayed no one would see the frail white arm reach for the keys. And she prayed Bessie would summon the courage to reach for them.

MacDougall bellowed, covering any jangle Bessie might let slip from the heavy ring. "They're red! 'Tis true! Have you ale down there?"

Christina covered her panic with rage. Had Bessie been brave enough to leave the wineskin at the man's side? But they couldn't go down to look now. She snorted. "No need to look! Can you not smell it? Can you not see how he gapes as if he's addled even now? Take him to Duncan!" The faster she could clear them from the courtyard, the better. Though Bessie knew the other way out of the kitchens, Niall did not. She couldn't risk Bessie panicking, perhaps bumbling up the stairs, in front of everyone, dragging Niall into plain sight. She pushed the guard. She seized MacDougall's arm. She turned on the tears. "How could you have?" she cried, careful not to tell the poor man what he'd done. The longer she avoided saying it, the longer before he insisted the prisoner was still there, the safer for Niall and Bessie. She berated him, browbeat him, begging God to forgive her, and drove him before her, the force of her anger swirling everyone in her wake, up the opposite stairs, to Duncan's chambers.

Inverness, Present

Angus had a small home, one in a row of attached homes. As Amy's thoughts jumped from her failure to find the flattened S to the news she had to give him, he opened his front door to reveal a house like her own. Stairs ran up on the left side, and a hallway raced back to the kitchen. Her eyes landed on the crucifix on the wall. Bisque-colored palms fanned out behind it. Pictures of Mary and Christ hung on either side of the fireplace in the living room. He'd never mentioned God or religion. He would, even more than other men, dislike learning she was pregnant, she thought with regret. She'd felt close to him in the tower, alive with possibilities—and hope. Telling him would end everything. She tore her eyes from the pictures. Her palms felt clammy. She strove to keep her voice light. "Something smells great. Did you make dinner?"

"Oh, well, no. I mean, I always put something on." His ruddy cheeks turned a shade darker. "But I'll take you out for a bite."

"No, you don't have to. It smells great. What is it?"

"A bit of a specialty of mine." His concern relaxed into a smile. "Nothing fancy, now. I just threw some things in the slow cooker. Would you like a drink? What do you Americans do? Beer, wine, a cocktail?"

Her hand drifted to her stomach. "Water's fine." She smiled, touched at his eagerness to please, and feeling guiltier, still, because of it.

He led her down the short hall.

Behind him, her smile subsided. He was investing time in her, standing close, making meals. She had to tell him.

"Dinner." Angus stepped aside, revealing a small kitchen. A round table, covered in a navy blue cotton cloth, frayed at the edges, held two place settings of beige stoneware plates, and dull, battered forks and knives. She bit her lip, holding back a smile. Shawn would have had fine linen, bone china, crystal, and silver, on his large mahogany table in his oversized dining room. He would have laughed this to scorn.

She liked it. It felt genuine.

She breathed in the smell of roast chicken, lemon, and pepper. "I didn't know you cooked." She didn't volunteer that Shawn had loved to, also.

Angus beamed. "If a man's going to eat, he may as well enjoy his food." He glanced at the table. "I just threw an extra setting on, before I left, that's all. Just in case. Sometimes my sister stops by."

She smiled. "Does she?" Her stomach gave an odd little flutter. If Rose hadn't assured her, his behavior did. Angus really liked her. Trying to get information wouldn't leave him so flustered.

"Not that I don't want you here," he added hastily. "If she stops by, I'll not kick you out."

Amy laughed. He was as nervous as she was. Shawn would have a heyday watching the two of them. Nothing had ever made him nervous. But she had to tell him. Instead, putting off the moment she dreaded, she asked, "Do you want help with anything?"

He waved her off, already yanking the plug on the slow cooker and lifting the pot over to the trivet waiting on the table. He turned back, a quick step across the small room, and took a bowl of salad from the refrigerator. Seated, he bowed his head in quick prayer. When he finished, he heaped chicken and potatoes on her plate. They sent up curls of steam.

It was a lousy time to mention she was pregnant. She'd work it in during the meal, as they talked. She cleared her throat as she lifted her fork. "I'm at a disadvantage. You knew plenty about me before we ever met. Tell me about your family."

"I've two parents, a sister, and a brother," he said. "Eight years on the force." She was right, she thought, in guessing he was eight to ten years older than her. "My life has not been so interesting as yours."

She cocked her head. "You think my life is interesting?"

"Playing with an international orchestra, dating...." He stopped.

"Yeah, him." She poked her fork into a potato, and took a bite. "Delicious. I told you I broke up with him. What I didn't say is, it's because he cheated and lied. It's not interesting. It's painful."

His fork dropped to his plate with a soft *chink.* "I'm sorry."

"His other antics got out. That part never did. Which makes me wonder if I'm crazy after all."

His hand stretched across the small space between them, touching her fingers where they rested at the edge of her plate. "Is that why you said I might think you're crazy?"

She frowned. "No." Her words, on the drive to Creagsmalan, and in Glenmirril's chapel, came back to her. She gave a nervous laugh and grabbed his explanation. "Yes. He always said I was seeing things."

Across the table, Angus let out a breath. "Of course. It protected him. In eight years on the force, I've found women have a good instinct. I'm sorry. I shouldn't speak ill of him."

He was apologizing! Shame burned in her. While she withheld a thing like being pregnant, he was apologizing. She set her fork down. "Angus, I have to...."

The doorbell rang, a sharp peal. He swiped at his mouth with a napkin as he rose. "I'm sorry," he mumbled. "Bad timing."

"No, it's okay." She laughed nervously. "Maybe it's great timing."

Several more thuds landed on the front door, and two young voices shouted, "Uncle Angus! Mam says sure you're home but we can't walk in this time!" Amy bit her lip, holding back a laugh. Color climbed up Angus's cheeks. Without a word, he headed down the hall.

The door flew open. Two small boys and a large black lab burst in, enveloping Angus, jumping into his arms. The dog leapt up, woofing and licking his face. Amy watched from the doorway, smiling. Moments later, a bright voice rose above the din in the hallway. A dark-haired woman erupted from the crowd at the front door and rushed into the kitchen, hauling the boys with her. "You're Amy!" She let go of one of the children to push a flop of dark curls out of her eyes. Before Amy knew it, she was wrapped in a warm embrace. "Oh, what beautiful hair!" She lifted a lock of the hair falling to Amy's waist. "Angus did say so."

"He did?" Pleasure flushed Amy's cheeks. She looked to him.

Angus kept his eyes on the children jumping around his knees. One of them bumped into the kitchen table, rattling the plates and silverware. "Uncle Angus, have you sweets for us!"

"This is Mairi," Angus managed to gasp as the children dug in his pockets, toppling him half off balance. He caught himself against the counter. "My wee and verra intrusive sister." The dog woofed, wiggling through the forest of legs.

"It's nice to meet you." Over bouncing heads, Amy shook hands.

"Get out of there, you two," Mairi scolded. "You've too much energy for this small kitchen!" Her cheeks were as ruddy as Angus's. "Your Uncle Angus'll not give candy to bold children. I'm sorry," she said to Amy. She noted the half-eaten meal. "Angus, I didn't mean to interrupt."

"You did indeed," he said, but he sounded amused.

The dog woofed again, nosing Amy's hand, till she scratched its ears.

"No, really," Mairi insisted. "I just came to leave that magazine you wanted." She handed it over the boys' heads. Angus took it with one hand, while reaching in his pocket with the other, producing candy for the children.

They fell to tearing at the wrappers even while shouting a chorus of *Thank you, Uncle Angus!* as loud as the girls that used to scream for Shawn.

"Gavin and Hamish." Angus introduced them to Amy. They smiled shyly and ducked behind his legs. The dog plunked itself on its rump, its tail swishing furiously across the floor. The younger boy's hand reached back out, offering her his stick of hard candy, already sampled.

She squatted down, meeting his dark blue eyes, and accepted it. "Thank you. Are you Gavin or Hamish?"

"Hamish." He ducked back behind Angus's legs.

"Off with you now." Mairi shooed them down the hall. "Go show Uncle Angus your new dog." The boys yelled, their shyness forgotten, and raced ahead, dragging Angus, one on each hand. The dog bounded behind them, barking loudly.

The front door slammed, dropping silence around them. Mairi gripped Amy's hands. "He did say you were lovely. Since Julia eight years ago, he's dated a bit, but his heart was never in it. We've worried about him so, but he can't stop talking about you. He's the loveliest man, the kindest you'll ever meet."

"Yes, he's...." Amy had no time to say more before the front door burst open again, Angus trying to enter as the boys and dog jumped in front of him.

"He'd give the shirt off his back!" The whirlwind that was Angus's sister squeezed her hands, kissed her abruptly on each cheek, and hurried out after the boys calling, "Thank your uncle and tell Miss Amy it was nice to meet her." And in the same flurry in which they'd arrived, they were gone. Amy was left with the sticky candy in her hand.

In the doorway, Angus grinned. "You needn't eat it."

She smiled. "It's a shame she didn't stay."

"'Tis a *verra* good thing she didn't stay. How much did she manage to tell you when she had her minions drag me out?" He put a hand on her shoulder, guiding her back to the table.

"You know her well." Amy looked uncertainly at the candy in her hand before placing it on the plate beside her chicken. "She said you're lovely and kind." She paused. The issue of pregnancy burned on her mind. But so did Mairi's comment about Julia. "You know all about my boyfriends. What about you?"

"I've had none," he said.

She blinked, then laughed. "Girlfriends."

He sat down. "One in high school, a couple in college. One a few years ago. I've dated a bit since then, but none struck my fancy."

She pushed at her potatoes.

"She told you about Julia, didn't she?"

"She mentioned the name."

"Yes, well, I hope I don't come across as less than honest. 'Twas a long time ago, sure. I suppose my family regard her as a bit like Shawn. She fell in love with someone else and didn't like to hurt me."

"She cheated on you."

He shrugged. "'Tis no matter now. I've dessert when you're done."

Amy lifted her fork, her stomach resuming its churning with the need to tell him.

"Is the chicken not good?" he asked.

"It's wonderful," she said. "It's just...I have to...."

The door bell rang. "That's the last time I tell them anything," Angus muttered. The door flew open before he reached it, and a short, barrel-chested man with thin brown hair burst in, wearing denim jeans and a dark blue t-shirt. "Angus!" He pumped his hand and slapped his arm. He peered over Angus's shoulder, jumping at sight of Amy. "Why, you didn't tell me you had company, or I'd not have burst in!"

"No doubt Mairi told you which is *exactly* why you burst in," Angus grumbled. "Clive, Amy. Amy, me mate, Clive Chisolm."

"We've met," Amy said.

Clive pushed past Angus, taking Amy's hand and shaking it vigorously. "A pleasure, Amy. And I do apologize if I seemed to be badgering you, at the hotel. I was only trying to do my job now, you know. Now it just so happens I brought a bottle of some very fine Scotch. Nice and smooth, aye?" He steered her into the front room, calling over his shoulder, "Angus, get us some glasses. Now, then." He ushered Amy onto Angus's leather couch. "Did you know Angus was on the telly just this past summer?" He seated himself beside Amy. "Has he shown you his awards? Has he told you about being written up in the paper?"

"No." Angus came in with three glasses. "We were just after eating." He glanced from the bottle in Clive's hand to his watch. "I'd say the Scotch will last an hour and a bit, so is my brother scheduled to show up in two? Or do my parents come first?"

"Now, you've an awfully suspicious mind." Clive took a glass and poured the Scotch, a smooth waterfall of amber. It reminded Amy of the crucifix in the chapel. Clive handed it to her, ignoring her protests. "Finest Scotch out there," he said. "You should see Angus swim. He was awarded a medal...."

"'Tis my job." Angus accepted a glass of Scotch. "Perhaps you'd like to hear what Amy does."

"We know all about Amy. Why, didn't we watch her come in with the orchestra on the telly just last June?"

Amy raised her eyebrows at Angus. "You watched me on TV?"

He sipped his drink, not meeting her eyes. "The telly was on at the station, that's all."

"And didn't Angus look up when you and your man came through the gate and say, 'Now there's the loveliest woman I've ever seen.'"

"Amy was quite taken with Glenmirril's crucifix," Angus said loudly.

Amy smiled. Her thumb tucked under her fist, feeling the ring on her finger. "Very," she said. "It's stunning workmanship."

"The woodworking equivalent of Angus's rescue work," Clive declared. "You've never seen such wind blow up on the loch, and out of nowhere. We got a call at the station, three boys out in it, and their mothers in a panic now, and the chief says, if it's water, send MacLean."

"And I did my job. Amy, you don't like Scotch?"

"It's fine," Amy said.

"He was awarded a commendation," Clive added. "D' you mean to say he told you none of this?"

"Amazingly, I did not." Angus set his glass on the end table. "Thanks for stopping by. Let my brother know we're going for a drive, so he'll be ringing the bell on an empty house. Help yourself to dinner if you like, and there are some movies on the shelf there."

Tucking her mouth down against the laughter bubbling up, Amy took Angus's outstretched hand. "It's a pleasure to meet you when you're not a police officer, Clive," she said, and followed Angus into the cool night.

Creagsmalan, 1314

Niall rose early, too agitated to sleep. Yesterday's hammering of the gallows had echoed through his nightmares, jarring him awake as he dreamed of jolting to the end of a rope. Today, he left his dank, cold prison and the rats, by low road or high. He tried to pray; worries preyed on him instead. His restless mind leapt from one fear to another. What if...what if...*what if?*

He paced the small cell, told himself the guard did not need unusual activity to alert him, and forced himself to his knees. He wanted his crucifix to calm his mind; he prayed for Allene, hating the thought of her left alone, grieving. Anger flashed up in him, like the Beltaine fires high in the hills, flaring to life in an instant, crackling and burning. He'd been promised her hand in marriage, and one thing after another had prevented it. He wanted, at least, to die having known all the love between them, maybe with a child to carry on his name and memory. He vowed if he got out of this, there would be no more delays. *None.*

With fiery claws of anger digging in his gut, he tried to slow his breathing. He pushed his thoughts to praying for Amy and her child who would not be born for seven hundred years. It helped. He took a steadying breath, and prayed for Bessie, murmuring over and over, "Grant her courage, My Lord, please! Grant her courage!"

He rose again, felt his legs tremble, and added, "Please, I need courage, too." His heart cried out to see and touch Allene one more time. "Please, God, just let me see her!"

The tiny bit of the world outside the grates turned gray. Mist hovered beyond the bars. A pair of feet and a sapphire skirt swished at the grate. "All will be well," Christina's throaty voice breathed down, and she hurried by. He clung to the hope. Anything could go wrong.

He prayed *Aves* and *Paters* and *Glorias* while the mist outside turned from gray to pink, and finally white as the sun rose higher. He wrapped his two cloaks around him, determined to be ready, and peered through the bars on the door to see the guard snoozing peacefully. Squinting, he made out a flattened wineskin by the man's feet. Hope struggled higher, a weak flicker in the shadow of his anger of moments ago. The wineskin had been Bessie's job. Though a small thing, it helped the overall picture. More importantly, Christina had hoped, it would give Bessie courage to see she could do one small thing.

A voice beckoned him back to the grate. Ellen pressed her peaked face against it, forcing biscuits and a wineskin through. "A dozen ladies are in the chapel praying for you, Fionn," she whispered. Her voice trembled, tottering on the edge of tears. "It must come aright." She reached down thin fingers to touch his, her head pressed against the bars. Tears rolled down her cheeks.

"Go pray with them, Ellen," he finally told her, though he hated to be left alone. When she had gone, he ate and drank, despite the stone in his stomach. He must have strength. He thought of Allene, of her angry words to him, only months ago in the tower, telling him how awful the waiting was. He knew now. He understood, helpless here in the dark, with nothing to do but wait, blind and deaf to events unfolding outside. He crossed himself. "My Lord, my God, forgive my impatience with her. I didn't understand." He wanted to wrap her in his arms, apologize, and swear he'd never again be angry with her, if he could just get out of this and marry her as they'd planned for so long.

A clattering rose, far from his small window, a far-off stampeding of hooves on cobblestone. He ran to the door. The guard still slept. All the better. He crossed himself, begging, "My Lord, give Bessie courage." From outside came shouting, a woman screaming, a man bellowing. Hair prickled the back of Niall's neck. He gripped the bars and peered through. The guard slept on. From the street, the voices grew louder. "To arms!" someone shouted. Townspeople yelled. A flurry of feet raced past his cell window. Niall paced, trying to out-walk the frosty grip of nerves.

Another several agonizing minutes, every muscle taut, and he heard the voice he'd waited for, a man bellowing down the hall for the jailer. Niall backed up against the wall next to the door, out of sight, in case they looked in. He swallowed, forcing himself to stand still, begging, *God, don't let him check the cell.* The guard mumbled, yelled back.

"I've no notion what's wrong!" the first voice shouted. Niall pressed himself more tightly against the wall. "Milady's in a rage and wants ye ten minutes ago. Move!" The sound of feet running through the dark hall buoyed his heart. He spun, knowing he shouldn't touch the door, and gave it a sharp rattle of desperation, anyway. He strained to see through the torch-lit flickering shadows of the hall. The guard was gone! He gave the bars another hard shake, knowing he should stay back, too desperate and scared to do what he should. "Bessie!" he hissed into the empty hall. "Let me out!"

The hall remained silent and empty.

Chapter Fifteen

Inverness, Present

They parked by the river. Last time she was here, Amy thought, she'd been running for the bridge with Niall, running from a man with a knife, and before that, walking south to the hotel, holding his hand, thinking he was Shawn. Now, she was here again, needing to break unpleasant news to someone she'd come to like very much. Her stomach twisted with nerves.

"Shall we walk a bit?" Angus asked. "Wait." He jumped out of the car and rounded it, opening her door. They walked the pebbly shore of the Ness, with the moonlight glinting off the river, toward the hotel. Memories flooded her. When she and Shawn had flown to Inverness planning the tour, they'd walked by the river, too, past the lacy, white bridge. They'd sat on the shore, and later, walked along it to the first rehearsal in Inverness, just five months ago.

It had all somehow happened so fast with Angus. She glanced at him, walking beside her, his hands tucked in his dark blue pea coat. Except nothing had happened. They'd spent a great deal of time together, traded jokes. Nothing more. "I've been thinking," he said. "Niall went with James Douglas. How about we follow the trail of Douglas's raids? Who knows what we'll find?"

"We don't know it was really him." Amy burrowed her hands into her own pockets. Her mind jumped from Niall, and gallows, to pregnancy. "Creagsmalan's archives say he was in MacDougall's dungeon at the same time."

Angus shrugged. "I'd trust sources claiming he was knighted before MacDougall's dungeon records."

Amy kicked a pebble on the shore. "That would be a road trip."

"I've hols coming up. It's my treat. I've wanted to make this trip for a long time."

Amy smiled, ducking her chin deeper into her scarf. Everyone was dishonest in their own way.

"You're quiet," he said. "Dinner was cut short, but there's a nice place over the bridge, if you'd like a bite to eat and a wee drop."

"I'd love it," she said. But her emotions churned. He was offering a road trip. He'd put his arm around her shoulder, made her dinner. The carved Christ with its amber-honey tones loomed in her mind, not condemning, but remonstrating, gently persuading. *You need to tell him. Now.*

They ascended the few steps up to the bridge, the lacy, white one, fragile and delicate looking, and stopped in the middle, looking out on the water. Flashes of moonlight danced on it. Angus leaned his arms on the rail, looking across. After a minute of silence, he touched her hand, ran his finger up and down the back of it. A fish leapt in the water below, a bright flash of streetlight on gills, and landed with a small splash. Her every nerve stood on end. She wanted to turn her hand and twine her fingers in his, wanted to keep walking this path he'd just offered her. But she couldn't, not until he knew everything. She swallowed hard, but couldn't pull her hand back.

He stopped. "Something's bothering you. Is it all of them stopping by and making assumptions?"

"No." For an instant, Shawn's solution looked good—a quick trip, a flash of pain, and she'd never have to tell Angus. Nothing to ruin this beautiful moment under the stars. Tears stung the corners of her eyes. She'd vowed never again. The pain had not been over in a flash, at least not the pain in her heart. The river slapped softly against its banks. She gave a sharp sniff, trying to hold back tears, but they slid out. She brushed futilely at her nose.

He wrapped his arms around her; she turned, pressing her face into his dark, wool coat. Six months ago, life had been entirely different. Now Shawn was dead and she couldn't tell anyone. Memories of him crowded every path. She loved him, hated him, was pregnant with his child, and felt guilt about everything, including Angus's family and friends making assumptions while she kept such a big secret from him.

"Rose said we have things to talk about," he said. "Is it Shawn?"

She gave a short, unhappy laugh. "Yeah, it's Shawn. It's always Shawn." She snuffled into his jacket; wiped at it, apologizing.

He laughed. "'Tis not the worst that's gotten on it."

"It's everything," she said. "I still have feelings for him. It's very recent. And I haven't told you everything."

"About Shawn?" His voice tightened.

She shook her head irritably, then changed her mind. "Well yes. Not really. Not anymore."

"You're making no sense, Amy. Is this about why you think he's not coming back?"

She pressed her fingers against her eyes, trying to shut it all out. Even telling him she was pregnant was better than telling him that.

"Amy?" He spoke softly, his cheek against her hair. "Whatever it is, tell me and we'll deal with it together."

She took a deep breath, calming herself, wondering if there was any chance he could possibly still want to deal with it together when he knew. Niall would pray. She breathed a silent prayer, and, somewhat calmed, said, "Understand, please, I didn't know the right time to tell you. All of a sudden, you stopped being just a friendly stranger, and became someone who had a right to know. I've waited too long, but I was afraid it was presumptuous, before. And all of a sudden, we're talking about a road trip, and your family thinks...."

"Aye, well, don't worry about my family." His voice was tight. "Worry about you and me. What is it?" He sounded gentle. Kind. His arms were warm around her. If she hadn't started crying, he would have been kissing her already, she knew. He looked good in the moonlight, broad and strong, his eyes intense. She'd much rather kiss him than tell him she was pregnant and watch him walk away.

But she had to. She tried to ease into it, to build her courage. "You know Shawn's reputation." It wasn't entirely honest, she chided herself, and tried again. "I can't blame him. I'm an adult. It was my decision, too."

He stiffened and pulled back. "The counterfeits?"

Her fist flew to her mouth, laughing, that he'd think such a thing. "No!" She said it again, realized she was repeating herself, and managed to say, "I would never do that. No, I think that was really just sort of bad luck on Shawn's part."

He took her shoulders. 'Take a deep breath."

She did, squeezing her eyes shut and said, "I'm pregnant."

It got still and quiet. The water lapped below. Everything sank inside her. She opened her eyes; her stomach plunged at the shock on his face. He stared at her. She pulled back. His arms fell to his side. "I don't blame you," she said. "I'm sorry. I wasn't trying to keep secrets. I just didn't know you at first, and all of a sudden...." She started across the bridge; turned, and said, "Please, I just need a ride to the hostel."

He jolted and said, "Amy, I'm sorry...." He strode after her, took her shoulders again. "I don't know how to react. Give me a minute." He dropped his hands from her shoulders abruptly, spun, and walked to the far end of the bridge, toward his car. He turned and walked halfway back to her, his fingers pushing his forehead like he couldn't understand something, then spun and crossed the bridge, descending the steps. From the shore, he turned and looked back at her, frowning.

"Please don't look at me like that," she said. "I know I shouldn't be pregnant, but...please. You don't know how it was with Shawn. I wanted the wedding night, I valued that, and he promised he'd respect that. He *promised.*" Her voice came faster and faster, trying to make him see. "And then when he'd worked his way into my heart, he started pushing. I was so afraid of losing him by then. And Dana was telling me...."

Angus stared at her quizzically.

She took a deep breath, trying to calm herself. "I can't blame them. I should have told you sooner. I just didn't know when."

He climbed the stairs, came back across the bridge and pressed her head down on his shoulder, his hand in her hair. "I just need a minute," he said. She thought she felt him shaking, but maybe it was her own trembling. He kissed the top of her head. "You're shivering. Let's get in the car."

They sat in the warm, dim interior, not talking. He started the engine and drove. Finally, with dark mountains rising on the right, and the loch keeping pace on the left, he said, "I just don't know what to say."

"If that's the end of archives and museums, that's what you say." She wrapped her arms around herself, willing away the chill. The car slowed as they entered the village. "I understand. I really do, and I'm sorry. I just didn't know the right time. I know I'm not exactly anyone's dream date."

He pulled up at the hostel, killed the engine, and looked at her. He touched her cheek and ran two fingers down the length of her hair. "I think you're every man's dream date."

He leaned back against the head rest. After another few minutes, he took her hand and asked, "What does this mean to us? What am I to you? Were you looking for a father? A friend who shares an interest?"

"I didn't bring you coffee," she reminded him. "I have money in savings, a professional skill, royalties coming in. I can support a child. If I just wanted a father, Rob's begging."

He stared at the ceiling.

"I'm sorry," she said. "I understand."

"Do you?" he asked. "Do you understand I just need a few minutes?"

"I said I do. I really enjoyed our time. Thank you." She got out.

The window hummed behind her. "Amy," he called. She turned.

The window went up, and he got out of the car. He took her hand, going with her into the hostel. They sat by the fireplace. It crackled. The flames danced. Finally, Angus spoke. "Am I just another complication? A friend? Someone you could love?"

"I just lost someone," she said. "Yes, someone new this soon is a complication. Yes, I consider you a friend. I get excited when you're near me. I look forward to seeing you, I think of you at night, and I want to pick up the phone and call the station just to hear your voice."

His hands clenched between his knees.

"There's never been anyone but Shawn. I don't want you to get the wrong idea about me."

"I'm in no position to judge, if that's what you're worried about." He stared into the crackling flames. "It could just as easily be me telling you this." The flames cast shadows over his face. "'Tis just dumb luck I didn't get pregnant meself."

He said it so calmly that it took a second to sink in, the absurdity, the humor. She smiled, her eyes finally meeting his. He laughed softly and took her hand.

She stared at their clasped hands, as afraid of her next words as she had been of telling him she was pregnant. "I promised myself next time I'm true to my values. Is that...." She cleared her throat, dreading his answer. "Is that going to be a problem for you?"

"You saw my house." He stared into the hearth a moment before returning his gaze to hers. The flames flickered shadows across his face. "It's not just decoration."

Her breath came out in a warm sigh of cautious relief.

He squeezed her hand. "I think my sister and Clive gave you a good idea of my feelings. About you, I mean."

Amy nodded. "They care a lot about you."

Angus chuckled. "More than I care for at times. Tonight being one of them."

"No, tonight was good," Amy said. "I learned a lot about you."

Angus stared into the fire. His forehead puckered. "This must be what Rose said we had to talk about." Appearing dazed, he rose. "I've things to think on." His hand slid from hers and, looking dazed, he rose.

"Angus?"

He left without looking back.

Her stomach sank.

The Glen Beyond Creagsmalan, 1314

Shawn pounded hard through the sparse wood, Niall's sword clutched in his hand. Lachlan and Owen galloped on either side, separating only to speed around a tree now and then. A look back showed no sign of pursuit. But it would come. They dodged firs and tore under the bare limbs of oaks and birches, racing for the small group of mounted men rising from the mist. They reined in their mounts with a twisting and whinnying, and bucking of the animals' heads, biting at the bits. "He's gone back to the castle," Shawn gasped.

Without a word, MacDonald yanked his reins, wheeled his horse. The men followed, cutting east into the foothills, and up the steep slope. Allene worked her horse in beside Shawn's, her face pale. She reached her hand to his. Their fingertips touched. "I've never been so helpless," he said.

"You're not helpless. Niall. You've done your part. Now you pray while Bessie and Fionn do theirs."

He stared at her, impressed by her presence of mind, in the crisis, to remember who was who, as far as her father's men were concerned. But his words were, "God and I, we're not on the best of terms. He doesn't want my prayers."

"He wants everyone's prayers," Allene said. "D' you not know of the prodigal son?"

"No, I don't, actually. And if it involves God, I don't want to."

The horses struggled up the steepening slope, across scrubby grass and around boulders. Stones skidded under their hooves. The animals slowed, their front legs bucking, back legs leaping, trying to climb. The men pushed to the tree line for cover, before dismounting, helping the animals on now, pulling them upward. Shawn turned, watching the glen below from the cover of the pines. As the first of MacDonald's men reached the crest above him, MacDougall's men appeared at the northern edge of the glen below him, dozens of them, charging south, stirring the mist that bubbled in the glen.

Allene pulled his sleeve. They stood alone. Her horse whickered beside her, nudging her. "There's naught more to be done. They've come, just as we hoped. We must go now, reach our land and see if he made it."

"If he didn't?"

"We dasn't think on it." Her voice trembled. "Come now, lest they look up and see us."

"The trees will cover us." But he backed up, watching from the ridge, as the storm cloud from Creagsmalan rolled directly beneath them. Hoof beats and men's shouts reached up the walls of the glen, sounding oddly near. It looked like the whole army had followed them, but it would take only one man, left behind at Creagsmalan, to stop Niall.

And it all rode on a fearful girl summoning the courage to do her part. Even now, she might be cowering somewhere while Niall remained locked in his cell, helpless.

Shawn cursed himself. He should have insisted on a more direct plan. They should have stormed the castle. They should have sneaked in all of MacDonald's men and launched an assault. They should have....

"Come," Allene said.

Shawn turned his eyes from the enemy, and led his horse over the crest. They followed the men, leading their horses gingerly down the other side, feet sliding, stones rolling, and congregated at the bottom. MacDonald looked around at his men, and made the sign of the cross. "'Tis in God's hands." They solemnly repeated his motion, and immediately mounted, riding hard to the north.

Inverness, Present

I sit on my bed for what feels like hours after he leaves. Angus, Shawn, and the unborn baby jostle for room in my thoughts. I'm shocked and crushed that Angus walked out. But I stood for my child this time, instead of giving in to fear, and I feel good—strong—in reclaiming another piece of who I used to be. My hand settles on my stomach, my love growing for the unseen baby. If I have to choose, I choose my child. I choose to be a mother, to love and protect, no matter what it costs me this time.

My thoughts travel back. It happened when we came to arrange the orchestra's tour. We went to a castle out on a spit, crossing the causeway as the sun rested its drowsy head on the western sea, and Shawn found a way in. Shawn always found a way.

I felt as if we'd slipped past the guarding angel, into the ancient, abandoned garden of Eden. Wild trees burst up sporadically in the court-yard, wild flowers and grasses grew everywhere, and birds sang from an empty hall. We climbed what was left of the ramparts. Red and white signs warned us not to. Danger! Stay out! We went up anyway—an analogy of my entire life with Shawn.

The tide had come in, shutting off the castle. He grinned and said, "No one's leaving and no one's coming. It's ours for the night."

I said, "You knew, didn't you?" He laughed, his head thrown back the way he did, so full of life, and then kissed me, setting off explosions inside me. I can't believe all that life and energy are gone forever. A candle—no, a roaring bonfire—has gone out in the world, with all its warmth and all its danger.

My thoughts drift from the castle, and Shawn, to sitting by the fire with Angus, everything his sister and Clive said, his rescue of three boys. If Shawn had done such a thing, he'd tell everyone. Angus wanted Clive to stop. Shawn's job was entertaining people, kissing women, and glorifying himself. It sold albums, and lifted the whole orchestra with him. Angus's job is risking his life and brushing it off as nothing.

Shawn swirled women into his charismatic vortex with his utter belief in his own charms. Angus's good looks and humor dawned on me only slowly, like a flower blooming, as I spent time with him.

I lie awake while the window turns from black to deep blue. I tingle when Angus stands close, my stomach flutters when he smiles, my heart flips over at his name in my e-mail. With a sigh, I throw off the covers, accepting that it's another night of no sleep. A warm shower is better than lying here worrying. I gather my things.

If Shawn were alive, if Shawn were ever coming back, I'd be torn. I'd remember the apology and fly straight to him. But Shawn is gone, and my heart wants Angus.

I slip from my room into the hall, hoping he'll be back.

Creagsmalan, 1314

Niall gave the bars another shake of frustration, craning to see down the gloom of the empty hall. "Haste, Bessie," he muttered. "*Haste!*"

And then, his salvation! She ran, a slight, hooded figure, through the shadowy hall, with little sobbing gasps. "Bessie!" He reached one hand through iron bars, the other pressed against the rough, wooden door. She touched his fingers. Tears streaked her tiny face, looking up to him. "Give her your strength," Christina had said. He willed it to flow through his fingers to hers. "You put out the wineskin, Bessie. You did it. Find the key."

She gulped up at him, hiccuped back a sob, wiped her nose with the back of her hand.

"The key," he urged. He peered frantically into the gloom, desperate to be out before MacDougall and the guard returned. The smoke of the torches stung his eyes and burned his nose.

She fumbled, spilling the ring to the ground with a clatter loud enough to draw down the whole army. Her gaze shot back to his, her face pale.

"It's aw' right." He willed his hammering heart to slow. "Pick it up."

She did so, tried a key, breathing hard, the keys rattling against the lock. She tried a second, while he whispered any soothing, comforting thing he could think of. She dropped the keys again. He strained, listening for the guard, or MacDougall, storming down to prove he was still here. She tried a third, while he fought back panic, urging her gently on. She tried a fourth, and the lock clicked. She gave a sob. He yanked the door open, squeezed an arm around her shoulder. "Good lass. You're ready to go, aye?"

She nodded mutely, her face ghostly pale and tear-streaked in the flickering torchlight. She gave another gulping sob.

"Take us out," he said.

They ran down the dim hall, past the kitchens, with Niall whispering, "Ave Maria, protect us." Shouting rang out above. Bessie paused. She took his hand in hers, squeezing like the frightened child she was. She backed up against the wall, edging up the stairs. Niall held her hand tightly, willing his courage to her, though his own knees trembled. They reached the place where the stairs split. Sunlight from the courtyard reached from the left fork, almost touching their toes. Voices shouted in the bailey. Bessie darted into the right passage, up three stairs, and down a hall Niall had never traveled. He was dependent on her now, blind, with no knowledge of his whereabouts. He could only pray panic did not overtake her, child that she was.

She ran down the dim hall, her feet skimming the flagstones. Torches were far and few between. She pulled him into a small room off the side. Light streamed in a window, and fresh air. A pan of water waited there, and a razor. "Quickly," she whispered. He knelt, bared his throat to her, praying her shaking would stop. She moved swiftly, splashing him with water still warm, scraping. The mustache was gone in moments. She grasped the hair on his head, and soon he was bald. She studied him, her face pale, and took another careful swipe over his head. "The north gate," she said.

He wanted desperately to go back for Christina. He'd argued with her till she said she must go. But he knew there was no way to draw her from the distraction she herself was creating for him. He followed Bessie, with no choice but to trust her, twisting through halls, out a back entrance that spilled them into the stable courtyard. She threw a helmet at him, and grabbed a horse. He vaulted up, dragging her after him, and squeezed her in front of himself, hiding her under his cloak, and they stormed out, down a side street, to the north gate, with a lone soldier still guarding it.

"Open up!" Niall bellowed. "The prisoner is loose! Haste else you swing in his place!" The man complied, in a rush of fear over Duncan's temper. Niall slapped the horse, bearing its double burden, and rode, bending over Bessie, hiding her from any lookouts on the parapet, for the northern glen.

Fifteen miles, and he'd be in MacDonald's land, in a glen with a deep ravine, and a waterfall, and if all went well, the Laird and his men would meet him there. He drove the horse hard, into woods that would shelter them. Shawn's job was to lead MacDougall south. He prayed no guard would look north. It would take only one competent man to end the ruse, even now.

Chapter Sixteen

Inverness, Present

Fresh from her shower, Amy cheered herself with a soft jersey tunic with four brass buttons running up the cuffs of narrow sleeves. Rose would approve its vivid garnet red. Leaving her hair hanging free to her waist, she went to the kitchen. Damp tendrils of black hair curled around her cheeks as she filled the kettle. A little coffee, and she'd be okay, despite the sleepless night. The window over the sink showed gray sky beyond the lace curtains. She tried to imagine going back to being alone. She'd been happy on her own. She'd be happy again.

"Amy." The voice sounded behind her, deep and rough.

She spun, banging the pot against the sink. Cold water sloshed over her hand.

"Good morning." Angus stood a foot from her.

She smiled tentatively, unsure what he'd thought or decided. Maybe he was only decent enough to come back and tell her in person. Her breath rushed out. "Good morning." She didn't want to hope.

"You're up early."

"I couldn't sleep." She turned on the burner under the kettle, willing her nerves to stop dancing.

"I brought cinnamon rolls." He held up a box and a paper cup. "And a mocha. Hazelnut."

"Thank you." With the kettle going, they found a table in the dining area, and stared at each other. An electric field shivered around Amy's heart, relieved and overjoyed to have him back; afraid to touch him. She cleared her throat to say more, but a thin, bearded student wandered in, gazing bleary-eyed around the dining area and at each of them, before going to a cupboard and pulling down a loaf of bread.

Amy waited till he'd disappeared into the kitchen. She swallowed, afraid of the answer, but someone had to say something. "You thought things out?" She'd been okay before Shawn, she told herself, and before Angus. She'd be okay.

Angus nodded. "I did. I have a confession, too."

Amy tilted her head, trying to guess what he meant. A prelude to explaining why he was ending it with her? "You can't possibly have any skeletons in your closet."

"Not in my closet." A frown creased his forehead. "In the Glenmirril archives. I've kept a secret, too."

Fifteen miles north of Creagsmalan, 1314

Niall and Bessie sat in the glen, beside a stream. The rocks strewn up and down the bank were cold to the touch, and the wind icy on Niall's face and shorn head. Bleak limbs, bare of all life, scraped the gray sky above. Evergreens sheltered them from the worst of the wind, and the approach of any who might come from Creagsmalan. A small waterfall trickled over rocks, giving an oddly cheerful sound to the landscape, like Yule fires in the dead of winter.

Bessie huddled on a large rock, shrinking into her cloak and shivering, even with Niall's second cloak, the one from Ellen, covering her shoulders, while Niall listened for his clansmen—or enemies. They'd reached the place only minutes ago. He knew the others had a longer route, and their numbers would slow them. Still, the seconds ticked by like torture. MacDougall would not stop at his own border. And Niall was defenseless, alone against any number that might show up. He wished desperately for his father's sword. He had not even a spare knife for the girl to use, should they be attacked.

Niall paced the small ravine, his leather boots soundless on the rocky bank. The wind rippled the edge of his tunic, above his knees, and tugged his cloak, billowing it outward every time he let go of it. "You did well," he told Bessie, partly to encourage her, partly to distract himself from worry. Things could still go wrong. He could still end the day with a rope around his neck.

She raised a pale, chilled face to him. The wind lifted a tangle of dark hair. She pushed it back off her cheek. He thought, at first, she wasn't going to answer. Then she asked, her voice thin, "What of my future?"

Niall scanned the ravine, listening, searching for the approach of men, before saying, "MacDonald will welcome you at Glenmirril, so long as you swear fealty."

"Aye," Bessie said. "Ye've no idea what ye've saved me from."

Niall did not add to her cares by saying he'd heard enough to have a disturbingly good idea.

"I'll be a kitchen maid forever. I can have no husband or children."

"Why not?"

She simply stared, breezy gusts reddening her pale cheeks.

"Oh," he said. "But surely—you'd no say in the matter."

"Think ye it matters? I'm a ruined woman."

Niall checked up and down the ravine once more, listening over the burble of the stream, before joining her on the rock. He tugged his hood up against the cold cutting into his ears. "Surely you didn't wish to be left."

She hung her head, her face hidden by her hood. "I don't mean to seem ungrateful. My apologies, Fionn. You nearly died today, for trying to get me out the first time."

"You've repaid it." Niall covered her cold hand with his. "You got me out just now, aye? We look forward from here on."

"Forgive me." She lifted her small face, meeting his eyes. "I *will* make bold. Is there naught to be done for Milady?" Tears glittered in the corners of her eyes.

"Surely he can find no fault in her?" Niall asked.

"He need find no fault. He's brutal, he is. He pressed a hot poker into her ankle the first time, though he could prove nothing against her."

Ice ran down Niall's spine. "He didn't."

"He did." She reached a timid hand, clutching the edge of his cloak. "I daren't think what he'll do if he suspects she had aught to do with this."

Niall's ears picked up the smallest echo on the wind. He eased the knife from his boot and rose. He heard the sound of hooves pounding the earth, the steady roll of many men and beasts. His heart hammered. His knuckles whitened on the handle of his knife. He was grateful at least there was no snow to leave their tracks, as he edged her behind him, backing under the thick boughs of an ancient fir tree. There they waited, barely breathing, to see whether MacDougall or MacDonald had found them first.

The Glenmirril Archives, Present

"You mind I've done a fair amount of work and study at Glenmirril?" Angus guided his mini through the gray morning.

"I get the impression you know every stone," Amy said. Outside, mist curled into strange shapes along the surface of the road.

"Every stone, every character history has remembered for us. At least, I used to. I've forgotten quite a bit. But I understood what you said back at Creagsmalan, feeling they were real, because they were that real to me, too, I once knew them so well." He eyed the road as a car flashed by on their right. "Well, I knew them like internet friends, people you know well, but never see their real face or hear their voice."

As the heater warmed the car, Amy loosened her blue coat. He'd said nothing about where she stood with him. She refused to ask.

"Except the one," he said. "The Glenmirril Lady."

"The Glenmirril Lady?" Amy asked faintly, wondering where he was leading. "Is that someone from Niall's time?"

"I dinna ken." Angus shrugged. "But 'tis she who sparked my interest in Glenmirril. I'd a cousin who worked in the archives years ago, you see. One day when I was seventeen, we were going to see the Rangers—the rugby team," he clarified. "He'd promised me a Guinness afterward. He had to stop and fetch his ID he'd left at work. He took me back to the archives, and I saw a piece of parchment his mate was working over." He fell silent, skimming the car around a bend.

"What happened?" Amy asked, when he didn't speak again.

The castle came into sight around a curve, its rugged stone tower jutting against the early morning loch on their right. Angus cleared his throat. "As I tried all night to think how to say this, I realized you may question my intentions, even my character."

Amy wanted to touch his hand, where it gripped the clutch, but held back. If this was an excuse to drop her, instead of admitting he was upset about the pregnancy, she *would* question his character.

He eased the car into Glenmirril's empty lot, pulling into the same spot Rob had, so many months ago. She and Rob had sat, watching the rising sun climb like Kilroy, inch by inch over the castle. Now she and Angus sat, watching another dawn rise over the walls. October was chillier than mid-June. He left the car running, the heater humming.

"I've never fancied myself much of a romantic," Angus said. "Always practical and well-grounded. And it was only a picture, ancient, worn and faded about the edges. But it captured my fancy, see? And I think it's why I've had few girlfriends. Every time I meet someone, I feel something's missing."

Amy closed her eyes, her breath stuck in her throat. She twisted the Bruce's ring. "So this—this thing between us?" Shawn was right. She was a terrible judge of men. Even Rose was wrong this time. Angus was as good as telling her it was over, and blaming it on an old scrap of parchment.

Angus switched the engine off. "Let's go in, aye? You don't think I'm mad, fancying an old picture for so long? Chasing a woman from a medieval drawing?"

He opened his car door. She climbed out her own door, numb with disappointment. It was because she was pregnant. "No, of course not."

He laughed, taking her hand as they pushed through swirls of mist to the offices across the lot from the castle. "You're being polite, just like when you said the information about Niall Campbell was helpful."

"No, really." But anger welled in her chest. He could at least be honest. He was no better than Shawn. Her vision darkened at the edges.

Angus opened the glass doors, greeted the secretary, and ushered her down a flight of stairs. At the bottom, a man opened another door. He greeted Angus, but his eyes flew to Amy.

"Amy, Charlie, Charlie, Amy," Angus said.

Charlie stared, leaned back in the room without taking his eyes off her, and called, "Marjory, come and meet Angus's friend."

Marjory's voice floated ahead of her. "Jack's gone to collect that book. He'll be here with it soon." She appeared, a middle-aged woman with flyaway graying auburn hair. "Oh, my!" She stopped short. Her eyes skittered to the side, and back to Amy's face.

Amy touched her earrings, wondering what was wrong.

"You don't remember us, do you?" Marjory asked.

"No," Amy said. Everything felt hazy. Their words echoed from a distance. She scanned their faces. "Should I?" Angus was letting her down easy. Why like this, with an audience? She glared at him.

The man, Charlie, laughed, pulling her bewildered attention back. "I owe you an apology. Last time you saw me, I was wearing breeks and a leather apron and shoeing a horse. I'm afraid I was staring."

"Me, too." Marjory spoke in a breathless rush. "I'm sorry."

As Amy looked from one to the other, their faces became clear. They had been among the living history actors, when she'd come to the castle with Shawn in June.

"It's just, we were shocked," explained Charlie.

"I was right," Amy said softly. "I told Shawn so. He said I was imagining it. He said you recognized him from his promotional posters. But —why?"

"Come in." Angus put a hand on her back, leading her into the archives, to the long black table. "You put it out?" he asked Charlie over his shoulder.

"On the table," Charlie replied.

Amy reached the table, and stared at the medieval drawing, the Glenmirril Lady, startlingly lifelike. She wore a flowing black skirt and a black blouse with billowing sleeves. Thick, dark hair flowed to her waist. She held a violin upright on her knee. A heavy ring with a square stone, worthy of a king, adorned her right ring finger. Amy's hand drifted to her earrings, the same as the Lady's.

She sank into a chair. Darkness tunneled in around her. She forcibly pushed it back with slow, deep breaths, and managed to whisper, "That's me."

North of Creagsmalan, 1314

The sight of Niall emerging warily from the tree, his face shadowed by a hood, compared to nothing Shawn had ever experienced. He wanted to fall to his knees, shout in sheer gratitude. He wanted to return Niall's sword to him, grateful he was still alive to take it back. But sense must reign. He stayed to the back of the group, the sword on his back. He lifted his own hood to shield his face from Bessie, and gripped Allene's arm, giving a shake of his head to remind her. Today, in front of these men, he, Shawn, was Niall to them and to her. She gave Niall himself barely a glance, and Shawn could only imagine what it cost her.

"Fionn of Bergen will be joining us," the Laird told his men. "He's on the Bruce's business. We've a hard ride."

Niall pulled the girl, pale-faced, onto the horse behind him. And they left the glen behind. They rode hard, through the afternoon, through ravines, gullies, forests, and moors. Allene pounded along beside Shawn, trying to keep her eyes off Niall, who rode ahead with his hood pulled far over his face, and Bessie clinging to his back.

"Soon enough," Shawn murmured, catching Allene looking again. "Help me learn the way." It would take her mind off her longing. She pointed out landmarks, told him what they'd left behind, what was to come, and which lochs, hills, towns and rivers lay east and west of their route. He repeated it all, reviewed it in his head, and asked for more. It passed the endless monotony of galloping, cantering, galloping again.

They splashed across a stream, a baker's dozen of horses, and kept going, chewing hard bannocks as they rode, and stopping only once, at dusk, high in the hills where they could look down and see anyone approaching. MacDonald pulled Niall from the group, leaning close and speaking intently while Shawn and Allene sat together, looking down into the valley they'd just left, into the evening mist rising among the trees. "D' you think they'll follow us?" Allene asked. "They know Niall will go sooner or later to Glenmirril."

"They have no proof it was Niall in their dungeon," Shawn reminded her. "Will they really risk attacking one of Bruce's biggest supporters right now? They're skating on thin ice as it is, with him."

Allene looked at him quizzically.

"They're on shaky ground," Shawn explained. Still, they watched the valley for signs of pursuit, and were relieved when none came, and more relieved, still, when Allene's father called for them to mount up and ride. Bessie rode now behind Owen, giving Niall's horse a much-needed rest from its double burden.

As the hills turned purple and the last light slipped from the fir trees, leaving the birches ghostly silver in the night, they slowed their mounts to a walk, weaving in and out among the shadowy trunks in single file, pushing through rising mist. MacDonald joined Allene and sent Shawn forward to ride with Niall so they could trade stories, a furlong ahead of the group, in hushed voices. Shawn kept his hood up as he had all day, to avoid awkward questions from Bessie.

"You were knighted by Bruce," Shawn said. "We raided Appleby and Brough." He told who he had commanded, of his growing friendship with Lachlan, tending Taran's injured arm, and every detail he remembered—

except leaving marks in each church.

Niall asked questions, repeated important details, and took his turn telling his story.

"What of Christina?" Shawn asked.

Niall hesitated.

Shawn's nerves leapt to full alert, as sharp and cold as the silver moon shining down through the trees. "What happened?"

"Weeks ago. The first time I tried to get Bessie out, Duncan pressed a hot poker to her leg. She's aw' right. Mind the hills to the...."

"*All right?*" Shawn interrupted. "He burned her with a hot poker and you say she's *all right?*"

"She's alive," Niall argued. "I call that aw' right. You saw her in the confessional after it happened. Did she not seem aw' right? Beyond those hills...."

"No, I don't call that all right."

Niall shrugged. "We've different standards."

"But we have to get her out."

"There's naught to be done at the moment."

"Well, you can't just *leave* her!"

"D' you think I like it any better?" Niall's eyes snapped to Shawn's, his voice angry. "What would you have me do?"

Shawn shrugged, hating his own lack of an answer.

Niall pointed through the moonlit forest, his shoulders still stiff. "Northwest is the Isle of Skye. Take heed; you must know this."

"No, I don't need to know this." Shawn shook his head. "We're heading back to Glenmirril." The thought of walking off, leaving Christina, bothered him. But Niall would take care of it. He'd make sure, get a promise out of him, before he left. It wasn't really his world or his problem. "I'm going home, remember?"

Niall turned startled eyes to him.

"Let me guess," Shawn said. "That hasn't been at the top of your list. How about the middle? Not even the bottom, huh?" Gloam reached to his stirrups, as thick as it had been the night they'd first switched. Surely it would happen again.

"I've no idea what to do," Niall said.

"Well, you figured something out last time."

"I guessed," Niall said. "What do you think we might do?"

Shawn wondered if he imagined that Niall didn't sound enthusiastic. Then again, the man had barely escaped hanging. He might not be excited about anything but a bed safe inside his own castle walls. MacDonald had been adamant about pressing on, despite the dark, despite the women sagging in their saddles. He would not hear of sleeping in the open, with MacDougall on their heels.

"I thought I would just go to sleep in the tower," Shawn said. Niall looked at him askance. Even with a full moon shimmering down, lighting his shaven face like ivory in the dark night, Shawn could not guess what the look meant. He shrugged. "Okay, you're tired. We'll talk about it later. But if you did it a second time, there's got to be a way for me to do it, too."

"Aye," Niall said, with no enthusiasm. "How's Allene keeping?"

"Tired. Wants to be with you."

It brought a small smile to Niall's face, and in view of his exhaustion, Shawn reluctantly resolved himself to waiting till later to discuss his concerns.

Glenmirril Archives, Present

"You don't think I'm a stalker?" Angus peered at her through the tunneling darkness, frowning.

Amy's mind registered the far-off click of a door, and the empty spot where Charlie had been. "A stalker?" She couldn't take her eyes off the drawing. Light shone down on the woman with the violin. "Why would I think that?" She felt dizzy. The pieces didn't fit. With effort, she focused on Angus's face.

"She fascinated me," Angus said. "Knowing every step of the way I was being fanciful. Shortly before you came here on tour, they showed a clip of your orchestra playing on the telly. Charlie called me at the station, frantic, yelling, 'Turn on the telly now!'" Angus chuckled. "I told him calm down, the Rangers will get by without me cheering them on the once. He didn't laugh. He said, 'That American orchestra is on. Hurry!'"

"So it's us and the Rangers for him?" Amy asked faintly. "We don't get quite as muddy when we play."

"Well, except for being prepared for Kleiner's antics, I didn't care about any American orchestra, but I turned it on. He was in that much of a panic, you see. I was lucky in the timing, and I saw what had him so excited. It was the Glenmirril Lady sitting there playing. You. I can't tell you what I felt, Amy. I'm a practical, sensible man, and I told myself it was a strange coincidence, and whoever was on stage was not herself in the drawing."

Amy's mind churned. Of course she was the woman in the drawing. But how? Shawn couldn't draw. "Was Niall artistic?" she asked.

"What? How would I know that?" Deep lines wrinkled Angus's forehead. "What's he to do with this, anyway?"

"Nothing." She forced a laugh. "You're right, just a coincidence." She knew it wasn't. "But how does that make you a stalker?"

"I was at the hospital." He stared at the floor. "I didn't ask to be sent. I'd not barge in on someone in crisis, no matter my feelings. Nor did I ask to be sent about the counterfeits, or after he disappeared."

"I thought you were staring. But Shawn always said I imagined things. And I thought it was because I was making such a fool of myself."

"I tried not to," Angus said. "I'm sorry. Can you imagine the shock of a medieval drawing coming to life before my eyes?"

"I can imagine lots of shocking things lately." Amy couldn't take her eyes off the picture. She'd never seen Niall draw, but then he'd had weightier things on his mind than sketching.

"I hope you'll forgive him, but Mike called up in Inverness and told me you'd come to the Heritage Centre. It was too tempting that time, and I drove down. I told myself I was being practical, that I'd find you were just like any other woman—not herself at all."

She reached for him, needing to feel something solid. His hand wrapped around hers, large and warm, giving her something real to hang onto. A deep breath of air rushed into her lungs and sighed out again. "There has been absolutely nothing sane in my life since the second I turned and saw—Shawn —holding that knife behind the castle. You're the closest thing to sanity there is."

"You don't hold it against me? I thought I'd see you weren't hers, but the more I saw of you, the more I liked you for yourself, no matter who you were or weren't."

She laughed, seeing in one colorful burst every ugly, mean thing Shawn had ever done. "You're apologizing for loving me and being kind?"

"I wasn't honest. I didn't tell you the whole truth."

She glanced around, reassuring herself they were alone. "Yeah, well, it's like being pregnant, isn't it? Not the kind of thing you blurt out the first time you meet someone." She studied his short, dark curls, his dark blue eyes, and ruddy cheeks, his tall, broad form. "I'm glad you kept coming down."

"You can live with knowing this started with an irrational fancy for a medieval drawing?"

She wanted to tell him she was the woman in the drawing, but there was no explaining that. She wanted to warn him the shocks and surprises might not be over. But she desperately hoped they were. Shawn was dead, after all. Niall wasn't coming back. It was over.

Angus took her hand. "I was wondering," he said, "knowing this, if you'd stay an extra couple of days?"

Her heart picked up an extra beat, even as the baby in her womb gave a flutter and a turn. "You want me to stay?"

"I'd like to introduce you to my family." The corner of his mouth quirked up wryly. "Those who didn't barge in last night."

Amy smiled. Then she laughed. "You're sure?" she asked.

"Verra sure."

"They can't possibly approve of me." The crucifix and Christ and Mary on Angus's walls daunted her.

Angus squeezed her hand. "My family is lovely. They already approve of you."

She let him wrap her in his arms, kiss the top of her head, hold her tight. Shawn was dead. She'd put it all behind, and there would be no reason, ever, to tell him her 'missing' boyfriend had been sucked through time and killed by a medieval warrior, or that the medieval Niall Campbell of Glenmirril had drawn her picture centuries before her birth.

Glenmirril, 1314

"We've a problem," the Laird announced.

He roused them out of bed before noon, despite the long night ride into the early morning hours. He'd given Shawn ten minutes to don hose, boots, a shirt, and heavy vest, before pulling him across the solar, into Niall's bed chamber, and yanking the draperies on the bed apart.

"A bigger problem than nearly being hanged?" Niall threw back his covers, rubbing his neck and squinting in the noon sun. He got out of bed, followed MacDonald back to the solar, and went to the gray stone window, staring out over the loch, sapphire in the stark autumn light. His white nightshirt hung to his knees. "Things look quite good to me right now."

"With the exception of Christina," Shawn said. "We need to get her out."

"How am I supposed to do that?" MacDonald asked.

"Well, gee." Shawn let a touch of his old sarcasm into his voice. "I don't know, but she has herself a nice scar from a hot poker, thanks to her first attempt to get Niall out. She's in danger there."

"I'll think on what I can do," MacDonald promised.

"Think on it?" Shawn said incredulously. "She's...."

"Shawn," Niall warned. "We *must* think on it. We cannot simply storm in."

MacDonald plunked himself at the table, and with a jab of his finger, ordered Shawn to join him. Shawn obeyed, grumbling. "We could all think on things a lot faster with a latte."

"Enough," snapped the Laird. "We've a scullery maid who thinks Niall is Fionn of Bergen, and may know MacDougall says Fionn of Bergen is Niall; she can't see Shawn in the hair she just shaved off Fionn, and we've a dozen men who think Shawn is Niall."

"Have we explained to those men why we rescued a traveling minstrel from Chez MacDougall in the first place?" Shawn asked.

"We said Fionn of Bergen is on the Bruce's business." Niall turned from the window, scratching his stomach. "But the Laird's word is law. They do as they're told and don't ask questions." His eyes fell on his father's sword, hanging on the wall. His eyes lit up. He crossed the room to lift it down, took a cloth from the wardrobe, and joined MacDonald at the table, polishing the blade.

"Weird," Shawn said. "They have no curiosity whatsoever? Your time is weird." He lifted a tankard of ale. "Except this beer for breakfast thing. I'm loving this."

"'Tis ale." MacDonald shook his head. "What else would one drink? Among our problems, Niall's mither, sister and nephew all wish to see him, and they can only see you." He looked pointedly at Shawn. "As we've no explanation why Niall would shave his head."

"This is not a problem," Shawn said. "Tell them he's tired. Niall's hair will grow out in a few months, and I'd like to sleep at least that long, since there's no coffee around here. Wake us up when we look alike again."

Niall lifted his head, pausing in his care of the sword. A corner of his mouth quirked up. "A twice as high mocha, aye? 'Twould taste good now."

Shawn laughed. "Double tall." He turned to MacDonald. "What else did you have in mind?" he asked.

MacDonald stared at him, unamused. "I've a woman preparing to dye your hair back. Then you, Shawn, will greet Niall's kin, and you'll both take the information to the Bruce. His parliament meets at Cambuskenneth in a week. Shawn, I've already set the cordwainer to making you a duplicate of Niall's boots. The moment they're done, you leave."

Niall's hands became still on the sword. "Cambuskenneth?"

Shawn, too, stared at MacDonald, as he considered the long, cold journey back to Stirling. "You do remember I don't belong here," he said, "and it might only be fair to at least let me try to get back. I'm sleeping in the tower from now on, and sooner or later, I'll just wake up in my own time."

MacDonald and Niall looked one to the other. Niall frowned. "You must let him try," he said.

MacDonald grumbled. "Well, aye. I see no purpose in it. We don't often have people appearing and disappearing from our tower. But we still must see to it that the lass doesn't call Niall Fionn, aye? Or see Shawn with hair, or hear the men calling Shawn Niall. And everyone expects Niall to have hair."

"The thing is," said Shawn, dismissing MacDonald's concerns, "you've gotten good mileage out of this, but do you intend it to go on forever?"

"How else do we explain your presence?" MacDonald asked. "But to say you're who you look like?" He rubbed his thick silver and red beard. "We can't tell Douglas he had an imposter with him."

"We don't tell him. We say it was the imposter in MacDougall's dungeon and the real Niall with Douglas."

"Aye, a good plan." Niall lifted his father's sword, studying the sheen on its blade. "I proved to MacDougall I'm not Niall by showing him I've no scar. Shawn showed him the scar back at Stirling."

They discussed and argued, back and forth, trying to get one story that accounted for everything, until Shawn burst out, "But what's the point! Either I get back, or I end up stuck here, in which case, am I supposed to be his *stunt double* forever?" He threw in English where he had no Gaelic.

Niall and MacDonald stared at each other and back to Shawn. "Stun dubble?" Niall asked.

"Movies, they're guys who...."

"Movies?" Niall rubbed his bald head.

"You must have seen the TV in my room," Shawn said impatiently.

Niall's eyes widened. "Aye, the people in the box."

"They're not real people. Just pictures." He smacked his forehead. "Forget it. That's not the point. Are you expecting me to be Niall's secret other self forever?"

"It's been useful," MacDonald said, unperturbed.

"Useful!" Shawn snorted. "That's meant to be my goal in life?"

"Is there a better one?" MacDonald's face wrinkled in perplexity. He leaned forward, waiting for an answer. Niall, too, waited to hear what else one could want out of life.

"You're kidding!" Shawn looked from one to the other. "Yeah, I'd like to be my own man again, not having to hide all the time and cover my face and pretend to be someone else. Not to mention, he's constantly getting credit for everything I do."

"D' you not see what matters, Lad?" MacDonald looked at Shawn with something akin to pity. "It matters only that Scotland survives. It matters that our people live in freedom. In a hundred years, none will care which of you did what. Your names will be forgotten."

Shawn laughed, a dry sound with no humor. "Well, that's not quite true. Seven hundred years later they're still looking at a tapestry of Niall stealing MacDougall's cattle."

MacDonald frowned. "Those were our cattle."

"Yeah, sorry. I'm just saying."

"Just saying what?" MacDonald half-rose from his chair.

"Just saying, that's all. Just saying what I just said."

"You said we stole MacDougalls' cattle," Niall reminded him. He rose from his seat, the great sword at his side.

"No!" Shawn stood up, turning in agitation, raking his hand through his hair. "That's not what I meant."

"It's what you *said*."

"Can we just move on, please?" Shawn stomped around the table, and threw himself onto the window ledge. He pulled his legs up on the sill, braced against the opposite edge.

"I believed I was getting used to his ways," MacDonald said to Niall. Niall shrugged, shaking his bald head.

"So I don't matter, only Scotland matters?" Shawn stared out over the loch, glittering with light on the crest of each small wave, out to the mountains beyond. It was less than five months since he'd first entered this room with Amy, since Niall's closest friend, Iohn, had spoken to him here, warning him to watch how he spoke to the Laird, and asking Shawn to let him, Iohn, make the journey to Hugh instead. Niall had said nothing in all this time about killing his best friend, turned traitor, at Bannockburn.

Shawn looked back to MacDonald, who, last June, had pushed him to his knees to pray, before ordering him out this very window, clinging to a rope, with the moon shining down and the wind whipping all around. It had been only a few months, but a lifetime away. The twenty-first century, Amy, Conrad, the orchestra, and his mansion on twenty acres, all felt oddly like a dream. But one he very much wanted to get back to. It had been a pleasant dream.

Niall hung his sword back on the wall. "Aye, you understand. Only the future of our country matters. Not me, not you, not the Bruce. What matters is a better life for our children."

Shawn leaned his head back on the stone wall of the window, staring at the arch above. "I've got a child," he said softly. "When do I get a chance to make a better life for *my* child? You can't keep me here."

He and Amy had—would—walk those hills in seven centuries. He wished he could call out, send his voice across the years and tell that fool who had walked with her that day to smarten up, see a good woman when he still had the chance, quit being so stupid and listen when she tried to talk. He turned to stare at Niall and MacDonald, watching him from the table. His life was in their hands.

The Glenmirril Archives, Present

The archives door slammed open. Amy gave a start. Angus jumped back, as Jack burst in, cradling a book like a new baby, on a piece of cloth.

"It's back!" His eyes glowed. He settled the tome gently on the black table. He caressed the old leather cover, and Angus didn't seem to find that odd. Amy bit her lip, amused. She shouldn't be, she knew. It was an ancient book, obviously in need of careful handling.

"'Tis a copy of a much older one," Jack explained. "A history of Glenmirril. There's a chapter on Niall Campbell himself!"

Amy's amusement faded. The book suddenly became as valuable in her eyes as it was in his. "Can I see?" Her words slid out on a hushed breath.

Jack was already turning pages, thick, heavy, cream-colored leaves now and again with watermarks or black spots of mold, over which he murmured as if it were an injured child. "Here." He offered the open book like a jewel.

Amy touched the words centered on the right hand page: *Niel Cambel.*

Under his name in small font were the words *Fourteenth Century.*
She looked up at Angus. "If he lived long enough to have his own
chapter, MacDougall can't have hanged him, right?"

"I still say Creagsmalan's records are wrong." Angus turned to Jack.
"We found an order there for gallows for Niall Campbell."

"Well, now, I never heard he was hanged by MacDougall," Jack said.

"I don't think he was," Angus answered. "Because he was knighted by
Bruce on the border at the same time he was supposedly in Creagsmalan's
dungeon. I suppose we should just read and find out."

Amy hesitated. It could as easily be bad news as good.

"Go on," Angus encouraged. "It's exactly what you wanted."

Amy lowered her eyes to the page. Fear and excitement made it hard to
focus. She read the words twice. *A fascinating character, with a larger than
life reputation. Sir Niall married MacDonald's daughter in October 1314
just before being summoned to Bruce's parliament at Cambuskenneth.*

Excitement hammered Amy's heart, as vibrantly as if her best friend had
just sent a wedding announcement. But the implication of an October
wedding sent an even greater thrill through her. "October 1314." She turned
to Angus. "If he *was* in the dungeon in September and October, but he
married in October, then he got out, right?"

"But he was knighted by Bruce during that time," Angus reminded her.
"Why would you believe Creagsmalan's records?"

"I found his mark on the wall in the chapel."

Angus scratched his head. "How do you know...?"

"When was Cambuskenneth?" Amy turned quickly to Jack.

"November 6, 1314, of course," Jack said.

"Of course," she murmured. Relief, for herself, and for Allene, coursed
through her. "Thank God," she breathed. But the smiled slipped. "Are you
sure? Because 'he was summoned,' doesn't mean he went."

"I think 'tis as close to hard proof as you'll find seven hundred years
later," Angus said. "Now about this mark...."

"I think it was in one of the Professor's books. What about the rest?"
Amy reached for the ancient tome. Angus edged it closer to her, a small
frown playing on his face. The book's musty odor rose; she found it a
wonderful smell, bringing news of an old friend.

*He attended parliaments and councils with Bruce, raided with James
Douglas in Northumbria, and fought with Robert Bruce in Ireland.*

"Ireland." Angus stopped, raising his eyes to her. "There you are!"

Amy thought back over her notes. "1315?"

"*Robert* Bruce went in 1317." He grinned. "So Niall lived that long."

She smiled, and lowered her eyes, hiding the relief unfurling inside her.
She offered a silent prayer of thanks, wondering how MacDougall had gone so
far as to build gallows, yet let him go. She kept reading.

*Niel was devout, though his behavior was at times inconsistent,
perhaps as a result of injuries received in the cattle raids between the
MacDonalds and MacDougalls. He was a man of great humility. Once,
after taking dinner in his chamber, he carried his platters to the kitchens
himself, brushing aside the servants' attempts to do their duty. Further
surprising the castle folk, he reappeared in the great hall, insisting the
servants sit, and he, himself would serve. He proceeded to do so, saying,*

"Did not Christ Himself say the greatest must serve?"

He often took his son to the stables from the time the child was an infant, or walked the shore behind the castle with him.

"Unusual for his time," Angus murmured.

Amy smiling, pleased at the image of Niall holding a child of his own.

Angus leaned closer, reading aloud. "We know few details of Niel Cambel's life, but he was colorful, capable, and accomplished; a warrior, musician, and diplomat; a man of humility and kindness."

Amy turned the page, hoping for more. But that was the end. She tried to keep the warring excitement and disappointment in, not wanting Angus to know how terribly important it was to her. It warmed her, knowing he'd continued in the kindness she'd cherished. But she wanted to know so much more, wanted to know about Allene, MacDonald, and Hugh. The book told so little. Then again, she thought, she was grateful the book gave no clue when MacDonald died. She wanted him to stay as vibrant and alive in her mind as he had been the day Niall had talked about him on the train.

"Serving the servants," Angus mused. "I've never heard that one."

"The original was dated 1712," Jack said. "So they were closer to the sources, maybe more access to oral history that hadn't yet been lost." He glanced at his watch. "I've a meeting. You'll give the book back to Marjory when you're done?" With Angus's nod, he left the room.

"Incredible!" Amy breathed in the silence, touching a gloved hand to the heavy cream paper. "So detailed, and yet so little." She felt giddy. For just a moment, the past had reached out to touch her, fingertip to fingertip, through the thin veil separating them.

"Amazing, is it not?" Angus asked.

"Like the past is real," she agreed. "I mean, of course it is, but it usually doesn't feel like it. Not like this."

Angus slid the book from her hands, shutting it gently. He studied her face.

Her smile slipped, warning bells going off.

"I've known Glenmirril's history all my life, as have my friends here," he said. "None of us knew about a mark Niall Campbell used or that he was so devout. How did you know?"

Glenmirril, 1314

In the windowsill, Shawn stared out at the loch. Leaving his sword hanging on the wall and returning to the table, Niall said, "There's another problem with going immediately to Stirling."

"What is that, Niall?" MacDonald raised bushy eyebrows in surprise.

"I was promised your daughter's hand in marriage long since." Niall met his gaze directly. "By the time we get back, we'll be into Advent, and it will be put off again."

The Laird glowered. "D' you think I like it any better, the disruption to our lives? What would you have me do?"

"Let us marry now, before I go."

The Laird harrumphed. "You can't be seen before all Glenmirril like that!"

"It need not be public," Niall argued. "Lachlan and Margaret spoke their vows in his father's home only this morning."

MacDonald shook his head. "You know well more is expected for the Laird's daughter." He looked to Shawn, frowning.

Niall's eyes became harder still. "I'm past caring what any man expects. I want my wife. You are the Laird. Your word is law."

"Do you want folk asking questions?" MacDonald demanded. "They'll say 'twas done on the sly. They'll question her virtue."

"You've given all in this castle good reason to have faith in her," Niall countered.

"Niall," MacDonald sighed. "I've lost my own son to this war. You may have to wait till after Christmas for your wife."

Niall shook his head. "I've waited long enough." His voice became hard. "I almost died without marrying her as promised. I vowed in that dungeon such a thing would not happen. I won't go until she's my wife."

MacDonald's eyes strayed to Shawn, staring morosely out the window.

Niall caught his look, and shook his head. "No."

"No, what?" Shawn turned to them.

"D' you want your wife now, Lad?" MacDonald's grin, beneath his bushy red eyebrows, gave him the distinct look of a fox.

Inverness, Present

A promise to search the professor's books had stopped Angus's questions, though it increased Amy's anxiety. Still, she found herself relaxing in the buzz of conversation and laughter that filled his home that evening. Maybe he'd forget by the time he returned to Bannockburn. Or she could feign a search, and say she'd been mistaken, when no such book turned up. Her only consolation was that, unlike Shawn, it wasn't her own choices that had forced her into the shadowy world of half-truths and evasions. Still, the look on his face told her he knew she *was* telling half-truths and evading.

The smell of grilled burgers and hotdogs drifted in from the backyard, despite late October's chill. Hamish and Gavin darted in and out among the guests. Angus's hand rested on her back, and he beamed—she couldn't remember the last time Shawn had beamed over her—as his mother pulled her in for a hug and kisses on the cheeks. She was short and round, the picture of motherliness with a warm smile and soft gray curls. The smell of apples and cinnamon hung around her. "Angus has said so much about you," she said.

His father, an older version of Angus, with the same height and solid build, but graying curls, kissed her cheeks next, saying, "We watched your last concert. Wonderful orchestra!"

"She arranged their music, too," Angus added. Once more, her mind flew to Shawn. He'd rarely volunteered that information. When people praised the music, he'd smiled, and said, "Yes, I really enjoyed that piece."

"Come along to the garden, now." Mairi breezed in, taking Amy's arm. "Angus's mates want to meet you."

Angus's friends and family kept Amy hopping, till her head spun with names and faces: Roddy, a bit round; William with his height, red beard and quick laugh; Donald, thin, sallow-faced and black-haired; Angus's brother Ken, the spitting image of both Angus and their father. Her face hurt, in the best possible way, from smiling, and a parade of stories marched through her head. Angus hovered by her side, as proud as a new father; and she realized how often in the last year Shawn had made cutting comments. *Are you ever going to do something different with your hair? Was everything else in the wash? Your playing was off tonight, what's up with that?*

"There was a teacher everyone hated," William confided, when Angus went to check on the burgers. "Angus kept telling us we didn't know what we were on about. Well, Jimmy was going to hide a rat in her desk drawer, you know now. Angus took it right back out. Nearly got himself rabies in the process. Then didn't we find out she had cancer, but kept working to support her old mother." He stopped abruptly as Angus, in his heavy peacoat, piled a plate with burgers from the grill and strode toward them.

Clive appeared at her side, gulping a hotdog, when Angus went to help his young nephew out of a tree. "He's still not told you about rescuing those boys, has he?"

Amy tilted her head. "No." She glanced at Angus, stretching his arms up to Hamish, who clung stubbornly to a limb, eyes wide, shaking his head.

"He wouldn't, now. Three of them got themselves in a wee mess, not watching the weather, and all of a sudden it turned. They got their boat in as far as a sandbar, d' you see, but the water was rising. Angus was called. He always is for this sort of thing, being the strongest swimmer and knowing the water so well."

He glanced at Angus, and Amy did, too. He was coaxing. Hamish shook his head. His lip began to quiver.

Clive lowered his voice. "We launch the rescue craft in no time, and in no time, the wind blows it right over and tosses our men in the water. Angus here says 'No matter,' and sets out for the boys. He takes the youngest, keeping the others calm, gets them to hang onto their boat, promising he'll be back." He gave another covert glance at Angus, who reached for a branch and swung himself up.

Clive's constant checking on Angus sank in. "People keep telling me stories when Angus isn't around," Amy said.

"Oh, aye!" Clive looked aghast at the thought of the alternative. "He'd not like us telling tales."

"I'd think he'd be proud."

Clive shook his head. "You've one fine man there. As honest as the day is long, full of honor and far too humble for his own good. He'd not like to feel he's bragging or letting others make him out as something special. But he is." He paused, and they both looked once more at Angus, a great bulk in the tree, convincing Hamish to climb on his back.

"We were trying to launch a second craft," Clive continued, "and having trouble." His normal cheer slipped from his voice, and he became grave. "Angus swam out a second time, and was halfway out again for the third, when we finally got it in the water and managed to bring him and the last boy in. It was on the telly."

Amy watched Angus shimmy down the tree, reassuring Hamish the whole way. She found herself wondering if in a year or two, Angus would change, too. *But I knew who Shawn was from the start,* she reminded herself. *I let him convince me he was different from what I saw at rehearsal.* The stories of Angus's family and friends showed her Angus was exactly who he seemed to be. Better, in fact. To Clive, she said, "He's let me think he directs traffic and does paperwork."

By the tree, Angus swooped the child off his back. "No more trees till you can get down, too, aye?" He patted his head, and returned to Amy. "Now what's Clive telling you?"

Amy handed him a hotdog, smiling. "He says you're the best paper-pusher at the station."

Angus narrowed his eyes at Clive, who nodded vigorously, slapped his shoulder, and said, "You cross your i's and dot your t's. That's what I told her." And he disappeared into the crowd, calling for Ken.

Dundolam, 1314

Christina knelt by the jailer's straw mattress. The house around her was no more than a pair of dim, dirt-floored rooms. His sons played in the narrow street outside, where his wife had herded them, giving Christina a glare before she went. Unnerved, Christina peeled back the bandages clinging to the man's seeping wounds. "Gently now," she soothed. "It may sting a wee bit."

Wincing at the sticky blood and lacerations under her fingers, she smoothed the balm on. She'd gotten it from Joan, fearful of Duncan finding she'd spoken to the physician. Duncan had had the guard flogged in the square before he, MacDougall, and their men rode for Glenmirril, shouting for Niall Campbell's head. They would be back in three days. She must do all she could for the man and his family before then, as anonymously as possible. And it may well have been for naught, anyway. She dreaded the sight of either Niall, or the man, Shawn, being dragged back, a noose already around his neck, perhaps bloodied and beaten on the way, in Duncan's rage.

With the jailer's wife and children out, she spoke softly. "Forgive me, Martainn." She dared explain herself no further. MacDougall might fly into a rage worse than any of Duncan's, if he ever suspected he'd been used; if he ever suspected he wasn't as desirable as he believed. She'd knelt before the Blessed Sacrament for hours, praying for Martainn's recovery, asking God's forgiveness. With a man outside the confessional while she talked to Shawn, she'd grasped at the first plan she thought of, to get keys from a man she'd barely ever looked at. Only when she'd seen them drag him to the courtyard, ripping his shirt from his back, had it dawned on her—she had endangered more than herself.

"My Lady," he said weakly. "I've thought a wee bit, this past day. I did naught for you or Bessie when I saw what he was doing down there."

"Had you tried, he'd have killed you." Christina lifted her fingers from his sticky back, wiping them on a cloth. "I brought this on you directly." She lifted a jug of water from the stand by his bed.

"Is this worse than what he did to Bessie?" The man paused as she tilted the jug to his mouth. He sipped the water, with her hand cupped under his chin. "With time to think...." He twisted his head to peer at her in the dark. "I know why ye did it. He was going to be hanged unjustly."

"Jesus, Mary, and Joseph." The jug clattered to the floor. Her heart thumped against her ribs. "Don't say such a thing. They'll kill me if they think that. That Fionn of Bergen, he took Bessie, he's awful. I truly believed you were drunk. I beg your forgiveness."

Martainn reached awkwardly for her hand. "I'll not say it to any man. You're forgiven. Have I not seen you take on his anger time and again to protect the lass? Ye saved a man from hanging and got her away."

Christina fell silent. Her disclaimer had not swayed him in the least. She spoke softly, knowing she was admitting the truth to a man who could use it against her. "You paid the price."

"I know ye, Milady. Had ye thought of another way, ye'd have taken it."

"I didn't think at all," Christina cried.

"I'll tell my wife. I'll not have her speak ill of ye."

"Tell her naught," Christina breathed. "Better my reputation broken than my neck. I beg you." Sweat turned her hands clammy; cold with fear.

"'Tis unjust," the jailer murmured.

"'Tis *safe*," she insisted. "Let her believe as she does, for my sake." At his reluctant acquiescence, she added, "I've left food for your family." She reached in her pocket for a bag of gold coins, and pushed them under the bed. "There's money, and new shirts. I beg you, Martainn, never tell anyone what ye think. I'm that sorry," she whispered. "I've left balm. I dare not come back."

Behind Glenmirril, Present

"I'm not overwhelming you, am I?" Angus asked. They sat on the patch of shore behind Glenmirril, after the barbecue. Pink and orange clouds hovered behind the castle, while the eastern sky, across the loch, deepened to royal blue.

Amy huddled in her thick blue coat, his arm around her. Her hair hung free under her white knit hat. "Of course you are!" Her face glowed. "I haven't had so much fun in a long time. Your friends and family are wonderful, and I learned a lot about you."

He grimaced. "Then we'd best stop meeting them."

"No!" She gripped his free hand. "It's a good thing. And you know it. You're surrounded by people who tell me you're straightforward and honest, everything you seem to be."

His face sobered. "Of course I am. Why would a man want to be anything else?"

Amy shrugged. "Some do." Shawn hovered between them. She ran her thumb under her palm, feeling the ring. "Clive told me about the boys stranded on the sandbar."

Angus waved it off. "Any of the men would do the same."

"Clive thinks you go beyond what anyone else would or could do." The water lapped at the shore. "Weren't you scared?"

"Of course." Angus laughed. "I thought sure I was going to die. But I'd want someone to do it for my nephews. I kept thinking of their mothers, waiting on shore, and telling myself, just a bit further, just another minute, and praying. And here I am, safe and sound, am I not?"

She studied him. "I didn't expect to meet anyone so soon after I broke up with Shawn."

"Well, that was foolish of you." Angus grinned. "I bet the men were in line."

Amy blushed, staring at her knees. "Rob said the same thing."

"There you go. Rob's a bright man."

"I thought Rob was only talking about himself." She spoke softly, poking a pebble with her toe. But Niall had seemed to like her, too. She couldn't admit to Angus how much Shawn had made her doubt herself.

Angus touched her cheek, a trail of warmth compared to the cool breeze blowing off the loch. "I think most men would feel lucky if you gave them a second look." He wrapped one large hand around hers. "I don't want to rush you." He touched her chin, turning her face to him. "It's only been a few months."

"I'm not going to lie and say I'm over him." Amy studied his dark blue eyes, the heavy lashes, ruddy cheeks, and short black curls. "You need to know that." She wasn't sure anymore what she felt for Shawn, but her feelings for Angus had grown steadily.

"I think you're worth waiting for." His fingers, on her chin, moved to her cheek, to her ear. "Maybe you should throw me in the loch there, if you want me to stop."

Amy smiled. "I don't think I could budge you, much less throw you."

He grinned. "Well, that's no fair, then, is it?" He stood up, taking a step toward the water. A crest brushed the tip of his toe.

"Now, that's *really* not fair," Amy laughed. "I have to either kiss you or watch you freeze your toes? That's out and out blackmail."

He edged his toe closer, grinning.

"Come back!" Her heart beat faster; warmth flooded her insides. "Please." And then he was beside her, his hands in her hair, backing her up to the castle wall out of the cold wind, pressing his mouth on hers, the smile gone, running his finger over the arch of her eyebrow and down the slope of her cheek, kissing her again, while warmth shot through her; he was holding her tightly, pressing her head against his warm chest.

She wrapped her arms around him, safe against the warm sweater under her cheek, with his arms around her, till her own heart slowed down.

Glenmirril Chapel, 1314

Shawn stood at the altar, watching Allene come down the aisle of Glenmirril's kirk. His mustache was gone, his face clean-shaven. His hair was once again his and Niall's own golden chestnut brown, yanked and pulled back to its real shade by an old crone with her hands dipped in some goo whose smell made Shawn swear it contained lizards and internal organs of some sort.

Unreality swept over him. He was about to make false vows to a girl who had died hundreds of years before his own birth. Dizziness swirled over him. He swallowed, telling himself it was the weight of Niall's finest court tunic, sewn with jewels, the thick, gold chain of knighthood hanging on his chest, and the heat of a church packed with the nobility of Glenmirril, all watching him lie before God and priest and man.

Niall had insisted on an immediate marriage. MacDonald had remained steadfast that Niall's stubble-short hair would raise too many questions. "You'll have them make false vows?" Niall had demanded again this morning. His fist had pounded the scarred wooden table. Never had Shawn seen Niall angry with the Laird. He personally had not cared one way or the other, and leaned back in a chair tipped against the wall, watching in amusement. Allene stood by the window, her eyes red with unshed tears of frustration and worry, clenching her hands one in another. Through the door connecting the rooms, Shawn had heard her argue with her father the previous night that she did not want anyone but Niall speaking the vows.

"He's but a proxy. The vows will be valid," MacDonald had insisted. "You'll repeat your consent before me afterward."

At the altar now, Shawn wished he hadn't mentioned how weddings were done in his time. He should have seen that a man who insisted on daily church attendance would be intrigued with the idea of weaving marriage directly into the Mass. Shawn's weak knees longed for the brief ceremony on the church porch that Niall had described as their custom.

"Lying to a priest!" Niall had raged. "Can we not at least validate them, me and Allene, before a priest here in my room afterward?"

"And have one more person know the secret?" MacDonald demanded. "Christina MacDougall knows, and that girl in the village may guess."

Shawn shook his head. "She's too busy talking to think."

MacDonald scowled at him, and added, "God knows your hearts. Shawn is but a proxy, to protect us all."

Niall's jaw tightened more, though that hardly seemed possible. He glared at MacDonald. "He's to have *my* wedding feast with *my* bride!"

"'Tis but *food*," MacDonald raged. "You'll have the marriage and the wife, which is what matters."

MacDonald won. Angry though Niall was, he respected authority. "I'm sorry, Niall." Shawn had apologized, belatedly, realizing he did care about the outcome of the argument, for Niall's sake. Niall had grumbled, shot Shawn looks of irritation, and disappeared into Shawn's room, while a team of valets dressed Shawn in Niall's finest.

Now, Allene came down the aisle, her eyes downcast. She wore a kirtle of deep blue, embroidered with jade green flowers, over a gold underdress. A gold belt skimmed her waist, sewn with jade-green chrysoprace, pale blue chalcedony, and emeralds for virtue, closeness to God, and Christian hope. Orange blossoms, interspersed with red jasper for love, crowned her auburn hair. With a glare and a toss of her head, she'd refused Niall's tongue in cheek suggestion to wear plenty of white jasper for gentleness. Still, she came meekly down the aisle, clutching a bouquet of herbs for luck and fertility.

She walked, with Gil piping on the recorder, past rows of family and friends, past pews holding men who had fought in England beside Shawn, past James Douglas himself. She reached Shawn's side, looked once into his eyes and lowered hers again. The priest stood before them, and the enormity of his lie washed over Shawn.

"I'm sorry," he whispered. He should have insisted, with them, that it mattered. He could have refused to participate.

She didn't respond.

"Join hands," the priest said. Shawn reached for her reluctant hand, the words of the ceremony running numbly over his mind. Marriage was different here and now, he'd gathered from Niall. Consent was all that mattered, and Niall and Allene would do that with MacDonald as their witness. An expectant pause in the flow of words snagged his attention. He looked up to the waiting priest. "I do," he said. The ceremony went on, with his stumbling interjections whenever the priest paused. Not that they'd know if he made a mistake, he reminded himself. This was not their way. Allene's hand lay clammy in his. His mind wandered back to the night he'd said to Amy, "What would it be like, if we got married?"

It had been at the top of a Ferris wheel. Carnival music and city lights spread far below, twinkling like a sea of stars. He remembered thinking at the time, he'd never ride a Ferris wheel with any of the other women. And he liked it. He liked being with her in every way. He'd promised himself again she'd never find out, he'd never upset her or hurt her. Maybe, if they got married, he could even change his ways. She'd looked at him with trust and love. Her black hair shone in the lights, lying over her shoulder. It was eighteen months since he'd first kissed her, just days before she told him she was pregnant, before she found the cell phone and started asking questions; before distance had grown between them, and he'd been afraid to bring it up again.

"Kiss the bride."

The priest's voice jolted him back to the present. To the past, he corrected himself with dull humor. Allene waited with lowered eyes. He leaned down, giving her a brotherly kiss on the cheek. "Smile," he whispered. "Dinner can't last forever. I'll eat fast."

She looked up, met his eyes, and laughed. He smiled, pleased he hadn't lost his wit, and they walked down the aisle, nodding, smiling to those he'd come to know—Lachlan, Owen, Gilbert, Niall's mother, his sister Finola, the Morrison twins looking like a medieval double mint commercial, the tiny widow Muirne to whom Ronan had given his one sheep, and Ronan beside her, grinning over his stringy red-gray beard. Niall's mother stepped out, hugging Shawn. "God bless you, Son," she whispered, and kissed his cheek. His heart pounded, waiting for someone to call him for the fraud he was, to recognize what he'd just done.

No one did, and he and Allene pushed out the church door into thin October sunshine. The common folk of the castle waited there, strangely silent. Not one of them cheered, as he would have expected. The sound of the loch washing the shore outside the castle walls thundered over their silence.

Above all, Shawn knew these people loved the Laird, Niall, and Allene. The brief moment of lightness sank in him. He looked around, over the heads of the silent crowd. And there, at the back, he saw them: men in black leather, on jet black horses. MacDougall's men.

Chapter Seventeen

"Did you find out about the marks?" With a large floral-patterned oven mitt on one hand, Rose greeted Amy at her front door with excitement.

"Nothing." Amy set her suitcase and the backpack with her laptop at the bottom of the stairs. She could feel her cheeks glowing with happiness. "But Angus's friend found a book proving Niall didn't hang at Creagsmalan!"

"He did?" Rose embraced Amy in a warm hug. "I'm so glad! What a load off your mind!" She pulled back, frowning. "But how, if the gallows were already being built?"

"I have no idea."

"And the tower?" Rose gripped Amy's shoulder with her bare hand, peering into her eyes.

"We went up after everyone left." Amy laughed. "Rose, the guilt just sort of melted away. I don't understand it."

"Don't try," Rose advised. "Just enjoy finally putting it in the past."

"I will." Amy glanced at the mitt on Rose's hand. "Whatever you're making, it smells great."

"Crab. The seafood in the Orkneys is to die for! I brought back enough to keep you for months!"

"How's Ina?"

"She's great! Tea's on." The kettle emphasized her words with a long, slow hiss. Rose hurried down the hall to rescue it. "Are you going to tell me now why you stayed longer?" With her mitted hand, she lifted the kettle high off the glowing burner before turning to study Amy's face. She broke into a smile. "Angus? I was right about him, wasn't I?"

"You always are!" Amy reached for a teacup, holding it out for Rose.

Rose poured a steaming arc of water. "Did you tell him?"

Leaning against the counter, Amy wrapped her hands around the warm cup. "Some of it."

"Which some?"

"That little part about being pregnant." Her cheeks grew warm.

"How did he take it?" Rose set the kettle on a hot pad.

"That's why I stayed. He asked me to meet his family." Amy felt a smile grow, thinking of the first kiss behind the castle—and the second, and the third. The smile hovered on her lips, as she stared into the depths of the hot tea, reliving the cold October wind behind Glenmirril, the castle wall against her back, his hands in her hair. "It was a very good week," she said.

"Apparently so," Rose said archly. "He's a good man." She lifted one eyebrow. "But very different from Shawn. No more backstage excitement." She set sugar on the table. "There's something special about that."

"No more working side by side," Amy added. "I miss that with Shawn." But then, she thought, no more questions and suspicions, gnawing like medieval rats at her insides. She lifted her eyes to Rose's. "No more surprise trips to Hawaii, no more lies."

"Is it a good enough trade-off for you?" Rose opened the oven door, pulling out a pan of scallops and crab.

"It's beside the point. Shawn's dead." She sipped her tea before adding, "It's not as if I have to choose between them."

"What if you did?" Rose asked.

Amy closed her eyes, her hands wrapped around the cup. "Don't even say that. Something finally, really changed in him. We have a child together. How could I turn my back on that? If he was alive, if there'd been any chance of him coming back, I never would have let myself feel anything for anyone else. There was only room there because Shawn *is* dead, because it's over, no matter who he became in the end." She took milk from the refrigerator, adding, "It would be horrible to be put in that position. But he's dead. So why would you even ask?"

Rose piled crab, scallops, and shrimp high in a serving bowl. "Because there are other men in the circles you're used to—world travelers, composers, musicians. Will you be content with something so different from the life you had?"

"Yes." Amy set her tea down and opened the refrigerator to find a bowl of salad. She put it on the table. "You know I never went looking for someone like Shawn."

"Hm. Well, there *is* no one quite like Shawn. Speaking of whom, what else did you tell Angus?" Rose set the seafood alongside the salad.

Amy's lips tightened as she poured French dressing on her salad. She stared at the pool of dressing, orange-red against crisp green lettuce leaves. "Rose, I *can't* tell him the rest. Shawn's gone, he's dead. There will never be a reason to tell Angus, ever, that I believe something so insane as that my boyfriend—ex-boyfriend—disappeared into medieval Scottish mist."

"So you've thought up stories to explain the crucifix and how you know so much about Niall?"

"No." Amy returned her gaze to the untouched salad, her appetite sliding away. "And I feel like gum on the bottom of someone's shoe every time I lie to him." She sighed. "I guess it's a matter of time before he wonders if I'm dishonest about other things, too."

Rose reached across the table, covering Amy's hand with her own. "Which is why you *have* to tell him."

Amy laughed with a touch of bitterness. "So I can either have him think I'm crazy or think I'm a liar. It's barely begun with him, and I can already see it can't last because of this. Shawn's not even here, and he's still wreaking havoc in my life. Maybe I should just end this with Angus right now."

Rose squeezed Amy's hand. "Don't do that, Amy. Take it day by day, and trust that something is going to make this work out, for you, for him."

Amy nodded, wanting to believe Rose. But her joy from the weekend faded. They ate dinner to the accompaniment of Rose's attempts at conversation, telling about the Orkney Islands. Finally, Amy pushed her plate away, saying, "I'm tired."

"I'll clean up." Rose's eyebrows drew together. She glanced at Amy's barely-touched meal. "Get a good night's sleep. Things will look better in the morning."

Amy nodded, her mind jumping between Shawn and Angus. She retrieved her suitcase from the foot of the stairs and tugged it up behind her, the backpack slung over her shoulder. At her bedroom, she stopped. The office stood open. There would be e-mails to answer, almost certainly one from Angus, but something else niggled at her. She entered the office, took out her laptop and pulled up her e-mail.

I've called a few times, Rob complained. *Where are you?*

I went to Glenmirril, she typed, and hit send.

Are you coming home for Thanksgiving? her mother asked. *We worry about you. We'll buy your ticket. How are you feeling? Is there any word about Shawn?*

Amy stared at the words, thinking of Rose's story, at the Hermitage. Anger and compassion for her mother mingled in her heart. *Hi, Mom, I'm staying here,* she typed. *Don't worry. I'm seeing a doctor, eating well, all that good stuff.* She didn't mention Angus. *There's no word about Shawn.*

There never would be.

I'd have let you know. She added a dutiful *Love, Amy,* and hit send.

Celine and Dana had sent lengthy e-mails detailing life in and out of the orchestra.

She saved Angus's e-mail for last, excited and sad all at once. *I've been thinking about you all day at work. I miss you already.*

She pressed her clasped hands to her mouth. There was no way she could tell him the truth. And there was no way it could last, as long as she was forced to lie to him.

How was your train ride home? The men at the station say I'm smiling a lot today. I have time off for our trip following Douglas's route. I can stay with Mike Monday night and pick you up early Tuesday.

A dozen emotions, options and possibilities swarmed her. She closed her eyes, trying to face them one by one. She should end it now, before he got more involved with something that couldn't last. But there would be no explanation for abruptly ending it, either, not after meeting his family, not after kissing him behind the castle. He'd be hurt, bewildered, angry.

She didn't *want* to end it. She *wanted* to make the trip with him. Maybe Rose was right, and she should just give it a chance, hope for some miracle to solve the problem. Maybe she could think up a story about the crucifix and Niall and gradually, Niall would drift out of their lives, and there would be no more lies.

Her eyes traveled to Angus's next line.

Here's the world's oldest joke. How do you entertain a bored pharaoh?

She scrolled down for his answer, smiling.

You sail a boatload of women dressed in fishing nets down the Nile and urge the pharaoh to catch a fish. He'd added an asterisk and his own note. *Historians suspect it lost something in translation.*

A grin tugged at the corners of her mouth. She typed, *I'm smiling a lot, too. I'll see you Monday night. I'm looking forward to it.* From downstairs came the clatter of dishes in the sink as she added a joke. *How do you recognize Russian composers?* She typed the answer, *By their accents,* and hit send.

Her inbox flashed on the screen, showing Angus's name. And suddenly she knew what had been in the back of her mind. *He's far too humble for his own good.* She pulled up Google and entered *Angus MacLean.*

Glenmirril, 1314

MacDonald stepped out behind Shawn and Allene. The merry sounds of chatter emerged from the church, voices falling silent as one after another burst into the sunshine and saw the silent crowd and MacDougall's men. MacDougall himself snapped his reins. His horse snorted and pranced down the aisle between the castle folk, its head as high as its master's. Duncan followed close behind on his own mount.

"Niall, I'm at your side," came Lachlan's voice softly in his ear.

"I'm here," echoed Hugh, not far behind. "He'll not take you."

Niall's mother laid her hand, like a feather, on his shoulder.

Behind, Shawn heard the whisper of dirks sliding from boots. The Laird raised his hand to his men, signaling peace. He stepped forward. "What do you mean, showing up with men and weapons at my daughter's wedding! Where are my guards?"

MacDougall's mouth twisted up. "Your guards were persuaded they'd live longer by letting us in. Hand over my prisoner."

Allene's hand tensed in Shawn's. More people spilled from the church, pushing them down the stone stairs, almost nose to nose with the great black beast. The Laird spoke at Shawn's side. "Who d' you mean, MacDougall?"

"Niall Campbell who came to my son's castle as Fionn of Bergen."

Lachlan's head snapped to the side, staring at Shawn. "'Tis naught," Shawn assured him. "The man is mad." Niall's mother tightened her grip on his shoulder. Shawn could hear her quick breathing. She must surely be thinking of her six dead sons. Allene's hand clenched his. She stared straight ahead at MacDougall. A cold wind lifted her hair.

A hushed wave of whispers ran over the crowd. Steel rang on steel as MacDougall's men pulled their swords from sheaths.

"I know naught of any Fionn of Bergen." MacDonald laid his hand on Shawn's other shoulder. He smiled. "But by God's own name will I swear this man was never your prisoner."

If his heart had not been pounding with nerves, Shawn would have smiled. MacDonald's reputation for revering God's name would stand him in good stead, with such an oath.

Indeed, a moment of uncertainty flickered across MacDougall's face, before he said, "Stop your games, MacDonald. I saw him myself."

Shawn stepped back, leaned close to MacDonald, and breathed in his ear, "Christina," hoping MacDougall did not have sharp ears, hoping the Laird did, and would take his meaning.

The Laird pushed him back; faced MacDougall for a tense minute, then said, "I say he wasn't." He paused, while the horses under MacDougall's men pawed. "A wager, MacDougall. Prove me wrong and he's yours."

Allene drew in a sharp breath. Her hand squeezed Shawn's so hard, he thought the bones would break. He turned to see her face pale beneath the orange blossoms and vivid hair.

"If I'm proven right," the Laird continued, "you send Christina to live under my protection." He fixed a harsh stare on Duncan.

MacDougall laughed. "Christina is safe enough."

"Do you agree?" MacDonald's bushy eyebrows quivered.

"Aye. Duncan, is this not the man who was in our dungeon?"

"Aye," Duncan snarled. "'Tis himself, despite the changed hair."

"Ragnald!" MacDougall shouted. Another horse clopped forward. "Is this the man who was in our dungeon in September and October until two days ago?"

"Aye, My Lord." The man nodded. His horse snorted.

"Hand him over," MacDougall snapped, satisfied with his proof.

"Lachlan," MacDonald called, without turning. Shawn's comrade and friend from the raids stepped forward. "Tell us where Niall was throughout August, September, and most of October."

"Northumberland, My Lord. I was with him."

MacDougall's face flushed. "He's lying!"

"Owen, Taran," MacDonald called. One by one, men stepped forward, affirming Shawn had been with them.

MacDougall's face darkened with each one. "Lies!" he roared.

James Douglas stepped to Shawn's side, taking the place of Niall's mother, laying his hand on his shoulder where hers had rested. "This man was with me. He was knighted by the Bruce. This man was not in your dungeon, My Lord."

MacDougall's face turned brick red, looking from one to the other. "I saw him myself! You've heard three of us testify!"

"And you've heard a dozen swear he was in England at the time."

"He showed me his injury!" MacDougall sputtered. "The injury from Bannockburn is gone! Let us see, as proof, and then he must be hanged for witchcraft, for we all know 'tis impossible for such a scar to disappear."

"God works in all things!" Allene breathed. Her fingers relaxed. "Show them." A smile touched her lips. "Niall."

Shawn rolled his eyes. But the hammering of his heart slowed. "I'm getting a little tired of baring it all." He couldn't help but note the irony in Shawn Kleiner saying such words. Perhaps God existed and had a wicked sense of humor. He himself didn't find it very funny. "Could we at least go inside where it's warm?"

"Show him," Douglas rumbled. "Before all, so there be no question." To MacDougall, he said, "Tell them all what you saw on the man in the dungeon!"

"Nothing!" MacDougall shouted triumphantly. His dark eyes swept over the people. A twitter of laughter rippled through the crowd, quickly silenced by the threatening looks of MacDougall's men. "This man was cut near in half at Bannockburn. I and ten other men saw the scar only weeks ago at Stirling, you among them, Douglas. In the dungeon, this man, Niall Campbell, lifted his shirt and showed me there was nothing there."

James Douglas nodded to Shawn. "Show them."

"And when you see the scar is gone," MacDougall demanded of Douglas, "you'll stand by my claim?"

"Aye," Douglas said. "I so swear it."

"And when you see the scar is there, Christina will be delivered safely to us without a mark on her." Shawn spoke, his eyes boring into Duncan's. "Or you'll have identical marks. Starting with the hot poker on the ankle." Duncan blanched. Shawn loosened his belt, handing it to Allene, who faced MacDougall, her chin high and eyes blazing. He lifted Niall's jeweled tunic, lifted the white shirt underneath. Cold autumn wind whistled across the courtyard, across the jagged, puckered scar, viciously red, more than an inch wide, stretching from one side clear to the other, and halfway around to his back. He turned, holding up the tunic, making sure everyone saw. Some men gasped. Ladies turned, or lifted hands to shield their delicate eyes.

MacDougall's eyes widened. "'Tis impossible!" he gasped. "I *saw* him!" He shouted now. "*There was no scar!*"

James Douglas stepped forward, grabbing the horse's reins, biting out each word. "I've no idea who was in your dungeon, MacDougall, but your son's failure to swear fealty already puts you on dangerous ground, without storming in on the marriage of a man knighted by Bruce himself, making false accusations and demanding to hang him. You've three days to return with the Lady Christina, as you've sworn before all this day, or the Lord of the Isles will harry your coast, and my men will attack from the east!"

"Three days!" bellowed MacDougall. He glared around the crowd, as if expecting their support. "'Tis barely enough time!"

"Then you'd best ride hard!" Douglas threw the reins from him, barked at the horse, and shouted to MacDougall's men. "Three days!"

Shawn yanked his tunic back into place. "I'll be waiting with the hot poker in the fire, Duncan."

Allene grabbed his face between her hands and kissed him on the lips, throwing her arms around him and hugging him with the grip of death he'd just once again narrowly escaped. He held her back, breathing deeply in gratitude. "Damned good luck I didn't side with Niall," he whispered.

"The Lord works in all things," she returned.

Shawn threw his head back, laughing. They'd never agree. Either way, Niall, alone in his room, had just escaped the noose a second time.

Bannockburn, Present

"I thought his job was mundane." It was a week and several more searches on Angus's name before Amy mentioned it. She hurried with Rose through Bannockburn's chilly morning streets, enjoying the last day of her teacher's visit, before the plane would whisk her away again. "Shuffling papers, standing around Eden Court while royalty visits." She laughed ruefully. "Occasionally asking questions of distressed American musicians."

"Did he tell you more about his work?" Rose asked.

"No. Clive did." Amy buried her hands in the pockets of her blue coat. Her hat shielded her ears from the biting wind. "And I googled. He's called in for big things." A list had sprung up on Google, *Angus MacLean* in bold over and over. She'd paged through, more amazed at each link. "Awards, commendations, water and mountain rescues. The list went on and on. Why hasn't he told me any of it?"

Rose tugged her wool hat down firmly. "Because he's not Shawn."

"Miss Amy!" Sinead's piping voice interrupted them. She danced up and down in the door of the co-op. Her red jacket set off her freckles and black hair. A bag of apples swung from one hand. "My teacher asked me to play for the talent show next week! She said...."

Mrs. Gordon appeared, juggling an armful of groceries. "Now, then, young lady, perhaps Miss Rose and Miss Amy were talking! Rose, so good to see you back. How are ye, Amy?"

"Good," Amy said, amused as always by the girl's energy. "Do you have something picked out?" she asked her. They chatted as they walked, until they reached the Gordons' street and Sinead skipped away with her mother, swinging the apples.

Amy waved good-bye and returned to the subject of Angus. "There was one particular rescue in the mountains. Four hours on his stomach in the snow, hanging onto a man who fell over a cliff, till they got equipment to pull him up. He was awarded a medal for it."

"And well-earned," Rose said. "He's a fine man. I hope you've reconsidered this breaking up with him business?"

"He's already got time off for the trip." Amy stuffed her hands deep into her pockets. "I could hardly tell him I'm canceling."

"And you're excited about going," Rose pointed out.

"Yes." Amy smiled, her face aglow with memories of her time with Angus. "I am." The smile slipped. "But I just can't see a good ending from letting this continue."

"There's a third option of stepping out in faith." Rose lifted her hand to wave at an older man coming down the street toward them, huddled into his scarf. They met him at a corner. "Hello, Mr. Graham! How are you today?"

"Wonderful, Rose, and yourself?" He stopped briefly to chat, shaking Amy's hand and expressing his pleasure at meeting her.

"Is there anyone in Bannockburn you haven't met?" Amy asked when he'd passed.

"Hm." Rose thought about it. "I haven't made it to the nursing home to meet his wife yet. Maybe I'll do that this afternoon."

Amy laughed. "I have no doubt you will."

Rose returned to their conversation as they waited for a break in the traffic to cross the street. "Angus is smart. He took the reports. He's seen the crucifix. He's asking himself why an honest woman is hedging."

Amy gave a delicate cough. "Such a polite word for lying."

"When we had our drink," Rose continued, "I told him to think outside the box, asked him what's the wildest thing he could think up to explain it all, and he said that Shawn and Niall are one and the same."

"And what did he think of that?" Amy asked curiously.

"He laughed," Rose admitted. "Said Shawn Kleiner is obviously not a time-traveling medieval warrior."

Amy sighed. "No, he certainly wasn't."

"But at least he opened the door to the impossible," Rose said. "It's percolating in his mind. He's a logical man, Amy, and logical men know that when you've ruled out every other possibility, what you're left with is the answer. Give him time, and one day, your gut is going to tell you he's ready for the whole truth. You may be pleasantly surprised."

"Maybe." Amy tugged her hat more tightly around her ears. "Here's the clinic," she said. "Thank goodness. I'm freezing."

Rose stopped her, a hand on her arm. Her perpetual smile slipped from her face. "You'll make this trip with him, Amy? You'll give this a chance with him?"

Amy stared into her teacher's blue eyes. Something besides her own lies still held her back.

Rose squeezed her arm. "Promise me."

"Yes." Amy nodded, wondering why she still felt unsettled about seeing Angus.

"Good." A weight seemed to lift off Rose, and her usual cheer returned. "Let's see about this baby, then!"

♫

They pushed through the door into the doctor's office. Sinead sat in the waiting room, her red jacket on her lap. Amy gave a start. "Hello!"

The girl smiled. "Hallo, Miss Amy. Hallo, Miss Rose."

"A shame we didn't know you were coming here, too," Rose said. "We could have walked together."

A nurse opened a door. Sinead popped out of her seat, saying, "Here I am, Miss!" She bolted to the nurse, throwing a grin back at Amy.

"What was that all about?" Amy murmured, but a moment later, she was called back herself, and all thought of her student was swept away in the thrill of listening to the swift, fluttering pulse of her baby's heart.

Rose beamed, squeezing her hand.

"Nice and strong." The doctor smiled, coiling up his doppler.

When he left, Amy laid her hands on the small mound of her stomach. "Shawn was so good with my cousins."

"For all his faults," Rose agreed, "he did like children. He would have been a good father."

Amy bit her lip. "I wonder what he meant by *Iona J.*"

"We'll never know," Rose said.

Amy sat up abruptly, yanking her shirt down. "Well, it doesn't matter. He won't be here to be a father to his child." Shawn and Angus danced in her mind, and suddenly she knew what it was that left her unsettled.

Wedding Feast Glenmirril, 1314

They would feast all night, in honor of their future Laird's marriage. As a host of Douglas's men ushered MacDougall across the drawbridge, Shawn and Allene ran, laughing, across the courtyard to the great hall, decked with tapestries, ribbons floating from the beamed ceiling, hundreds of smoky candles scenting the air, and viols, lutes and recorders playing in the gallery. Allene's eyes lit with joy and gratitude when she looked at Shawn, and she danced and feasted with a liveliness all would take for a typical new bride, hugging him at intervals and thanking him again and again in hushed whispers.

When Niall's mother claimed her for a warm embrace, Shawn whisked one of the Morrison twins into a reel—at least he thought it was a reel—and spun back to Allene. While the Morrison twins and Lachlan's sisters surrounded her in a gaggle of giggles and blushes, he downed another ale, listening to Adam's grieving widow reminisce about her own wedding, holding both her hands between his. He did his best imitation of a strathspey with one of her seven daughters, while Hugh swung Allene to the bright melody of the recorder. Her face glowed. Candlelight and firelight glinted in her auburn curls.

Shawn danced something stately with Niall's mother. A veil held her tawny hair back, framing her patrician face. She studied him from under feathery eyebrows. "You seem—changed—tonight. In unusually high spirits."

He leaned close. "Next time you see me, remind me you like me best as I am tonight at my wedding." He grinned and winked. "Don't forget!"

"Niall." Allene appeared at his side, flushed with dancing, and glowing as only a bride could. "Your mother likes you best *as you always were.*"

His mother smiled. "I'm rather enjoying his humor tonight."

"See," Shawn smirked. "She likes me best."

"Come away now, *Niall.*" Allene's fingers tightened on his arm. "'Tis time for us to be going." They slipped toward the stone staircase, but an immediate flurry of calls and shouts dragged them, creeping, back. Allene's smile slipped a notch to courtesy. The blossoms in her hair seemed to droop.

Ronan claimed a dance from Allene, less thrilled with the festivities than she had been, while Shawn downed another ale, traded jokes with Lachlan, and did something circular and lively with another Morrison twin. "You look familiar," he said, and moved on to a dignified dance with the widow Muirne. "They're telling me stories!" he exclaimed. "You're far too young to have six children!" She beamed up at him from her five feet. He moved into another dance with one of Lachlan's sisters. "I just married the most beautiful woman in Glenmirril." He leaned close. "But you are a close second! You have gorgeous eyes!" She blushed and laughed.

Allene minced away from Owen, into Shawn's arms. "Come, *Niall.* Let us be away."

"She can't wait to get me upstairs," Shawn told Lachlan's sister with a broad wink, and, taking Allene's hand, made for the stairs.

A drunken, bawdy Gil spotted them. "Niall, where are you rushing to in such haste!" Men guffawed knowingly. "What could you want upstairs?"

"You've got all night for that," roared Ronan. He tossed back what was most definitely not his first, third, or even fifth, ale. "Come back and dance!"

With a sad face, Allene followed Shawn back to her wedding celebration. Shawn's gaze followed a thin-waisted girl, batting her eyes back at him. "Just how many Morrison twins are there?" he asked. "Have I danced with you yet?"

Bannockburn, Present

"Rose?"

In the front room, lively gypsy music skipped to a stop. Rose lowered her violin and opened her eyes.

"You leave tomorrow. Can I ask a favor?" Amy lifted a bottle of Merlot and two china cups. "Sorry, I don't have wine glasses."

"Anything." Rose laid her violin in its velvet lining.

"Come upstairs." In her room, Amy turned on the lamp. Moonlight shone through the window. Outside, beyond the lace curtain, the bare limbs of the tree swayed in a night breeze. Shawn's heavy, white robe lay across the peach and lace duvet. Amy settled next to it, handing a tea cup to Rose, and poured wine into each cup. They clinked the china rims together, and drank.

"What's the favor?" Rose lowered her cup to her lap.

"Something was bothering me today, when you asked me to promise to move ahead with Angus."

"Mm," Rose said. "Considering you *like* him, it was the most trepidatious promise I've ever heard."

"Is that a word?" Amy asked.

"Of course it is," Rose said. "I just used it, didn't I?"

Amy smiled, despite the serious concerns on her mind. But she said, "I know what else is holding me back. Apart from being forced to lie to him."

"And what is that?"

"Things never really ended with Shawn. I broke up with him, but who knows what would have happened if he'd come back."

"You need a *coda*," Rose stated. "A solid five-one cadence to end the piece."

"Yes." Amy nodded. "It's time to put this away." Amy touched Shawn's fluffy, white robe, running her fingers down the edge. "There was never any burial, no closure, and I need it. This is the closest I'll get and it seems right to have someone here."

Rose squeezed her hand. "Do you have one of his CDs to play?"

"On my ipod." Amy took it from the nightstand drawer. It had been a gift from Shawn. "I only have earphones." She plugged them into the ipod and handed one to Rose. "Which song, do you think?"

They leaned close, scrolling through the many pieces. "Here." Amy touched the words *I'll Remember You,* off his first CD. Almost immediately, the first strains of Amy's own violin drifted into their ears. She leaned back against the headboard, remembering every moment of arranging the piece in Shawn's sunny music room, and of the recording session. The violin faded away into the rich chords of Shawn's brass quintet. Amy closed her eyes, remembering watching as Shawn, Rob, Dana, and the rest of the quintet played. After the intro, a singer joined, with a low, throaty voice.

Amy sipped her Merlot, eyes closed, letting the day replay itself in her heart. Her hand rested on her stomach, thinking of a child who would never know its father. When the song ended on a *pianissimo* chord, she opened her eyes, turned off the ipod, and asked, "What now?"

"A eulogy," Rose declared. "He made people laugh. He was generous."

"He always had gifts for my cousins," Amy said. "He loved his mother."

"He was a great musician, a great leader. He got incredible music out of other people. He had drive."

"He sacrificed himself to save a child," Amy whispered. Her hand tightened on her stomach. Tears stung her eyes. "It's so unfair. It doesn't really make sense to pray for someone long dead, does it?"

Rose took her hand. "It can't hurt, right? Fold up his robe."

Amy did so. She pulled his suitcase from under the bed, and settled the robe on top of his other clothes.

"God, watch over him wherever he is," Rose murmured, and added an *Our Father.*

Amy zipped the suitcase shut, and with a heavy sigh, pushed it under the bed. "There." She stood up, met Rose's eyes, and gave a sound somewhere between a sob and a laugh. "What kind of pathetic memorial service is this?" She sank back onto the bed. "If he'd died the normal way—but when did Shawn ever do anything the normal way—he'd have had a service with thousands of crying girls."

"There's not much precedent for funerals where the rest of the world thinks he'll turn up." Rose wrapped Amy in a hug, and they sat for some time before she added, "I think this is more fitting. He died a different man. He should have a different sort of funeral."

Amy nodded. "Shawn would have seen the humor in it. Just the two of us for the world-renowned Shawn Kleiner." They sat quietly for a moment before she asked, "What would he think of Angus? Of someone else being with me and his child?"

"If he redeemed himself in the end," Rose said, "then he became a man who would be happy you have Angus in your lives." She swung her feet to the floor, and refilled her glass with Merlot. "You're wise to lay him to rest this way." She raised her glass in a toast. "To a beautiful future with Angus."

Glenmirril, 1314

Shawn threw back ale like he'd been doing it all his life. In the gallery, the musicians piped a lively reel. He leaned in to Allene. She was beautiful in her gown, with flowers decking her auburn hair. "I don't have a clue clue clue how to dance this do," he slurred in a stage whisper.

"Follow me," she said, and in an undertone, "and hope they're too drunk to notice." He fumbled through, copying other men and following Allene as well as he could. The blazing fires in the hearths, on top of exertion and liquor, flushed his face. He became less concerned with steps, throwing himself whole-heartedly into the fun, spinning her and laughing at her horror that he'd done the dance wrong. Other couples clapped in time, laughing, seeing his improvisation as Niall's usual humor.

Allene glanced at the stairs leading to her real husband. Her face lengthened. The crowd pressed around them, growing louder and more boisterous as servants hurried with casks of wine and frothing ale. Shawn raised another overflowing tankard high, shouted *Slainte!* and drank it down. A crowd of bearded men raised theirs in return, shouting and drinking.

"A *troika!*" Shawn bellowed. He dropped to a squat, arms crossed over his chest, kicking his legs out in time to the rhythm in his head. "None of you ever seen the Russians dance? Get down here!"

Owen and Lachlan tried first, landing quickly on their less than sober rears. "I can do that," Gil boasted, and was instantly beside Shawn, doing a passable impression of a Cossack, giving sharp kicks of his legs, arms crossed and elbows high. Taran and his one-eyed father joined him, but quickly fell on the floor on top of one another, laughing uproariously and pounding one another's backs in mirth.

Shawn leapt to his feet, and danced back to Allene. He looked her over with an appreciative eye. The way she'd kissed him on Coxet Hill, the night before battle, filled his drunken brain. He spun her around. "I should kiss you. Just for show, you know."

She smiled, pressed her lips close to his ear, and whispered, "Niall will rip your teeth out one by one if you do." She waved at Niall's sister, across the hall, holding the new bairn of Adam's widow.

"I like my teeth where they are, but you're beautiful," Shawn replied. The roaring fire threw shimmers of copper over her hair and sparked off the jewels on her belt. "If you'd been around in my day, there'd've been a Scottish bikini team, instead of Swedish."

"I've no idea what that is." Allene rolled her eyes. "D' you think we can get out yet?"

"Douglas is watching. I don't think so. Just smile. Bikini teams smile."
He pulled her closer under pretext of a dance. "Midnight's coming, aye?"

"What does that mean?" she asked.

"I turn into a pumpkin and you get the real prince." He suspected he'd
had enough alcohol. But it was high time he had a little fun in this place. "In
the meantime, I'm better looking than him."

She sniffed. "You look exactly the same."

"Well, I'm not the worst substitute you could be stuck with," he retorted
indignantly.

"Aye, Duncan MacDougall would be worse."

Behind them, Gil toppled in a heap on the floor. Several of the young
men tried to help him up, one of them falling on him instead, while the older
men roared in laughter.

"Thanks." Shawn spared a glance at the graceless dancers. "At least try
to look happy. How about I tell a joke? A jest?" He racked his brains for a
clean one. Couples swirled around them, laughing, women with heads
thrown back and white teeth shining.

"They said you all have bad teeth in medieval times," he mused.

"You're drunk," said Allene. "What of this jest?" In the gallery, the viol
and fife skipped from note to note.

"Okay, okay, I got one. There's this guy." Shawn took her hand, leading
her into the dance. "He walks into a bar. What a klutz."

Allene didn't smile.

"He walks into a tavern," Shawn clarified. "You're not getting this.
Pretty clumsy to walk into a building, right? Okay, forget it." He swung her
around, making her skirt spin. "Try this one. A guy walks into a tavern with
his...." Lacking Gaelic, he substituted English. "...his *giraffe*."

"His *certainly*?"

It took him a moment to realize she was hearing Gaelic. "No, not
dearbh," he said, "gir*affe*."

"That's what I said."

"But it's not what *I* said."

The dance called for switching partners. Shawn handed Allene off to
Hugh and found himself with a Morrison twin, red cheeks shining above her
blue kirtle, smiling shyly. "How many of you are there?" he asked, spun her
around and worked his way, arms linking with a dozen women in turn, back
to Allene. "You've never seen a giraffe? It's like a pony but with legs as tall as
me, and a neck long enough to reach the leaves of trees."

She laughed.

"Wait, that's not the punch line," he protested.

"Surely you jest. There can be no such animal."

Before he could answer, he found himself passed off to another woman,
did a bit of a waltz with her, moon-walked his way through the next one, and
tried some Macarena with the third.

"What are you doing?" Allene demanded, when he reached her again.

"It's how we dance." He laughed at her annoyance. "Now they think
Niall's funny. Would you smile?" The shawm skipped through the refrain.

"You promised me a jest," she reminded him curtly, "and so far, you've
done naught but tell tall tales."

"Very funny." He spun her around, and brushed off another woman, whose turn it was to take Allene's place.

"You can't do that," Allene gasped.

"I'm trying to tell a joke!" Shawn snapped. "And you're taking it too seriously." Nearby couples turned their heads. He grinned at them. "A jest." To Allene, he said, "The guy says, 'A drink for me, a drink for my giraffe.'"

"You're ruining the dance," Allene objected.

"You're ruining my joke and making people think you don't want to marry Niall, with the long face. The guy says, 'another drink for me, another one for my giraffe.'"

"Of course I want to marry Niall," she hissed. "I'd rather be with him now."

"No one will think so, the way you're looking," he retorted. "So after a couple hours, the giraffe is drunk and passes out."

The music shifted to something like a minuet. Shawn took a long slug of ale from the table laden with food and drink. It went delightfully to his head, making the room spin pleasantly, making everything bright and cheerful. The women's long dresses blurred into a burst of garden blooms.

"That's ridiculous," Allene said, as he took her hand and stepped back into the dance. "How does a man give ale to a twenty-foot pony? From a trough?"

"He just does, okay!" Shawn glared at her. "Besides, you're too late to argue about whether a giraffe *can* drink. It's *already* drunk and passed out on the floor."

"'Tis unlikely," sniffed Allene.

"'Tis very likely," Shawn mimicked her. "So the guy walks out the door, leaving the giraffe on the floor."

"I'd not leave my pony like that."

"It's a *joke!*"

Taran's father gaped at him in surprise, his one eye wide.

"A jest!" Shawn beamed back. "She's really happy to be marrying me!"

"Stop it, Shawn!" Allene hissed. She minced back a step, holding his hand high in the air. "What happened to the *dearbh?*"

"It just lies there. But the innkeeper says to the guy." The room spun, making him laugh. Her hand was warm in his. Colors sparkled around him; firelight danced off swirling dresses. "The innkeeper says 'Hey, you can't leave that lyin' here!' And the guy says, 'That's not a lion! That's a *giraffe!*'"

Allene circled around him, her feet keeping delicate time to the music. A frown marred her features. "Where did the lion come from?"

Shawn reviewed his words. One fact worked its way into his liquor-logged brain. "It doesn't translate well, does it?" he asked. "Try it in English. *Laighe,* lyin,' *leomhann,* lion, get it?"

She frowned. "Certainly."

They minced another circle around one another.

"Could you at least laugh at me, if not with me? The goal here is to look happy."

The musicians stopped playing at that moment. A hush swept over the crowd; it lasted only a heartbeat before a man called, "*The Falkirk Lament!* Play for us, Niall."

Shawn's heart knocked hard in his chest, two erratic swinging eighths.

He had no hope of playing and singing it as Niall did. Allene's hand squeezed his. She held her breath. Shawn let out his. He knew subterfuge as well as he knew music. He gave a hearty laugh, throwing his head back. "A lament at my wedding feast! This is a *happy* occasion!"

"Play the *Lament*," called Taran. Beside him, Niall's mother and the widow Muirne nodded.

"No, really." Shawn grinned from ear to drunken ear. "I'll play a happy song."

"Play the *Lament*," Lachlan shouted, and several young men beside him joined in. "Ye've ever played it at wedding feasts."

"Whyever would you refuse?" Niall's mother tilted her head at him.

His smile slipping, Shawn looked to MacDonald.

Bannockburn, Present

"Rose, I'm going to miss you!" Amy could feel her cheeks glow even as she spoke.

Red wool hat on her head, a matching cape hanging from her shoulders, and her floral suitcase at her feet in Amy's front hallway, Rose kissed Amy on each cheek before holding her back, gripping her shoulders. "But not like the last time I left." She looked up and down Amy's black leggings and black long-sleeved t-shirt under a long, knit vest that showed the small mound of Amy's stomach. "You look wonderful. And happy. And you're going to have a beautiful baby. You're going to let me know when you leave for the hospital, right?"

Amy nodded. "I wish you could be here."

"I wish so, too, and maybe I will be, but you'll be okay. I told you life would get better, and I was right, wasn't I?"

"You always are," Amy said with a laugh.

"You did the right thing, putting Shawn's robe away. I felt the confident, talented girl I sent off to the Midwest show up again."

"I felt the weight lift off," Amy said. "I feel like I can really let go of him, finally, and move forward."

"Speaking of which, when's Angus getting here?" Rose asked.

"Not until this evening."

"A shame I couldn't meet him again."

From outside came the sharp beep of the taxi.

Rose gave Amy another quick hug, grabbed her suitcase, and hurried through the blue door, into the gray November day, clamping her hat to her head against the wind. Amy shivered in the cold of the open door, one arm clutched around herself, waving while Rose climbed into the cab. The car slid away as drizzle began trickling from the gunflint clouds overhead. Amy smiled, watching Rose wave from the back window, and thinking how right Rose was. She felt, once again, like the confident Juilliard graduate who had hugged her teacher good-bye at the airport, not so long ago, and flown to claim her chair with a professional symphony.

She shut the door, closing herself in with cheerful electric lights that held the gloomy day at bay, and the soft crackle of the fire in her front room. In a short time, she had chicken in the crockpot, ready for when Angus arrived that evening, and went upstairs. She lifted the picture of Shawn off the dresser, studying his face, remembering all the good times, thinking of the apology on the rock. *A, so sorry. Iona J.*

She wished she could have known the man he became. But he was gone. She held the picture against her chest for a moment, before rounding the bed, opening the suitcase, and sliding the framed picture inside Shawn's robe. She glanced at the ring on her finger—Bruce's heavy gold and garnet ring. Maybe it should go in, too. She gave her head an unconscious shake. No, it would stay on her finger, a small testament to his last sacrifice, to his redemption. She pushed the suitcase under the bed, and went back downstairs to practice until her first student arrived.

Glenmirril, 1314

Allene turned to her father, her eyes wide. MacDonald gave a crinkly-eyed grin through his big red and silver beard. The scar running from eye to cheek wrinkled in a fine white line. "And why would we want a lament at a wedding!" He raised his tankard, splashing ale over his fingers and down his wrist. "To a dozen grandchildren! Drink to my daughter and new son!" He threw back his ale, encouraging the men to do likewise, and the demand for the *Lament* sloshed back down dozens of drunken throats. MacDonald signaled the musicians, and they kicked into another lively dance.

At the end of it, Allene looked to her father, with a heavy sigh. He nodded, and raised his hand to the musicians. They finished with a trill and flourish, the dancers skidded to stops, panting, and she broke into a smile. "My father says we can go!"

"I've never had a woman so thrilled to get away from me," Shawn grumbled.

"Dry your eyes!" She beamed as she grabbed his hand and pulled him through the crowd, through ribald comments flying as thick as confetti. People clapped and cheered. At the bottom of the stairs, Niall's mother hugged him and kissed Allene. Color climbed up her cheeks, across her run-away smile. Shawn almost blushed himself. Never had a private moment been so public. Even in the orchestra, the men had jibed him about his exploits with a modicum of subtlety. He returned their comments with winks, smiles, and nods, gritting his teeth at the irony of his cold, lonely bed waiting, and followed Allene in her mad dash up the stairs.

Laughing and out of breath, Shawn and Allene burst into Niall's room. Niall spun from the window, moonlight glinting off the short, dark stubble on his head, and rushed with un-lairdly lack of dignity to Allene. "How was my wedding?" He glared at Shawn.

"Dude," Shawn drawled the word. "I'd rather have the honeymoon than the wedding." He laughed at Niall's scowl before lifting the hem of the jewel-encrusted tunic. "Seriously? Diamonds? You got the better half of this deal."

"Niall, don't be angry." Allene buried her face in his neck.

"You missed your wedding," Shawn said, "but your marriage will be much longer for it." Turning his back, he disappeared into his own room. Allene would explain. From the other side, the bolt slid to with a sharp report, and there came soft murmurs and breathless laughter.

His head swimming with ale, Shawn peeled off Niall's finery. Clothes sewn with jewels! Even he didn't wear such things! He tossed the tunic at a peg in the wardrobe. It missed, sliding to the floor in a jeweled heap. He pulled on a nightshirt, and flopped on the bed. A moment later, he jerked up irritably, to add a log to the fire. Flames curled around it for a few seconds before shooting high. He climbed under the furs to ward off the chill that was quickly taking the pleasant edge off his drunkenness.

He lay under the sables and bear skin, letting ale-induced maudlin overtake him. He fingered the gold chain from Bruce that still hung around his neck, thinking of Amy, and imagining what their wedding might have been like. She wouldn't have actually married Rob. She couldn't have! When he got back....

He sat up abruptly! He could go to the tower *now*! He would wake up in his own time and walk to Inverness! He paused, his bare feet hitting the floor.

It was time travel. Maybe he'd wake up just a day or two after the re-enactment, no matter when he left. He could show up any time, couldn't he? Regardless of when he left. It would raise awkward questions if someone saw the groom wandering the halls alone on his wedding night.

He laid back down, pulling the furs up tight. He could wait a night and slip up there before MacDonald sent them to Stirling. He could use the extra day to plan out his raid on Amy's affections as thoroughly as Douglas planned his invasions of Appleby and Brough. He'd storm the halls of her mercy and forgiveness as he'd stormed the churches of Northumbria. Just a night or two, time to say good-bye to Allene, Niall, Lachlan, Hugh, Taran, MacDonald.

He'd start by confessing everything to Amy, coming clean. He thought about the women, too many of them, and tweaked his plan. He'd come clean about the ones she already suspected. No need to hurt her unnecessarily. But his intentions were honest, he consoled himself: start fresh, confess, even if not all the details, and never do it again.

Then he'd buy her flowers. Hundreds of them. He'd build that stable and buy her a horse, or two or three. He'd ride with her every morning. This horse business was growing on him. He'd take her on trips and give her necklaces and rings. No, scratch that, he thought. She wasn't the jewelry type. A really great violin would be her heart's desire.

He'd throw away the secret cell phone and get rid of all those e-mails. He'd give her the biggest diamond engagement ring she'd ever seen, or even imagined. He'd spend every day with her and their child. He tried to imagine what she looked like, pregnant. He'd heard it gave women a glow. And she already had an alabaster sheen to her perfect skin, against her dark hair, that he had loved.

He forgot about all the things he'd buy her, and lost himself in the desire to see her and touch her, to hold her close, in a slow dance before a fireplace the way she'd loved to do. He finally drifted into restless sleep, dreaming of her. He'd give them a couple nights. Then he'd sleep in the tower, no matter what MacDonald said.

Bannockburn, Present

Angus arrived as Colin, with his long hair, gave his shy grin and shuffled out into Bannockburn's dark evening. Angus shut the door, pulling Amy into a warm hug. "I missed you," he whispered.

Her heart fluttered as she reached up to wrap her arms around his neck. "I missed you, too." She'd missed him even more since putting away Shawn's robe, as if the action had freed her. She liked Angus, she liked everything about him, and the week had passed with agonizing slowness, waiting for each e-mail, each call, waiting to see him again. Rose's question drifted to her mind: *what if you had to choose between them?*

She never would have met Angus, had Shawn still been here. But she'd never see Shawn again. Choosing between them wasn't a question she wanted to answer, and thankfully, one she'd never have to.

"I can't wait to go on this trip." He released her from the hug, taking her arm and turning her. His other arm slid quickly behind his back.

A smile split her face. "Me, neither. But you're not half so clever as you think, Inspector MacLean. What are you hiding?"

He grinned, and with a flourish produced a paper cone she first took for a bouquet of flowers. Then she laughed in surprise. "Paint brushes!" Their bristles stuck up like blooms.

"And paints!" He pulled out the brushes to reveal more supplies below. "And colored pencils and charcoals. You've a wonderful gift. Do you mind?"

"Mind?" she asked in surprise. "Why would I mind?"

"That it's not flowers," he explained. "I stood in the florist asking myself what flowers would you most love to see in the cellophane, and realized *this* is what you'd most like to see. Or maybe tickets to a horse show. Or score paper." He grinned. "But I didn't want to overwhelm you, so I just got this."

Her heart warmed, touched by his thoughtfulness, and already seeing what she could do with the greater array of paints and pencils. "I love it." She fingered the bristles of one of the brushes. "Thank you." She reached to hug him again, feeling tears prickle the back of her eyes. Shawn had given her flowers while dismissing her music and artwork. She swallowed over the hot lump in her throat, not wanting to stray into the past, anymore. "I made you chicken and rice."

"My favorite. It smells delicious." He swung a backpack to the floor. "And then I have a dozen maps and brochures and we can plan our route."

An hour later, they sat on Amy's couch together, maps of England spread across the table, covered in highlighter marking the route they would take from one castle and town to another, visiting the places James Douglas had raided in the early 1300s. Finally, with the fire growing low, Angus folded the maps. He dug in his backpack for a small ipod and a pair of speakers, which he set on the mantle. The push of a button brought slow strains of a ballad lilting from the speakers.

He held out his hand, a smile touching his lips. "Would it be too corny if I asked for the last dance?"

Her heart fluttered in time with the shadows flickering over the plane of his jaw, in time with the silky arpeggios floating from the piano.

She settled into his arms, swaying in a slow dance. Her head sank to his shoulder, remembering what it was to feel safe and loved.

Chapter Eighteen

Creagsmalan, 1314

Just back from bringing food to a widow, Christina was hanging her cloak in the wardrobe when the door to her chamber crashed open, followed by Duncan's roar and MacDougall's deeper voice behind him. She sprang back, the pounding of fear in her ears covering their words.

Duncan grabbed her shoulders, shaking her, shouting, "What did you do? You'd summat to do with this!"

"Take your hands off her, Duncan."

Duncan thrust her across the room. She fell, twisting her wrist, before the fire, her hand just short of the hot embers. "A little closer," Duncan taunted, towering over her. His hand flashed out, slapping her. Pain stung across her cheek. Bells rang in her ears.

His father loomed over her. "Enough, Duncan."

"I'll do as I please," Duncan roared. "She's my wife!"

"Then you should have treated her as such." MacDougall's face burned crimson over the black beard. "Get out. I'll deal with this myself, since you're obviously incompetent to do so."

Fighting panic, Christina scooted across the floor, dragging her fine blue kirtle in the ashes. Duncan and MacDougall stared one another down. MacDougall's hand drifted to the hilt of his knife.

Duncan gave one last, baleful look, spat at her, and turned on his heel. She shrank into herself, as he stormed out, slamming the heavy wooden door. Niall was perhaps locked in the dungeons again already. And Bessie—what would Duncan do to Bessie for this? Her heart pounded mercilessly.

MacDougall dropped the bar in place across the door, and turned on her. "Duncan seems to think you'd summat to do with the prisoner escaping. I begin to wonder myself."

Glenmirril, 1314

"I get it," Shawn said over dinner in Niall's solar. He'd spent the day since the wedding with Allene, Hugh, the Laird, Niall, all of them, saying good-bye in his heart, though not in words. "But I don't. You saved Scotland. So what's wrong with going back to an easier time? Grocery stores on every corner, thinsulate jackets for this crapola weather Scotland loves, vacations. You'd never be hungry. Never in danger of being hanged. Never in danger of much of anything, really. So why do you act like that tower is something to be scared of?"

Niall twirled his goblet between two fingers. "Everyone I care about is here."

"So take Allene and the Laird with you." Shawn stabbed his knife at a chunk of meat floating in his trencher.

"They wouldn't go." Niall stared into the swirling mead.

"What if they would? You could give her a house of her own with wall to wall carpeting, hot showers every night, beautiful clothes, all the things women love."

Niall raised his eyes. "We've everything we need already."

"Vacation in the sunny Bahamas," Shawn pressed. "Think if you could give her that, let the Laird relax in a cabin on a lake, and spend the rest of his days fishing, instead of fighting."

Firelight flickered over the stubble on Niall's head. "Your time has its own dangers."

Shawn rolled his eyes and snorted. "I never got cut in half in my own time. You don't get thrown in a dungeon for sneaking off with a girl." He laughed. "You get a slap on the back. And if you do get thrown in prison, you get a bed and three squares a day."

"Squares?"

"Good meals. No rats." He gave an exaggerated shudder. "I do not like rats. I especially don't like them in the dark, crawling over my face. I never had to worry about that in my own time."

"You're talking about corporal dangers." Niall lifted his goblet, sipping.

"Corporal *Who*?" Shawn's knife poised over another chunk of beef.

"Of the body. I'm talking about dangers to the soul."

Shawn laughed as he speared the meat. "What, like we're all going to Hell? God is love. There's no Hell." He gulped his meal, chasing it with a heavy swallow of ale. "There's no danger to our souls."

Niall once again stared into his cup. Finally, he spoke. "Would you go to a meeting with Conrad, as you look now?"

Shawn looked down at himself. Apart from sleeping in a nightshirt, he'd been wearing the same billow-sleeved *leine*, hose, and vest since returning from Creagsmalan. He'd worked in it, sweated in it. He hadn't bathed since the wedding. The hair on which he'd prided himself would not impress anybody now, not even pulled back in a leather thong, as neat as he could make it. "Of course not. What's that got to do with anything?"

Niall leaned forward, speaking intently. "Souls get worn and stained, too. You'd no more take yourself before God like that than you would before Conrad as you are now."

"My soul is fine, thanks." But Shawn pushed a hand through his hair, more aware of its condition than he had been for some time. "Ask anyone who's heard me play jazz." He laughed at his own joke, and added, "Get the Laird to let me play his sackbut, I'll show you some jazz." At Niall's blank look, he clarified, "Music, remember? Fun stuff. Ba-dop, shoo-bop, skibbidy-doo-doo." He took Niall's recorder and played four bars of *Take the A Train*.

Niall smiled.

Shawn danced around the room crooning into the recorder like a microphone, about Harlem and Sugar Hill, exaggerating the long notes.

Niall laughed out loud.

"See." Shawn grinned. "I got plenty of soul."

Niall shook his head. "You and I will never understand one another. I found myself changing, in your time, thinking more and more of myself and what I wanted."

"So?"

Niall frowned, chin in hand, studying Shawn. "I thought you'd seen enough here to know if you think only on yourself, others suffer."

"Yeah, okay, I screwed up, I hurt Amy, I get that." Shawn set the recorder on the table, spun a chair backwards and straddled it, his arms on the table. "But a little balance, you know? Like a well-written symphony. I'm going to treat her right when I get back. Where's the danger to my soul, then? Where would be the danger to your soul?" He realized, with a shock, he *wanted* Niall to come with him.

Niall tipped his chair back on two legs, rubbing the stubble on his head. "D' you know nothing of the fruits and gifts of the Holy Spirit?"

"As much as you know about jazz." Shawn arched one eyebrow. "And I care even less. Life is about having fun, you know."

"Is there no suffering in your time?" Niall dropped the chair sharply back on the floor, and leaned forward. "Caroline, Rob, Conrad—they had everything you say, and they weren't at peace."

"Oh, was Caroline put out?" Shawn quaffed his ale. "Yeah, I bet she was." Despite his flippant words, something twisted inside him. Caroline left a bad taste in his mouth, especially in front of Niall.

"Och, look at her!" Niall rose, and paced to the window. "Is she ever happy? One has but to look and see she's not. When a man has the fruit of joy...."

"What's that?" Shawn cocked his head. "Like the fruit they ate in the garden? Are we talking apples here?"

Niall turned from the window, throwing up his hands. "Did they teach you nothing in your fine schools and churches! The fruits of the Holy Spirit, one of which is joy. If she had joy, if any of them had joy, 'twould show!"

"She was joyful enough with me." Shawn's irritation overcame the twinge of shame. "Maybe you were the problem." He poured more ale into his cup, and gulped it down.

"Och!" Niall spun back to the window, his hands planted on the sill. "We don't understand one another. My world has dangers, sure, but I'm at peace with myself and God. Why go to a place where I'd lose that? What good is a long and safe life if you've lost God?"

Shawn set his cup down, watching Niall's back. "Are you saying I shouldn't try?"

"'Tis your world." Niall stared at the arch of blue sea and sky filling the window. "You belong there. You've a child. Of course you must try."

After a moment's silence, Shawn asked, "Why is it so much easier for you to understand than MacDonald?"

Niall turned back, regarding him, his arms folded across his chest. "I met them, I saw them. They're not real to the Laird. I think a great deal on Amy, alone with the child."

Shawn snorted. "I'm sure Rob moved right in. She's not alone."

"Aye, he would. But she'll not have him."

Shawn frowned. "Why wouldn't she?"

Niall shrugged. "She didn't fancy him. She was unwilling...." He stopped, and turned away again. "You must try."

Niall's sudden shying away from the subject sent alarms ringing through Shawn's head. "Wait, back up. Unwilling...?"

Niall's shoulders stiffened.

Shawn rose. "Unwilling to—what?" Suspicion rippled through him, warm and slow. "Did you, uh—try to sleep with her?"

Niall spun from the window, his face red. "I'd not take advantage of a woman that way! Do you think of naught else?"

"Then what was she unwilling to do?" Suspicion grew to anger, despite Niall's disclaimer. There was something Niall wasn't saying. He advanced, blocking Niall between himself and the wall. Not that he had half a chance of outfighting Niall.

Niall glared. "I asked for her hand in marriage, if I was stuck there."

"You *what!*" Shawn's fist crushed the front of Niall's shirt. "You tried to marry my girlfriend?"

Niall threw his arms up, dislodging Shawn's grip. "She was not your *girlfriend.* Have you forgotten she cast you aside that night in the tower?"

"Yeah, well, still."

"Yeah," Niall mimicked. "Well, still. This is why I'd not go to your time. I might lose my power of speech and try to reason with such words. She thought me an improvement over you. She promised to think on it, if I came back. And why would you care? You were as busy as Edward Bruce with Caroline and Celine and how many others."

"Listen to the holy roller," Shawn snapped. "What happened to don't cast stones?"

Niall pushed past Shawn, and pointed at the dinner things. "Since you've the look of Niall, you'll have to stick your head out and call a servant to take these away."

"I'll take them myself." Shawn wanted nothing more than to leave. This was supposed to be his last night with Niall, his good-bye, and it had gone bad.

Niall threw himself into his chair, arms clamped across his chest. "The future laird does not carry dinner things."

"Whoa-hoa!" Shawn set down the goblet he'd picked up. "Isn't there anything about humility in those apples of the Holy Spirit?"

"Fruits!" Niall barked. "And humility is a virtue, not a fruit."

"Yeah, well, theologically ignorant though I may be," Shawn said, "even *I* am not too arrogant to take my own things to the kitchen. Guess what, future laird, you're going to be seen carrying dishes." He grabbed his tartan, gathered the trenchers and goblets, and threw the door open. "Get over it." From the hall, he added, "And just for good measure, you're going to be seen in the great hall carrying other people's things, too. Maybe you'll tell the servants to sit down and have a rest while you bring them food for a change."

"You'd not dare!" Niall bolted from his chair. "You'll upset the order we have!"

Shawn laughed. "What are you going to do about it?" He yanked the door shut on Niall's spluttering.

Creagsmalan, 1314

"No, My Lord, I am outraged." On the floor by the fire, Christina shrank back, though MacDougall stayed by the door. "He took Bessie." Fear dulled her acting. Even to herself, her words sounded flat and false.

MacDougall caressed the hilt of his sword, regarding her. "For a man you hate so, he's quite an interest in *you.*"

"He has?" Her heart pounded erratically. Niall, or the man Shawn? "Did you bring him back?"

"Get up."

She scrambled to her feet, cowering against the wall. He hadn't answered her. Fear for them and herself battled in her stomach, nauseating her. She edged away from him, her face burning with shame, trembling with fear.

"I'm not my son," he said. "Tell me what you know of the prisoner."

"Only...." She took a grain of courage that he stayed across the room. "That he called himself Fionn of Bergen and you say he is not. That he said he took Bessie and she is nowhere to be found." Her insides shook, hoping she was keeping all the stories straight. She wrapped clammy hands together, praying he would take her nervousness as fear of Duncan and his own temper.

MacDougall raked her with a sharp gaze. Heavy brows hooded his eyes. She fought the urge to back away.

"It seems," said MacDougall, "that we've several men who look like Niall Campbell. There's Niall." He paced to the window, peering out at black clouds scuttling across the night sky. "There's Fionn of Bergen who plays the recorder. And a man in a town to the east who plays the sackbut." He turned from the window, watching her.

Her heart hammered. She fought to keep her breathing deep and even, feeling faint from lack of air. He waited, for what she didn't know. "My Lord," she whispered, "I've no knowledge of all these men."

"Niall Campbell has scars on his back and across his stomach. The man who plays sackbut has not the first, and Fionn of Bergen not the second. The coincidence is remarkable." His eyebrows drew together more heavily still. "Three men who look alike, each playing a different instrument." He crossed the room, and circled her like a hungry wolf.

"What do you wish of me, My Lord?" Christina asked helplessly. Her arms trembled. Her stomach coiled itself once, twice, like a snake ready to strike, and tightened in knots.

"Have you been to the dungeons? Did you know Niall when you lived at Glenmirril? How did my messenger's missive come to be in your desk?" He fired question after question at her.

She followed the man, Shawn's, advice, giving the truth as much as possible. "I barely remember Niall. He teased my cousins. I know naught of your messenger's notes. Many people have access to my desk. I've been to the dungeons only when...."

He stepped closer. "When what?"

She stared at the floor. "I tried to protect Bessie. My Lord, he was hurting her."

"She's a servant." He dismissed Bessie. "What else did he do to you?"

His question took her by surprise. Fear gripped her throat. He indicated the linen chest at the foot of the bed. "Sit. You made promises, and I intend to collect."

She dared not object, in the face of his anger, dared not remind him that, strictly speaking, she hadn't exactly promised. It took a force of will, stronger than any she'd needed with Duncan, to obey.

"Remove your boots. Show me your leg."

She did so, closing her eyes to avoid the look of disgust that must surely touch his face.

He lifted her riding skirt with gentle fingers, probing a dozen bruises and scars. "Duncan did this?"

She nodded, wincing as he touched a tender spot.

"How long has this been going on?"

She couldn't meet his eyes. Shame filled her, letting her voice out in the smallest whisper. "Two years, My Lord."

"Alexander. You will call me by my Christian name." He rose abruptly, shouting for a servant. "Bring the physician, a hot bath, hot wine. Now!"

Glenmirril, 1314

Niall liked Jesus, did he? Shawn marched through dim, torch-lit halls to the kitchen, where he demanded to carry up the venison. "They said was a good man," he heard Bessie whisper as he passed.

Good man, bah! He stormed up the stairs, past smoky torches, bearing the platter high over his head. The real Niall was upstairs, too arrogant to lift a finger for himself!

Niall's mother, sister, nephew, and MacDonald himself, gaped when Shawn marched into the great hall, and dropped the silver tray heaped with venison with a loud report on the head table.

"Let the servants rest!" he shouted, turning and piercing Hugh, Darnley, and Morrison, one after another, with furious eyes.

Conal half-rose from his seat beside Morrison. "Niall...."

"Look at all of you sitting around!" Shawn planted his hands on the table, going nose to nose with the young lord. "Demanding to be served! Didn't Jesus say the greatest must serve? Didn't Jesus wash the disciples' underwear or something?"

Conal dropped into his seat. Ladies gasped. Allene's hand flew to her mouth. She looked to her father in horror. The Laird slowly gathered his jaw up, meeting Shawn's eyes. He planted his hands on the table, rising. Shawn glared back, challenging him.

Then suddenly, MacDonald smiled, threw back his head with a giant guffaw, and shouted, "Yes, do as Niall says. Let the servants sit!"

Creagsmalan, 1314

"Calling in your promise at the moment would hardly be the kindness you wished." MacDougall stared down at her as she trembled, freshly bathed and gowned in her night dress, beside the bed, her arms clutched around herself. The physician had done his best with the burns, cuts, and bruises on her legs, arms, and back. "But I'll stay." He pulled back the cover.

Covering her revulsion, she bowed her head. "Yes, My Lord."

"Alexander."

"Alexander." With eyes downcast, she climbed into the bed, dreading his presence, dreading any touch at all from him.

He climbed in after her, wrapping his arms around her, but doing nothing more. She discovered, with surprise, that she found comfort in having protective arms around her, knowing he'd warded off Duncan's wrath. Had he not been there, she'd be nursing a number of new bruises now, instead of being safe, bathed, warm, and comfortable in her bed.

He had a wife, back in his own castle. Sharp teeth gnawed at her conscience. She'd hinted at adultery. But then, she reminded herself, she'd been racing against time. She hoped saving Niall and Bessie outweighed both what she'd inflicted on the guard and her indecent suggestion. She hoped she *had* saved them. Perhaps, even now, they and the man Shawn were bloody and beaten down in the dungeons. She prayed silent *Aves*, wrapped in his arms, for herself, and all of them, and relaxed in the safety of her warm bed, into deep sleep.

Glenmirril's North Tower, 1314

Shawn stormed from the hall, from dropping the platter of venison before the startled Laird, straight to the tower, not waiting to witness the social upheaval Niall feared. It was more fun to imagine it. He stopped in the buttery on the way for a bulging skin of ale—if ever a man deserved a drink, it was him, today—and headed for the tower. The stairs twisted up inside the wall, like they had that night with Amy. He could almost believe he was back there—then—that she'd come up behind him any minute now.

He stopped halfway up the curving stairs, under the cross window, to gulp the ale. A fist clenched his gut, punched him in the heart. He gripped the wall, his head bowed. *I should have listened to her.* The words burned deep in his heart. It was only months ago they'd climbed these stairs together. The cold wall bit into his palm, but he couldn't move, missing her, missing the life he'd had, wanting it all back.

"Please God," he rasped. "My dad said You're a God of love. I told Niall so. I stood up for You. I did everything they asked, I've tried to be better, so can't You give me this one thing?" He forced himself upright, looking around the cramped stairs in the evening gloom, through the window with the stone cross, to the choppy loch outside, and climbed the rest of the way to the tower.

Wind swept over the walls, biting through his tartan. Mist floated on the black loch far below. Stars winked in the winter sky. The same stars would be burning over Amy in her time. He wrapped the tartan tight, and sank to the floor, his back sliding against the wall, remembering every detail of that night with her. *I was callous.* The thought hurt. *I was selfish and self-centered.* He'd once worn those words as a badge of honor. Now, they burned, scarlet letters on his soul. She'd begged him to listen. She'd tried to tell him she was pregnant. She'd told him she hurt from the abortion; told him she'd never wanted it.

At least, she'd tried to. He hadn't let her say it, hadn't listened.

He draped his arms over drawn-up knees, staring bleakly around the tower. He would set the basket there, in the middle, in seven hundred years. She would stand by the wall overlooking the loch. He'd look out over the hills to the north, sneering at her. He wanted to go back, go forward, wherever he needed to go in time, and fix it.

This is repentance. It's what you want, isn't it? he demanded of God. *I've learned my lesson. Now take me back, all right?* He sipped the ale, remembering his first weeks with the orchestra. He'd been taken with Amy's long, thick hair, the dark blue of her eyes, the way she leaned in in concentration when she played, the way she laughed with Dana. He'd wanted gentleness and constancy, something different from the normal women he pushed through the revolving door of his affections. She'd ignored him, refused his requests for dates. When he heard her mother was ill, he'd sat in his Jaguar, outside a church, ruminating on losing his father without saying good-bye, before buying the ticket and going to slide it under her door.

He smiled, remembering her voice, calling down the hall of her apartment building that night so long ago, ordering him to stop. He'd turned slowly, unable to run, reluctant to be caught in a deed so unlike the man he showed the world, the hard, stony man, incapable of being hurt, that he desperately wanted to be.

Amy's living room light, a soft yellow glow, lit her from behind. She stood in her doorway in a peach-colored robe, her black hair flowing, her voice like an angel, inviting him into Heaven. Her apartment came from the pages of a Victorian novel, draped in lace and old-fashioned things. He wanted to explore every inch of it and get to know her, and fell uncharacteristically quiet. His lines that worked so well with other women felt like sacrilege in her presence.

"Why?" She held up the ticket, tugging her satin robe close.

He had no smooth lines. The truth slipped out. "It's important to see your mother. You don't ever want to lose someone without a last chance to say good-bye."

She sized him up. "I wouldn't have expected such insight from you."

He stared at the large throw rug covering the wooden floor, and was grateful he didn't have a hat, or he'd be nervously working its brim, making a complete fool of himself. Then he muttered words he'd said to no one since the day it had happened. "My father died—unexpectedly. I didn't get to say good-bye."

"I'm sorry," she said softly.

He looked up and saw kindness in her eyes, kindness for him. And he knew he'd do anything to see that look again, to drink it in every day of his life.

"Do you want tea?" she asked.

She'd served it from a china pot echoing Jane Eyre, and he'd slipped back into the person he'd been long ago, before his father's death, leaving in the small hours of the morning with her gracious and heartfelt thanks, not so much as a kiss, and it had felt good to connect with someone in a real way.

The memory drifted away, leaving him alone in the cold, dark tower of medieval Scotland. He drank deeply from the skin, leaning his head against the tower wall, staring up at the stars. Filmy wisps of black cloud scudded across the pink sky, across the yellow moon. She'd put him off for six months, an eternity for him, leading him instead on moonlit walks, to movies, plays, ice skating. He remembered the feel of her hand in his, her cheek under his fingertips. He touched gingerly the memory of their first moments of intimacy, and her questions, asking repeatedly beforehand: *You love me? There won't be anyone else?*

Why *had* he cheated on her the first time?

He took a deeper drink, scowling. It didn't matter. It hadn't meant anything, and it didn't change anything between them. He loved her, wanted to be with her forever, and a woman whose name he didn't even remember didn't change that. He'd promised himself he wouldn't do it again, and that was good enough. He tugged the tartan around himself and curled into a tight ball on the stone floor. He'd wake up in his own time and make it all up to her. With that promise, he sank, finally, into deep sleep.

Coda

A pounding on the door jolted Christina awake in the gray morning. A voice shouted, "The men are ready, My Lord. We must leave anon!"

MacDougall scrambled to his feet, throwing an angry glance out the window, and swearing. He looked her up and down, as if she were to blame. "I slept too well. I'd planned to wake early."

She lowered her eyes, thanking God. "My apologies, My Lord."

"Alexander."

"Alexander."

He swore again, grabbing his breeks off the chair.

Another knock sounded on the door, followed by her maid's voice. MacDougall let the girl in, not the least embarrassed by his presence in Christina's chambers in his nightshirt, and all it suggested. Christina's own face flamed with shame. "Her riding clothes, and warmest cloak," he barked at the girl. "Haste!"

"Yes, Milord." She bobbed a curtsy. Though she'd say nothing to either of them, Christina knew rumors would swirl in the kitchens and over wash tubs and behind hands in the hallways as servants rushed and met one another. Defending herself in any way might result in putting out enough information for Duncan and his father to know for certain what she'd done. She lowered her eyes. She would have to live with that reputation.

Alexander yanked up his breeks and stuffed his shirt in. He pulled her close, hand possessively on her back, and kissed her, more than a fatherly kiss, while the girl, eyes averted, laid her garments on the tousled bed. Christina closed her eyes, trying not to think of the yellowed teeth, trying to be grateful for his kindness the previous evening.

He pulled back and shouted at the maid. "Five minutes!"

The girl jumped, startled, and murmured, "Yes, Milord."

"My Lord...." Christina began.

"Alexander."

"Alexander. Where are we...?"

"'Tis no concern of yours." His eyebrows bristled over dark eyes. Fear churned in her stomach. He stormed out the door.

Christina kept her eyes off the maid, her face burning, but her mind was already sliding from the scandal of MacDougall sleeping in her room, to fear of where they were taking her. He knew. Somehow or other, he knew. Her mind flew to anyone who might suspect, to the jailer, to Joan. Had they betrayed her? Or had MacDougall captured Shawn, Niall, and Bessie on the road and beaten it out of them? She barely registered the maid's gentle hands helping her into her warmest clothes.

"The thing is," Amy said over breakfast in a pub, "we don't know where Niall really was. He can't have been both in Creagsmalan and raiding

England with Douglas at the same time." She felt lighter this morning than she had in over a year; eager for a week with Angus, free of the past. She grieved the good parts of who Shawn had been, but she was ready to move forward. She still felt the glow of swaying in a slow dance before the crackling fire the previous evening, of Angus's arms around her.

"I'd believe the knighting source first," Angus said. "He could have left the mark at Creagsmalan anytime. Or someone else may have."

The waiter, with a shaggy collie trotting behind him, set their eggs and toast on the table. Thanking him, Angus continued. "Here was a man," he said, "who was only a minor player, historically, but we've heard outlandish tales that he walked through walls and across the Irish Sea, and from more reliable sources that he recovered miraculously from two serious injuries. The Stirling physician tells of a man cut nearly in half being up and about the next day. A Lord Kerr reports seeing a scar across Niall's midsection that would result from such an injury."

The image of Shawn, under the sword, flashed across Amy's mind. She frowned. "It's rather unlikely." Unlikely, she thought, that they had both suffered such similar injuries. So what had Lord Kerr seen?

Angus buttered his toast. "He walks away from a serious jousting injury, and goes immediately back to working twenty hours a day."

"But what's true, and what's just wild stories like the guy at the pub?"

Angus beamed. "That's the fun of it, aye? And now we have a man apparently in two places at once. Do we follow the one path? I say what can it hurt? *Someone* named Niall Campbell was there."

"But the stories are crazy," Amy objected. "One man couldn't do all that." A commotion at the door distracted her. A family burst in, a man and a chattering, bouncing girl. It was Sinead, being seated with her father. The girl promptly ejected herself out of her chair, and dashed across the small place, stopped to kiss the dog on its nose, and nearly bounded into Amy's arms, hugging her. "Miss Amy, Miss Amy, how's things!" She beamed at Angus, who shook her hand.

"Remember, you met him...." Amy started.

"Is he your boyfriend?" Sinead interrupted. "Are you going to Stirling, too? We're going up to the castle for the day."

Her father appeared at her side, apologizing. "Sinead, they may want to eat in peace." He extended his hand to Amy and Angus in turn. "Good to finally meet you, Miss Nelson." They chatted a bit, before he ushered his daughter back to their own table.

Amy lowered her voice. "Two hours a day each at dancing and violin. How does she do it and still have that kind of energy?"

Angus shrugged. "She likely doesn't actually do so much. A wee bit of exaggeration on her part, aye?"

"But she's so good at both." The baby chose that moment to give a hard kick. "Can you excuse me?" Amy asked. "Three cups of tea and a bouncing baby." She grinned, letting him figure it out.

In the restroom, she came face to face with her student, this time with Mrs. Gordon. "Hello again!" she said in surprise.

Sinead stared at her.

"Say hello now and be nice," her mother said.

The girl kept her hand clutched to herself. "Hello, Miss Amy."

"She's burned her hand," her mother explained. She held it out, showing Amy a blister rising on the palm. "We were just after running cold water on it."

"How did that happen so fast? I just saw her...."

Sinead's mouth twitched. She looked at the floor. Her mother glared at her, and huffed. "Have ye been playing games with Miss Amy?"

"No, Mum." But she stared at the floor, fighting a smile.

Amy felt the frown crease her forehead, even as she said, "She's been wonderful." She wondered what games Mrs. Gordon imagined. But she had to excuse herself.

Moments later, alone in the bathroom, Amy stared into the mirror as she washed her hands, wondering which of her features, and which of Shawn's, her child would have, missing Shawn, wishing he could have been here, the new Shawn who would leave an apology. But he was dead.

She snapped off the water, dried her hands and left the bathroom.

She took a step around a corner and saw Sinead and her family, and stopped short, her eyes wide, trying to get her heart beating again, trying not to laugh out loud, trying not to cry in elation as all the pieces snapped into place.

Western Scotland, 1314

Christina huddled atop her horse, shivering under her heaviest surcoat and warmest cloak. Pines rose steeply on either side of the dirt track. Two dozen mounted men accompanied her and MacDougall, filling the stale, cold air with the jingle of mail and scent of horses. Snow sprinkled the forest path.

MacDougall rode at her side, stiff in his black armor on his black steed, his face as angry as the winter clouds that glowered over them. Since leaving Creagsmalan, he'd driven his men hard, saying not a word. His men held their tongues.

Christina rode silently, fearful of rousing his temper. Possibilities filled her head. They'd killed Niall or Shawn and were taking her to a deep forest to kill her, too. They were going to leave her to starve or be torn apart by wolves. She feared, with MacDougall's desires, what he'd do first; imagined him hanging her from a tree and leaving her body for animals. She felt her face draining of more color at each new fear.

With her fingers bone-cold on the reins, she tried to fill her mind with good thoughts. Bessie had gotten away. Maybe. MacDougall had not called in her promise. Yet. The snow-capped mountains rising in the distance were beautiful. If she was to meet God this day or on the morrow, she'd lived as well as she knew how, despite the scandal and stories that now surrounded her name.

She looked to the mountains, their peaks gleaming white, and prayed, for Shawn, for Niall, for the jailer, for Bessie, for everyone she'd ever known. She might not have many hours left for praying, she feared.

Glenmirril

Shawn woke with a deep chill in his bones, despite the heavy tartan. The chill of the flagstones cut through his cloak. Cold winter air brushed his cheek, like his mother had years ago, whispering to wake up. He stayed in the dark behind his eyelids, locked in hope. He'd asked God, he'd defended God to Niall, setting him straight that God was Love, not Hell. He'd learned his lesson. God would surely bring him back, would work the magic in the tower again, slide the centuries up, one against the other and tip Shawn back into his right time. He opened his eyes cautiously.

The tower walls surrounded him, etched against the rising sun. Mist crept across the flagstones. It looked as it had last night. It looked as it had the night he and Amy had fought. The wineskin lay flaccid by his side, and his head thrummed with alcohol.

Voices sounded on the stair. He strained to hear if they were medieval Gaelic or modern English. It could be that dragon lady tour guide from so long ago! He sat up, slowly, putting off the moment of finding out whether the switch had happened, hoping. Footsteps fell on the stairs, light feminine steps. It was Amy! By some miracle, it was Amy, come back for him! He scrambled to his feet, his heart racing.

Bannockburn, Present

Still in the short hallway leading to the bathroom, hidden from Angus's view, Amy pulled her phone from her pocket, her fingers trembling, and hit *call* at Rose's number.

Rose answered promptly. "Amy, what is it? Aren't you on your way to England?"

"Rose." Amy's voice shook. Tears of shock and joy slid down her cheeks, even as her thoughts reached out with a hundred worries to Angus, waiting, unsuspecting, at the table for her; as her mind spun around the implications, flew to the many possible futures, to the choice before her, the choice she wasn't supposed to ever have to face.

"Amy?" Rose's voice rose in alarm. "Are you okay?"

"Rose," Amy whispered. "Rose, Shawn survived. He's alive."

Made in the USA
Monee, IL
06 March 2021